DON'T CLOSE YOUR EYES

"*Don't Close Your Eyes* has all the gothic sensibilities of a Victoria Holt novel, combined with the riveting modern suspense of Sharyn McCrumb's *The Hangman's Beautiful Daughter*. Don't close your eyes—and don't miss this one!"
—Meagan McKinney, author of *In the Dark*

"An exciting romantic suspense novel that will thrill readers with the subplots of a who-done-it and a legendary resident ghost seen only by children. These themes cleverly tie back to the main story line centering on the relationships between Natalie and Nick, and Natalie and the killer. Carlene Thompson fools the audience into thinking they know the murderer early on in the book. This reviewer suggests finishing this terrific tale in one sitting to ascertain how accurate are the reader's deductive skills in pinpointing the true villain."
—Harriet Klausner

IN THE EVENT OF MY DEATH

"*In the Event of My Death* is Carlene Thompson's blood-chilling new tale of vengeance, madness and murder."
—*Romantic Times*

THE WAY YOU LOOK TONIGHT

"Thompson . . . has crafted a lively, entertaining read . . . skillfully ratchet(ing) up the tension with each successive chapter . . ."
—The Charleston *Daily Mail*

St. Martin's Paperbacks Titles

by Carlene Thompson

SINCE YOU'VE BEEN GONE

CARLENE THOMPSON

St. Martin's Paperbacks

This is a work of fiction. All of the characters, organizations, and events portrayed in this novel are either products of the author's imagination or are used fictitiously.

SINCE YOU'VE BEEN GONE

Copyright © 2001 by Carlene Thompson.

For information address St. Martin's Press, 175 Fifth Avenue, New York, NY 10010.

ISBN: 0-312-35706-0
EAN: 978-0-312-35706-1

Printed in the United States of America

St. Martin's Paperbacks edition / September 2001

St. Martin's Paperbacks are published by St. Martin's Press, 175 Fifth Avenue, New York, NY 10010.

10 9 8 7 6 5 4 3

TO MY BROTHER KEVIN

Thanks to Vada Thompson, Jim Sprouse, Ada Roush, and Keith Biggs.

Special thanks to Guy Shawkins.

Prologue

His cape swirled dramatically. His piercing eyes looked from beneath the darkness of his hood. "You have joined the dark side," he intoned. He whipped out his light saber and grandly swept it through the air, electrified as it made its scary-thrilling hum of power. "I am Obi-Wan Kenobi, here to help you fight your way back to the light. Fight!"

His nemesis cringed in front of the awesome power of a Jedi Knight . . .

Suddenly he couldn't breathe. The light saber dropped from his hand and the face of his frightening adversary disintegrated as he struggled out of the mystical dream of *Star Wars*. He tried to open his eyes, but they were covered. He opened his mouth to scream and a sickeningly sweet-smelling cloth filled it. His breath rasped in his throat. His legs thrashed. His arms waved, his hand connecting with something solid. He clutched material, wondering if this was a part of the dream that was going so wrong. Mommy had told him there was a secret rhyme to make a bad dream go away. He hadn't had a bad dream for a long time and he tried to remember: *One, two, three, four / Bad dream out the door!*

Dizzy with fear and nausea, he didn't wake up. He couldn't see the comforting familiarity of his room with its *Star Wars* poster and the bowl with two sleek goldfish and the sparkling blue Lava lamp Mommy always left on until he went to sleep. He must still be asleep! He needed to try again. *One, two, three, four / Bad dream out the door!*

Nothing. Horror flamed through his slight seven-year-old body as he realized something awful, something real, was happening outside his dream world. He writhed wildly, although his energy was slipping away. The cloth pressed over his face, making his eyes burn, turning the inside of his nose raw. His tongue felt huge. Where was Mommy? Mommy, please *help*! He struck out with a hand and heard someone mutter "Damn you!" when he connected with a nose. What kind of nose? Big? Little? A man's nose? A girl's?

Fiery panic surged through him. He knew he was going to throw up. He was scared like a baby because his legs would barely move now. He shivered and he thought he might wet his pants. Something was pushed over his head, something like a hood, but not a good kind of hood like the one on Obi-Wan Kenobi's cape. Something rough and itchy and smothering and moldy that sucked into his mouth when he tried to breathe. And now he was having trouble thinking. Blinding spots of light flashed in front of his eyes.

With the little strength he had left, he closed his fingers around the leg of the stuffed dog he'd loved furless in places. Good, strong, loyal Tramp—forever his protector. Brave Tramp who saved the baby from the rat in the movie *Lady and the Tramp*. Tramp could help.

And Tramp tried. Someone forced loose his fingers but the dog clung, a hook on its collar caught on his pajamas. Don't let me go, he begged Tramp mentally. Don't let *go*!

"Time to leave," someone whispered harshly in his ear, into his fuzzy mind. "Say good-bye to all you know. This is the beginning of the end, little boy."

With a horror he'd never known in his life, he felt his light body being roughly lifted from the bed, the stuffed animal a dangling weight. In a minute the night air washed over him, seeping through his sweat-drenched pajamas, chilling his damp feet, touching his limp fingers.

He heard the distant bark of a dog and the high whine of a mosquito near his ear before he went still, sinking into a dreamless, unnatural sleep.

CHAPTER ONE

"This is WCWT in Sinclair, West Virginia, bringing you one of our favorite oldies, 'Bitter Sweet Symphony' by the Verve."

String music soared throughout the car and Rebecca Ryan rolled her eyes. "Since when does a song from 1997 count as a golden oldie?" Her Australian shepherd, Sean, sitting on the bucket seat across from her, looked back alertly. "I wonder what they call songs from the fifties? Prehistoric?"

Rebecca drained the last bit of strong, lukewarm coffee from her Styrofoam cup and stuck it in the plastic trash bag along with two other used cups. Her stomach churned, her eyes burned, and her hands trembled. Too much caffeine and too little sleep. And fear. It had coursed through her since last night, when her cousin Molly had called her in New Orleans and said, "Aunt Esther has cancer."

"Well, that's not possible," Rebecca had said inanely, thinking of the woman who'd radiated health and energy since Rebecca was a little girl. According to Molly, seventy-five-year-old Esther had just told the family she would have surgery and begin radiation therapy in less than two weeks. Esther wanted no sympathy and she wanted no one except immediate family to know of her condition. "She told me not to tell you in particular," Molly had said late last night on the phone after waiting until her seven-year-old son Todd had gone to sleep because she didn't want him to get upset. "Esther doesn't want you coming all the way from New Orleans, especially because Sinclair has such bad memories for you. So you have to think up an excuse for this trip."

An excuse? Rebecca was still working on that one, her

mind having been occupied with the flurry of the hurried trip. She'd been unable to make the earliest flights from New Orleans to Charleston, West Virginia, and had to wait until a mid-afternoon one with a layover in Pittsburgh. She hadn't had time to make arrangements for boarding her dog, Sean, and getting him unloaded from the plane and renting a car had taken extra time before the 60-mile drive to Sinclair. Through it all Rebecca had been unable to catch up on the sleep she'd lost last night and she was now tired and feeling slow-witted.

Rebecca flipped off the radio. Music that had helped to keep her awake now blurred into irritating noise. She glanced at Sean. "You look fresh as a daisy. No wonder. Thanks to that tranquilizer, you slept through both flights." The dog gazed at her, panting. "I know you're not crazy about kids in general, but I hope you like my nephew Todd. He'll be crazy about you." A drop of saliva rolled off Sean's tongue onto the seat. "My mother will like you, too, as long as you don't drip on any of her beautiful clothes."

When she was a child, Rebecca had adored her lovely mother Suzanne's thick, wheat-colored hair, azure eyes, and slender-boned body. She'd had quick, tinkling laughter and a personality that alternated easily between adult and child-like. One evening she could be the gracious, polished host-ess at a dinner party. The next morning she could wholeheartedly throw herself into one of Rebecca's tea par-ties or a game of hide-and-seek with her and her brother Jonnie.

A sudden pain reamed like a knife in Rebecca's stomach at the thought of Jonnie. Three years younger than she, Jonathan Patrick Ryan had been a beautiful, happy baby who'd grown into an agile, high-spirited boy with a cap of blond curls and a devilish glint in his bright blue eyes. When he was very small he had allowed Rebecca to dress him up and treat him like her own beloved baby. When he was older, he'd shrugged off her coddling and insisted on being treated as an equal. In later years they'd played to-gether, shared secrets, squabbled, tattled on each other, and managed to always remain best friends. She hadn't been able to imagine life without him. She hadn't thought she would ever *be* without him.

She'd been wrong.

Sean pawed at her arm, sensing her tension. "We're almost . . . there." She'd nearly said *home*, but Sinclair wasn't home and hadn't been for the eight years since Jonnie had been murdered. She hadn't visited since she'd left for Tulane University in New Orleans when she was eighteen. She'd intended never to return.

Her stomach tightened as she drove into the Sinclair city limits. To her right was the huge brick Baptist church that dated to 1870. Molly had told her a few ambitious parishioners had lobbied for an addition, but the historic preservationists had quashed the motion. Ahead, Leland Park overlooked the Ohio River. Rebecca had always loved the park with its tennis courts, rose gardens with brick paths, and two-story River Museum. She noticed that the eight acres of land were as beautifully maintained as always, benches, birdfeeders, and old-fashioned water fountains painted pristine white. Even the bandstand, built in the early 1900s and the site of summer night concerts, looked brand-new. Long ago, Suzanne had brought her and Jonnie to the concerts. One time Jonnie hid. Certain he'd fallen into the river and drowned, Suzanne had promptly lapsed into hysterics. Rebecca had found him hiding under the bandbox and was deeply disappointed when he didn't receive the spanking she would have for playing such a trick.

As Rebecca drove through town, she saw that Main Street looked just the same as when she'd left. About ten years ago several merchants had banded together in fury over the business drained by the huge new mall that seemed to erupt overnight on the outskirts of town. Their defense had been to make their establishments appear quaint, thereby charming customers away from the indistinguishable stores in the modern, Muzak-filled mall. The result was three town blocks that looked as if they could have been lifted from a Dickens novel. Rebecca found it unbearably precious. And to the best of her knowledge, business had improved for only a couple of years until the curiosity wore off. But the flagging enthusiasm of the merchants for their brilliant project showed only in the occasional set of faded shutters or rust-edged wrought-iron trim.

Rebecca slowed as she neared the former Vinson Drug Store, now Vinson's Apothecary Shoppe. She'd packed in a hurry and had spent part of her flight time ticking off a list of toiletries she'd forgotten. The place was still open and stopping here would be much faster than going to the mall. She parked and rolled down the windows a fraction so Sean could have fresh air

As she emerged from the car, she saw storm clouds billowing against the slate gray sky just turning black. Inside the store the attempt to keep up the Victorian motif continued with Currier & Ives prints on the walls. A few small wrought-iron tables and chairs had been placed in front of a minuscule soda fountain, behind which stood a bored teenage girl chewing gum and flipping through a magazine. At the prescription counter was an array of large, ornate bottles filled with "potions" that were really colored water. She knew the last touch had been the inspiration of Matilda Vinson, the store's owner and pharmacist.

Rebecca cursed the unlabeled aisles that made it necessary for her to cruise around until she found body lotion, disposable razors, toothpaste, and a bottle of soaking solution for her contact lenses. She picked up an overpriced bag of generic kibble for Sean, promising herself to get something better tomorrow, and headed for the checkout counter.

She paid no attention to the woman behind the register until she noticed the clerk wasn't ringing up her purchases. Rebecca glanced up to see silvery gray eyes regarding her coldly. The woman was young with short platinum hair, straight dark eyebrows, and thin scarlet lips. Rebecca felt color creep into her face as she realized she was staring into the face of someone who used to be a close friend.

"Hello, Lynn," she said without false friendliness.

"Rebecca." Lynn Cochran Hardison flicked her light eyes up and down Rebecca's slim height. "You're looking well. Life away from Sinclair must agree with you."

"I love New Orleans." Rebecca pushed her items closer to the cash register as she talked. "How have you been?"

"Fine. *Very* happily married."

"Good. I'm glad things are working out for you and Doug."

"Of course they're working out. We've always loved each other," Lynn announced as if expecting an argument. "I thought you'd come to our wedding. After all, Doug is your stepbrother."

"I knew you didn't want me there, Lynn."

"Why would I? You caused me a lot of pain, Rebecca." Rebecca sighed. "Lynn—"

"Is this all you want?" Lynn suddenly looked angry. "We're having a sale on aspirin. With all those so-called ESP visions rattling around in your head, you must get plenty of headaches."

Here we go, Rebecca thought dismally. The specter of the extrasensory perception that had first manifested itself when she was nine was still following her, more of a curse than a gift.

"Lynn, we can't change the past," Rebecca said evenly. "I'm sorry I've hurt you, but we're family now. Can't we work at healing old wounds?"

The speech sounded sententious to her own ears and Rebecca wasn't surprised by Lynn's scowl. "Forget what happened? That would be convenient for you, wouldn't it?" Lynn grabbed the toothpaste and jabbed buttons on the register. "Just wreak havoc, then go your merry way, live your good life in New Orleans, forget all the damage you've done here." She swiped at the razors and dog food. "And I heard you've written a book. Trying to cash in on your brother's murder? I'm sure you didn't mention how your fabulous ESP suddenly went on the fritz and you didn't save him."

Rebecca quietly absorbed the sting of hearing how she'd

failed Jonnie, looking down so Lynn couldn't see the pain in her eyes. How hard it was to believe this razor-voiced woman once had been a friend.

"My book isn't about Jonnie," Rebecca managed. "It's a murder mystery but it's fiction."

"I wouldn't know. I sure as hell wouldn't read it. And you owe twenty-two seventy-three."

Rebecca handed over thirty dollars, took her change, and picked up the plastic bag in which Lynn had stuffed her purchases. "Good-bye, Lynn."

"I'll give your regards to Doug, even though you didn't even bother to ask about him," Lynn called tartly as Rebecca headed for the door.

Rebecca closed her eyes when she heard Matilda Vinson utter a sharp "Lynn!" as she descended on her employee for what would surely be a dressing-down. It was deserved, Rebecca thought, but it would only deepen Lynn's resentment.

"Rebecca!" Miss Vinson called. "Rebecca, dear, please forgive Lynn. She's had a long day."

Rebecca smiled at the small, sixty-year-old whirling dervish of a woman who had worked in the drugstore for nearly forty years. "It's all right. Lynn and I understand each other."

"I see." Matilda still looked distressed. "Are you home for a visit or returning to us for good?"

"Just a visit." Lynn's silvery gaze seemed to burn through Rebecca and she felt desperate to escape the store. "I'll be going back to New Orleans in a week or so."

"That's a shame. We miss you around here. I remember when you were just a little thing and came in with your father. I always gave you a butterscotch candy and you acted like I'd handed you a piece of gold." Matilda looked out the front windows. "Good heavens, what a storm is brewing! You can't go out in this. Go back and have an ice-cream soda and wait it out."

"It's closing time," Lynn announced.

"I will decide when we close!" Color rode high on Matilda Vinson's cheeks and Rebecca thought that Lynn must not value her job to be so insolent. "Please stay for a few minutes, Rebecca."

"I can't," Rebecca said abruptly, heading for the door. "I left my dog in the car. He's terrified of storms. Besides, if I hurry, I can get home before it hits."

"Well, be careful, dear," Matilda called after her.

Outside the wind had picked up sharply. Tree limbs bent backward and a metal trash can rolled across Main Street. A few raindrops pelted her with stinging force. In the distance Rebecca saw a streak of lightning cast a blue glow against the dark sky. She forgot to count until the thunder rumbled, loud and ominous. If she believed in signs, she would have considered a storm her first night back in Sinclair a bad omen.

Wind snapped her long auburn hair across her face and plastered her slacks against her legs. She opened the car door and jumped in. Sean nearly leaped onto her lap. She grabbed his collar and pushed him back to his seat, speaking soothingly as he panted in agitation. She handed him a rawhide chew stick that he held in his mouth like a cigar, too nervous to eat it.

Slowly she pulled away from the curb and started down the street. She turned up the speed of the windshield wipers. Lightning viciously sliced the sky again and a wave of rain slapped the car hard enough to make her swerve. Main Street was strangely empty at nine-forty. The marquees of the two theaters valiantly tried to glow through the torrent of water. Rebecca doubted if many people had shown up for the second movie showing.

Less than a quarter of a mile ahead, Rebecca sat at what seemed an interminable red light. Across the intersection she noticed a large, white stucco structure with dramatic, sweeping lines. A sign on the front lawn bore the name DORMAINE'S RESTAURANT in black lettering bold enough for her to see through the rain.

She turned left at the light. An explosion of thunder followed a glittering spear of lightning, making Sean yelp and Rebecca cringe. The lightning had been too close for comfort, although she knew the rubber tires of the car protected them from electric shock. A dull throbbing had started at her right temple. It was a familiar pain, although she hadn't felt it for quite a while. She would think of something else, forget it, take some aspirin when she got home. Thank goodness it wasn't too much farther to the Ryan house, she thought, watching the wipers swipe uselessly across the windshield. Back and forth. Back and forth . . .

The rain-smeared windshield slowly blurred, then began to disappear. Rebecca tried to focus, to shut out all that was not tangible, but with dreamlike inevitability, she felt herself drift from her own consciousness into someone else's. . . .

Rough cloth was tied around his face and around his mouth. Blindfolded and gagged, that's what he was. Beneath him was something hard—wood, probably—and his right hip and arm were numb. Something was tied around his ankles and his hands were pulled behind his back and trapped by rope, the skin beneath it raw from fruitless rubbing. He felt sick, like he wanted to throw up, and his head hurt real bad. He thought he might cry, which would be awful because none of his movie heroes would cry and he'd feel like a complete baby.

He tried inhaling deeply in an effort to stop the crying, but the air was hot and smelled awful. Rotten. And he could hear thunder outside and rain beating against windows. Bright pinpoints of light sparkled in front of his burning eyes. He was afraid. Deathly afraid. Thunder boomed and he shuddered, pulling himself up into a ball. Uttering guttural sobs, he inched across the floor until his face touched something soft. Tramp, his stuffed dog. Tramp who saved the baby from the rat in *Lady and the Tramp*. Maybe Tramp could save him, too . . .

Slowly Rebecca's vision faded. The thoughts of the little boy were drowned out by the sound of rain pounding on her windshield. The hood of the car pointed toward something large and looming. Rebecca blinked, aware that she'd returned to her own reality but unfortunately too late. She jerked the steering wheel to the right, but the car plunged at a giant tree trunk. The noise of screeching metal seemed far away as the hood of her car crumpled. Rebecca had worn her seat belt, holding her body in place, but her head snapped violently forward. Her last sensations were of blood running down her face and her vision dimming into darkness.

Chapter Two

"She's waking up."

Rebecca felt her eyelids fluttering. Then they opened. She was certain they were open. But she couldn't see anything. Her hands flew to her eyes, delicately touching the open lids as panic surged through her.

"I'm blind," she whispered. Her voice rose. "I'm blind!"

"Calm down," a woman said in an expressionless voice.

"But I'm *blind*."

"Ma'am, calm down."

Someone pulled her hands away from her eyes and Rebecca felt herself being lifted and placed prone on the lightly padded surface of a gurney. "How bad is it?" Rebecca asked in the direction of one of the disembodied voices above her.

"We're going to take care of you."

"What other injuries do I have?"

"You just calm down and enjoy the ride. We'll be at the hospital in a few minutes."

"I want to know how bad it is! Where is my dog? Is he dead?"

No one answered and fear for herself and Sean struck her mute. She'd been in another car wreck, she thought. The last one had killed her father when she was nine.

Rebecca sank into unconsciousness.

"Open your eyes."

Open them to what? Rebecca wondered. Open them to perpetual darkness?

"Open your *eyes*."

She automatically responded to the authority in the voice. Her eyelids snapped open. She blinked against the light, then slowly focused on a man's blue-gray eyes. He grinned. "Is that better?"

"I can see," Rebecca gasped. "I thought I was blind."

"You crashed into a perfectly innocent tree, shattered your windshield with a limb, knocked yourself senseless, and got two nice cuts on your forehead. Some of the blood ran under your contact lenses. We took them out, rinsed with saline solution, and now those beautiful green eyes seem to be working just fine again."

Rebecca took a minute to absorb the information, then breathed, "Thank God."

"Gave you quite a scare, didn't it?"

"That's putting it mildly. What other damage is there?"

"So far all we've found are contusions and lacerations. We'll need to suture your forehead. The cuts are near the hairline and four or five stitches for each should do the trick."

"My dog. Where is my dog?"

The doctor frowned. "I don't know anything about a dog. If the paramedics who brought you in are still around, I can have someone ask if they saw a dog at the scene."

"Yes, please," Rebecca said urgently. "He was in the front seat. He's afraid of most people—a case of abuse when he was younger. I took him in as a stray. He means so much to me—"

The doctor placed a hand on her shoulder and she realized she'd been rising. "You lie still." He turned to a slender young man in hospital scrubs with stooped shoulders and gigantic brown eyes behind thick glasses. "Alvin, will you go out and see if the paramedics know anything about the dog?"

The young man stared at Rebecca for a moment and she realized she must have sounded hysterical, babbling on about the dog being an abused stray. "Alvin?" the doctor repeated.

"Sure, Doc," the young man said and nearly fled from the room.

The doctor turned back to Rebecca. "Alvin's one of our

best orderlies, but his mind seems to be wandering tonight. Now, how did this wreck happen?"

Rebecca couldn't imagine saying, "I had a vision and I could only hear and see through the consciousness of a little boy who's probably been kidnapped." Instead she improvised. "There was a terrible flash of lightning right in front of me. It startled me and I must have slammed my foot on the brake and then . . ."

"Hydroplaned right into Peter Dormaine's hundred-year-old oak tree."

"Peter Dormaine?"

"Yes. You wrecked at Dormaine's Restaurant." He frowned. "Didn't you even know where you were?"

"Oh sure," she said quickly. "I forgot for a second. I was pretty shaken up."

"No wonder. If you hadn't been wearing your seat belt, you would have been a mess, young lady." He paused. "You don't recognize me, do you? It's Clayton Bellamy."

Clay Bellamy? Her stepbrother Doug's friend who had sent her teenage heart racing and inspired a hundred ridiculously romantic fantasies?

Rebecca closed her eyes against the strong lights shining down on her. Her head hurt and she felt as if everything inside her was quivering. The rest of her body was remarkably free of pain, but she knew a dozen aches would kick into gear soon. "Hi, Clay," she managed weakly.

She looked at him again. His gray-blue eyes still had a slight downward tilt of the outer lids, and he still wore his thick golden blond hair a bit longer than most men's. His even white teeth were wreathed by deep dimples. It could have been a pretty-boy face, with its near-perfect features, but his eyes held a trace of sadness and his face more lines than one would expect of a man barely over thirty. The whiskey-edged voice also added a few years. Clay had aged well, but he was definitely a man now, not the striking boy he'd still been at their last meeting when he was 22 and she 17.

"How did you end up as my doctor?" Rebecca asked.

"I have my pick of the patients." Clay smiled. "It's good to see you, even under these circumstances, Stargazer."

Rebecca had forgotten the nickname Clay had given her when she was eleven because of her fascination with astronomy. She had never been certain whether or not he was making fun of her.

"Good to see you, too," she said weakly.

"You're in remarkably good condition given the seriousness of your wreck. We tried to call your family, but got a busy signal."

"You know my stepfather is a workaholic. I think he makes calls until midnight. Besides, they didn't even know I was coming. Molly does, though. You remember my cousin Molly?"

"Sure. First cousins and best friends. She was always at your house when I dropped by with Doug. We'll call her in a minute. First I have a couple of questions. Who wrote *Moby-Dick*?"

"Are you kidding?" Clay shook his head. "Herman Melville."

"Good. When did William Faulkner get the Pulitzer prize for literature?"

"You're being very strange." Rebecca scrunched up her forehead in deep thought, then announced, "It was the Nobel Prize in 1949."

"Nothing wrong with this noggin!" Clay crowed.

"You were testing me?"

"Have to make sure there's no memory loss."

"As if he'd know when Faulkner won his prize," the nurse joked.

"She sounded sure of herself and I do know who wrote *Moby-Dick*." Clay stood up and took Rebecca's hand as if they'd seen each other only yesterday. "You're as pretty as ever in spite of those cuts on your face."

He possessed the same easy charm, the tendency to flatter even when she was certain he was giving little thought to his words. In the space of a day he probably told several women they were pretty. "Thanks, Clay. Will I have scars?"

"No. The cuts are small and I'm a master of sutures."

"And *modest*." The nurse laughed.

Clay looked at Rebecca earnestly. "Stargazer, I get appallingly little respect around here. Sometimes my feelings are so hurt I have to go into the rest room and cry it out."

"You poor thing!" Rebecca giggled. "Your sense of humor hasn't changed."

"Certainly not." Clay grew serious. "Now we need a CAT scan and then to call Molly."

Rebecca rattled off Molly's number and the nurse wrote it down. "And please try to find out something about my dog. I know it must seem silly to you, but—"

"It doesn't seem silly at all," Clay said briskly. "I have one of my own named Gypsy and I love her like crazy. You try to relax."

Rebecca felt as if she would scream if she didn't get out of this place. She was shaken by the wreck, worried about Sean, and most of all rocked by her vision of a little boy being taken from his bed, then held captive in some awful place. Over the past eight years she had worked at suppressing her visions, shutting her mind to them until they had almost disappeared. But she could not have shut out this vision. It was too powerful, too insistent. Rarely in her life had she experienced one of such clarity.

Still, she didn't dare say anything to these medical people about her experience. She'd just been in a wreck; her tale would sound like rambling. They might decide she'd had some kind of brain injury not shown on the CAT scan and keep her overnight when she desperately wanted to leave and possibly unravel the mystery of what she had seen. Was a little boy in town missing? Was there something she could do? If she were alone would another vision come that might tell her more?

After what seemed an interminable time, the nurse reappeared and said, "Dr. Bellamy, may I talk with you for a moment?"

Clay, who had been frowning in concentration over his

stitches, looked up and smiled. "That's the sweetest tone you've ever used with me. What have I done right?"

"Nothing." Clay raised his eyebrows. "Well, I'm sure you've done a few things right today, but I just need to talk to you. *Now*."

Clay's smile wavered a fraction, then came back full force as he gazed down at Rebecca. "Don't look so apprehensive. This is no doubt about another patient. You're fine, I promise."

A dozen thoughts raced through Rebecca's mind in the two minutes Clay was gone. Something was wrong and it had to do with her. As soon as Clay returned she demanded, "What is it? Did they find my dog? Is he dead?"

"Your dog?" Clay blinked at her. "No, the paramedics said they didn't see a dog. I told you it was about someone else."

But his face looked tight and pale as he finished the suturing and he made no small talk. Rebecca's heart pounded. Where was her ESP when she needed it? Why couldn't she read his mind? The ESP seemed to have a will of its own and wasn't something she could command at will. It came and went as it pleased.

Growing more nervous as the minutes ticked by, Rebecca forced herself to sit quietly through the dressing of her two cuts as well as an injection of antibiotics and a tetanus booster. Then she gave an accident report to a policeman, carefully omitting any references to "visions." It was after eleven-thirty when, dressed in her damp, blood-splattered clothes, she walked out of the hospital with Clay solicitously holding her arm.

"You don't have to take me home," she protested.

"The nurse told me Molly isn't available, so we tried your house. Your stepfather isn't home, and your mother doesn't sound up to par."

Up to par, Rebecca thought. A polite way of saying her mother had been drinking. Rebecca wondered how many people knew Suzanne had become an alcoholic over the past five years. Most of the town? Word traveled fast in small communities.

"Of course, if insurance companies didn't dictate policy, you'd be staying within the hospital's hallowed halls tonight," Clay said.

"I'm glad I don't have to. I just don't understand why Molly isn't around. She knew I was coming. Of course I'm later than I'd expected, but I promised I'd get here sometime today."

"Well, lucky for you my shift is over, and I have a car."

"Clay, this is nice of you but unnecessary. We have taxi service in Sinclair."

"Not a taxi that will drive around and help you find your dog. What did you call him?"

"Sean! Oh Clay, will you really help me find him?"

Clay stopped at a black compact car. "I save lives and I help find lost dogs. I'm a full-service doctor."

"I'll say. You can't tell me you give all your patients this kind of service."

The remark sounded flirtatious and Rebecca regretted it, then told herself she was being too self-conscious because— much to her surprise—her old attraction to Clayton Bellamy remained intact.

"I've known you for years, Rebecca. If I can't help an old friend find her dog and then drive her home when she's hurt and without transportation, I'm a sorry specimen."

Well, so much for my believing he thinks I'm anything special, Rebecca thought with a slight thud of disappointment.

"Now hop in and don't trip over the Styrofoam cups on the floor. I'm a slob when it comes to the car."

Rebecca climbed in and immediately snapped on her seat belt. Belts had saved her life twice in auto accidents. She also noted that the car was spotless except for three cups and a candy bar wrapper on the floor.

"Clay, I don't know how to thank you for doing this," she said as he started the car. "Sean is an Australian shepherd. They're usually gentle, good around children, but he was clearly abused because he doesn't react well to most people. I think he was dumped in my neighborhood; for some reason he picked my house to seek refuge."

Clay finally looked at her and smiled. "The first time I met you, you were taking care of a tiny bunny. Kept it in a hamster cage. You said the vet had told you it couldn't live, but you refused to believe him. And it did live. After that you took in every abandoned rabbit and robin you found and never lost one."

"I can't believe you remember that."

"I wanted to be a doctor, so your talent as a healer made a big impression. Besides, I remember quite a bit about you, Stargazer, particularly your sensitivity." Rebecca felt herself blushing, then felt silly for blushing and blushed some more. "You also had quite an imagination. Of course you ended up writing a book. Murder mystery, isn't it?"

"That's what I call it. The publisher calls it 'psychological suspense.' I was lucky to get it published, but it only came out a month ago so I don't know much about sales. That's why I'm not giving up my job teaching in a private school."

"That's great. And I haven't read the book yet, but I will."

Rebecca laughed. "You don't have to."

"I *want* to. I also want my copy of the book signed. Deal?"

"Deal."

The storm had let up, leaving only a slow, dreary rain to fall in its wake. Streets glistened moistly, streets that were nearly deserted, unlike the perpetual busyness of New Orleans. Most of the houses they passed were dark and none bore the security warnings so common in the Garden District where she lived. Sinclair hardly ranked as a high-crime city.

"Are you feeling worse?" Clay asked.

"No. Why?"

"You're frowning and biting your lower lip."

"My head has felt better and the seat belt gave me quite

a jerk around my middle, but I'm okay. I'm worried about Sean."

"Well, we're back at Dormaine's. There's your car. Good grief, look at that hood!"

"Do I have to?"

"Not if it'll make you feel worse."

"It's a rental. I have no personal attachment," Rebecca said in an attempt at lightness. "I just can't believe the damage I did."

"Only to a car. When I think of what could have happened to you, when I remember how you looked when they wheeled you into the emergency room and told me who you were and that you might be blind . . ." Clay took a deep breath. "It scared the hell out of me."

Rebecca was taken aback by the emotion in his voice. She hadn't seen him for eight years, and at their last meeting, she'd been wraith-thin, all hair and dark-circled eyes, still grief-stricken over the murder of her brother Jonnie. And before that she'd been a giggling, blushing, clumsy thing whose teenage crush glowed in her eyes whenever she looked at him. He probably remembered her, all right— remembered her as a strange being who claimed to have ESP.

"The storm must have slowed down the wrecker service or the car would be gone by now," Clay said. "Where's your luggage? Trunk?"

"Yes, but you don't have to—"

"Why not? We're here. I'll bet the keys are still in the ignition."

Apparently they were because in two minutes Clay had opened the trunk and was carrying Rebecca's luggage to his own. "Nothing to it, and you'll have your things with you tonight," he said. "Now on to find Sean."

They had the street to themselves and Clay turned the car to face the restaurant, allowing the headlights to sweep the side of Dormaine's. "No sign of a dog. Of course if he'd been right here, the paramedics would have found him. But Alvin said they claimed not to have seen a dog."

A thought flashed in Rebecca's mind. "The orderly. Alvin. It's an unusual name. And he looked vaguely familiar to me."

"Alvin Tanner. He's Earl's son."

"Oh God," Rebecca whispered, remembering. Earl Tanner had been stabbed to death outside a local bar called The Gold Key. Police had immediately arrested a male suspect. Circumstantial evidence piled up against him until twelve-year-old Rebecca had told her uncle Bill Garrett, a deputy on the police force, that Earl had been stabbed to death by a woman named "Slim" who had waited for him in an alley outside the bar. Slim Tanner was Earl's wife. Just as Rebecca had predicted, police had found a knife stained with Earl's blood buried beneath a rhododendron bush on the Tanner lawn. Slim had claimed she'd killed Earl because he was beating her and Alvin. Nevertheless, she was doing a life sentence because of Rebecca.

"What's wrong?" Clay asked.

"You know what I did to Alvin's mother."

"I know what Alvin Tanner's mother did to his father. She wasn't fending off an attack—she was waiting for him. It was cold, premeditated murder. You saved an innocent man from going to jail for Slim Tanner's crime." Rebecca remained silent, lost in her memories. "There's a vacant lot beside Dormaine's," Clay said. "Sean might have gone there if he doesn't like people."

Clay pulled to the curb, ordered her to stay inside, and tramped around the damp lot with a flashlight. In a couple of minutes he returned to the car, his blond hair hanging damply over his forehead. "I see a dog behind a pile of wet boxes. I'm not going near him because he doesn't know me and I don't want to scare him away. One of Gypsy's leashes is in the backseat. Grab it and approach him. Be careful, though. It might not be Sean."

But it was. At the sight of her Sean bounded from behind the soggy mass of boxes, jumped up, and wrapped his front legs around her waist the way he'd done since the second day she'd officially adopted him. "I've been so worried about you!" Rebecca cried. "But you look okay. Wet but well."

She attached the leash and led him back to the car, then hesitated. "He has long hair that's sopping wet, Clay. I can't put him in your car."

"The seats are vinyl," Clay said. "Any mess he leaves can easily be cleaned. There's an old blanket in the back. Wrap that around him. He's shivering."

Within minutes Sean was warmly ensconced on the backseat. Rebecca was glad Clay had not pursued the dog in the vacant lot. Sean reacted with bared teeth and snarls at any sign of aggression, particularly from men.

"I don't think he's hurt," Rebecca said as they pulled away from the curb. "I could take him to the vet tomorrow, but those trips usually don't go well. When I get home, I'll look him over."

Clay nodded absently and Rebecca suddenly felt as if she'd become a burden, first by being unable to reach any of her family to fetch her from the hospital, then by having Clay haul her around until they found her wet dog, who was now dripping in his backseat. "I so appreciate all you've done for me tonight," she said hastily. "You've certainly gone above the call of duty. I'm sorry I've been such a pain."

"You haven't been a pain."

"I'll pay for having your car washed and cleaned inside. In spite of the blanket, I think Sean's long hair is making quite a mess—"

"Rebecca, there's something I haven't told you," Clay said abruptly. She looked at his face. It was taut, the jaw almost rigid. "You were so shaken up by the wreck, then so worried about the dog . . . I wanted to do as much as I could to calm you down before I gave you bad news."

"Bad news?" Rebecca echoed faintly, her stomach clenching. "I sensed in the hospital something was wrong. Not with me, though. It's my family, isn't it? That's why no one came to the hospital."

"Yes, I'm afraid so." He took a deep breath. "It's your cousin Molly. Or rather, Molly's son."

"Todd? What's wrong with Todd? Is he sick?"

"No, Rebecca." Clay slowed the car and looked at her, his voice growing soft. "Todd was kidnapped tonight."

Chapter Three

"Kidnapped?" Rebecca felt as if her voice were coming from someone else. "What are you talking about?"

"Apparently Molly was out. A baby-sitter was looking after Todd. Someone got into the house, knocked the baby-sitter unconscious—"

"And took Todd out the window. He didn't make a sound because he'd been drugged. But he had his stuffed toy with him. A dog named Tramp." Clay nearly stopped the car in the middle of the street, staring at her in shock. "And now he's bound and gagged in a place that's hot and reeks of something rotten. And he's terrified and half sick, probably from chloroform."

After a few beats of silence, Clay asked warily, "Rebecca, what are you talking about?"

"I'm talking about Todd. I'm talking about a vision I had. That's what made me wreck, not lightning. I saw it all so clearly. Or rather, I *felt* it. I couldn't see because I was in Todd's mind, and Todd was blindfolded. *He* couldn't see, so I couldn't either." Her voice had taken on a dreamy quality born of horror and the sickening inevitability of her ESP's return. "He doesn't know who took him. But he's not hurt. Not yet, anyway."

The blast of a car horn behind them jolted Clay back into action. He pressed down on the accelerator and they sped along the rain-slicked street for nearly a mile before he said, "Rebecca, are you trying to tell me you knew all along what had happened to Todd?"

"No. I had a vision but I didn't know who the child was. And I'd forgotten Todd had a stuffed dog named Tramp. How could I have forgotten that? When Molly brought him to visit me in New Orleans last summer, he had it with him. He was such a joy, so bright and inquisitive. And he had a wonderful time. We went to the French Quarter and the aquarium and horseback riding in Audubon Park and—"

"Rebecca!" Clay's voice was sharp. "Stop rambling. What are you saying? That you had a psychic vision?"

"Yes." She turned to him. "You don't believe in it, do you?"

Clay raised his shoulders and shook his head, as if trying to clear it. "I don't know. I don't understand it. I guess the scientist in me wants to see proof, statistics, test results . . ."

"There are statistics and test results, Clay. Lots of them collated by respected psychologists, not a bunch of New Age quacks. Besides, Doug must have told you about some of the things I did when I was younger. You saw some of it for yourself. What about the lost children I knew were in that abandoned well? What about Slim Tanner, for God's sake? I didn't even know the woman, had never heard of her. How could I have known she killed her husband?" Clay remained silent and anger surged in Rebecca, then ebbed just as quickly. "I don't care if you believe I have extrasensory perception or not. What we both know is that Todd is missing. He's only seven years old. Molly must be out of her mind with worry. Please take me to her house. Then you can go your own way and I won't bother you anymore."

"Rebecca—"

"I don't want to talk. My head hurts. Just please take me to Molly's."

Clay honored her request and said nothing else, but she stole a couple of glances at his face. She couldn't quite read the expression but it looked like a mixture of worry and regret. At the moment, though, Clay Bellamy's emotions were the least of her concern.

She thought of Todd as she'd last seen him, a slight boy with brown hair like his mother's, cinnamon-colored eyes, and a quick and slightly crooked smile. No one knew who Todd's father was. Molly had become pregnant when she was 19 and refused to tell even Rebecca the identity of the father. She'd spent her pregnancy in New Orleans with Rebecca, then surprised everyone by keeping the baby and returning to Sinclair. After his birth she had finished her college degree in West Virginia and went to work at the headquarters of Rebecca's family's business, Grace Healthcare, a national chain of nursing homes. During the next few years she'd devoted herself to Todd. As far as Rebecca knew, she rarely even dated.

And now that sweet boy, the center of Molly's world, was gone. He'd been taken just like Jonnie. History was repeating itself. Or was it? When Jonnie had vanished at age 14 on a Boy Scout camping trip, Rebecca had "seen" nothing. During the week when everyone had been scouring the area for him, when the local and state police and even the FBI had searched for him in vain, she had seen nothing. Finally his battered body had been discovered in a vacant lot downtown, dumped like a load of trash. No one ever knew who took him. No one ever knew where he'd been kept for a week. And most of the people who'd had faith in Rebecca's powers began to doubt her. She doubted herself. She had failed her own brother. Would she fail Todd, too?

No, this time would be different, she vowed. It was already different. She'd experienced Todd's thoughts after his abduction. And if she'd done it once, surely she could do it again.

Molly's house was about three miles from Rebecca's family's home, situated in an attractive yet definitely less prosperous neighborhood. Although Rebecca had never visited the house, Molly had sent her photos and even by streetlight Rebecca immediately recognized the tan ranch-style home with dark brown trim and shutters.

As they drew near the house, a policeman flagged them down. "No unauthorized visitors," he said. "Please move along."

"I'm Dr. Clayton Bellamy and this is Rebecca Ryan, Molly Ryan's cousin. Chief Garrett is Rebecca's uncle. If they're here, they will want to see Rebecca."

The deputy looked at them suspiciously, then spoke into a walkie-talkie. A voice crackled back and his manner relaxed. "Chief Garrett says for you to park in the driveway, Dr. Bellamy. He's inside with the other Miss Ryan."

Clay dutifully pulled into the driveway. "Thank you," Rebecca said formally. "May I keep Gypsy's leash for the evening? I'll have to tie Sean to the porch."

"I'm going in, too," Clay said. "This is going to be hard on you after the trauma you've just suffered. Also, Molly might need some sedation. I brought my bag."

Hurt pride over his skepticism concerning her vision made Rebecca want to insist that he not come in. Good sense told her a doctor was definitely needed in this situation. Molly was probably near hysteria.

Silently they emerged from the car, Sean in tow. Before they had climbed the three steps to the porch, Molly flung open the front door. "Oh God, you're here at last!" She almost fell down the porch steps, then threw herself into Rebecca's arms.

Rebecca held Molly tightly. Molly looked remarkably like Rebecca's father, Patrick, who had died when Rebecca was nine, complete with reddish-brown hair, freckles, and the cinnamon-colored eyes that she'd passed on to her own son Todd. Molly's sturdy body was hot and trembling.

"I just heard about Todd," Rebecca said softly.

Molly let out a choking sob. "He can't have been kidnapped, Becky. He just can't. He's run off or something. And on this horrible night. He's probably wet and cold and . . ." Another wrenching sob tore at her throat.

"Molly, calm down." Rebecca looked up to see her mother's brother, Bill Garrett, standing tall and lean on the porch. "Hi, Becky. You and Clay and Molly come in now. Bring the dog, too."

Bill's accent had always sounded southwestern to Rebecca. At 45 he was tall and lanky with rough sandy hair and light blue eyes, a dozen crow's-feet fanning onto weathered temples. Rarely was he without a cigarette in hand, although often he lit one and let it burn to the butt without taking more than one or two drags. Rebecca hadn't seen her Uncle Bill for eight years, but he looked and sounded just the same—soft-spoken and uncannily composed, a sharp contrast to his elegant, nervous sister Suzanne.

Rebecca entered Molly's home and took a quick survey. The house was comfortably furnished, although it lacked some of the finer touches of Rebecca's. Rebecca had always been careful with the money that had been held in trust for her until she was 21, but now and then she indulged in a nice painting or an expensive crystal ornament. Molly made a good salary at Grace Healthcare, but with a child and no convenient trust fund like Rebecca's, she couldn't afford luxuries.

Sean, still shivering, lay down near the door. Clay set his medical bag close to the dog, then took a seat across the room, seeming as if he wanted to be as unobtrusive as possible. Bill looked at Rebecca closely. "That nurse who called said you'd been in a wreck."

"You didn't tell me!" Molly gasped accusingly at Bill.

"I'm not seriously hurt," Rebecca said quickly. "Just a couple of cuts. I was taken to the emergency room. Clay took care of me. When the nurse called Molly to come pick me up, she found out about Todd."

"Are you sure you're all right?" Molly asked anxiously.

"As her doctor, I can assure you that in a couple of days she'll be good as new," Clay said. "She was lucky."

Another police officer walked through the room, nodding to Bill before he went out. Bill looked at Rebecca. "We're tapping the phone lines."

Rebecca nodded, feeling cold inside. She remembered the same routine eight years ago, when a frantic Boy Scout leader had called to tell them Jonnie had been missing for hours from a campsite in the hills. Less than 24 hours after that call had come the ransom demand. Then the FBI entered the scene, the ransom drop had been bungled, and Jonnie had been killed. And now Todd, Rebecca thought with a shudder. This just couldn't be happening again.

She looked at Molly. She wore jeans and a red plaid cotton blouse. Her shoulder-length hair was skimmed back with a blue headband and her brown eyes were red-rimmed and swollen. She'd never been a beauty, but her sparkling eyes and brilliant smile usually made her radiant. Now she looked plain and older than her twenty-seven years. Her wire-rimmed glasses rode low on her button nose, pink from crying.

"Please tell me what's going on," Rebecca said, determined not to say anything about her vision yet. "All I know is that Todd is missing."

Clay shot her a narrow look, but Rebecca ignored him. Molly closed her eyes. "I had to work late tonight. Well, I didn't *have* to, but I knew the work needed to be done as soon as possible and I thought I could be home before you got here because of all your flight delays."

"Was Todd angry with you for going out?" Rebecca interrupted.

Molly shook her head. "I keep trying to convince myself that he was mad because I deserted him on a Saturday night and he ran away. But he wasn't. Oh, he did seem disappointed until I told him Sonia could sit with him. Sonia Ellis. She's seventeen and beautiful and he adores her."

"And you feel she's reliable?"

"Goodness, yes." Molly tried to smile. "She's our high school valedictorian. She's headed for the University of Virginia in the fall but she's already taking classes this summer through an extension program. She works at The Jewelry Box downtown during the day. Very ambitious. Her mother works at Grace Healthcare. She's Frank's secretary."

Frank Hardison, Rebecca's stepfather, had taken over running Grace Healthcare shortly after the death of Rebecca's father, Patrick. Her mother had married him a year after Patrick had been killed in the wreck that had almost claimed Rebecca's life, too. If not for Frank, Rebecca felt the family and the business would have fallen apart.

"Frank was here earlier," Molly said. "After Bill had

finished questioning Sonia, he took her to the hospital."

"We missed them somehow," Clay said. "It was a busy night with the storm."

Bill nodded. "The girl had been hit on the head. She said it happened a little after nine. She was watching TV. She was still unconscious when Molly got home."

Rebecca leaned forward, looking at Molly intensely. "You haven't come in contact lately with anyone who seems odd, have you? Someone who pays too much attention to Todd, someone who says things like they'd love to have a boy like him?"

"Bill has already asked me all of this." Molly shook her head. "Since school is out, Todd has been staying at Mrs. Lomax's during the day, but then so do about six other kids. We've been to the movies a few times and last Saturday we went to one of the concerts at the park. But I didn't see him talking to any adults or anyone watching him with particular interest."

"Well, I see I'm just covering the same ground as Bill," Rebecca said. Of course she knew all the questions to ask. The same ones had been asked about Jonnie. "But what about the neighbors?" she couldn't help continuing. "Did they see anything?"

"People in the house on the right are on vacation," Bill answered. "Couple across the street say they didn't see anything unusual. A nurse lives next door. She does some private-duty work at nights looking after an elderly lady. She leaves about seven."

"And the baby-sitter, Sonia, saw and heard *nothing*?"

Bill answered again. "Said she looked in on Todd just before nine. He was asleep. Molly's told me he can be a pill about going to sleep—wants some special light on, keeps asking for glasses of water—but I guess he'd played pretty hard today and wore out early. Sonia claims she was lying on the couch watching something on TV. All at once she was aware that someone was in the room and then she felt a pain in her head before she could even sit up. She does have a nasty bump."

Molly stared at a framed eight-by-ten photo of Todd prominently displayed on the mantle, clearly not paying attention to the exchange between Rebecca and Bill. Her fingers knotted and unknotted a couple of times before she finally asked almost timidly, "Becky, will you do something for me?"

"Anything."

"Go into Todd's room. Spend some time and tell me what you see."

A tingle of discomfort rippled through Rebecca. So often in the past she'd been asked to perform this feat of "seeing" what others couldn't. She'd already "seen" something, but she didn't want to mention it in front of Molly, who was clearly fragile. First she wanted to discuss with Bill her vision of Todd being chloroformed and carried out the window. But at the moment Molly was looking at her with both hope and desperation in her eyes. As much as Rebecca disliked trying to stir her drowsing ESP back to full wakefulness, she couldn't turn down Molly.

"Okay. But you realize I haven't done this sort of thing for years. I'm not like I was when I was sixteen. The visions don't come—"

"Rebecca, *anything* you can do will be a help," Molly said beseechingly. "Please try. For me."

Only someone with a heart of stone could have turned down the frantic mother, Rebecca thought. All of her life she'd loved Molly. She'd waited in the hospital while Molly gave birth to Todd by cesarean section. She'd begged Molly to stay in New Orleans, but Molly had insisted on returning to Sinclair. She stood up. "Show me his bedroom."

Bill rose with Molly. As they walked down the hall, Rebecca felt her chest tightening with stress. The exhilaration that had once accompanied ESP insight now triggered dread so strong she was near nausea. Still, she managed a tight smile for Molly as she entered the bedroom.

In her vision she'd known only what Todd knew and

his eyes had been covered by a cloth. Her knowledge of the room came from Todd's thoughts—the blue Lava lamp Molly left on at night for comfort, the goldfish in a large, sparkling clean bowl. Her gaze went to the window set only two feet above the floor, nothing in front of it except a red and blue throw rug. How easy it would have been for someone to climb through it holding a slight, limp seven-year-old. "Could he have left prints beneath the window?" she asked.

"We haven't had rain for two weeks until tonight," Bill said. "The ground was hard. But no one said he came in through the window."

"I just assumed the doors were locked," Rebecca said to Bill, who was looking at her suspiciously. He'd been the first person to accept her extrasensory abilities when she was a child, and now he'd already guessed she knew more than she was saying.

"But I might have left the window unlocked!" Molly blurted. "I should have checked it before I left, but I didn't! Oh, God."

Rebecca put her arms around Molly. She was trembling violently. "Molly, if someone was out to kidnap Todd, they would have just forced the window open even if it was locked. It's not your fault." She leaned back and smiled into Molly's blotchy face and wide eyes. "Now you and Bill go back to the living room and leave me alone. Maybe I'll come up with something."

"Oh, Becky, thank you," Molly said.

"I can only try. I can't promise anything. You know how this works, or doesn't work most of the time . . ."

Bill put his hand on Molly's shoulder, steering her away from the room. "Take your time, Becky. And relax."

Rebecca had rarely felt less relaxed. Her nerves thrummed and her shoulders ached from the weight of everyone's expectations. She walked around the small room, trying to concentrate on her surroundings but instead replaying every negative remark that had been made over the years about her "magic powers" and her "hocus-pocus."

Usually she had been able to shrug the gibes off because she had a degree of faith in herself. Her mother's mother, Ava, had had the same power. She had never suffered an insecure day in her life and she'd tried to instill the same unshakable self-faith in Rebecca. Ava had never been entirely successful. But now Rebecca had to dig deep for some of her old confidence and try, for Molly's sake.

Rebecca trailed her fingers over the red, white, and blue patchwork quilt covering Todd's bed, a bed she knew police had already searched for fingerprints, errant objects, torn clothing, and blood. Above the bed on the north wall hung a *Star Wars* poster. On the east wall was a magnificent framed photo of a wolf standing in snow taken by Todd's grandfather, Molly's father, who had abandoned the running of Grace Healthcare to become a wildlife photographer, leaving the company in the hands of his brother Patrick.

Rebecca walked to the maple dresser. At one corner sat a globe. In the center two goldfish swam peacefully in their bowl with blue gravel and a castle in the bottom. On the edge of the mirror hung a medallion on a red ribbon reading, "First Place, Junior Swimmers." Last year's trophy for Todd's performance in swimming class. Rebecca smiled. After years of lessons, she still could not swim although she wasn't afraid of water.

Dimly Rebecca heard a roll of thunder. Was the storm coming back? She shivered, not for herself but for Todd. She knew he was terrified of storms. She scanned the room again. She could almost feel Molly and Bill vibrating with anticipation in the living room. She wanted desperately to tell them she'd seen something beyond the ordinary in the room, but there was nothing.

When she walked into the living room, Molly took one look at her face before her tears began to stream. "I'm sorry," Rebecca said awkwardly. "I didn't see anything . . ."

In the bedroom, she wanted to add, but she knew it was best to keep Molly in the dark for now; she'd tell Bill about her vision in the car as quickly as possible, though. Not that it would be all that helpful. She couldn't give him a description of Todd's abductor or where he'd been taken.

"It's all right," Molly said hollowly, wiping at her face with a tattered tissue. "I really didn't expect anything."

But of course she had and the sobs that tore at her throat a minute later said so. Rebecca rushed to her and held her shuddering body close. Clay rose. "I think Molly needs something to help her relax," he said gently.

Molly shook her head. "No! I have to stay alert so I can help Todd."

"You can't help Todd in this condition," Bill said. "Let Clay give you something. Then you'll think more clearly."

Molly didn't argue. She simply cried raggedly on Rebecca's shoulder as Rebecca's own tears began. It had been Molly who had cradled her when she'd cried over her father's death when she was 9, Molly who had comforted her after Jonnie's death when she was 17. Now their positions were reversed, although Todd wasn't dead. Rebecca knew this, but she couldn't say anything yet, she couldn't raise false hopes with a vision so vague.

Molly didn't flinch as Clay injected her. "Ativan," he said. "You'll feel drowsy in a bit."

"Drowsy? I don't want to be drowsy," Molly protested. "I want to be alert."

"You've had a bad shock, Molly. You need to sleep it off. When you wake up, you'll be calmer and better able to help your son."

Rebecca helped Molly into her bedroom, into her pajamas, and into bed. "Will you stay with me for a minute?" Molly asked after Rebecca had tucked her in like a child.

"Sure." Rebecca sat down on the bed and gently smoothed Molly's brown hair back from her face. "Remember when you used to spend the night with me when we were kids?"

"So often. My parents were always gone. And you know what? I didn't care. When they were home Dad seemed so restless and Mom asked incessantly what he was thinking, where he was going, who he'd been talking to on the phone until he'd lose his temper. It was different at your house. So much fun." Molly's smile became slightly lopsided as the tranquilizer took effect. "Remember how we used to stay up watching horror movies?"

"The *Halloween* group were my favorites. I wanted to grow up to be Jamie Lee Curtis. Mother threatened to ground me if I didn't stop standing on the back lawn practicing my screams."

"You were a *great* screamer. And how about Jason in his hockey mask? No summer camps for us! Summer at your house was perfect." Molly had begun slurring her words. "Even affer your dad died it was still good. Oh, he was wunnerful and I missed him but then Frank came along and he was gennel and kind . . . not as much fun as your favver but loving . . . and zen . . ."

And then Jonnie was murdered. Rebecca couldn't talk about Jonnie's murder with Molly, not when Todd was still lost. She was searching for something to say when she looked down and saw Molly's eyes closing. Thank God.

She went back to the living room where Clay and Bill were talking quietly. "She's asleep," Rebecca said. "Bill, I didn't want to bring this up in front of Molly, but is there a chance Todd's father took him?"

"The father was my first thought," Bill admitted. "But Molly told me he's dead."

"Dead?" Rebecca was shocked. The possibility had never occurred to her. "When? Who was he?"

"She wouldn't tell me who he was. She just said he definitely couldn't have taken Todd because he died several years ago. I pressed until I thought she was going to get hysterical, but I couldn't get any more information. I thought you might know something, Becky."

"I don't. Honestly, Bill, I wouldn't hold back at a time like this if I knew *anything*. I was in New Orleans when she got pregnant. Mother was in better shape then and took care of her." Rebecca frowned. "But I've always thought maybe the father was married. She never said anything definite, but I got the feeling he was just unavailable, not unwilling to be with her. Maybe he was one of her professors. She might be protecting his family from ever knowing he had an affair."

"That would be like her," Bill agreed. "Always thinking of other people."

Rebecca closed her eyes. "Oh, God, what a thing to happen to Molly. Todd was her world. *Is* her world," she corrected herself in horror. Todd would be returned. He had to be. "Of course I'll stay with her tonight."

Clay shook his head. "That's not a good idea. Your body has suffered quite a shock. You're not up to caring for Molly tonight." He looked at Bill. "Is there someone else who can stay with Molly?"

"There will be cops here taking care of the phone, handling people who have heard the news and will start coming by. And I'll be in and out. I might be some comfort to her. Molly and I have been seeing each other a bit lately."

"You mean dating?" Rebecca blurted in surprise.

Bill's color rose slightly. "Well, I guess you could call it that. We're not related by blood after all," he said defiantly. "I'm *Suzanne's* brother, not Patrick's and Molly's father's."

"I know the family relationships, Bill," Rebecca said, smiling. "You don't have to defend yourself to me. I think it's wonderful that you're seeing each other."

"Anyway, I know a friend of Molly's who would probably be glad to come and stay with her. I'll give her a call."

"I still think I should stay," Rebecca protested.

"No, you shouldn't," Clay said firmly. "I'm driving you to your house, and I want you to get a good night's sleep. You need it more than you realize."

"All right," Rebecca said reluctantly. Then she looked at Bill. "Before I go, there's something I have to tell you. It's the reason I had the wreck." Bill's expression quickened. "I had a vision about Todd."

"I knew it earlier when you asked about the bedroom window!" he said. "Tell me everything you saw."

Chapter Four

1

The next morning Rebecca awakened disoriented and sore. Her head throbbed. She opened her puffy eyes, glanced around her former bedroom in the Ryan home, and closed her eyes again.

Her mind spun back to when she was nine and she and Daddy had been driving down a curving hillside road. Daddy always drove fast and they'd been singing along with the radio. She remembered being just about as happy as she'd ever been when she heard a noise like an explosion and suddenly they were plummeting down the hillside, rolling over and over. Daddy didn't make a sound. All she heard were her own screams and the sound of shattering glass. Then they landed upside down and rocked back and forth twice, the car creaking, before the world went dark.

The next thing Rebecca recalled from that time was a jolt that stiffened her body, arching her spine. Then shouting. "Again!" Another jolt. "Time?" "Four minutes." "Again!" Another jolt. Then mechanical beeps. She'd opened her eyes and demanded, "Where's Daddy?"

Daddy—Patrick Richard Ryan—was dead. She'd already known he was gone forever: Before she'd blacked out in the car, she had seen his head twisted at that odd angle, the eyes open but flat, unseeing.

Mommy had just cried every time she looked at Rebecca's bruised, swollen face. It was Uncle Bill who'd explained that she'd had an operation. She'd only have a few scars, including a tiny facial one beside her right eye shaped like a crescent moon. She also had a few broken bones and she'd have to wear some uncomfortable casts, but in a couple of months she'd be her old self. Jonnie and Molly were too young to be allowed in for visits, he'd explained, but they couldn't wait to see her. Daddy's best friend Frank Hardison was rushing home from a meeting in Pittsburgh, and he would help Mommy take care of the business, where he was already vice president. Soon she would be home and everything would be fine. The news didn't make up for losing Daddy, but she'd felt slightly cheered.

Then in the middle of one endless night when her broken ribs ached and she couldn't sleep, a pretty young nurse Rebecca liked had crept into her hospital room to check on her.

"Hi, sweetie. Can't sleep?" Rebecca shook her head, and the nurse made a soothing noise. After taking her pulse and jotting some notes on a chart, she held Rebecca's small hand in hers. "You like me and you'll tell me the truth about something, won't you?"

"I always tell the truth," Rebecca said virtuously. "Well, almost always."

"That's my good girl." The nurse looked serious. "Before the doctors made your heart beat again, did you go down a tunnel?"

Rebecca was confused. "We didn't go in a tunnel. Daddy's car crashed down a hill."

"I know that, honey, but your heart stopped after you got to the hospital. You were *dead* for four minutes. Didn't you know that?" Rebecca had gone rigid as the nurse leaned forward, her breath hot on Rebecca's face. "Were you drawn to the bright light at the end of a tunnel? Did you turn away from the light? Is that how you came back from the land of the dead?"

A chill had rippled through Rebecca and she was suddenly terrified of the pretty nurse she'd liked so much. "I didn't see a tunnel or a light and I wasn't *dead*!" Rebecca had hidden her horror behind loud petulance. "Don't touch me! Go away! Go *away*!"

The nurse had fled, afraid her supervisor would write her up for frightening the child, but her words had echoed in Rebecca's head: "You were *dead* for four minutes." She'd fallen silent and refused to speak for two days until she was released from the hospital. The nurses said they were disappointed. They'd thought she was such a sweet, brave little girl. But she hadn't felt sweet and she hadn't felt brave. She'd felt angry and terrified because she had died and come back like some creepy, awful being in a movie.

About a month after the accident she began having visions. They frightened her a little even though there was nothing scary about them. The first time she'd pictured one of her mother's earrings, missing for a month, in the toe of a pair of her evening shoes. A few more times she'd been able to locate lost items. She'd even found Molly's lost cat, Taffy. Then when she was twelve, she had "seen" a man standing unsteadily in a badly lit alley talking to someone named Slim. Rebecca didn't know the man. She didn't know Slim. She only knew Slim was a woman who'd said, "I hate you, Earl," before she'd drawn a knife from her purse and stabbed the man over and over. That had been the Earl Tanner case. Some people said she was a hero for saving the innocent man who'd been arrested for the crime. Other people had been afraid of her. She'd been a little afraid of herself.

Rebecca opened her eyes and returned to the present, to her warm and beautiful bedroom in the Ryan home. During the night Sean had jumped up on the bed. He now touched her arm with a slender paw. She patted it, then gingerly turned her head to look at the clock. Nine-thirty. Why had the family allowed her to sleep so late on a day when Molly needed her?

As if on cue, someone tapped lightly on her door. Probably Betty, the housekeeper, who had greeted her and fussed over her last night. "Come in," Rebecca called in a husky voice.

Her mother Suzanne took two steps into the room and clapped a hand over her mouth to stifle a gasp. "I'm sorry the dog's on the bed," Rebecca said quickly.

"I don't care about the dog." Suzanne drew nearer. She wore a pale blue silk robe and the tightened belt showed how painfully thin she'd grown. Her silky blond hair was sprinkled with silver and her eyes were lost in mauve hollows. "Why on earth didn't you wake me when you got in last night?"

When Clay had dropped Rebecca off at the house, she'd been surprised when Betty said her mother was sleeping. How could she sleep when Todd was missing? Then she remembered being told in the hospital that her mother wasn't "up to par." Suzanne had no doubt flown to the bottle upon hearing the news about Todd and by midnight was probably incapable of standing. "I didn't want to disturb you," Rebecca said.

"But you had a wreck. Betty told me. Your head . . ."

"Just a couple of cuts, Mother, and some bruises. No broken bones."

"You could have been killed!"

Rebecca was startled by the passion in her mother's voice. She'd fled to New Orleans mostly because of her mother's cold resentment that she hadn't been able to find Jonnie. Their relationship had never been close, but the manifestation of the ESP destroyed it forever. During the next few years Suzanne had turned more and more to alcohol and away from her daughter. They'd grown so far apart Rebecca didn't think Suzanne really gave her much thought anymore.

"I'm really okay."

Suzanne suddenly looked angry. "Someone should have told me last night! No one ever tells me anything. They think I can't handle it."

"There wasn't any reason to upset you, what with Todd and all," Rebecca said lamely.

"Todd! Dear God." Suzanne drew nearer and sat down on the bed. Up close Rebecca could see the thin, unhealthy look of her mother's skin. "He can't have been kidnapped, Rebecca. I won't believe that could happen again. I believe he's just run away."

Humor her mother or be honest? Rebecca had trouble being anything but honest. "Mother, the baby-sitter was knocked unconscious. Todd is only seven years old. He's not capable of that."

"Maybe she was lying."

"She had a bump on her head. Frank took her to the hospital. Haven't you talked to him this morning?"

"No, she hasn't." Her stepfather, Frank Hardison, strolled into the room. "Good morning, Rebecca. I'm so glad you're all right."

"Leave it to me to try to sneak into town and end up making a big entrance," Rebecca said dryly.

Frank smiled. "You don't have the kind of personality that lends itself to *sneaking*."

Although Frank was only of medium height, his perfect posture and slenderness made him seem taller. With his salt-and-pepper hair and aquiline nose, Rebecca had always thought Frank was the most distinguished-looking man she'd ever seen. He was only three years older than her father, but she'd always thought of Frank as being much older than Daddy. Where Patrick was exuberant, Frank was grave. Nevertheless, she'd always been comfortable with Frank and quickly came to love him after he married Suzanne.

"Frank, has there been *any* news about Todd? Mother says no one will tell her anything."

Faint impatience crept into Frank's hazel eyes. "Suzanne is paranoid. No one is keeping anything from her." Their gazes met and a flash of the old fire appeared in Suzanne's before she looked away. "There simply hasn't been any news unless something has happened in the last couple of hours that I don't know anything about. I'm headed down to the volunteer center now. They'll know of any recent developments."

"The what?"

"The old fabric shop on Elm Street closed about two months ago and I bought it. We're using it as a center to coordinate volunteer efforts to find Todd—you know, copying leaflets with his photo, gathering calls about sightings, organizing civilian search parties."

"It was wonderful of you to offer the place, Frank."

"He bought it for Lynn," Suzanne intervened caustically. "It seems he thinks his daughter-in-law has a great flair for ceramics that is wasted at Vinson's Apothecary. She's going to sell her wares out of her very own store."

"She *is* talented, Suzanne," Frank said tiredly. Clearly this was an old argument.

"Not that I can see. But we must keep Doug and Lynn happy."

"Do you have a problem with my son being happy?" Frank asked tightly.

"Not your son. He's a good teacher, a good man. It's Lynn I have the problem with." Suzanne looked at Rebecca. "I didn't sleep well last night. I think I'll lie down again for a few minutes. I'm glad you're home and that you weren't hurt last night, Rebecca." She glanced at Sean. "And please get the dog bathed today. I don't mind dogs in the house as long as they're clean."

"He was thrown free of the car during the wreck and was out in the rain for hours," Rebecca said in Sean's defense. "He doesn't usually look like this."

"Yes, whatever," Suzanne said vaguely as she wafted out of the room, seeming to have already lost interest.

"She looks much worse than when you two were in New Orleans three years ago," Rebecca said quietly to Frank.

"The drinking."

"We have to do something."

Frank shrugged. "I hate to humiliate her by having her hauled off to rehab. Everyone in town will know. I keep hoping for some kind of miracle."

"Well, it looks like we need more than one miracle now," Rebecca said. "It was wonderful of you to offer the building."

"An empty building. Big deal. The county and state police have been brought in on this. There are ground and air searches. And this morning we got Molly pulled together enough to tape a plea for Todd's return that will run on all the local television stations. They'll show his photo and she repeats his name a number of times to humanize him, make him seem like a *child*, not an *it*, to his abductor, pleads desperately for him to be brought home, assures the kidnapper there will be no consequences. She did a good job with it, but frankly I've never had much faith in a kidnapper being moved by a televised plea."

It was all too sickeningly familiar. The same frantic activity had been set in motion 24 hours after Jonnie's disappearance. People had swarmed over the countryside where he'd disappeared. Helicopters had scanned a hundred-mile radius. Leaflets papered every tree and telephone pole. A ravaged Suzanne had appeared on morning, noon, and evening television broadcasts. None of it had helped. "They still don't have any idea who could have done this?" Rebecca asked.

"Bill says no, but I have my doubts about the baby-sitter."

"The baby-sitter? I thought she was knocked unconscious. You took her to the hospital."

"I did and she does have a head injury. Her mother is my secretary. Mrs. Ellis is efficient, loyal, intelligent, the widow of a minister. She has two teenage children. Sonia, the elder, is nearly a paragon of teenage responsibility."

"Then what's the problem?"

Frank frowned. "Her boyfriend. Randy Messer. He's been in a lot of trouble. Oh, nothing big. Shoplifting. Possession." He smiled. "And I know you think I'm being terribly judgmental since my own son saw his share of trouble as a teenager. Well, I know how I sound, but Douglas was different. His mother deserted us, then died, I didn't devote enough time to him, and he didn't feel welcome in this house after I married your mother. Oh, you were always great to him, but Jonathan—" He broke off uncomfortably. Frank had always called Jonnie *Jonathan*. "Anyway, Doug was never malicious and he's completely turned his life around. Randy Messer is a different matter. Sonia's mother worries about the relationship."

"Then why doesn't she make Sonia break it off?"

"You don't know Mrs. Ellis and you don't know Sonia—spun sugar and cast iron. And Sonia's mother has been at sea since the death of her husband two years ago— he thought he had a direct line to God's ear. He ran a tight ship and Mrs. Ellis deferred to him about everything for nearly twenty years. She's just getting her bearings. Anyway, Bill has promised me he'll check out the Messer kid." He stood. "And now I'll leave you alone to get some rest."

"First I have to make some calls and get things straightened out about my car with the rental company."

"I've already taken care of that. And while you're here, you can drive your mother's Thunderbird. No sense going to the trouble of renting another car when that one just sits in the garage."

"Oh, Frank, thank you," Rebecca said.

He came over and planted a light kiss on her forehead. "You're welcome, dear. I'm just thankful you're all right. At least we didn't have two disasters last night."

After he'd left, Rebecca didn't know why she hadn't told him about her vision of Todd. She'd never felt the need to hold a vision so closely in her life.

2

Betty arrived five minutes later with a tray bearing poached eggs on toast and a thermos of weak tea. An invalid's breakfast. She fussed and sympathized and tucked a napkin in the neck of Rebecca's nightgown as if she were a child. At last she produced a leash from her apron pocket. "Sean needs a walk and something to eat. I sent Walt out for some dog food this morning. That other stuff you brought looks like gravel. You do know that I got married, don't you? That Walt is my husband?"

"Of course I know you got married. You sent me pictures of the wedding." Betty had stood small and round in an unflattering fussy pink suit, smiling broadly. Her groom had been tall and thin with a strong resemblance to Abraham Lincoln. "How is Walt?"

"Fine. He's always fine. He has the constitution of a horse," Betty announced proudly. How romantic, Rebecca thought, trying not to grin. "He does all the lawn work around here and all the maintenance, too."

Rebecca dipped into her poached egg. She hated poached eggs. "Even though I arrived at night, I could tell the lawn looked especially nice."

"Not one patch of crabgrass in it. Walt won't abide crabgrass. He does work at the Business, too."

"The Business" was the headquarters of Grace Healthcare, the chain of nursing homes started by Rebecca's paternal grandfather. Rebecca often wondered what would have happened to the company if Frank hadn't been there to step in when her father was killed.

"That's how I met Walt," Betty was going on. "Your stepfather sent him from the Business over here to do some work. Walt's real good with dogs. He'll take to Sean."

"The question is if Sean will take to him. I told you he's skittish around men."

"I'm tellin' you the truth, honey, Walt has a gift with animals." She carefully attached Sean's leash and began talking to him in a baby voice. "Now you come along with your Aunt Betty and meet your Uncle Walt. You two are going to be the best of friends."

"If they aren't, tell Walt I'll pay for the hospital bills," Rebecca called as Sean reluctantly followed Betty out of the room.

As soon as she finished her breakfast, Rebecca called Molly's. Bill answered. "I thought I'd get Molly or another cop."

"I just walked in ten minutes ago. Molly got a good, long sleep. How about you?"

"The same. I'm just fine this morning."

"I'll bet."

"I'm coming over as soon as I get dressed."

"Ah, Becky, I don't think you should," Bill said. "The

press has gotten wind of this as well as half the town. You wouldn't believe the crowd outside. I had to call in some deputies to help keep the mess under control."

"Then I'll just fight my way through them."

"No, honey, please don't. That nurse who lives next door, Jean Wright, is here with Molly now. I guess they're pretty good friends."

"Well, surely Molly can have more than one woman with her. And I didn't know she and that woman were good friends. Molly's only mentioned her once or twice."

"Becky, people around here know who you are. Or, more important, what you've done. No one has forgotten your work with the police a few years ago. You're a celebrity. We're having enough trouble keeping a lid on things here as it is. I'm afraid if you show up, we'll completely lose control."

"Oh," Rebecca said slowly. "I hadn't thought of that."

"I know. And I know Molly would appreciate having you here, but we've already talked about it. She agrees with me that it's best for you to keep away right now. But I told her about your vision and she's ecstatic that you've made some kind of contact. She said you could do more good concentrating on getting some other vibes about Todd than sitting here holding her hand."

"Concentration doesn't help," Rebecca said as she felt the weight of people's expectations descend on her. "Your mother had ESP. My mother doesn't understand how it works, but you do."

"Suzanne doesn't understand it because she doesn't want to. It scares her and she's always run from what scares her. That's why she got so distant with you when you started manifesting it. I don't completely understand it, but I accept it—both its limitations *and* its strengths. And you've already had one vision. There's no reason why we shouldn't be optimistic about you having another one." Rebecca heard him turn away from the phone and speak to someone else. "Got to go, Becky. Besides, we don't want to tie up the phone line. You get some rest. I'll tell Molly you called."

He hung up without saying good-bye. Rebecca sighed and lay back against the pillows, feeling helpless. She couldn't just lie here hoping another vision would strike, so she climbed painfully from the bed and took a shower. She then called her best friend in New Orleans, briefly explained about the situation with Todd, and asked her to water the plants and keep an eye on the house. Next she E-mailed her agent, saying only that she was in West Virginia and leaving a phone number. The agent was waiting for the proposal for Rebecca's next book, a proposal that was due at the end of the week. Rebecca doubted if she would get one word written this week and didn't care.

She tried to lie down again, but after ten minutes in bed she knew she was too restless to spend any more time shut in her room. She got up and took two aspirins, hoping to work some of the soreness from her body. A look in the mirror almost scared her. Bandages covered the cuts on her forehead. A long scratch ran along her jaw and a bruise discolored her right cheekbone. Her eyes felt too irritated to accept contact lenses, so she dug her metal-framed glasses out of her purse, put on slacks and a T-shirt, and went downstairs.

On her way to the kitchen, Rebecca passed through the living room. Decorated in tones of cream, hunter green, and antique gold, it remained just the same as when she'd left home. At one end of the room sat a Steinway piano; at the other was a Hammond organ. Both she and Jonnie had taken music lessons. Rebecca had practiced diligently but at best managed only to plunk out the standard beginner's fare. She'd been bitterly disappointed with her failure, as had her mother. Jonnie was a different story. Although he'd complained loudly about the forced tutelage, he'd shown remarkable talent.

Rebecca flipped on the organ and sat on the bench, picturing her brother with his golden hair and a rapt look in his eyes as he'd played. Their father's favorite song had been a haunting remnant of the sixties, "A Whiter Shade of Pale" by Procol Harum. He'd listened to it so often, Suzanne told him he'd wear out the tape. And years after Patrick's death, Suzanne cried quietly in the audience when Jonnie had played the song with tremendous skill and feeling in a talent contest, dedicating it to his father. He'd won the contest and been ecstatic. Three months later he had been murdered, all his joy, all his promise brutally cut short.

Rebecca managed the first few chords before her fingers froze. Even if she'd possessed Jonnie's talent, she couldn't have played the song. It had belonged first to Patrick, then to Jonnie. She would never hear it again without thinking of the two males she'd loved most and lost.

Abandoning the organ, she walked into the kitchen. "What are you doin' up?" Betty demanded as she worked on tuna salad for lunch. "You need sleep."

"I slept long enough and I'm restless."

Betty inspected her face in the light, then shuddered. "The thought of you in another wreck frightens the life out of me. Child, I do wonder about your luck sometimes."

"So do I," Rebecca said dryly, "although a lot of people would say I was lucky to survive two wrecks."

"That's right, I guess. By the way, I like your glasses. You wore them until you were twelve. You were cute as a button then."

"Great. I look like a cute-as-a-button twelve-year-old. My day is truly made."

"You're cranky. You need to go back to bed."

"Then I would be crankier." She looked at a man looking up from a plate of bacon and eggs at the kitchen table. "And this must be Walt." His long, thin arms and legs splayed at all angles and his high-cheekboned face was seamed and brown as leather. He gave her a shy look and stood up, bumping into the table and setting everything rocking, and bowed slightly as if to royalty. "How do ya do, ma'am?"

"Hello, Walt." Rebecca went forward, hand extended.

Walt rubbed his on his pant leg before shaking. "And I'm Rebecca. *Ma'am* makes me feel at least a hundred."

"Yes ma'am, ummm, Rebecca."

"Walt wanted to lay those new flagstones in the garden before the day got hot," Betty explained. "That's why he's eatin' breakfast so late. Want some bacon and eggs, honey?"

"No thanks." She glanced at Sean, who lay beside where Walt's big feet would have been. "You two getting along?"

"He's a fine dog, ma'am," Walt said earnestly. "Takes a gentle hand, but he's smart as a whip. Loyal, too."

"You can tell he's loyal?"

"Oh yeah. I can sense it in a minute."

"Walt's got a real affinity with animals," Betty said.

Rebecca picked up an abandoned half of buttered toast and smiled. "Hear that, Sean? You've made a couple of friends. Walt, please sit down and finish your breakfast before it gets cold."

Walt obeyed, banging into the table again.

"So if you won't go to bed like a good girl, what's on your agenda today?" Betty asked.

"Frank said I could drive mother's car instead of renting another one."

"Missus told me so this morning." After all these years, Betty refused to call Suzanne "Mrs. Hardison." She'd gone from "Mrs. Ryan" to "Missus." "Keys are on the Peg-Board in the pantry. Missus doesn't drive much anymore. Hasn't had her car out for weeks, in fact."

Rebecca was both saddened and relieved to hear this. Suzanne used to love driving as much as Patrick did and got a new, fast car every two years. But now that she was drinking heavily, her decision to abandon driving was for the best.

"You leavin' right away, honey?"

"Yes. Uncle Bill doesn't believe I should visit Molly this morning. There's a crowd and the press." Betty shook her head and clucked disapprovingly. "I think I'll go see Aunt Esther."

Betty's face fell. "Oh, that poor dear. 'Bout broke my

heart when I heard about her cancer. But I thought you weren't supposed to know."

"You didn't think Molly would keep it from me, did you? I also need to see if Happy Tracks will take Sean in today since it's an emergency. He got soaked last night, and Mother wants him to have a bath immediately."

"I could bathe him," Walt said.

"He needs some clipping done. That's usually a two- to three-person ordeal. Thanks for offering, though. He'd probably prefer a bath from you."

"I told you Walt has a way about him," Betty said sagely.

"Apparently. He convinced you to marry him."

Betty's cheeks pinked. "You and your teasin'. You keep under the speed limit today and pull right off the road if you feel dizzy or sick. Walt'll come pick you up."

In the garage Rebecca found a red Thunderbird with every imaginable option. It was three years old but the odometer showed only a little over 4,000 miles. Betty wasn't exaggerating—Suzanne certainly hadn't done much driving lately. Sean hopped onto the passenger's seat and she backed out of the driveway.

Since she was a child Rebecca had called Esther Hardison aunt, although she was Frank's aunt and no blood relation to any of the Ryans. After the death of his parents when he was twelve, Frank's Uncle Ben and his wife Esther had taken him in. Later, Rebecca, Jonnie, and Molly had learned to love her and feel as if they were truly related. Even after Rebecca had moved to New Orleans, she still spoke to Esther once a month on the phone, and twice Esther had come down for Mardi Gras.

Esther still lived five miles out of town on a ten-acre piece of land called Whispering Willows Nursery. At one time most of the ten acres had been used for growing flowers, shrubs, and trees. Now the widowed Esther had reduced the business by half, keeping a staff of only two.

A large white sign with WHISPERING WILLOWS NURSERY written in green script sat beside the highway. Rebecca turned off onto a narrow asphalt road. Green fields spread on either side and in a minute she saw Esther's sprawling, white two-story nineteenth-century house, which sported a wraparound porch and a glass cupola that reflected the sun. For as long as Rebecca could remember, Esther had been threatening to sell the five-bedroom house that was far too large for one person, but Rebecca knew she never would. Esther had come here as a bride and had lived alone for the past ten years since her husband died.

Rebecca pulled up in front of the house and, knowing no one would be inside on this beautiful day, led Sean around back. Esther emerged from one of the greenhouses, immediately spotted Rebecca, and rushed to her, hugging her fiercely. "No one told me you were coming!" She leaned back and frowned. "Sweetheart, I heard about your wreck."

"First night home and I ran my car into a tree. I'm fine. I'm not so sure about the tree."

"Trees can be replaced. So can cars. You, my girl, cannot." Esther glanced down at the dog. "And this must be the temperamental Sean you've told about in your calls. He's beautiful, but we'll let him make up his own mind about me."

"I think you'll be on the acceptable list."

Rebecca looked at Esther closely. She'd feared the woman would look ill, debilitated, but she seemed just the same as she swept off her straw hat to reveal curly, shoulder-length silver hair that had never seen the inside of a styling salon. She had a weathered face, but her bright blue eyes belied her 75 years. Her tall body was slim as a girl's; she wore jeans, a loose checked shirt, running shoes, and an ever-present tiny gold cross on a chain around her neck. "Frank didn't call me about Todd until this morning," she said, tears welling in her eyes. "I can't believe it! I wanted to go to Molly's, but when I called, Bill told me to stay away for now."

"You and me both. I guess it's a madhouse of reporters and sightseers around Molly's."

"Disgraceful!" Esther swiped at a tear that had run down her cheeks, then frowned. "But Todd was taken only last night. You couldn't have gotten here so quickly even if they'd told you immediately."

"I . . . I . . ." Rebecca, the writer of fiction, went blank. "It was just a coincidence that I came home at the same time."

"Oh phooey, Rebecca Ryan! Molly spilled the beans about my cancer. Oh, don't gear up for a big denial. I see it in your eyes. But don't you worry about me. I'm going to be fine. I'll be running this nursery twenty years from now. I'm just burned up that I have lung cancer when I've never smoked a cigarette in my life!"

"Oh, Aunt Esther, you're wonderful!" Rebecca laughed as she hugged the woman again. "I should have known your spirits wouldn't flag. They never do."

"Thinking the worst doesn't accomplish anything except to make you too depressed and upset to help yourself. And that's what we all have to do. Help ourselves—and others, of course. You came here to see about me and now it turns out you're here just in time to help Molly."

"Oh, I don't know, Aunt Esther. I certainly wasn't much help to Jonnie."

"I've always believed that was because you were too close to the situation. The tie between you and Jonnie jumbled up your ESP—not that I really understand the whole concept, and not that I don't have more than a little trouble accepting that such a thing can exist. But I saw it work too many times to doubt it anymore. And I do believe that God works in mysterious ways, even through something like ESP."

"I wish everyone were as levelheaded as you about the phenomenon. Some completely doubt it, some think it's the work of the devil."

"When that Tanner man was killed, you saved an innocent man from being punished for murder. I don't call that the devil's work, and I dare anyone to say it is!"

Rebecca had always loved Esther's spunk, her general acceptance of life and all its joys as well as vicissitudes. She only wished her own mother had some of Esther's spirit. "Come inside," Esther said. "I made a fresh batch of lemonade and some gingersnaps this morning."

Esther always had lemonade and gingersnaps when Jonnie and Rebecca visited and the children stuffed themselves. Esther loved and understood children. When she was young, she had taught grade school for years and had been a great favorite among the children for her patience and sense of humor.

Half an hour later one of Esther's employees came to the door to tell her about a problem. Esther turned to Rebecca. I have a lot of loose ends to tie up before I go to the hospital. I'll hurry."

"Take your time," Rebecca said. "I'll walk Sean around the grounds. I haven't seen them for a long time."

Rebecca hoped Esther didn't see how often Sean lifted his leg as they hurried past the two greenhouses and back toward the pond. It hadn't been dredged for a few years and water lilies grew on its surface. Rebecca remembered her and Jonnie's delight and the sound of spring peepers in the evenings as they ran around catching fireflies in jars, then freeing them after they'd seen who'd caught the most. Now, large dragonflies hovered over the pond and tall cattails and sedge edged the murky water. Rebecca wondered if Esther had not dredged the pond because her funds were low. She had always refused to take money from Frank, but it was a shame to let this beautiful spot slip into neglect because she was too proud to accept a little help from relatives.

She turned Sean's leash loose, knowing he wasn't fond of water and wouldn't jump into the scummy pond. Instead he ran aimlessly for a couple of minutes, then headed toward the log cabin about fifty yards from the pond. Rebecca followed him, recalling how the cabin had intrigued her, Jonnie, Doug, and Molly. Built around 1770, it had shel-

tered one of the first families in the area, a couple named
Leland who farmed the land and reared three children to
adulthood and lost two more to smallpox.

Rebecca tried the cabin door although she knew it would
be locked. She peered in one of the windows that had replaced the greased paper used by the original Lelands. The
inside was bare except for an old wooden table in the middle of the main room and a rocking chair in the nearest
corner. Along one wall sat a stone fireplace and in the op-
posite corner was a built-in china cabinet. Rebecca doubted
if the Lelands had had much fine china to display. Perhaps
the cabinet had been built in anticipation of luxuries to
come. A garden spider had constructed an impressive web
between a juniper shrub and the door frame.

Rebecca turned away from the cabin. Sean bounded happily toward her, stood on his hind legs, and wrapped his
forelegs around her waist. She bent to hug him and dropped
a kiss on the top of his head, touched by his affection for
her in spite of his general fear of humanity. He dropped
down and headed for the pond, seemingly entranced by the
few brave sunfish that remained. He dipped a paw in the
water, then fastidiously drew it back.

The movement sparked a memory in Rebecca. She had
been eleven and devastated when she'd awakened to find
her hamster Melvin dead. Frank had brought her and Jonnie
and their Irish setter Rusty to Esther's, knowing how much
Rebecca loved the nursery. In spite of everyone's attempts
to cheer her, though, Rebecca had continued to droop. Then
Jonnie abruptly stripped off his T-shirt and jeans to reveal
garish bathing trunks. He dived into the pond, displaying
the aquatic acrobatics at which he'd excelled since age four
while Rebecca remained unable to swim more than two feet
without sinking straight to the bottom. In the midst of his
showing off, 100 pounds of dog leaped in beside him, mis-
taking his whoops of delight for cries of despair. The two
flailed until Rusty got a firm hold on Jonnie's arm and
pulled him, protesting and gasping, through the weeds to
the shore. While Jonnie lay helpless with giggles, Rusty

shook vigorously then looked around proudly at Rebecca, Esther, and Frank, clearly awaiting kudos for his bravery. Rebecca had bent double with laughter, the hamster temporarily forgotten.

Rebecca giggled at the memory. Jonnie had been trying to brighten her mood and he had, only not quite the way he'd intended. But he hadn't minded his own embarrassment as long as he'd made her laugh. He'd always wanted to entertain, to see people have fun. He'd possessed a basically kind, joyous, and expansive spirit. . . .

A fish bobbed, sending ripples flashing in the sunlight, out and away, out and away, slighter and slighter . . .

The sun dulled. The sound of bees buzzing in a nearby clump of larkspur grew distant, inaudible. Rebecca no longer felt the heat of the day or the sting of perspiration running into the cuts on her forehead. She knew what was happening but she was powerless to stop it. This time she didn't *want* to stop it . . .

The room was chilly. His ankles and wrists were rubbed raw from chafing against their metal cuffs and his jaw ached from being forced open by a gag. His head throbbed. His chest felt tight. He was dully afraid.

His fear sharpened when he heard footsteps coming toward him. The rustle of clothing. The smell of sweat beneath something else. Cologne, old and tainted. He lay still, waiting. A hand grabbed his finger and bent it backward until he moaned. "They screwed up the ransom," a voice rasped. "Your loving family wanted to make sure they didn't lose their money, so they brought cops in. FBI. They knew what would happen if they did that. They were warned." The tormentor jerked the finger until the bone snapped and he screamed against his gag. "They signed your death warrant, Ryan . . ."

"Rebecca?" A voice floated languidly from far away. "Rebecca, you're walking into the water." A hand clamped on her shoulder and pulled her backward. "Rebecca, stop!"

She heard Sean growl before he lunged and clamped on

someone's leg. There was a shout; Rebecca focused on Douglas's shocked face, and then she commanded, "Sean! Halt!" He clung to the leg and she kneeled, running her hands down his sides. "Sean, stop it," she murmured. "Good boy." He immediately loosened his bite.

Rebecca looked up at her stepbrother. "Doug, are you okay?"

He took two slow steps away from Sean and rolled up the right leg of his jeans. Just above the ankle was a shallow bite, blood barely showing in four spots. "Has he had his shots?"

"For every known dog ailment."

"Then I'm fine. Thank goodness for heavy denim."

"He's not a bad dog. He thought you were hurting me."

"Relax." Doug smiled. He had his father's black hair and hazel eyes, but not the patrician features. His nose was broader and his cheekbones less prominent. He was barely five-foot-nine and slightly stocky. In fact, in the last eight years he'd put on about 20 pounds, Rebecca noted. What in high school had been a "cute" face was now turning into a pudgy one. His dark hair was also receding from his forehead. Rebecca was surprised by the change in him.

"I was standing over there watching you look at the pond and suddenly your face went blank," he told her. "Then you started walking into the water. It's dirty. Besides, I know you can't swim and there's a sharp drop about two feet past the bank." He frowned at her. "You were saying 'FBI.' You said it a couple of times. What did you mean?"

"I . . . I don't know." She'd entered a mind that was hearing about a ransom drop that had failed because the FBI had been brought into the case. But there had been no ransom demand for Todd. The FBI was not involved. Her stomach clenched. Jonnie. For Jonnie there *had* been the FBI and ransom.

The truth hit Rebecca like a blow to the head. This vision wasn't about Todd—it was about Jonnie. A moment ago she'd glimpsed into the mind of someone who had been dead for over eight years.

Rebecca swayed and Douglas caught her. "What's wrong?" he demanded. "I heard about your car wreck. Are you dizzy? Let me carry you back to the house."

"No, please, I'm fine," Rebecca said thinly, knowing she'd never been less "fine" in her life. My God, she thought, all those years ago when Jonnie needed me, I saw nothing. Why now, when it doesn't matter anymore? What the hell kind of sick cosmic joke is this?

"Joke?" Doug asked. "What's a joke?"

Now she was speaking her thoughts aloud. Douglas had been her stepbrother for 16 years but she felt as if she barely knew him. She certainly didn't want him to know about the images flashing through her mind. "Maybe I *have* overdone it today." Rebecca tried to sound calm. "I can walk back to the house, though. If you try to carry me, Sean will probably tear off your leg." Impulsively she linked her arm through Doug's. "Walk with me."

"Gladly." He gave her a sideways glance. "I'm sure you know all about Todd. Have you 'seen' anything?"

"No." Rebecca would not discuss what she'd seen with anyone except Bill and Molly. She did not want gossip spreading, resulting in half the town looking at her as if she were an oracle and half looking at her as if she were a lunatic. She was already angry that she'd blurted out her first vision in front of Clay Bellamy, but that could not be helped now. Still, Doug had no right to probe her thoughts. He wasn't close to Molly or Rebecca. "I haven't been any help at all, which is why I am avoiding the subject of Todd," she said firmly. "Tell me about your teaching."

Doug looked taken aback by the rebuff, then reacted gracefully. "Well, I teach history to seventh graders. The students can be a handful, reaching adolescence and all that. And most of them aren't riveted by the subject." He smiled. "If anyone had told me when I was in the seventh grade that I'd end up teaching history, I'd have laughed myself silly."

"You weren't exactly the scholarly type."

"Too busy picking fights, although I dreamed of being

a flashy cop. Then I started hating the police . . ."

"After Larry was shot by the police. Of course he wouldn't have been caught if it weren't for me, for which your wife will never forgive me."

"Larry is Lynn's brother," Doug said coolly. "Certainly you can understand how she feels, even if she isn't being fair. It's hard to be rational where family is concerned."

Esther had spotted them walking slowly toward the house. She must also have noted the linked arms and interpreted the contact as a sign of something amiss.

"Rebecca, you're pale as a ghost. Go right inside and sit down. Or lie down. I knew you were overdoing it. Should we call a doctor? What happened to your slacks?"

"I don't need a doctor and I went wading in the pond."

"*You?* Wading?"

"I guess I was daydreaming." Rebecca had a believable explanation for what even she didn't understand.

Esther shook her head. "Those pretty linen slacks will never be the same." She turned to one of her staff members, a young man with huge biceps carrying a three-feet-tall holly tree. "Jake, that's for Mrs. Emerson. Don't put it with the others. She seems to think there's something special about that particular one." Esther turned back to Rebecca and Douglas. "People and their ideas! It's a wonder to me the world keeps turning. Becky, inside. Douglas, get her some lemonade and aspirin. I'll be there in five minutes. And get the dog some water. His tongue is hanging out."

Doug insisted Rebecca sit while he gave a wary Sean water and poured lemonade. "Are you sure you're all right?" Rebecca asked as he handed her a tall glass.

"My friend's bratty two-year-old son gave me a worse nip on the ankle last week, and the human mouth has more bacteria than a dog's."

"Most people don't know that."

"I like dogs. Like to have one, but Lynn doesn't care for them."

"Does Lynn care about anything anymore?" Rebecca snapped.

Doug gave her a long look. "Me. Lynn loves me completely. *She* always has even when I didn't deserve anyone's affection." He paused. "And she loves her brother. Two losers, but she found it in her heart to care about us. That takes someone special, Rebecca, whether you with all your extrasensory powers can see it or not."

3

"Does she know anything about the kid?"

Lynn Cochran Hardison looked at her brother. His light brown hair was heavily sprinkled with gray although he was only 31. He hadn't shaved for days, making the deep scar along his jaw stand out even more prominently. The scar was the result of a prison fight that had almost killed him six years ago. Since then he'd grown leaner and more muscular as he'd prepared himself for more battles. It seemed to Lynn that even his eyes had acquired a wolfish look, as if he'd transformed into a predator before his parole.

Even after his year of freedom, he still wore a hunted look. And no wonder, Lynn thought. It seemed the police were looking for any reason to harass him even though he'd never missed a day of work at Maloney's Garage, where he was a mechanic. He had also scrupulously obeyed the law, not even getting a parking ticket. But Larry was surly and neither his boss nor his co-workers liked him. He was also drinking too much. He now poured another shot of Jim Beam and limped back to the stained wing chair he'd bought at a garage sale. His right leg had been permanently damaged when Bill Garrett shot him while Larry was committing a robbery.

"I haven't talked to Rebecca except for when she came in Vinson's last night," Lynn said. "I'm sure Doug will see her today. He'll find out what she knows."

"Why would she tell him? She doesn't know about this

great transformation your husband experienced. She thinks he's still a creep like me."

"Don't take that sneering tone when you talk about Doug," Lynn flared. "He knew he couldn't go on with the drinking and the heroin, especially after what happened to you. He's worked damned hard to change. He's trying to live a good life, that's all. He's great to me, he's trying to be a good friend to you—he doesn't deserve your ridicule."

"While he was busy turning himself into a model citizen, I was in the penitentiary," Larry said bitterly. "Have I ever told you what it was like in there?"

"About a hundred times."

"I love it when you get sarcastic." Larry took a slug of bourbon. "You and Doug did everything I did. You just didn't get caught."

"We didn't commit burglary and pull a gun on a cop. That was your bright idea."

"But you didn't mind doing the drugs I scored from my ill-gotten gains," Larry snarled.

Lynn's eyelids dropped over her piercing gray eyes. She stared at her lap for a moment, then sighed. "I'm sorry for everything that's happened to you. And you're right—technically Doug and I were just as guilty as you. We were all crazy back then. But it wasn't because of us you got caught robbing those houses. That was Rebecca."

"Rebecca who somehow found out what I was doing and set her uncle on me. He *shot* me."

"You pulled a gun on him, Larry," Lynn said softly.

"I wasn't going to shoot him. I just freaked. And look what happened to me. I'm a damned wreck. My leg hurts all the time, I can't afford anything . . ."

"Why *can't* you afford anything? You make a decent salary, certainly enough to pay for this apartment and your living expenses. You even bought a stereo." Lynn looked around. "At least I thought you did. Where is it?"

"I didn't like it. I got rid of it."

"You loved it." Larry drained his glass and looked sullenly out the window. "You *had* to sell it, didn't you? What are you into?"

"Nothing. I'm not in debt, but I know you'll draw your own conclusions, negative as always." He glared at his sister. He was only three years older than she, but he looked at least ten years her senior, with deep furrows in his forehead and lines of petulance and discontent etched around his eyes and mouth. "I'm doin' okay, but not like that Ryan bitch. Why does she get to ruin my life then go on like nothing happened? Now she's written a book so she'll make even more money. She better not have talked about me in her trash."

"She didn't."

"You read her damned book?"

"Doug bought it. I wasn't going to read it, but I couldn't resist even though I told her in the store I'd never look at it. Anyway, it doesn't seem to be based on anything about her life in Sinclair. Not even Jonnie."

Larry's head shot up when she mentioned Jonnie. "Does she know what happened to him?"

"What do you mean?"

"His *murder*. Does she know who killed him?"

Lynn lifted her hands. "How should I know? I think if she had any idea, she would go running to her Uncle Bill and someone would be in a world of hurt. That family thought the sun rose and set on Jonnie."

"He was a little shithead. Arrogant little twerp. Like brother, like sister."

Lynn stared while her brother poured another drink. "Rebecca used to be my friend," she said. "Becky, Molly, and me."

"If you say you were the Three Musketeers, I'll vomit."

"If you don't lay off the bourbon, you'll vomit."

"And you always exaggerate how good a friend you were to Rebecca and Molly. *You* weren't a Ryan. As for the bourbon, it improves my mood. Might improve yours, too, as well as your memory. Want one?"

"No. I don't drink anymore." Lynn stood and walked

toward her brother. She was tall, slim-hipped and full-busted. She had developed early and been sought after by males of various ages since she was 14, but she'd always been faithful to her childhood love, Douglas Hardison. They used to look striking together. Now they looked rather odd, Lynn with her lean platinum hardness, Doug with his darkly round physique. But as Lynn's husband grew rounder, eating compulsively from some nervous discontent he refused to discuss, her brother grew thinner and more taut from relentless workouts to make up for his impaired leg. But their love had only deepened with the years. "Why are you so upset about Becky Ryan?" Lynn asked Larry.

"After what she did to me you have to ask? I hate her."

"She was young when she blurted out to Bill Garrett about you being the one robbing houses. I hate her for it, too, but it was a long time ago. You act like it happened yesterday. And you act like you hate her more now than you did then."

"She's back because of that kid."

"Todd? What's that got to do with us?"

"She sees all, she knows all."

"She didn't see or know a thing when Jonnie disappeared. She probably won't have any more success with Todd Ryan." Lynn's eyes narrowed. "But what would you care if she did know something about Todd? What's your problem, Larry?"

Larry tossed back the bourbon, grimaced, then hurled his glass against the wall.

CHAPTER FIVE

1

SUNDAY, 11:00 A.M.

Deputy G. C. Curry entered Bill Garrett's office slowly. He felt embarrassed about the information he'd come to deliver.

"Got a few minutes, Chief?" he asked.

Bill looked at him with tired blue eyes. "Sure. What's up?"

"You told us Todd Ryan might be in a deserted building." Garrett's niece had given him this brilliant heads-up. Curry had great admiration for Garrett except for his one weakness—his belief in this flaky woman who claimed to have ESP. Yes, Curry had heard the tales from older deputies of her successful leads in the past, but it was his opinion the kid had merely said something that got Garrett's mind working in the right direction and for some unfathomable reason, he'd given the girl credit. Whatever. If he didn't report what he'd just heard and it got back to Garrett some other way, Garrett would be furious with him. "We've checked every deserted building within a two-mile radius and come up with nothing."

"Damn."

"We might do better tomorrow."

"Damn," Bill repeated. "Sorry. I know everyone's doing their best. I appreciate it."

"I have a five-year-old boy," Curry said. "If someone snatched him . . . well, let's just say I couldn't live with myself if I didn't push to the limit to find this child. Anyway, I've got a piece of information, but I don't know how reliable it is. Not very, I'd say, considering the source, but you said you wanted to know *everything*—"

"Just tell me, Curry."

"Well, you know old Skeeter Dobbs."

Bill nodded. Everyone in town knew Skeeter Dobbs. His family had once been near-royalty in Sinclair, owners of the Dobbs Saltworks just outside of town and the opulent Dobbs Hotel on Main Street. Skeeter's grandfather Carson lost everything in the Wall Street crash of 1929 and jumped from the Presidential Suite on the sixth floor of his hotel. Skeeter had not been born until the early forties, but his father never tired of recounting the family's history. Unfortunately, the highlight for him was describing in grisly detail Carson's suicide: While his young son stood wailing on the sidewalk, Carson had sat in a window for a few minutes, contemplating his options, before hurling himself forward, barely missing the child with what would have been the fatal impact of his body. Carson's skull had burst against the concrete, spraying brains and gore. It had been nearly ten minutes before shocked bystanders could calm and drag away his screaming, blood-splattered son.

Years later this son had been graced by the birth of a child with below normal intelligence and several other mental problems that had remained untreated. However, the boy did have a vivid imagination, making him a perfect audience for his father's lurid recounting of his own father's suicide. Finally the child came to believe witnessing the suicide had been his own horror and, along with his other inadequacies, it had twisted and confused him. Now Carson Randolph Dobbs III was known as Skeeter, had never held the most menial job more than a few months, kept himself soused in wine, and constantly watched the top floor of what had been the Dobbs Hotel, convinced the building still belonged to him and that the Presidential Suite was haunted by his grandfather.

"What about Skeeter?" Bill asked.

"He's here. Been in and out of here all day but wouldn't say until a few minutes ago what his business was. Seems he's got a story. I listened, tried to humor him, but he insists on talking to you."

"What does he want to talk about?"

"Klein's Furniture Store, what else?"

"The old Dobbs Hotel, you mean. Has he seen the ghost again?"

"Oh sure. Old Carson Dobbs must be the busiest damned ghost in the world."

Bill grinned slightly. Curry was right—according to Skeeter, Carson was one active spirit.

"But Skeeter swears this time things were different at the hotel. He says last night Carson was acting strange and was in the deserted attic." Curry shrugged. "I know he's nuts, but the 'deserted' detail got my attention. Besides, he's planted out front again and this time he says he's not moving until morning unless he finally gets to talk to you."

"I can spare him a few minutes since we're getting absolutely nowhere. I'm just sitting here taking up space. Send in Skeeter."

In a few moments Skeeter shuffled in. One shoe bore a loose sole that flapped when he walked, exposing a sock that might once have been white. He wore khaki pants, clearly a handout because they were too big, rolled twice at the ankles and held up by a lady's tattered pink belt. His thin, faded shirt was covered by a circa 1920s wool suit jacket that was much too short for the skeletal Skeeter. The hem rode a few inches above his waist and his sleeves were almost three-quarter length. Bill believed the jacket must have belonged to his grandfather because Skeeter had owned it since he was a young man. Once Bill had forced him to remove it after a couple of punks had roughed him up, and he'd seen a Saville Row label sewn in the back. Skeeter wore it throughout the summer, even when the temperature hit the nineties and the humidity was unbearable.

"How do, Chief Garrett," Skeeter said. "Did Deputy Curry tell you what I seen?"

"A little. Want some coffee, Skeeter?"

Skeeter appeared to consider this. "Well, don't mind if I do."

"And we've got some nice fresh pastry here. How about a doughnut or a Danish?"

The man was rail thin, his cheekbones sticking out cadaverously under his grayish skin. He thought some more, a formality since Bill knew he was starving. "I'll have a Danish. I like foreign food."

Bill poured a bit of milk in a Styrofoam cup then filled it with coffee he'd just made. He placed an apricot Danish on a paper plate and handed both to Skeeter. The man smiled, showing dingy, crooked teeth. "Napkin, please." Bill gave him a paper napkin. Skeeter never forgot his manners, even when he was dead drunk.

Bill sat down behind his desk and fiddled with a potted plant. Skeeter took a few bites of his Danish.

"He was actin' funny last night."

Bill's attention snapped back to Skeeter. "Who was acting funny?"

"Grandfather."

"So you were outside Klein's Furniture last night?"

Skeeter looked annoyed. "I was across from the Dobbs Hotel. It's been in my family for a century."

"Okay. The Dobbs Hotel. Exactly where were you?"

"I was sittin' in the doorway of Vinson's. Takin' the air, you know. Pretty night."

It had stormed. Skeeter had ridden out the rain and lightning in a doorway bolstered with only a bottle of cheap wine. The realization made Bill feel bleak.

"Go ahead, Skeeter."

"May I have another piece of that foreign food?"

"Sure. Try the apple-filled. They're my favorite."

Skeeter's dirty hand shook as he reached for the plate Bill offered. The chief didn't want Skeeter plunging that hand into the pastry box. "It was before ten," Skeeter said abruptly. "Rain had stopped. I noticed the time on the courthouse clock. I'm real precise about time. My grandfather jumped from the window at seven-oh-one. P.M."

"That's interesting, Skeeter. Do you usually see your grandfather at the hotel in the evenings?"

Skeeter looked at him reprovingly. "I've *told* you I do. Pacin' back and forth in front of that big window in the Presidential Suite. He did that for quite a while that evening, you know. Then he sat on the window ledge a few minutes. Then he jumped. I was standin' right there. I had his blood and brains all over me. I screamed and screamed." He shook his head. "What a terrible thing."

Skeeter narrated without emotion. He'd told the story countless times and Bill knew he was convinced that it was he who had been standing on the sidewalk when Carson jumped, not his father.

"You said this time your grandfather was acting funny," Bill prodded.

"At first he was normal. Pacin' back and forth in the Presidential Suite. Maybe tryin' to figure out a way to pay his margins. That's what caused the stock crash. Margins." Bill knew Skeeter had no idea what "margins" meant. He was merely repeating what his father had told him about the margin calls that had broken the financial backs of so many stock market investors in 1929. "Or maybe he was tryin' to get up the nerve to kill himself. Killin' yourself. That would be real scary. Anyway, he paced and paced through the Presidential Suite."

Klein Furniture used the first three stories of the old Dobbs Hotel. The next three stories had been converted into apartments. For the last 30 years a couple named Moreland had occupied the apartment that had been the Presidential Suite.

Skeeter took another bite of Danish and chewed with the slow deliberateness of a cow before he swallowed. "The storm was bad. Leaves went flyin' off trees. Twigs. Trash blowin' down the street. That girl who reads minds had a wreck. I don't like her bein' back here."

"She's no concern of yours."

"I know she's a relation of yours, but she's not natural, that one. She's the devil's handmaiden, I say."

"That's enough of that crap," Bill said sternly. "There's nothing evil about her. Now get on with your story."

"The storm let up. I thought about takin' a walk, but somethin' told me to keep watch on my hotel." Skeeter was under the impression that as the last Dobbs, he still owned the building. "Well, I was right because I saw Grandfather again. Only he wasn't in the Presidential Suite. He was on top of it."

"What do you mean 'on top of it'? On the roof?"

"*No*. Grandfather wouldn't stand on the roof in the rain. He had more sense than me. My dad told me. He said I woulda been a big disappointment to Grandfather."

Nothing like building confidence in your child, Bill thought. Skeeter might be a delusional drunk, but his father had been self-pitying and malicious, largely responsible for turning Skeeter into the mess now sitting in Bill's office.

"Grandfather was on the floor right *under* the roof. The attic."

"Are you sure?"

"He had a flashlight only it must've been a big flashlight 'cause it made more light than the little ones. He moved back and forth maybe five times in front of the window."

"Did you see his face?"

"No sir, I didn't, but then I never do."

"How many times have you seen your grandfather in the attic?"

"Never. That's my big point, why I had to tell you. And I never seen him past midnight. I think ghosts have to go back to wherever they stay at midnight. It's some kind of rule."

"I see." Bill fought to hide his rising excitement. "Did your grandfather do anything else unusual?"

"Well, I saw his outline at the window because of the streetlight right below. He looked up and down the street. Maybe three times each way. Sometimes there's people out even after midnight comin' out of the movie theaters and the bars like Landy's and that other one, The Gold . . ."

"The Gold Key. But last night, after the storm, the street was empty."

"Right. I hunkered down in the doorway. I don't think he coulda seen me. But Grandfather *never* looks out, all sneaky-like, like he don't wanna be seen, so I usually don't have to hunker. All that lookin' out—that was odd. I knew

I had to tell you because my daddy always said Grandfather would get his revenge on this town for not treatin' Daddy like he deserved for bein' a Dobbs, and with Grandfather actin' so peculiar, I thought maybe he decided the time had come. And that girl with the second sight comin' back is a bad omen, too. I want her to go away."

Bill wished Skeeter would stop focusing on Rebecca. He thought the guy was harmless, but he couldn't be certain. He was certain, though, that Skeeter had seen unusual activity in the Klein building last night. In the attic. And Rebecca had "seen" Todd bound and gagged in a dusty, hot space with a wooden floor and mice. Just like an old attic.

2

An hour later Bill Garrett, Deputy G. C. Curry, and Herbert Klein entered a glass door on the right side of Klein Furniture. Inside a narrow, well-lit hall was a set of nine mailboxes. Each of the three floors above the furniture store contained three spacious apartments. Stairs led upward, but the three men opted for the old elevator.

Herbert Klein—sixtyish, portly, high-strung—was a wreck. He'd gone into near-hysterics when Bill called to ask permission to search the building for Todd Ryan based on the sighting of lights and movement in the attic. Klein had been too flustered to ask what concerned citizen had spotted the activity and Bill volunteered no information. He didn't want Klein turning him down when he heard the citizen was Skeeter, therefore making it necessary for Bill to get a search warrant. Instead Klein offered full cooperation. Now he alternately talked and wiped his bald, sweating head with a handkerchief.

"In all these years I've never had any trouble here," Herbert Klein assured Bill for the fifth time. "I have older, stable tenants, none of this drinking and arguing you get with young folks." Apparently he believed people over forty didn't drink or argue. "I think it's impossible the child is in this building."

"Why? Have you been in the attic?" Bill asked.

"No. Our storage is on the second and third floors. I don't have any reason to be clear up in the attic."

"Then you wouldn't have heard anything if the child was up there today even if the store were open."

Klein looked stricken. "Oh, you're right. Oh dear. Oh no. This is awful." Klein vigorously wiped his head as the elevator stopped on the sixth floor. "Only one of the apartments up here is rented. Helen and Edgar Moreland. They've been here for thirty years. They're late seventies. No, Edgar's eighty. Oh dear. They're fragile. And here it is after midnight. Please don't ask them any questions."

"They live below the attic," Bill said. "I'll have to question them."

"Oh God. Edgar will have a heart attack."

"Maybe not. I'll be gentle," Bill promised solemnly, aware of Curry's mouth twitching. Bill wondered how Mrs. Klein could bear living with this fretting, overwrought specimen.

As they walked down the hall toward the attic entrance, a door opened and an elderly man stepped out. His thick, silver hair waved back from a high forehead and the clear, azure eyes of a boy looked at them alertly through wire-rimmed spectacles. "Found me at last, eh? Thought I got away with that bank robbery back in thirty-nine."

"Edgar, stop carrying on," a woman said sharply. "They'll think you're serious."

"I am serious about them taking so long to get here."

"Since nineteen thirty-nine?" Curry asked good-naturedly.

"Since almost nine hours ago when the wife heard noises in the attic."

Klein let out something like a squeak and Bill stiffened. "You heard something?"

"*I* didn't. Had my hearing aid out. But Helen did. Helen, get out here and tell the cops what you heard."

"Stop calling them cops. It's disrespectful." A small, pert woman with short, curly gray hair appeared at the door with a shy smile. "How do you do? Helen Moreland."

Bill nodded. "Hello, ma'am. It's a pleasure. I'm Bill Garrett and this is Deputy Curry. Now what's this about noises?"

Mrs. Moreland's color heightened. "We were gone over the weekend, visiting our daughter in Ohio. It should only have taken us two hours to get home, but Edgar insisted on driving and he kept getting lost—"

"I was taking shortcuts!" Edgar said defensively.

"Anyway," Helen Moreland continued, ignoring her husband, "it took us four hours to get home, around nine o'clock. I couldn't sleep all night. I was nervous and tired and my hip was bothering me. Before dawn I thought I heard something in the attic. Now that's nothing new. Sometimes we get rats up there."

"No rats in this building!" Klein burst out. "I run a clean house!"

"Settle down, Herb. You sound like you manage a brothel." Edgar Moreland laughed. "Rats aren't a disgrace in an old building as long as you do something about them, which you do." He addressed Bill. "Puts out poison. Sometimes the smell from dead rats gets fierce in the summer, but what are you going to do? Can't catch the little devils and haul them out to the country to romp? Now you go on, Helen."

Bill didn't even nod at him. *Rats*. Rebecca had said Todd was in a hot, dusty place with rats.

Mrs. Moreland took a deep breath. "Well, rats make a skittering sound. And sometimes you can hear them gnawing on things. I'm used to it and I knew all I had to do was tell Herbert and he'd take care of the problem. But the skittering stopped. Then there were footsteps. I swear. Slow and . . . well, *stealthy*. I hate to sound melodramatic, but someone was trying to be quiet. Sneaky. I got out of bed, went into the far end of the living room, and stood right

under where I heard the footsteps. Then there was a shuffling sound. Then more footsteps, only heavier. I ran in and
tried to wake up Edgar, which was near hopeless."

"Did you follow the sound of the footsteps?" Curry
asked.

"When I went into the bedroom, they seemed to be heading that way." She motioned toward the door to the attic.
"Edgar finally roused himself a little. He told me to call the
police. Or rather he shouted it."

"I didn't have my hearing aid in!"

"I know. It's all right," Mrs. Moreland soothed. "Anyway, when I came back to the living room, I didn't hear
another thing."

"And no one at the police department responded to your
call?" Bill asked.

"Actually, I didn't call." Edgar looked at her in surprise.
"How seriously would they have taken an old woman calling up to say she heard mysterious noises in a locked attic
at night?"

"Mrs. Moreland, did you see anyone leave the attic?"

"No. And I am so mad at myself! I think whoever was
up there came down when I was trying to wake Edgar.
They might have even hurried when they heard him yell
for me to call the police. Then that person could have gone
out the back, down the fire escape. If I'd just opened my
door, my front door, I would have seen who it was!"

"I'm very glad you didn't open your door," Bill said.

Edgar's attention quickened. "Why? You think maybe it
wasn't some harmless prowler up there? And hey, what are
you doing here if Helen never called the police? What's
going on?"

Bill did not want to get into specifics. "We're not sure
what's going on, Mr. Moreland. Deputy Curry and I just
need to check the attic. Mr. Klein, you wait here with the
Morelands."

"This is *my* building," Klein blustered purely from reflex, then mopped his head again. "But you go ahead. Here's the key."

Bill and Curry walked to the end of the hall. Bill stooped and looked at the old-fashioned lock on the attic door. "Scratch marks. It's been picked. Wonder low long it's been like this?"

Curry didn't answer. Bill pulled on latex gloves and opened the door. Hot, stinking air washed over them. "I hope that smell is just from dead rats," Curry muttered. "Footprints in the dust."

"Step around them," Bill said unnecessarily.

As they climbed the stairs, a pulse beat in Bill's stomach. The sweet, rotting smell grew stronger and hot water seeped into his mouth. Molly's round face with her hopeful eyes flashed in front of him. Please, he silently begged a universe he usually found implacable. *Please.*

The attic was poorly lit by a few incandescent bulbs. Bill didn't know what he'd expected to be up here—relics of the once-opulent Dobbs Hotel? Instead the attic was nearly empty, with only a few sets of metal shelves bearing sealed boxes along the walls. In the middle of the space sat a garishly printed plastic patio set complete with fringed umbrella looking as if it waited for a party of ghosts. Skeeter's grandfather and friends, perhaps.

"Chief, take a look at this."

Bill walked to where Curry stood over a rumpled, rough-textured white blanket and a gray stuffed animal. Kneeling down, Bill took in the animal's floppy ear and silly grin. "It's Todd's dog Tramp."

Curry pointed toward a big rust-colored splotch on the dog's white chest. "Did the toy already have that stain?"

"No." Bill swallowed hard. "And that stain looks like blood."

CHAPTER SIX

1

Bill wasn't sure why he first called Rebecca with the news of finding Tramp. Maybe it was because she'd given him the tip about Todd being in a hot, dusty, deserted place. Maybe it was because he was putting off telling Molly as long as possible.

Rebecca agreed to meet him at Molly's. News like this should not be delivered by phone, nor should Molly be without the support of her closest friend. Right before he left the office, Bill impulsively called Clay Bellamy. Bill thought Molly might be in need of a doctor to administer another tranquilizer. She might even need hospitalization. Clay had just gotten off his shift at the hospital but said he would immediately head for Molly's.

As Rebecca neared Molly's house, she was dismayed to see at least six cars and a news van stationed in front, even though it was past midnight. She parked nearly a block away and walked casually toward the house, wishing she knew a way to dart around to the back door. But on her first visit she'd noticed that a chain-link fence enclosed the back lawn. The front door would be her only choice.

She lowered her head and turned in the front walk. Almost immediately a woman appeared beside her and said, "Excuse me, are you family?"

Rebecca looked up. The woman was young with perfect features, avid blue eyes, and artfully messed hair the color of butter. "Who are *you*?" she asked.

"Kelly Keene, WPCT News. We've heard there's been a break in the case."

"I don't know anything about a break and I'm in a hurry."

"Certainly you know about Todd's bloodstained toy being found in the attic of Klein Furniture."

Shock coursed through Rebecca that this woman knew about Tramp, but she rigidly controlled her expression. "I don't know about a toy."

"Look, Ms. Ryan, don't stonewall me," Kelly Keene said with false earnestness. "All we're trying to do is help."

Rebecca looked into the avid blue eyes. "Somehow I don't think helping Todd Ryan is at the top of your agenda, Ms. Keene. I think helping your ratings is. Now please stop trailing after me."

"You *are* family." Kelly Keene pursued her up the walk. "You're her cousin, aren't you? Rebecca Ryan."

"My name is none of your business, although I have a feeling you already knew it."

"Ms. Ryan, do you have any idea who took Todd? Have you had any visions?"

Rebecca ran up the front steps onto the porch, pounded on the door, and yelled, "It's me!" The door opened barely enough for her to slip in. She came face-to-face with a slender woman in her early thirties. Her dark brown hair was short, her expression humorless.

"You're Molly's cousin?" Her voice held no warmth, no welcome.

"Yes. Where's Molly?"

"In the kitchen. I'm Jean Wright."

She had even features, a sensuous mouth, and large, long-lashed brown eyes. She could have been stunningly attractive, but there was no smile and no welcome in the eyes. Her face was tight, her slender body was almost rigid with restraint, as if she were controlling an impulse to push Rebecca out the door.

"You're Molly's next-door neighbor," Rebecca said in an effort at friendliness.

The woman's eyes flickered. Rebecca couldn't tell if it was anger or dislike. "Yes, but I was gone the night Todd was taken."

"It wasn't an accusation," Rebecca said coldly, already disliking the woman.

Molly walked in carrying a dish towel. "I didn't know you were coming, Becky! You've met Jean?" Rebecca nodded. "She's heard so much about you she probably feels like she already knows you. How about some iced tea? Or a soft drink? Or a hard drink? Or wine? I have something in the kitchen that's supposed to be really good. It has a cork and everything!"

Molly looked exhausted. She giggled too loudly, she was talking too much, and she acted like this was a casual social gathering early in the evening. Rebecca knew Bill hadn't forewarned her of bad news, but Molly probably sensed it because of the people descending on her at this late hour.

"I'll have some of that good wine," Rebecca said, thinking that uncorking the bottle might take up some of Molly's time until Bill and Clay arrived. "Not too much, though. I'm driving."

Molly hurried off to the kitchen and Rebecca turned to meet Jean's hard stare. "You came to deliver bad news. What is it?"

"Bill Garrett will be here any minute. He'll want to be the one to tell Molly."

"Molly may need medication. I need to be warned so I can help her."

"A doctor is coming."

Jean paled. "Todd's dead."

"No."

"But you said Chief Garrett is bringing a doctor. What for? What doctor?"

Rebecca was losing patience with the woman's presumptuous tone. "Clayton Bellamy."

"Bellamy! He's barely beyond his residency! I've been a nurse for twenty years."

"Good for you." Rebecca gave a false smile when she saw Molly entering the room.

"Here you go." Molly handed her the glass of white wine. Rebecca couldn't stand white wine if it was warm.

She also hated extremely dry wine. This was both. She took a sip. "Delicious!"

"It has some totally unpronounceable name." Molly beamed. "Suzanne gave it to me."

Another knock at the door. Molly started toward it but Rebecca cut her off. She didn't want Molly seeing the crowd of people outside.

Clay faced the door while Bill stood at the edge of the porch facing the crowd. "There is no news here," he said firmly. "Meanwhile, you're obstructing the street with your vehicles."

Rebecca heard Kelly Keene's trained voice. "Is it true you found evidence that Todd Ryan was being held in the Klein Furniture Building?"

"No comment."

"Do you think he's dead?"

"Ma'am, no comment means no comment. This is *not* a press conference and you are trespassing on Ms. Ryan's property. Now leave. *All* of you."

A host of voices rose. Clay had already stepped into the house. Bill ducked in and nearly slammed the door behind him. At last everyone looked at Molly, who stood frozen, looking small and stricken. "Well, don't tell me this is a coincidence," she said thinly. "Clay, I haven't seen you for . . . for . . ." Her hand fluttered to her throat. "I heard that woman. Oh God, what is it?"

"Molly, we did not find Todd." Bill's voice was calm but adamant. "We have no reason to believe he's dead, no matter what those vultures outside are saying. Do you understand?"

She nodded as blood flooded her cheeks, then vanished with alarming speed. Rebecca knew she was going to faint but Clay acted first, rushing forward and guiding her to the couch. She flopped down limply and Clay sat next to her, holding her hand. She swallowed twice, then said, "Just tell me, Bill."

He told her about Skeeter's sighting, the noises heard by Helen Moreland, and finding Tramp. He didn't mention the suspicious stain on the toy. "So we're pretty sure that Todd was held in the attic," he ended.

"And killed?" Molly whispered.

"I told you there's no evidence of that. I believe that the kidnapper simply moved Todd because the Morelands, who live in the apartment below the attic, came home."

"But you don't *know* he isn't dead," Molly insisted.

"*I* know it," Rebecca said.

Molly looked at her desperately. "Are you just trying to comfort me?"

"No. I wouldn't do that. I feel that Todd is alive." And she did. She hadn't "seen" anything, but she knew the child lived. "Molly, you can't give up. Todd needs you."

Molly's eyes filled with tears. She lowered her head in her hands and began to shudder. "What can I do? I'm not like you, Becky. I'm just an ordinary person."

"Molly, you're the strongest person I've ever known," Rebecca said sincerely.

Molly shook her head violently and Clay took her trembling hand. "You are Todd's mother," he said. "You are the most important person in his life and I really think that if you give up hope, he'll feel it. That observation isn't based on any sound medical evidence. It's just my own belief."

"And mine," Rebecca said.

"I want to believe it, too," Molly quavered. "But he's been gone since Friday. I know the more time that passes, the worse the chances are of finding him alive." She began to sob. "I'm just so tired I can't believe we'll find him because I can't even think . . . Where's Tramp?" She looked at Bill and almost shouted, "Where's Tramp?"

"The toy is evidence," Bill said evenly. "We have to keep it."

"I don't believe you! There's something wrong, that's why you won't give him to me!"

"Molly, I told you it's—"

"*He.*"

"Okay, *he* is evidence. We might find fibers on him that will tell us something about the kidnapper."

Rebecca knew this wasn't the whole truth and she thought Molly sensed it, too. Molly's eyes blazed. "You're keeping things from me! And don't think I don't remember that Klein Furniture is one block away from where Jonnie's body was found!"

They'd all hoped she wouldn't realize the proximity. Rebecca had pounced on it immediately as further proof that there was a link between the kidnappings, but Bill had argued her down, saying it wasn't important.

Now Molly looked at Rebecca, who in the face of her despair echoed Bill's words. "It's probably just a fluke," she said lamely. "The cases aren't alike."

Molly opened her mouth, clearly wanting to present her own point of view, but Clay took control. "Molly, you're ragged, physically and emotionally. I want you to get a good night's sleep—"

"I can't sleep! My baby is somewhere out there! I have to *do* something!"

"You have to get some rest."

"I'll give her a Valium," Jean said.

"No, I'm giving her an injection of Ativan." Clay headed toward a small medical bag by the door.

Jean placed her hands on her hips. Her sleeveless top revealed strong, well-toned arms. "I think a ten-milligram Valium will be sufficient," she maintained.

"I don't." Clay didn't look at the woman but Rebecca did. Resentment simmered in her eyes. Rebecca could tell she regarded Clay as an interloper, even though he was a doctor and had known Molly since she was a teenager. She also seemed to resent Rebecca. Rebecca decided to find out more about her. Maybe later Clay could give her some information.

Molly fussed about the injection but at last fell silent, as if she'd run out of air. Afterward she sagged, wiping half-heartedly at the tears on her face, as Clay disposed of the syringe.

"I'll spend the night here," Jean said. "I don't think Molly should be alone."

Clay nodded. "I agree."

"I can stay," Rebecca said.

Bill drew near and spoke softly in Rebecca's ear. "Honey, you know Molly expects something spectacular from you. She's gonna be watching like a hawk, waiting for you to burst forth with some revelation. It's going to be hell on both of you."

Jean had overheard. "He's right, Miss Ryan. And you look tired." Her tone had mellowed considerably. "I'll just run next door and get a few things. I'll be back shortly."

Rebecca still felt as if she were running out on Molly a second time, but what Bill and Jean said made sense. Besides, some pain was kicking in from the minor injuries she had received in the wreck. She realized she had stretched herself too thin with all the walking she'd done at Esther's. She, too, needed some pain medication and rest.

Rebecca helped Molly to bed and sat beside her until she began breathing deeply. Then she walked down the hall to Todd's room. Dim light filtered in from the living room where she heard Clay and Bill talking quietly. She wandered around, touching the swimming medals, looking at the fish swimming serenely in their bowl. She glanced out the window just in time to see a light go off in Jean's house next door. She would return soon.

Rebecca sat down on Todd's bed. She shut her eyes and began counting backward. When she reached 85, she stopped in frustration. She had never "conjured" a vision. When she was 12 her grandmother Ava had told her visions came or they didn't. "I was ten when I discovered I had the gift," Ava had recalled the year before she died. "I was frightened at first. I thought I was going crazy." She had allowed herself a small, sardonic smile. "Your mother thinks I am. My own daughter is afraid of me. But my husband accepted me. And Bill loves me. Your mother will never appreciate your power, Rebecca. It will always scare and repel her. It will cause problems between you. But you have your Uncle Bill. He understands."

He *had* understood, believed, accepted. So had Molly. They were both counting on her now. And she had nothing to offer.

Feeling defeated, she went back to the living room. "Is Molly asleep?" Clay asked.

"Yes. She looks peaceful."

"She needed an injection, something to kick in faster, even though it didn't meet with Ms. Wright's approval."

"Do you know her?" Rebecca asked.

"I've seen her at the hospital. Never had the great pleasure of talking to her until tonight." Clay smiled wryly. "Can't say I'm too impressed."

Rebecca nodded. "Molly's mentioned her on the phone. She's not at all what I expected. I can't imagine having her around all the time, but Molly seems to like her." She lowered her voice and looked at Bill. "I'm glad you didn't tell Molly about the stain on Tramp."

"I was going to until I got a look at her; I knew she couldn't take it. Maybe tomorrow."

"Definitely tomorrow, whether you think it's best for her or not," Clay said. "That Keene woman asked me about it outside. If the press has the information, you can't shield Molly."

Bill looked furious. "And when I find out where that leak came from, someone is going to be mighty sorry."

Rebecca glanced at the clock. "I saw Jean's lights go out about ten minutes ago. She should be here by now."

"Maybe she got waylaid out front," Clay said. He strode to the front window and parted the draperies. "Don't see her, but the group is turning into a crowd. Must be thirty people out there."

Bill erupted from the couch. "That's it. I'm calling in a couple of cruisers."

Clay raised his eyebrows at Rebecca with a hint of a smile. She knew he appreciated Bill's forcefulness as much as she did. Bill placed a call to headquarters, then opened the front door. Voices rose. He shut the door behind him and Rebecca joined Clay at the window.

A moment after Bill's appearance, the crowd quieted and only Bill could be heard, telling people that there was no news but that they were behaving inconsiderately, intrusively, and criminally by trespassing. He could and *would* arrest anyone who did not leave the premises. Within seconds of this announcement, a police cruiser arrived, lights flashing. The crowd began dispersing, some fleeing hastily, others languidly, grumbling, as if seeing how far they could push their luck. The only person who did not move one inch was the reporter Kelly Keene.

"Chief Garrett, you seem to forget that the people have a right to know—"

"You seem to forget that Ms. Ryan has a right to privacy." He took a step toward her. "I repeat, you are trespassing. Now, you might get a momentary thrill out of being arrested, but your adoring public will probably start thinking you're fairly stupid for getting yourself tangled up for hours in the booking and bail process when there's a big story you should be following. If you disagree, I will gladly have one of my officers escort you to the jail."

Kelly's eyes narrowed. Her whole face seemed to narrow, pinched with the frustration of a spoiled child. Then she turned with the grace of a dancer and strode toward the news van. She climbed in and slammed the door. Seconds ticked by. The news van didn't move. The people inside knew sitting in front of the house on the street was not trespassing. They intended to stay. Bill remained on the porch, glaring.

"This is a nightmare," Clay said.

"One I've been through before." Rebecca sighed.

"Which makes this even more bizarre—too bizarre to be coincidence." He looked at her earnestly. "This is a city of twenty thousand. To some people that's a small town. The crime rate is low. Folks feel safe about their kids here. But then something like this happens—to your family—not once but twice." Clay paused. "And I seem to be pounding you over the head with it. I'm sorry."

Rebecca felt a tremendous sense of relief flow through her. She knew Bill believed in her visions. It was her reasoning power he seemed to doubt. She couldn't talk to her mother about this and she felt that Frank believed her perspective to be clouded by her "delusion" that she had ESP.

"Don't be sorry," Rebecca told Clay. "You're just saying what I've been feeling, although Bill doesn't want to believe there's a connection in the kidnappings. I know he's trying to make me feel better, but it doesn't work because it isn't true." Her voice grew more intense. "And admitting there's a connection, looking for the similarities, is what's going to help us find Todd. As long as no one agrees with me, though. . . ."

Clay frowned. "I think other people don't want to see the connection because of how things ended for Jonnie. But if you of all people are willing to face it, then someone else should, too."

"I wish you'd tell that to my family."

"I don't think they'd listen to some guy they haven't seen for years," he said dryly. "But Rebecca, if there's any other way I can help you, please tell me."

Everyone offered to help, Rebecca thought, but people rarely thought they would actually be called on—and if they were, they seemed to feel put upon. But Clay looked sincere.

"Well, there is something you could do."

"Name it."

Rebecca plunged on before reticence got the best of her. "You can be a friend and a sounding board. You can hear me out and not try to comfort me but analyze what I'm saying, see if I'm being logical, help me find the link between the kidnappings."

"That doesn't sound like much help."

"It would be. Believe me."

Clay tilted his head slightly. "Okay, Rebecca. I'm your official sounding board."

The door opened and Bill walked in followed by Jean, spouting excuses. "Sorry it took me so long. I had to put food out for the cat. And just as I was leaving, my sister Wendy called. I told her I was in a hurry, but she chattered away. Something about deciding which boyfriend to see. She's *so* popular." For the first time, she smiled. "She's in college. You know how important these things seem when you're that age."

No one said anything and Jean didn't seem to expect an answer. "Molly's asleep," Clay told her. "I'll leave my number in case you have any trouble during the night."

Jean's smile abruptly disappeared. "I'm sure there won't be anything I can't handle."

"Take it anyway. You might just feel like gabbing to someone in the middle of the night," Clay returned with a flirtatious grin that clearly set Jean's teeth on edge. Rebecca almost laughed aloud as the woman's shoulders stiffened at the thought of calling up young Dr. Bellamy in the middle of the night for intimate chitchat. "Rebecca, I'll walk you to your car."

Outside, the van sat at the curb in front of Molly's house. Rebecca expected Kelly Keene to come leaping out at them, but she remained inside, perhaps intimidated by Bill's presence in the house. Clay said nothing until they reached the red Thunderbird. "I'm driving Mother's car since I bashed up the rental," she said. "Frank handled getting the car removed. I still haven't gone by Dormaine's to see how much damage I did."

"I wouldn't worry too much about it. But speaking of restaurants, would you like to go to dinner tomorrow evening?" Rebecca just looked at him. "I'm inviting you out, Ms. Ryan. It would give us a chance to talk."

She suddenly felt like the seventeen-year-old with a crush; when the idea of Clay Bellamy asking her on a date seemed ludicrous, unbelievable. She'd been feeling like that teenager ever since she returned to Sinclair. But she had to get out of the time warp and start acting like a woman, not a girl. Besides, she'd said she needed to talk with him. He said this would be a chance to talk. He probably didn't think of it as a date at all. She was being ridiculous and was glad for the darkness of night that hid her heightened color. "I'd like to have dinner."

He grinned, that old devastating grin that used to make her knees feel like they were melting. "Good. I'll pick you up at seven."

"Fine," she said abruptly, embarrassed over the knees and her whole girlish demeanor. "Good night, Clay."

He stood smiling as she opened the car door and got in, then fastened her seat belt. She gave him a brief wave as he lingered, watching her.

As soon as Rebecca turned on the ignition, music blasted through the car. Yet, on the way to Molly's, she had not been listening to the radio or the CD player. Rebecca went cold when she heard the familiar, haunting opening organ notes of "A Whiter Shade of Pale."

Jonnie's favorite song.

2

"My mom doesn't want me to see you anymore."

"So what else is new?" Randy Messer snapped a twig in his hands and tossed it. It was a beautiful night but they were a bit too close to Sonia's house for Randy's comfort.

"I wish we didn't have to meet in secret," Sonia said.

"It won't last forever." He reached out and touched a strand of straight black hair that had blown across her peachy complexion. He'd never seen eyes the color of violets like hers. She was a beauty. She was smart. She was crazy about him. He had no intention of losing her. "So your mother doesn't want you to see me. What's her latest complaint about me?"

"Oh, you're distracting me from my schoolwork."

"It's summer."

"I'm taking that composition class through the extension program. And you'll distract me when I go to college."

"Like I did in high school and you graduated valedictorian? That way?"

She grinned at him, showing perfect teeth. "I did manage to get in a few study hours, didn't I?"

"Enough to drive me crazy. What's your mother's *real* problem with me? My poor family from the wrong side of the tracks?"

"Partly. Also your earring."

"Which one? The gold hoop or the stud?"

Sonia smiled. "I don't think she cares for either one."

"I'll stop wearing them. Lost the hoop anyway. What other offenses have I committed?"

"Well, there's the shoplifting scrape."

"I was *eleven*!"

"The possession charge you racked up."

"It was marijuana, not heroin, I wasn't dealing, and I was *fifteen*." Randy looked to the sky. "Jeez, they don't let you forget anything in this town, do they?"

"You know what a straight arrow my mother is. My dad was a minister and neither one of them had a clue about real life. Mom just doesn't understand you."

"Oh hell, Sonia, it's more than that and you know it."

Sonia looked at his troubled face. James Dean. He looked like old posters she'd seen of James Dean in Rhondalee's Fifties Diner near school. Good bones, ash blond hair, blue eyes that could switch from soulful to dangerous. She'd loved Randy Messer since the first time she'd seen him in that diner two years ago. "This stuff about Todd Ryan has Mom totally creeped out," Sonia said meekly.

"No wonder. You were baby-sitting when he got snatched."

"I feel awful about it, Randy. Everybody thinks it's my fault."

"Nobody thinks it's your fault. Your mother sure doesn't."

"Well, no, she doesn't think it's my fault. Her problem isn't *me*. It's that people have been talking to her and . . ."

Sonia looked at him miserably. Randy stared back at her.

Then he smiled in a way she didn't like. "She thinks I had something to do with it, doesn't she? She actually thinks I knew when you'd be baby-sitting, sneaked in and hit you, then took off with the kid. And in her holier-than-thou Christian goodness she spouted her little theory around and that's why I got a visit from a deputy today."

Sonia's eyes widened. "You didn't tell me a deputy came to see you!" she cried reproachfully. "What did he want to know?"

"Nothing in particular. Where was I when you were baby-sitting. I told him I was with the usual suspects—my friends. That didn't win me any points. After he left, my old man went berserk. 'What've you done now, you little shit? Shouldn't never have had you. Don't even think you're mine.' Same old crap only he was drunk. I thought he was going to beat me. I took off. Haven't been home since."

"Oh, Randy!" Sonia cried. "I'm sorry."

"No big deal. I hid in plain sight—the park. Had a nice talk with Skeeter Dobbs."

Sonia liked it that Randy was never mean to Skeeter. "And what's new with Skeeter? His grandfather still haunting the furniture store?"

"Sure, only there's a new twist. Saturday night Grandfather was up in the attic and he *never* goes to the attic. Seems Skeeter was worried about that Ryan woman with the second sight being back. Had to protect his hotel from her so he was watching extra late. He thinks Grandfather's all disturbed over her."

"Did he mean *Rebecca* Ryan?" Sonia raised her eyebrows. "My dad used to talk about her. Naturally he thought she was some kind of dangerous woman. She's my mom's boss's stepdaughter. Is she in town?"

"I guess. She had a wreck. Didn't kill her, though. According to Skeeter, he saw her driving, I quote, a blood-red car. He agrees with your dad—calls her the devil's handmaiden and says he's got plans to drive her out of town. I told him to stop talking about Rebecca Ryan *and* his grandfather being in the attic."

"Why? No one pays any attention to anything he says."

"I'm not so sure about that. Bill Garrett took the time to talk with him this afternoon about old Grandfather Dobbs."

"So? Why do you look so worried?"

"I'm not *worried*. It's just that he should stop making threats about Rebecca Ryan and carrying on about his grandfather prowling around in the attic."

"I agree with you about the Ryan woman, but who cares what he says about his grandfather?"

"Yeah," Randy said carelessly, although his forehead was creased with concern. "Unless there really *was* someone in the attic."

3

MONDAY 1:20 A.M.

Skeeter had heard people say Sinclair was boring, but at night he liked the near-empty streets. After midnight the quiet became so profound it seeped into his own head, calming the sound of his father's carping and his grandfather's scream as he plummeted from the sixth floor of the Dobbs Hotel, a scream that to Skeeter sometimes seemed like a memory and sometimes like a dream.

Skeeter prided himself on his organizational skills. He kept string, rubber bands, and paper clips in his right trouser pocket. He kept his grandfather's Bulova watch in the left jacket pocket, although the watch had not worked since his grandfather's death. He kept his money—a few dollar bills and some change he collected during the week—in his right jacket pocket. And he never forgot to buy two bottles of wine on Saturday because his favorite liquor store was closed on Sundays. He held the second bottle now, comforted by the thought of the joy it would bring him tonight.

The day had had been hot but not uncomfortable. Really, it had been an exceptional day. He got to confer with Chief

Garrett, which made him feel very important. He'd had two cups of good coffee and two pieces of foreign food that were delicious. He'd visited with a number of beings in the park, some of them human. Yes, it had been a good day, but now it was night and Skeeter had a number of weighty things to think about and some plans to work out.

He looked up at his hotel. The light in the Presidential Suite was on. He wondered who was occupying it. No doubt someone rich. Sometimes he prowled the building at night, looking for his grandfather. He never entered any of the rooms, knowing that privacy was sacred, but one time the attic door had been left unlocked for about a week and each night he went up. He was staggered when he saw the beautiful patio furniture, complete with unfurled, fringed umbrella. One night a pitcher of apple juice and a plate of shortbread cookies rested on the table. He'd sat at the table for an hour, drinking juice from a paper cup, daintily eating cookies with a dirty hand, saying intelligent and witty things to imaginary guests, and generally acting like the golden boy of a distinguished family. The next night the attic was locked again, but that was all right because he'd been given one of the best memories of his life.

There had been a lot of activity in the attic today. Skeeter knew Grandfather wouldn't like it. Having a hotel full of fancy guests was one thing; having policemen tramping around the place was another. But Skeeter was responsible for the building and something fishy was going on. There wasn't a better person he could have gone to than Bill Garrett. He would settle down Grandfather and make him stop prowling the attic, if indeed that *was* Grandfather he'd seen Saturday night. During the afternoon he'd decided he wasn't quite so sure whether or not Grandfather had been messing around up there. But unfortunately Chief Garrett wouldn't do anything about the girl with second sight because they were related. No, Skeeter was going to handle the girl himself, scare her out of town . . . with a little help.

Skeeter entered the recessed doorway of Vinson's Apothecary Shoppe, placed his back against the wall, and slid down to a sitting position. His knobby knees nearly poked through the thin material of his trousers. He'd have to find something heavier by winter. Father Brennan was usually real good at finding clothes for him.

His hands were shaky because his evening drink had been delayed by all his important business. He uncapped his wine and took a long, satisfying draw and then another. Stars were out tonight. Before the Ryan girl got her second sight and he grew fearful of her, Skeeter used to talk to her when she came to the park with Chief Garrett. She told him that at night the stars formed pictures of bears and a cow, but he could never make any sense of them. Still they were pretty, all sparkly like the diamonds in the window of the jewelry store. The Ryan girl had also told him the light of the stars came from long ago. She said the stars were so far away, it took *years* for their light to reach Sinclair. But that didn't make any sense to Skeeter either. He thought she'd just been fooling him. Maybe she'd been bad even then.

He took another generous drink of wine. He'd had nothing to eat except the heavenly Danish and the wine seemed to hit his system harder than usual. When he narrowed his eyes, the stars shimmered and danced. He looked at the Dobbs Hotel again. He'd passed by at 7:01 P.M. and as usual seen the spectacle of his grandfather crashing to the sidewalk. Skeeter was used to no one else seeming to notice. He didn't take it personally, but he was always relieved when the fall was over.

Someone was walking down the street toward him. He squinted but it was dark and the person was looking down. Skeeter could make out jeans and some kind of jacket—not a fine, wool suit jacket like his—something bright blue and nylon. Used to be you could tell men from women. Now they all wore jeans and those huge white shoes they called running shoes although they never ran. And girls were taller than when he was young. Once Sonia Ellis told him girls wanted to be tall like supermodels. He didn't know what a supermodel was and she showed him some pictures in a magazine called *Vogue*. Skeeter thought the women looked gigantic, muscular, and scary like they could wallop the dickens out of any man. He was glad they didn't have any supermodels in Sinclair.

He looked at the courthouse clock. One-thirty. Soon he might see Grandfather in the attic again. And this time he might get a better view. Chief Garrett had asked him over and over to describe Grandfather's face the way it had looked last night, but he couldn't. He'd given the matter a lot of thought, though. He still could not describe Grandfather's face, but he'd remembered something outstanding: Grandfather's hair. In old photographs, Skeeter had seen a man with fair hair that was very short, parted in the middle, and plastered close to the skull. But in the attic, Grandfather's hair looked longer and fuller. And definitely darker. Of course he'd been a ghost a long time—his hair could have grown. But didn't ghosts remain the same as when they died?

Photographs had also told Skeeter Grandfather was a slight man. Daddy used to say, 'He was an elegant man, not a big, shambling hulk like you.' The photographs were *real* old—maybe Grandfather had grown. Still . . .

The figure walking up the street slowed. It wore a windbreaker with the hood tied close around the face. Now that was odd, Skeeter thought. There was no wind.

"How do?" he called politely. "Nice night." The figure nodded. Then it looked up and down the street. "You lost?" Skeeter asked.

"Lost? No. Just . . . tired." The voice was breathy, barely above a whisper, and a shadow fell across the face. "And lonely."

"No need to be lonely," Skeeter replied. "My daddy always said I was poor company, but I'm better than nothin'. Have a seat."

The figure ducked its head, then slowly approached Skeeter and hunched into the doorway. "Cozy."

"You can see all up and down the street from here at

Vinson's. Not so warm in winter, but just dandy in summer. Would you care for some wine?"

Skeeter might have been offering a fine Château Margaux. His guest took a dainty drink from the bottle, then said, "Good. It's kind of you."

"It's a big bad world. Folks got to be kind to each other. Father Brennan says so." Skeeter tried to get a better look at his guest, but his vision was really fuzzy tonight. It seemed his hearing was much worse than usual, too. And he felt a little dizzy and nauseated.

"See your grandfather tonight?" the visitor asked.

"Right on time. Jumping out of the Presidential Suite at seven-oh-one P.M."

"But not in the attic?"

"It's not time yet. He showed up in the attic later." He paused. "How'd you know about that?"

"You told everyone. Even the police."

"It was my civic duty. And I wasn't even tipsy. Left my bottles outside in my hidey-hole when I went to see Chief Garrett."

"Your hidey-hole outside Klein—I mean the Dobbs Hotel?"

"You're on to me!" Skeeter crowed. "I didn't think anyone knew about my hidey-hole!"

"*I* do."

Skeeter grinned showing all his stained teeth. Then his eyes narrowed. "Hey, you're not *her*, are you?"

"Who?"

"The girl with second sight."

A scoffing sound. "Oh, *her*. No. I don't even *like* her. She scares me. I wish she'd go away."

"Me, too!"

"I think she will. Real soon." The guest leaned from the doorway of Vinson's Apothecary. "Look, there's a shooting star!"

Skeeter stared upward, mesmerized by the streak of silver light. His face bore the wondering expression of a child. "Isn't that just like magic? The world is a beautiful place."

"Yes, it truly is," his guest said slowly. Unnoticed by Skeeter, its hand slipped into a windbreaker pocket. "There's only one problem."

Skeeter leaned back in the doorway, frowning. "What's that?"

"You're just like the girl with second sight."

Skeeter shook his head vigorously. "No, I'm not!"

"Oh yes, I'm afraid you are," the voice said gently. "You *see* too much. Way too much."

The hand whipped out of the windbreaker's pocket. With violent speed an ice pick glittered beneath a streetlight before the pointed shaft plunged directly into Skeeter's left eye. His whole body shuddered before it slammed against the wall. As the hand relentlessly drove the spike deeper into Skeeter's confused brain, his mouth fell open, his expression dulled, and blood poured down his creased face and dripped off his jaw onto his cherished wool suit jacket.

Another shooting star streaked across the heavens, but this time Skeeter did not see it.

CHAPTER SEVEN

1

MONDAY, 7:25 A.M.

A rushing, muttering Matilda Vinson literally tripped over the slumped body of Skeeter Dobbs while fishing for the keys to the front door of Vinson's Apothecary Shoppe. Incensed, she launched into a tirade about lazy, worthless, smelly drunks before she noticed a gooey, reddish stain all over one of her new white shoes. She used the toe of the shoe to roll Skeeter over and when she saw the ice pick sticking grotesquely from his left eye, she let out two short, piercing shrieks before fainting onto the sidewalk.

Three minutes later Matilda awakened to find several people standing over her, staring at her as if she, too, were a corpse. Someone bent to help her into a sitting position and she saw that her skirt had ridden up to the top of her thighs. While she pulled at it, a child quavered, "Did you kill that man?"

"Don't be absurd!" she snapped. "Quit looking at me. All of you! Call the police!"

"Someone went to get 'em," a man said. "Would that be Skeeter Dobbs? Sweet Jesus, look at that eye."

Unfortunately Matilda did. Her world swirled briefly before she fainted for the second time in her hardy life.

When Matilda opened her eyes again, a pair of cool gray ones were only two inches away. She almost screamed but got control of herself. "Lynn?"

"Yes, Miss Vinson." Lynn Hardison kneeled on the pavement beside her. "Just be still. The emergency squad will be here in a minute."

Matilda's gaze shot around. People were backing away as a man in uniform barked orders. He blocked her view of Skeeter and she was able to draw a deep, steadying breath. "Help me up, Lynn."

"But—"

"Don't talk back! I will not lie here making a spectacle of myself." She sat up, pulling at her skirt again. She caught a glimpse of her gory shoes and her stomach lurched. "Take my arm and lift."

Lynn obeyed and Matilda stood, wobbling. Bill Garrett appeared in front of her. "Miss Vinson, you've had a bad shock and a fall."

"I know very well what I've had. Why is everyone treating me as if I'm a hundred? I'm fine and this is my establishment. I need to be in charge."

"You need to be checked out—"

"I-am-in-charge." Matilda turned to Lynn. "Of course the store will be closed today. The police will have lots to do taking care of *him*." Her lips trembled slightly. "Drunken, foolish layabout, always prowling around babbling about that grandfather of his. Well, at least he won't be haunted anymore." She looked fiercely at Bill. "You concentrate on finding who did this horrible thing and leave me alone. All I need is to clean myself up and have a nice strong cup of coffee."

"Let me ask one question, Miss Vinson," Bill said gently. "I notice the blood on your shoe. Did you move Skeeter?"

"I stumbled over him. Then I . . . well, I poked him with my foot. I thought he was just passed out. His body fell sideways . . ." She drew another deep breath. "That's all."

"Okay. I may need to ask you a few more questions later. And why don't you have Lynn drive you home?"

Lynn looked daggers at him but said sweetly, "Yes, Miss Vinson, let me. I'd feel much better about you."

Matilda didn't want to be driven by Lynn, but she had to admit her stomach didn't feel right. She simply could not be sick in front of all these people or in her freshly cleaned car. "If I'm not needed, a ride home would be much appreciated," she said formally. "Chief, please call to let me know when I can enter the store. There is some work I should get done before evening."

"Will do, Miss Vinson. You take care."

He couldn't help the hint of a smile as Lynn gently led away her employer. He knew Lynn detested both Matilda and her job at the drug store, which Suzanne had told him might be short-lived. He couldn't imagine Frank buying a store for Lynn's ceramics, but apparently he had. Maybe he thought it would sweeten her disposition.

Bill realized he was stalling, not wanting to deal with the horror that was now Skeeter Dobbs. He looked across the street at the Klein Furniture. Skeeter had been huddled in the entrance of Vinson's when he'd seen someone in the attic.

"Curry, any sign that the body was moved here?" he asked abruptly.

G. C. Curry was stooping by the body. "Don't think so. If he was moved, the killer brought Skeeter's wine bottle with him. It's partly covered by his right arm."

So Skeeter had been murdered in the same spot where, approximately 36 hours earlier, he had seen someone in the attic of Klein's, someone who had apparently been holding Todd Ryan prisoner.

Bill walked closer and looked at the body. Skeeter's long, skinny legs were splayed, his feet in their ragged shoes pointing outward, his frayed khaki pant legs pulled up to expose gray nylon socks that had once been white. Skeeter was folded at the waist, the upper part of his body partially hanging over his right leg and leaning against the door of the drugstore. His head was turned slightly to the left, clearly showing a metal handle protruding from the eye socket. The whole left side of his face and neck was a mass of dried blood, already drawing hungry summer flies. His left hand lay upturned, the fingers stiffened by rigor mortis.

"Get tape around this scene," Bill said unnecessarily to Curry, who knew his job. Bill suddenly felt sad for this poor wreck of a man who'd never stood a chance in life and died a brutal death. "And where's the damned coroner?"

"On his way, Chief. You know he always takes his time."

"He'd like it if he called the cops and we took *our* time."

"That's the truth."

Bill knew he was near babbling and Curry was diplomatically easing him along. Curry was ten years younger than Bill and never seemed affected by anything he saw. Bill hadn't decided whether the man had a basically hard core, or he just reserved any tenderness for family. He didn't understand how Curry could seem so matter-of-fact about this murder. Of course Bill was more emotional than usual, rubbed raw by the abduction of Todd. Until the boy was taken, Bill hadn't realized how strongly he felt about the child.

He'd also been shaken by Rebecca finding a CD with "A Whiter Shade of Pale" in her car last night. She'd looked like death when she came tearing back into Molly's house to tell him, Clay Bellamy hot on her heels. The car had been unlocked, there had been a crowd on the street, and she'd driven the car all day. A lot of people could have realized she'd commandeered the red Thunderbird, and a lot of people could have easily opened the door and slipped in the CD. Then there was Jean Wright's half-hour absence and her return a good fifteen minutes after Rebecca had seen the lights go out at her home. She'd had plenty of time to place the CD in Rebecca's car.

"Do you think Skeeter's murder had anything to do with what he told us?" Curry asked.

Bill's gaze moved between Skeeter and the attic windows of Klein Furniture. "If it doesn't, it's a hell of a coincidence. My niece keeps talking about coincidences and I haven't wanted to face them, but I'm afraid there are just too many for me to ignore." He frowned. "What we need to find out is who knew Skeeter saw someone in the attic."

"That's the problem," Curry said dourly. "He spent all day Sunday telling everyone he saw."

2

Amy Tanner had been disappointed when she'd arrived at the volunteer center at 8:10 and found only eight other volunteers. But she had to remember this wasn't the police command center. Mr. Hardison had donated this building, but that awful county sheriff Lutz hadn't let all the efforts be coordinated from one place. He had a lot of policemen and computer people working at another building across town, which seemed like a waste of manpower to Amy. Also, it was Monday morning. People were returning to work. Some would probably drift in later and surely more would come this evening.

Normally she would be behind the counter of the 7-Eleven, but this was her vacation week. Last year she and her husband Alvin had taken a vacation together. They'd gone to Kings Island amusement park and acted like a couple of kids for three days. But even that modest trip had set them back more than they'd expected. This year Alvin had insisted on skipping his vacation time from the hospital where he was an orderly. He'd even been working overtime because the baby was due in three months and they were financially strapped.

Amy drew a cup of coffee from the urn and rubbed her back. She hadn't slept well. She never did without Alvin beside her, but he was on night shift. He promised to get his schedule changed by the end of summer. She smiled. By autumn, they would have a baby boy.

A woman turned from the copying machine where she was running off more leaflets bearing Todd's photo. "Are you feeling all right?"

"Yes. Just a little tired this morning."

"You should sit down. I remember when I was as far

along as you—twice. My legs and feet gave me the most trouble with all that swelling."

Amy looked down at her own slender legs and narrow feet in white Keds. "Thank goodness that hasn't happened to me."

"*Yet.* Then there are the hemorrhoids. And God, the stretch marks afterward!" the woman said and turned back to the machine, laughing. She sounds like she wants me to have swollen legs and hemorrhoids and stretch marks, Amy thought, hurt. She knew she was too sensitive, but she couldn't help it. She was gentle and easily wounded. Perhaps that was what had drawn her to Alvin. They'd both had rough childhoods. They were battered from old tragedies and slightly at sea in the world. They clung to each other for hope and strength, although Amy's hope seemed much stronger than Alvin's.

A phone rang and Amy quickly set down her coffee, grabbed a pen and paper, and answered. A woman reported seeing Todd Ryan in the company of a bald man on a Greyhound bus headed for Cleveland.

"When was this, ma'am?" Amy asked, trying to contain her excitement.

"Thursday night."

"Did you say Thursday?"

"I certainly did. Around eight o'clock. The boy looked terrified."

Amy's elation faded. "Ma'am, Todd Ryan was abducted on Friday night."

"I know what I saw," the woman said emphatically. "Are you accusing me of lying?"

"No ma'am. I thought you might be mistaken about the night."

"I'm not."

"You're sure it was Thursday?"

"*Yes.* Are you deaf?"

Amy sighed and asked the woman for her name and phone number. Chief Garrett had instructed volunteers to take this information, even if the caller was obviously a crank or a crazy. As she hung up, Alvin walked in looking especially tired, almost haggard. His straight dark hair, in need of a trim, hung over his forehead and his eyes were red-rimmed behind their glasses.

"Good heavens, Alvin. You look awful!" Amy exclaimed.

"It was a long night. I called home before I left the hospital and when I didn't get an answer, I figured you were here."

"I expected you home before I left." Alvin was five-ten and she had to stand on tiptoe to kiss his cheek. "Are you sure something hasn't happened?"

He smiled wanly. "Not to me. Did you hear about Skeeter Dobbs?" She shook her head. "He's dead."

"Oh." Amy was twenty-two but she had the voice of a little girl. "Well, he wasn't all that old but considering the way he lived—no proper food, all that liquor—I guess it's no surprise."

"He was murdered."

Amy's pixie face blanched. "Oh! Oh my! How? Why?"

"I'm going on hospital gossip. Someone jammed something in his eye. I've heard screwdriver, knife, ice pick." He lifted his stooped shoulders. "I don't know why. Skeeter wasn't the type to brawl."

"Oh gosh." Amy shook her head slowly. "I remember when I was little and I'd see him in the park talking to squirrels. I was scared of him. Mama told me not to say anything except 'hi' if he spoke to me. She said he was one of God's unfortunates."

"Your mother constantly talked about God, about how good He was. It must have been hard for her to explain Skeeter to herself."

Amy drew back, half afraid of any implied criticism of God. "God doesn't create everyone equal. I mean, in His eyes they're equal, but not in ours." She smiled. She wasn't sure that reasoning was correct, but it sounded good. "Anyway, she said Skeeter was one of God's unfortunates and

I decided right then that although they deserve our pity, I didn't want to be one of *them.*"

Sadness flickered in Alvin's dark eyes behind the thick glasses that had a tendency to slip too low on his narrow nose. "You didn't exactly hit the jackpot with me."

Amy cocked her head. "Now that's just your tiredness talking, Alvin Tanner! Of all the things to say! I'm the luckiest woman in the world."

"I can't even afford to take you on a vacation."

"I don't need to go anywhere. I'm happy staying in Sinclair."

"I guess you'll have to be." He glanced around. "Why are you here? You spent all day yesterday at this place. You took your vacation time so you could rest."

"Being here is nothing like being at the store," Amy said quickly, hoping he would not insist she leave, even though Alvin wasn't one to insist on anything. "I sit a lot and I'll only stay a few hours today. Besides, I keep thinking about how I'd feel if our little boy was lost. If I can help in any way to get Todd back to his mother, I'll do it."

"You feel really bad about that kid, don't you?"

"I feel awful about him! You do, too, don't you?"

Alvin nodded. "Sure. But you had cramping. You should be resting. And you shouldn't go back to the 7-Eleven job at all."

Amy smiled. "Alvin, I *have* to. We need the money. And after the baby is born—"

"After the baby is born you won't be working. You're going to get to stay home and be a full-time mother!"

Color tinged Alvin's high cheekbones and perspiration had broken out on his upper lip. Amy, suddenly looking worried and surprised, stroked his arm. "Honey, that's just not possible."

"It *is,*" Alvin said passionately. "I'm going to make it possible."

Amy had never had much in the way of material things in her life, but she'd always been an innately cheerful, hopeful person who believed in the basic goodness of the human heart and the benevolence of a God who loved all His little children. Alvin, on the other hand, had little faith in people besides his adored wife. He also had a tendency toward deep depression. Amy always thought the fate of his mother caused his depression. Slim Tanner sat wasting away in prison for murdering her husband, which everyone knew was because he'd been beating her and nearly killed Alvin with his savagery. Alvin never talked about those days. He'd also never let Amy visit his mother, saying the prison environment would upset her too much; he returned from his own visits looking worn and desolate. Lately, though, his usual mildness had given away to flashes of temper directed not at Amy, but at their situation. She thought he was worried about the baby. They both wanted him desperately. They wanted to give him what neither of them had when they were children.

"Alvin, honey, you're awful tired. You go on home. I'll only stay another hour if it'll make you feel better. And you quit worrying about things. We'll be fine."

Alvin nodded, the fierceness seeming to leak out of him. "I know we will."

"God will provide."

"I've learned not to count on God to provide anything," Alvin said bleakly. "*I* will provide for my wife and child. You'll see, Amy. Our lives are going to change."

3

After forcing herself to make a few pleasant comments to a thankfully subdued Matilda Vinson, Lynn raced for home. She had a feeling Doug would be headed for the volunteer center and she was right. He was picking up his car keys, starting out the door. They almost collided.

"Lynn, what are you doing here?"

"You will not believe what's happened."

Doug's expression froze. "They found Todd."

"Todd? No. You would have known about that before me. Why are you looking at me like that?"

"I just . . ." Doug swallowed. "Got my hopes up, that's all." He looked tired, his eyelids slightly swollen from lack of sleep. Lynn was unhappy to see him wearing his oldest pair of jeans and a faded green T-shirt he'd obviously pulled from the dryer without waiting for her to iron it. She liked for Doug to look good. His recent weight gain and his sleepless nights weren't helping, but he could at least wear decent clothes, she thought in annoyance. People would think he was unhappy with her and that she was a bad wife who didn't even take care of his wardrobe.

"Doug, that shirt—"

"Don't carp about my clothes. Come in and tell me what's going on."

Their house was small and spare, much newer than Molly's but less lavish and built of cheap materials. Frank had offered to buy them something nicer, but to Lynn's frustration Doug had turned him down. He wanted to live on what they earned. He still wasn't happy about the store Frank had bought for Lynn, although Frank agreed to let Lynn pay him back over time. Douglas and Lynn had argued over that one. Argued, made up, argued again. And finally Lynn had prevailed.

She didn't like her house, but she kept it spotless and had just finished painting the kitchen and living room. She pulled Doug over to a hard blue couch she hated and sat down beside him. "Skeeter Dobbs has been murdered. Miss Vinson found him in the doorway of the store. Fell right over him."

"Murdered?" Doug repeated woodenly. "You're sure he was *murdered*?"

"Someone jabbed an ice pick in his eye." Finally she looked repelled. "I got a closer look than I would have liked. It was gross. The thing must have gone clear into his brain. The blood—"

"*Stop.*" Douglas looked away. Lynn reached out and touched his palm. Her hand was thin and pale with long nails painted scarlet. Doug made no move to close his own thick hand around hers.

"Well, I didn't think you'd take the news so hard," Lynn said tartly. "You never treated Skeeter like a pet like so many people around here. He was just a half-loony, lazy drunk. He should have been shut up someplace."

"I guess he was a pretty sorry specimen," Doug said grudgingly.

"You *guess*? What did he ever do? Couldn't earn a living. He never helped anyone."

"Helped?"

Lynn looked annoyed with his slowness. "Yeah. Like you teach. You contribute. He never *helped* anyone."

"He might have," Douglas said faintly.

"Oh yeah? You have something specific in mind?"

"Todd."

Lynn stared at him. "I don't get it."

"Skeeter is the one who told Bill about there being someone in the attic of Klein's."

"They checked up there and found Todd's stuffed animal. That's all you told me last night." Lynn's voice rose slightly. "You didn't say anything about Skeeter."

"I'm telling you now. It was Skeeter who told Bill about someone in the attic. He thought it was his grandfather, but Bill decided to check it out."

"Oh." Lynn looked at him. "Well, what does that have to do with anything?"

"I wonder if the person he saw in the attic killed him."

"But you said he thought he saw his grandfather."

"Well, clearly he didn't, Lynn. Use your head. Skeeter saw the person who had Todd stashed up there. He looked right at Skeeter. He might have killed Skeeter as a witness."

Lynn's gray gaze went flat. She drew two shallow breaths before she said, "But Skeeter didn't identify anyone, did he? You would have told me. Bill would have arrested him."

"Like I said, Bill said Skeeter thought his grandfather was in the attic," Doug said wearily. "Bill had a feeling if

Skeeter took some time, though, he might come up with more information about what the person looked like."

"Skeeter? I don't think so."

"We can't be sure of that. Sometimes Skeeter could surprise you."

"Well, he won't now."

"No, someone saw to that."

They sat in silence. Lynn twisted her narrow wedding band. Douglas tapped his fingers on an end table. A boy rode by on a bicycle and yelled to a friend. The woman who lived beside them opened her front door and screamed for the family dog. Finally Lynn and Doug looked at each other, exchanging false smiles. "I'm going to the volunteer center," Doug said. "Want to come with me?"

"There are a dozen things I could do around here with my day off," Lynn said quickly. "Miss Vinson will probably make me work overtime to make up for this unexpected reprieve. She can think up more unnecessary work than anyone I ever knew. It's not like we're doing a landslide business."

"Yeah, too bad for Vinson's," Doug said vaguely. "I'll be on my way, then. Got a couple of errands to do, too. I'll be back for dinner."

"We're having pork chops. Peas and mushrooms. I might make some biscuits—"

"Good. Fine." He brushed her cheek with his lips. "See you later."

Lynn couldn't manage a good-bye. She waited until she heard Doug start his seven-year-old car, then crept to a window and peeked out until she saw him clear the driveway, stop at the end of the street, and make a right turn. When she turned away from the window, she felt dizzy, even nauseated. She clenched her hands and found them damp. Lynn had never been high-strung. She prided herself on rarely panicking in her life. But at the moment she felt as if she might pass out. Or scream.

Lynn's friendship with Molly had cooled years ago. Molly would not abide an unkind word about Rebecca, and

Lynn couldn't help taking potshots at her on every opportunity. She also resented Molly's loyalty to Rebecca instead
of to her and Larry. They had all been friends. Nevertheless, Molly had always been kind to her. And she'd been
through a hard time having and keeping her baby. Lynn
had even liked the kid the few times she was around him.
No one knew who his father was, although everyone had
opinions.

But one man Lynn knew could *not* be Todd's father was
her brother Larry, who had been in prison when Molly got
pregnant. Larry had no affection, no gentle feelings, for
Todd or any child. Larry, always burning with anger, had
been a powder keg lately. And he needed money. She
didn't know for what, but he needed it. And now Todd had
been taken.

Lynn had considered, rejected, considered again, then
feared he'd kidnapped the child for ransom, inspired by the
abduction of Jonnie Ryan. But Larry wouldn't kill the kid.
He wouldn't kill anyone. This had been the one certainty
that had comforted her.

Now someone had murdered Skeeter Dobbs, who had
seen the person who kept Todd prisoner in the Klein building. Maybe whoever took Todd killed Skeeter. Or maybe
not. And maybe Larry had nothing to do with Todd's abduction. Would he actually attempt such a dangerous
scheme? No, he had too much sense.

Except when he was drinking, which he'd been doing
to excess for a month.

"Oh God," Lynn moaned, thinking she might throw up.
She'd always adored her older brother and felt guilty for
his being shot and sent to prison. She and Doug hadn't been
in on the robberies, but Larry was right—they'd been there
to accept part of the spoils. And Larry was the only one
who'd paid. He'd never been the same since he'd been shot
and gone to prison. She didn't really know him anymore.

Lynn took a deep breath, fighting for control. Nothing
was ever gained by going into a tailspin, she told herself.
You didn't think clearly, you didn't act effectively, and

Larry might need her help more than ever. If so, this time she intended to be there for him.

She went to the phone and called Larry's apartment. No answer. That was good. It meant he was at work. She picked up her purse and car keys and headed to Maloney's Garage.

4

MONDAY, 6:45 P.M.

Rebecca took one last look in the mirror, smoothed her pale green dress, gave Sean another chew bone to occupy him for the evening, then shut her bedroom door and went downstairs. As she passed Frank's study, he called out to her. She paused in the doorway.

"You look lovely. I like that dress."

Rebecca pirouetted for him the way she used to when she was a teenager dressed for a special occasion. "Thank you, sir."

"We'll miss you at dinner."

Rebecca doubted this. Her mother had bitten and snapped all day, first at Walt for mowing too early and awakening her, then at Betty for trying to cajole her into eating, and finally at Rebecca for everything. After their third encounter she'd flung off to her bedroom with a headache. "Well she's a breath of fresh air," Rebecca said to Betty. She'd tried for cool disdain and failed. Hurt had vibrated in her voice.

"Honey, it's four in the afternoon and your mother hasn't had a drink since yesterday," Betty had said gently.

"How do you know?"

"She told me. She said I was to ignore her if she got mean-tempered. You do the same. It's hard on her but she's trying."

Now Frank seemed to be expecting a pleasant dinner with Suzanne. Rebecca felt pity for him, although she knew pity was the last thing this proud man would want. "It feels strange to be going out on the town," she said lightly.

"You need an evening out." The fading evening light shone on his black and silver hair. "This hasn't been a pleasant trip."

"I haven't been much help so far. I shouldn't be going out to dinner."

"Nonsense. A change of scene might give you fresh perspective." Frank leaned back in his chair, smiling. "Why don't you go upstairs and when young Bellamy calls, I'll answer the door. That way you can make an entrance."

Rebecca tried to look starry-eyed. "That sounds *fabulous*! And can I stay out an hour later than usual?"

"You're not that grown-up. At least not in my eyes."

The doorbell rang. "Hark! That must be young Bellamy now!" Rebecca trilled.

Frank laughed softly. "I have missed you, Rebecca. Have a good time tonight."

Ten minutes later she sat in Clay's car looking at him with reluctance. "Dormaine's? Clay, I can't go to Dormaine's for dinner. I nearly knocked down the place Saturday night."

"You didn't nearly knock down the restaurant. Just the ancient, prized tree on the lawn."

"Oh, that's different. What do I have to be embarrassed about?"

"That's what I'd like to know." Clay grinned. "Look, you had an accident in a pouring rainstorm. It's not like you were gunning for the place. This will give you a chance to apologize to Peter Dormaine."

"And assure him that my insurance will cover all damages, although I'm sure Frank has already done that. Still, a personal appearance might look more sincere." She sighed. "All right, Dr. Bellamy, Dormaine's it is."

Rebecca had been nervous all day about the date and chided herself, both for being silly and for being shallow. After all, Todd was still missing. How could she care about anything else? How could she even want to go out to dinner? Then she reminded herself that this wasn't an ordinary date. Clay had presented himself as possibly the only really objective sounding board in her circle. She needed to talk to someone who could be less emotional than the family.

When Peter Dormaine built his Art Deco–style restaurant on the corner of First Avenue and Grove Street two years ago, most people in town predicted failure. Even Frank had told her he feared Peter would be closing the elegant doors in a year. He had therefore dined at the restaurant once a month with Suzanne, held the Grace Healthcare holiday luncheon in the banquet room, and recommended the place to all his friends. "We must support local business," he'd told Rebecca. "Sinclair is a beautiful city. We want it to flourish."

"Do you eat here often?" Rebecca asked as they walked toward the front door, then could have bitten her tongue. She might as well have asked Clay how many other women he'd brought here. Her cheeks grew hot.

"I've been here twice," Clay said offhandedly, clearly pretending not to notice her gaffe. "I'm ashamed of myself for not coming more often this last year since I've been back in Sinclair because I've known Peter for ages. But my schedule has been pretty tough."

They entered the double doors and crossed gleaming black-and-white tiles that looked like marble. Against one wall sat a pale apricot couch; four lush chairs upholstered in amethyst satin surrounded a geometric-style glass table. Above the couch hung a framed poster for the movie *The Thin Man* and a beautiful chandelier sent down a prism of color.

The next few minutes were taken up with confirming reservations and being seated. "This place is beautiful," Rebecca murmured as the hostess left them with their menus and drifted back to her post.

"I think it's pretty impressive."

They both looked around at the clean lines of the large room with its continued color scheme of apricot and amethyst. Purple gladioli stood in tall fluted crystal vases. A large, white brick fireplace dominated one end of the room and above it a long silver-framed mirror reflected the tables and well-dressed guests. The song "Someone to Watch Over Me" completed the elegant ambience.

"I just might move in here," Rebecca said.

Clay smiled. "Sure beats McDonald's."

The waiter came and took their wine order. "Have I told you how pretty you look?" Clay said after the waiter disappeared into the back.

"Thank you. I didn't bring many clothes with me."

"The green of your dress brings out your eyes. I don't think I ever noticed just how green they are."

Rebecca laughed. "I loved my father dearly but when I was young I was devastated that I had his auburn hair and green eyes, not my mother's pale blond hair and blue eyes. But I've accepted what nature bestowed."

"I never knew your father."

"I think you would have liked him. Everyone did." She smiled. "He was fun-loving and outgoing. That's why people were so surprised that he was such a successful CEO of Grace Healthcare. At least that's what my mother has told me. I guess there was never any question of his taking over when his father died because his older brother had made plain his complete uninterest. But Grandfather was worried. He didn't think Dad had what it took."

"He proved him wrong."

"Yes. He loved the business." She grew solemn. "What a shame he died so young."

"I remember there was a wreck. I don't recall what caused it."

"We were driving down a hill in a wooded area. It was autumn—hunting season. Apparently someone was a poor shot and hit our tire."

"Good God!" Clay exclaimed. "That bad a marksman didn't deserve a hunting license. Who was it?"

"They never found out, although some people had seen a couple of young guys in the area carrying shotguns. They acted drunk, but no one was able to identify them. I hate hunting to this day."

"No wonder, but at least you weren't killed in the car accident, too. Your mother must have been grateful for that."

"I guess." Rebecca was glad the waiter brought their wine. Hers was Chablis, deeply chilled the way she liked. "Anyway, after the wreck my mother was so devastated by Daddy's loss I'm not sure I really existed for her for a while. She also might have been a little resentful that I lived and Daddy didn't, although she'd never admit it. Everything was chaos. Thank goodness Frank was around to step in. Daddy had always been closer to him than to his brother. He was an executive at Grace and knew everything about the business. Mother trusted him, too. She depended on him for everything. Sometimes I think Frank married her because she was so helpless and he was so loyal to my father."

"He married her out of obligation?"

"Not entirely. But maybe a little." She paused. "And that was extremely unkind. I can be a real bitch sometimes."

Clay shook his head. "Don't I feel like a fool! All these years I've thought you were a *witch*. Don't you fly on a broom and dance naked under the full moon?"

He'd turned her dark mood into a joke and she laughed. "In Sinclair I indulge myself in these activities only on Halloween. New Orleans is a different story. They understand my kind down there and I just have a high old time."

The waiter materialized to take their order, then vanished back to the kitchen. "And how was your day?" Rebecca asked, wanting to turn the conversation away from herself.

"Three broken legs in one day. That's a record. One vicious migraine. Food poisoning from ham salad left out too long on a Sunday picnic." He grinned. "And a kid brought in his dog. Hit by a car. I'm not supposed to, but I did a little work on him before I talked one of the nurses who was going off duty into driving the kid and the dog to the veterinarian. I called the vet a couple of hours later and he said the dog would be fine."

"I'm glad. I know you have a dog named Gypsy."

He nodded, smiling. "Mixed breed, medium sized. Maybe a beagle and German shepherd mix. Maybe a dozen other things. Golden brown face with a black back. Looks like a horse from the front."

"A *horse*?"

"Maybe that's just my perspective."

Rebecca giggled. "I *hope* so. Good heavens!"

Clay laughed. "Her ears are probably burning and I'll be in trouble when I get home. Anyway, I found her, a lovable little vagabond. I'm usually too embarrassed to admit how much I like her."

"So you took in a stray," Rebecca said approvingly. "So did I, only mine is a purebred Australian shepherd—who's not from Australia like most people think. Strictly American breed. Fast and used for herding, although I believe Sean would be insulted to the core if I asked him to do chores. I took him to Happy Tracks Grooming Salon yesterday and they put a bow in his hair. Terrible for the macho image."

"I should think so!" Clay laughed.

"I'll take it out tomorrow. He just looks so cute. Anyway, you probably didn't notice the other night, but his right eye is partly blue. It's not unusual for the breed. I did tell you he's skittish around men. So far the jury is out on Frank and he nipped Doug, but Sean's crazy about Walt Sykes, who's married to Betty. Do you remember Betty?"

"Sure I do. Fabulous cook. Great personality. Always seemed to like nothing better than a gang of boys in her kitchen to feed."

"She hasn't changed. She should have had a dozen kids of her own. I'm so happy she got married. My family has been her whole life for too long."

"Then I'm happy for her, too, as long as she hasn't given up her cooking. I still miss those Toll House cookies of hers."

"Maybe I can talk her into making you a batch," Rebecca said, then lost patience with herself once more. She sounded as if she was making any excuse to see Clay again.

She was grateful when their salad arrived at that moment and their conversation halted while they watched the waiter toss the contents. Rebecca had not eaten Caesar salad for a couple of years, and she found this one especially good. "Like it?" Clay asked with a faint smile, and she realized she'd been shoveling it in.

She swallowed. "I've lived alone too long and lost my manners. I also haven't eaten all day."

"That's not good for you. Blood sugar and all that."

"I know, but I've had a lot on my mind. Some people eat when they're nervous. My appetite abandons me."

"Nervous nibblers would envy you, and frankly, picky eaters annoy me." He looked at her solemnly. "But you've had every right to be nervous. Has Bill been able to find out anything about that CD you found in your car?"

"Not that I know of, but he hasn't had a lot of time to devote to it. I've been doing my own investigation, though." She took a sip of wine. "First of all, my mother stored everything of my father's. Miraculously I found the original Procol Harum album. I also found Daddy's cassette tape with the song on it."

"But no compact disc?"

"Remember, the car wreck was seventeen years ago, before most people had CDs."

"But the stereo in the house isn't that old."

"No, but I only found three CDs. They're Frank's—that generic easy-listening stuff."

Clay finished his salad and wiped his mouth absently, frowning. "All right, this must have been a new compact disc."

"I stopped by the two record stores in town. Neither carries the CD—the CD was from the original album dating from 1967—and neither place showed records of having ordered it within the last few months. The same with the two music stores at the mall. That leaves one resource—"

"The Internet."

"And good luck trying to track down *that* order."

Clay rolled his eyes. "Well, hell."

"My sentiments exactly."

Clay leaned nearer. "And now we come to the *really* important question: Who knew Jonnie loved that song?"

The waiter arrived with sherbet over which he poured champagne to cleanse the palate. They both ate in silence, their spoons clinking against the sides of the glass dishes. When they finished, Clay looked at her again. "Okay, people in the family knew about 'Whiter Shade of Pale.' I'm sure Doug heard Jonnie play it."

"Doug?" Rebecca echoed. "You don't think *he* took Todd and is now trying to scare me?"

"Absolutely not. But it's important to hit all the bases. Another person who knew Jonnie loved the song was Betty. Not that I suspect Betty, but she could have told Walt, who could have told God knows who. Innocently, of course, but they're still a source of information. So is your mother. She talks about Jonnie all the time, or so Doug says. Doug could have told Lynn, who could have told Larry. Larry could have told a girlfriend. And on and on."

Rebecca looked at Clay closely, noting how his boyish smile could so easily distract one from the keenness of his blue-gray eyes, his joking manner mask the constant clicking away of a computerlike brain.

"I hadn't even thought of all those potential sources," she said faintly. "Only immediate family. But there's another huge source. Jonnie played the song in a talent contest just months before he disappeared. He won. The news was in the paper along with the name of the selection he played."

"I'd forgotten all about that," Clay said. "Well, so much for tracking down a few leaks. The whole damn town could have known about the song. Hell, even old Skeeter Dobbs could have known."

"If you try to convince me Skeeter ordered a Procol Harum CD from the Internet and sneaked it into my car, I'm going to completely lose faith in you."

"Actually I don't think Skeeter was big on surfing the Net. I'm just trying to give you an indication of the number and type of people who could have known about the song."

Rebecca closed her eyes. "Poor old Skeeter. I remember when I was young and Bill would take me to the park. I used to talk to Skeeter. Then he grew afraid of me."

"Afraid? Why?"

"My ESP," Rebecca said wryly. "It terrified him."

"Is that right?" Clay frowned. "And someone obviously put that CD in your car to frighten you. Probably to scare you out of town."

"Not Skeeter. He never wandered more than two or three blocks from Klein Furniture. Even if someone had given him the CD and asked him to put it in the car—"

"He wouldn't have gone all the way to Molly's to do it. But you might have spooked someone else as much as you did Skeeter. You left town once before because of Jonnie. Maybe someone thought reminding you of him might send you away again." He looked at her intensely. "Whoever took Todd doesn't want him found, and they'd have to be particularly afraid of you."

"And it's probably the same person who murdered Skeeter," she said reluctantly. "After all, Skeeter is the one who saw Todd's kidnapper at Klein's, even if he didn't recognize him."

Clay lowered his voice and pinned her with his gaze. "Rebecca, you know whoever murdered Skeeter might go to the same lengths to get rid of you. Are you sure you want to face this kind of danger?"

Rebecca looked down to avoid his keen gaze. Yes, as much as she wanted to help Todd and Molly, a part of her remained timid, wanted to run away from the responsibility, the weight of another agonizing failure, the fear of danger to her own well-being. But the years had also changed her, hardened her more than she'd realized. "I am not leaving Sinclair," she said quietly. "Not until we find out something about Todd, one way or another."

Clay looked at her solemnly. "I admire that but I'm also worried about you. Aside from the possible danger you're in, I know what this situation is taking out of you."

"A lot of emotion without much to show for it." She forced herself to sound casual. "But enough about my mental state. I'm disappointed by my failure to track down the CD. Playing private detective isn't as easy as it looks on TV."

Clay drew back with his cocky grin. "Nonsense, my girl! We've only scratched the surface."

Rebecca couldn't help grinning back. Things didn't look nearly so bleak in his company. Maybe that was because he wasn't directly involved. Or maybe it was because he possessed an indomitable natural optimism.

Their food arrived and Rebecca was delighted with the large portions of shrimp with lobster sauce and lemon chicken. Clay was going to think she had the appetite of a horse, but she didn't care. She wasn't Scarlett O'Hara trying to fit her waist into a corset drawn to seventeen inches.

"No wonder this place has earned four stars," she said. "I haven't tasted finer food even in New Orleans."

"I do thank you for the compliment!"

Rebecca looked up to see a man in his fifties with impossibly blond, lacquered hair and a blue-and-red paisley ascot. She'd never met a man wearing an ascot. "Peter Dormaine, Ms. Ryan. So nice to meet you."

"A pleasure to meet you, too, and I'm so sorry about your tree," Rebecca said in a rush. "I'm usually not a reckless driver. I feel just awful—"

Dormaine held up a well-manicured hand bearing an ostentatious sapphire ring. "No need to apologize. I'm simply glad you're all right. And so is the tree. Mrs. Esther Hardison of Whispering Willows Nursery rushed right over with some foul-smelling potion she smeared all over the gash in the tree. She guarantees me the tree will not only live but thrive. And the lawn has been reseeded. All is well."

After he'd left, Rebecca leaned toward Clay. "He's nice but a bit flowery. That accent! I can't quite place it."

"Try a Berlitz course after spending his first eighteen years deep in a West Virginia hollow. He's a good guy.

He's just pompous. At least you got past your apology. Wasn't so bad, was it?"

"Not at all. I have a feeling the night it happened he wasn't quite so calm about the damage I'd done to his perfect lawn. I didn't know Aunt Esther had been called to the rescue."

Clay frowned. "I always get this confused. She's not really your aunt, is she?"

"No. She's Frank's. She and her husband raised Frank after his parents died, and she's always felt like family to me." The day when she'd flashed on someone telling a boy his family had blown the ransom drop and now he would die. A boy she knew was Jonnie.

"What's wrong?" Clay asked. "You wouldn't believe how your expression changed."

"Oh, something happened out at the nursery. It was probably nothing." Clay raised an eyebrow at her. "Okay, it was something weird and probably important."

"Then let's hear it. I *am* your sounding board, remember?"

Briefly Rebecca told him about seeing into the mind of someone she'd first thought was Todd. Then the someone had mentioned the family bringing in the FBI and signing his death warrant. "It was Jonnie, Clay. The FBI isn't involved with Todd's abduction. And whoever was speaking to the victim broke his finger. Jonnie's finger was broken."

Clay leaned back in his chair. "Have you had flashes about Jonnie before, since the kidnapping?"

"Never. Not one thing. When it happened yesterday, I was walking into the pond at the nursery. I can't swim but I was oblivious to the water. Doug stopped me."

"Doug is close to Esther?"

"Very. She was always loving and supportive of him, even when he was going through that bad time a few years ago."

" 'Bad time.' That's a polite way to put it. We were a bunch of punks."

"You? Clay, you were nothing like Doug and Lynn and Larry."

"Well, I wasn't the clean-cut, all-American boy. I probably would have gotten in a lot more trouble if I hadn't had so many chores to do on the farm." He frowned. "We were just an unhappy group and there was no reason for it. None of us had bad home lives."

"Doug didn't want his father to marry Mother," Rebecca said. "I never understood it. She was always kind to him. I think he had some idea his own mother would come back."

"He was crazy about his mother. Didn't he ever talk about her to you?" Rebecca shook her head. "Well, to hear him tell it, she was an angel on earth and he couldn't accept her death or his father marrying anyone else. He also didn't feel comfortable in your house. He knew Jonnie didn't like him."

"I don't think it was that Jonnie didn't like Doug. He just felt the way Doug did: He couldn't let go of Daddy and he didn't want Mother to remarry."

"It's a shame they didn't understand each other," Clay said. "But my point was that Larry, Lynn, Doug and I had okay lives—not perfect, but who does? But we chose to go around feeling misunderstood and abused by the world in general. We were all mad about something and we sort of kept each other fired up. It was stupid."

"You never got in trouble like the others."

Clay shrugged. "I was two years older than Doug and Larry. Maybe I had a *little* more sense. And then there were the drugs. I did my share of drinking, but I never experimented with drugs. I guess that's what my early interest in medicine did for me—gave me knowledge about their dangers that outweighed my curiosity. It was the drugs that really messed up Doug and Larry. They graduated from some occasional coke-sniffing to heroin. Doug came out of it all right, but Larry . . ." He shook his head. "You shouldn't feel bad about being the one who revealed he was behind all those robberies, Rebecca. If he hadn't gone to the penitentiary, I know he'd be dead of an overdose."

"Lynn doesn't feel that way," Rebecca said quietly.

"Lynn is strong, but she doesn't always have the best sense in the world, particularly when it comes to her brother. And she's jealous of you."

"Of *me*?"

Clay smiled. "You mean you didn't know?"

"It never occurred to me. She's pretty and smart and she was much more popular in school than I was. Good Lord, most kids thought I was a freak."

"Well, Lynn didn't think so. She used to talk about you when she'd had too much to drink. She admired you, envied you. She was also scared to death Doug was going to fall in love with you and dump her."

Rebecca gaped. "Doug fall in love with *me*? That's the most ridiculous thing I've ever heard!"

Clay shrugged. "I know. The very idea of anyone falling in love with you is ludicrous, but people get strange ideas."

"I should tell you flattery doesn't work on me," Rebecca said drolly.

"You're immune to my charm?"

"Completely. Now tell me about Lynn."

"What's to tell? She's always been crazy about Doug and she's always been possessive. It used to bother him. He cared about her, but he wanted to play the field a little."

"And did he?"

"A gentleman doesn't tell." Clay grinned. "Besides, if he did, he never confided in me. But why are you so interested? I know it's not for the sake of gossip."

"Thanks for the benefit of the doubt. Really, I've always been surprised by their total devotion to each other. Or what I thought was total devotion. I never dreamed Doug looked at anyone else, and despite what Lynn might have thought, he certainly wasn't looking at me. I don't think he even liked me."

"He didn't dislike you. That's all it took for Lynn to be jealous."

The waiter came with more wine, a ten-year-old Pouilly

Fuissé, a compliment of the house. They sent thanks to Peter, then sipped. "This is excellent," Rebecca said. "Now I'd like to ask your opinion about someone else. I'm not impressed with Jean Wright, Molly's new watchdog. Molly has only mentioned her a few times to me, but now the woman is like one of the family. Maybe her intentions are good and she's only trying to help or maybe she's, well, this sounds silly, but maybe she's keeping an eye on things."

"You mean trying to get in on all the action?"

"Or something more serious."

"You mean she knows more than she's saying. Or maybe she's involved." He looked into Rebecca's earnest eyes. "Jean works at the hospital. I'm sure I can find someone who knows her. You played private investigator today about the compact disc. I'll play it tomorrow about Jean Wright."

"Oh, Clay, that would be so helpful. Would you mind?"

"Mind? I'd love it. Mike Hammer will have nothing on me. I'm going to map out my strategy tonight. Here's to luck!"

They clinked their wineglasses. Rebecca felt lighter than she had since she'd arrived in Sinclair, as if some of the weight of responsibility for finding Todd had been lifted from her shoulders. She had help, now. Not official help like Bill's, but help in the form of a friend who didn't scoff at her fears or try to make light of her deductions or her worries no matter how tangential they might seem to the main issue . . .

Clay was smiling at her, his gray-blue eyes crinkling at the corners, the dimples deepening on either side of his mouth. Rebecca tried to smile in return, even when his eyes began to blur, their color to dim as if someone had placed a drift of pale chiffon over her own vision.

With dread Rebecca felt her consciousness leaving her body. Her hands turned cold while perspiration popped out on her forehead. Her breath quickened. From somewhere far away she heard Clay saying, "Rebecca, are you all right? Rebecca?"

Her lips moved but no sound came out. Clay's face completely vanished. The sound of other diners chatting, the strains of "I'm In the Mood for Love," disappeared. She felt as if she were falling into a bottomless well.

A small part of Rebecca held on to her own identity as the rest slid into another mind, a little boy's mind, where everything was dark. Not just dark because of the blindfold. He was in a dark place, pitch-black and cold and musty. He shivered, then sneezed, unable to wipe his nose because his hands were bound behind his back. His throat hurt a little and his lips were so dry they'd cracked painfully. He could smell where he'd wet his pants and he was bitterly embarrassed and damply uncomfortable.

He couldn't remember how long he'd slept this time. The Dark Warrior, as he'd come to think of the being who held him captive, gave him shots. At first he'd cried because he was afraid of needles. Now the pain of a needle prick seemed like nothing compared to his constantly cramped muscles, his headaches, and now his sore throat. In fact, he welcomed the shots because they meant he could go to sleep and forget everything for a while. He could even forget why Mommy hadn't come to get him. Almost.

The sound of high-pitched crying ripped the air. The wail was long and heartbreaking and also scary. Was a baby hurt, maybe being killed? Todd shivered violently . . .

By now Rebecca was gripping the tablecloth in her fists. Her green eyes were wide open but unseeing as she pulled the cloth and all the dishes shifted toward her. Clay stood and rushed to her side, gently putting his arm around her shoulder. "Rebecca, come back," he said softly as the voices of other diners trailed off and they began to stare. "Rebecca, turn loose of the tablecloth. Calm down. Come on, Stargazer. Come back to me."

But Rebecca didn't hear Clay. She heard the same heart-wrenching crying as Todd and chills ran up her arms. Clay looked at the fine, raised hairs against the golden skin, the tightened biceps, the face smooth as marble and sheened with sweat. "Rebecca, where *are* you?" he murmured frantically.

Todd was hyperventilating. The awful wailing continued. Something was hurt. He couldn't bear it. He was scared, so scared. He wished he was dead just so he could stop being afraid. And then he heard another noise. Footsteps. A creaking. The Dark Warrior was coming back again.

He sobbed, a sound so rough it hurt his lungs. Last summer when he'd visited his cousin Rebecca in wonderful New Orleans, she'd told him whenever he was scared, he should think about being in a good place where there was nothing to fear. He'd been crazy about Rebecca 'cause part of her seemed like a kid. And Mommy had told him Rebecca had special powers, although she didn't tell him what kind. So he decided to do what Rebecca said and tried to put his mind in another place. He would go into the world of *Star Wars*. He was Obi-Wan Kenobi. Obi-Wan was afraid of nothing. He was a skilled fighter. He knew magic tricks—

"And how are you liking your stay here, little boy?" the Dark Warrior asked in that terrible, grating voice that didn't even sound like it belonged to a person. "Cooler than the attic, wouldn't you say? No, I guess not. You can't say anything."

Please, please, *please* don't hurt me, Todd thought frantically, now afraid that seconds ago he'd wished he was dead. He really didn't want to die. He just wanted to go home to Mommy.

But the Dark Warrior didn't hurt him. He felt a blanket being spread over him. It was rough and scratchy but warm. Then his gag was removed. The terrible crying outside had waned into pitiful mewling. "What's that sound?" he whispered.

"Nothing you need to worry about. Now eat." The Warrior shoved his mouth full of bits of food—something that felt like a sandwich—but he was too dry to swallow. He gagged and the food sprayed out.

"Don't spit at me! Don't you dare—"

"Didn't mean to," Todd whimpered. "Can't swallow."

Todd cringed, waiting for a blow. Instead he heard the sound of liquid being poured. A plastic cup touched his lips. "Drink!" the Warrior commanded, and something wet entered his mouth and trickled down his chin. Water, but it tasted funny. He didn't want more, but he knew he had to have it or he couldn't eat. And he was so thirsty he could hardly stand it. He forced down four more sips of the moldy-tasting water. Then he had three bites of a peanut butter sandwich.

"Like peanut butter?" the Dark Warrior asked. "I did when I was your age. It's full of protein, but you don't know what that is. It'll keep you going, though. And I have to keep you going, at least for a few more days."

Todd was listening but the words barely made sense. The peanut butter stuck to his teeth, which hadn't been brushed for days and felt scummy. He hated the feel and Mommy would be mad. She was strict about tooth-brushing.

"Let's do something about those lips." Todd stiffened, not knowing what to expect, but in a moment a finger was running something creamy over his parched lips. It stung at first. Then he found he was able to stretch them without as much pain.

"Can't say I don't take care of you." Todd said nothing. "Well, *don't* I?"

Todd whimpered and nodded. "Y . . . yes."

The chilling sound of shrill crying started again. "What *is* that? Is a baby gettin' killed?"

"Do you care?" the Warrior asked.

"Yeah. I don't like for things to get hurt, 'specially animals or babies."

Another wrenching wail. The Dark Warrior chuckled. "I don't care if *anything* gets hurt. Except me. But not you. I don't care about you."

"Mommy does. And . . . and Rebecca."

Todd felt the Dark Warrior freeze. "What do you know about Rebecca?"

"She has special powers. Mommy told me. She might find me." He spoke with more confidence, not sure where the words were coming from, knowing he shouldn't say them but unable to stop himself. "She's here! She's looking for me!"

By now Rebecca's breathing came in short, ragged gasps. Perspiration dripped down her face, into her eyes, but she still didn't blink. A man rushed to Clay's side. "What is it?" he asked urgently. "Epilepsy? Should I call 911?"

"It's not epilepsy," Clay said grimly. "She'll be all right."

"She doesn't look all right."

"Hal?" the man's wife called tremulously. "Do something."

The man spread his legs slightly, taking on a fighting stance. "I'm calling the emergency squad. This woman needs help."

"Sir, I am a doctor," Clay said evenly. "I know what I'm dealing with. Now back away." He looked at the small group gathering around Rebecca. "Please, all of you, back away." And they did, like a group of frightened, wide-eyed animals, while Clay grasped both of Rebecca's shoulders. "Becky, snap out of it! Now!"

But Todd's mind consumed her. "Why are you doing this?" he asked the Warrior. "I never hurt you!"

"You shut up about Rebecca. You don't mention her, you don't think about her. And you'd better pray she doesn't find you or you'll never see your mother again!"

"No, *please*—"

"I've had enough of you." The Warrior roughly tied the gag around his head again, forcing open his jaw. Saliva flowed and Todd bit down on stale cloth already wet from long use. "I think you need to sleep now. A nice, long, quiet sleep." The Warrior paused. "But you've been a bad boy. I just hope you haven't upset me so much I put too much medicine in the hypodermic. Too much medicine can make you sleep forever. Would you like that? To die here in the dark where no one will *ever* find you?"

Todd whimpered as the needle pierced his skin. The last thing he heard was the terrible, piercing wail of something lost and hurt in the night, something just like him.

"Rebecca! *Rebecca!*"

She came back to her world with a jolt, spasmodically jerking the cloth off the table. China and crystal shattered on the floor. Food and wine splattered onto her dress, Clay's suit, and the apricot satin seat of her chair. A woman let out a shrill cry. The man who had wanted to call the emergency squad still hovered. Other diners stared, horrified.

Rebecca, trembling, began frantically wiping at the food on her lap with a napkin. "Oh, my," she mumbled weakly. "Look what I've done! I'm so sorry."

Clay took the napkin from her hand. "It doesn't matter. Let's get out of here. Can you stand?"

"I'm not sure. I feel . . ." I feel like I'm losing my mind, she wanted to say, but Peter Dormaine appeared, his color high, his ascot crooked.

"What's happened? Oh! The china! The chair! Look at the *mess!*" He was clearly appalled but managed to recover himself although he'd lost his atrocious attempt at a French accent. "Did she have a fit of some kind?"

"I don't think people have had 'fits' since Victorian times," Clay said dryly. "She's not well. Rebecca—"

"I can stand," she said hastily, nearly leaping from her chair. Pieces of chicken fell to the floor and her lap was soaked with wine. Never had she experienced such a public and violent reaction to a vision. "Mr. Dormaine, I'm so sorry. I'll pay for everything, of course. I . . . I don't know . . . I apologize."

Dormaine gave her a sickly smile. "Yes, well, these things happen," he said in a voice that told her these things did *not* happen, especially in his restaurant. "I hope you feel better," he added limply.

"Yes." Rebecca pushed damp hair behind her ears. "I'm fine."

People gaped at her as if she was a lunatic. She thought she might cry or faint. Clay pulled her close to him and she relaxed against the strength of his body. He looked calmly at the flustered Mr. Dormaine. "We *will* take care of the damage, Peter. Good night."

Clay had not apologized for her. In fact, he acted completely oblivious to the chaos, making Rebecca feel better, as if she hadn't humiliated him. That would have been the final blow she couldn't have stood.

Outside the night air was cool and fresh, the sky clear and star-studded. Rebecca drew a deep breath. "Clay, I'm so sorry—"

"I don't want to hear any of that. You have nothing to be sorry for. But I do insist on one thing."

"What's that?"

"You're coming home with me, have a drink or a tranquilizer or whatever you need, and you'll stay until you calm down. Gypsy and I are going to take excellent care of you. All right?"

"That sounds wonderful," Rebecca said gratefully. "Absolutely wonderful."

An hour later Rebecca sat on Clay's couch wrapped in his terry-cloth robe. Her own clothes were ruined and she'd had to take a shower to rinse away all the food and wine. He'd insisted she take a mild tranquilizer and by now the tension had flowed out of her body. Gypsy had cuddled close to her and Rebecca sipped a club soda and stroked the dog's silky ears.

She'd already related everything she'd seen in her vision to Clay. All during her teenage years, when she was supposed to have "seen" so much, he'd been slightly skeptical. His rational mind wanted to find other explanations for her so-called ESP. This evening had shattered the last of that skepticism. Saturday night she'd known the details of Todd's abduction without being told. Tonight he'd seen the torture on her face as she experienced what the terrified little boy must be experiencing. She wasn't acting. It wasn't all a coincidence.

"So what do we do now, Clay?" she asked. "We've talked to Bill, not that I had anything helpful to tell him."

"Don't be so hard on yourself. It's more information than we had this afternoon. Especially the fact that Todd's alive, Rebecca. After they found the blood on that stuffed dog, they weren't sure."

She sighed. "If only I'd seen more."

"You will."

"Not tonight. My brain is fried. I have to go home." She started to stand, then swayed. "Goodness. How strong was that tranquilizer?"

"Extremely weak. You're just worn out after the last few days. I have a proposition for you. Why don't you spend the night here?"

"Frank said I had to be home at eleven."

Clay grinned. "You're already past curfew. And over twenty-one, although I promise not to take advantage of that fact."

"Gorgeous *and* gallant. You're too good to be true, Clay Bellamy." Immediately Rebecca's face flamed. Her tongue had become entirely too loose. "I'll have to call home."

"You go in the bedroom. Lucky for you I changed the sheets yesterday. Climb in bed and I'll do the calling. You just rest."

Rebecca hesitated. How well did she know Clay? Oh, she wasn't afraid of being taken advantage of. She just wondered if he didn't think this whole situation was ludicrous, if she wouldn't be the object of fun tomorrow. Then she looked at him. His gray-blue gaze was kind, concerned, his smile gentle. No, Clay would not make fun of her. For some reason he was going far out of his way to take care of her.

Gypsy followed her to the bedroom. Clay didn't look like the type for pajamas, but she found an oversized sweatshirt lying on top of a laundry basket full of folded clothes. She shed the terry-cloth robe and slipped on the sweatshirt, then slid between the sheets, turning on her right side. Immediately Gypsy jumped on the bed, positioning herself close to Rebecca's chest in exactly the same position where Sean always lay. Rebecca fondled her ears.

In a moment Clay appeared in the doorway. "Gypsy! For heaven's sake, it's okay to sleep with me, but not with guests!"

The dog looked at him but did not move. "It's all right." Rebecca laughed. "I'm used to sleeping with Sean. And to tell you the truth, after the experience tonight, it feels reassuring to have a warm body beside me."

Clay sat down on the bed, reaching across Gypsy to touch Rebecca's face. He ran a finger down her cheek, then tucked a strand of her long auburn hair behind her ear. "You're cold," he said softly. "Need another blanket?"

"I don't think that would help. The kind of cold I feel comes from being scared and helpless and being alone in all this."

"You're not alone. I believe you completely."

"You do? After Friday night, when you said you needed tests and statistics to convince you—"

"The other night *I* was scared of what I didn't understand, but I'm not scared anymore. I just want to do whatever I can to help you."

Rebecca's throat tightened. She knew she was feeling sorry for herself, but she'd carried the load of people's expectations for so long. And she'd been alone. At least she'd felt alone, even though she knew other people believed in her. But with a few words, Clay had banished that frightening feeling of isolation. He'd made her believe that finally someone could actually help her.

"You really want to help me?" she asked shyly. He nodded, his gaze soft on her own. "Then lie down beside me."

In a few minutes Rebecca lay drowsing, Gypsy pressed against one side of her, Clay on the other. His arm lay lightly around her waist, and his warm breath touched her temple.

And for the first time since the car wreck that had killed her father and changed her life, Rebecca did not feel alone.

Chapter Eight

1

Clay Bellamy awakened with a sense of fierce purpose. When he heard about Todd Ryan he'd been shocked and saddened the way he would be hearing that *any* child had been abducted. Over the past few years he'd only seen Molly six or seven times and the boy once. An emotional distance had grown between him and the Ryan clan.

That emotional distance had been shattered last night. At dinner he'd felt more relaxed than he had for months. Over the years he'd occasionally thought of Rebecca Ryan, especially after he'd heard she'd written a book. Like most people, he'd assumed it would be about Jonnie's kidnapping, but someone told him it seemed to be pure fiction. He'd promised himself he'd read it someday and then immediately forgot it. A month later Rebecca had been brought into the emergency room.

Naturally Rebecca had changed since he last saw her, at Jonnie's funeral. He remembered her as tall and thin, looking older and younger than her years at the same time. He also remembered that Frank had hovered over a weeping Suzanne, who had never glanced at her stricken daughter. Clay had been more moved by Rebecca's silent, solitary misery than by all of Suzanne's tears. He'd known then that the girl who'd blushed and stammered in his presence, who had such an obvious crush on him, was gone. He'd felt oddly grieved by her loss.

But last night when he'd picked her up at her home he'd seen a vibrant, if worried, woman. Over dinner they'd laughed and they'd confided. Then he'd witnessed the drama of her vision. It had shaken him; although he'd tried not to show it, Clay had believed her completely.

He'd slept soundly in bed with her last night and they'd

laughed when they woke up to find that Gypsy had some-how worked her way between them without waking either. "She's jealous." Rebecca had giggled, and Clay had thought how lovely she looked in the harsh morning light even with no makeup and two bandages on her forehead. She'd insisted on taking a cab home so he wouldn't be late for work. On her way out the door, he'd barely glanced her cheek with a kiss, not wanting the cabbie to think they'd spent a passionate night together. He wondered why he cared what the cabbie thought, then realized it was because the cabbie would blab the news all over town and Clay did care about Rebecca's reputation. Oh well, people could do no more than talk.

Now he felt refreshed and ready for a full day. He drained his coffee mug, then dropped a good-bye pat on Gypsy's golden brown head. She looked up from her food bowl with gentle eyes. "Don't get in any trouble while I'm gone today. Just watch your soap operas and take it easy." She licked his hand, then turned back to the more important task of finishing her breakfast.

He was walking out the door when the phone rang. The answering machine picked up and he heard his mother's voice. He went back.

"Hi, Mom. I was on my way to the hospital."

"We're having your dad's birthday next Sunday," she'd said without a hello. "You going to be able to make it?"

"Of course I'll be there."

"I never know." Her voice took on a plaintive note. "You hardly ever come around."

"I drop by every two or three weeks."

"More like once a month. It hurts your dad."

Clay gritted his teeth, guilt battling with anger, resent-ment sizzling through resolve. "Dad hardly talks to me when I do come by."

"That's not true."

"It is. He talks to Ben, not to me."

"Shame on you! You sound like a little boy." Her rebuke made him angrier than ever because it was true. "Now Clay, be fair. You know you hurt your dad by becoming a doctor instead of a farmer. He doesn't have any particular liking for doctors and he's put his life into this farm."

The last was an understatement. Hoyt Bellamy had inherited the lucrative 300-acre dairy farm from his father and devoted himself to caring for it above all other things. He'd worked his sons Ben and Clayton hard, teaching them all he knew, trying to instill in them his love of farming. With his older son Ben, he'd succeeded. Clay had been another matter. He'd always been more interested in diagnosing the cows than milking them. When he was eight, one of the cows got sick with an ailment Hoyt had never seen before. Clay had hung around the vet who treated the valuable Holstein, absorbing all he could of medical terminology. He'd sat up at night with the cow and cried when she died. His father had grown furious, called him a sentimental sissy, and told him he'd better start acting like a Bellamy man if he expected any respect in this family. He didn't understand Clay and he didn't care to. He just wanted Clay to be like Ben and himself and if he wouldn't conform, he could damn well suffer his father's rejection.

"Mom, I don't have time to get into this now," Clay said, struggling to sound calm although his heart rate had increased. "Even if I had time, it's a pointless argument. I'll be there Sunday. Two o'clock lunch as usual?"

"Yes. I'll put the roast in the oven before we go to church. We still attend the Baptist, but apparently you've forgotten your way there." Clay rolled his eyes. "Ben and Elaine and the kids will be here for dinner." Another of the unnecessary details his mother always added. Ben and Elaine had a house on the farm. They never missed a family function. "You don't need to get a gift."

"Okay, Mom."

"If you were to get a gift, though, it would mean a lot to your dad."

No, it wouldn't, Clay thought. But certainly he would buy something as a gesture. "Have to go, Mom. See you Sunday."

Clay felt bad about rushing his mother off the phone even though he knew she had not minded. Just as his father's and brother's minds revolved around the farm, hers revolved around them. Clay had always been the outsider, certain he'd been switched at birth with some strapping, uncomplicated clone of his brother. The other boy probably lived with a family who wanted him to be a doctor when what he wanted to think about were cows and how to increase milk production. He would be as frustrated as Clay, always trying to win approval and always feeling guilty when he failed.

As he drove to the hospital, Clay semi-successfully pushed the whole family matter from his mind to concentrate again on Rebecca. Rather, on the questions Rebecca had raised about the kidnapping, he reminded himself sternly.

Clay pulled into the hospital parking lot still turning it all over in his mind. But as soon as he walked in and saw the Emergency waiting room full, he focused on work. He did not allow his thoughts to drift until he took a break for a quick lunch at one o'clock.

The hospital dining room was still pretty full. In spite of the running jokes about hospital food, Clay thought this particular cafeteria served an above-average menu. He rarely sent out for food from Village Pizza Inn like most people. At least not for lunch. He thought he was probably their most frequent dinner patron. He ran his tray down the metal rails, picking up coffee, tossed salad, chicken and noodles, and the biggest piece of coconut cream pie he saw. "You'll get fat, Doctor," the girl at the register teased, tossing her hair and flashing her teeth.

"Never. They work me too hard. Charge it to my bill."

"As if you have to tell me!"

She laughed loudly as if they'd had a hilarious exchange. A few people in the dining room turned to look. Her raucous flirtation with Dr. Bellamy had become a matter of minor interest.

Clay, trying to look nonchalant amid the stares, was

headed for an empty table when he spotted Myra Kessle, a middle-aged nurse who worked in the pediatric unit and whom he'd gotten to know when his nephew was in for an appendectomy. "Mind if I sit with you, Myra?"

"I'd be honored, but what will your girlfriend at the register say?"

He shook his head and smiled. "*Girl* is right. She must be all of nineteen."

"She's twenty-one and available."

"Are you matchmaking?" Clay sat down and withdrew his flatware from his napkin. "You seem too sensible for that kind of nonsense."

Myra's brown eyes twinkled from a web of crow's-feet she'd had since her thirties. "I wouldn't presume to know your taste in women, but I'd guess it wouldn't be a young lady with a voice like a bullhorn."

Clay nearly burst out laughing. "I thought you nurses were supposed to be warm and compassionate."

"This one is brutally honest." Myra took a sip of her coffee. "So what's new with you?"

"Not much." Clay dug into his salad. "Except that I've seen Molly Ryan."

Myra's smile immediately vanished. "The mother of the kidnapped boy?" He nodded, mouth full. "Oh, that poor thing. I have felt terrible ever since I heard about the child. They haven't found him, have they?"

"Not as of last night."

"I read about their finding Todd's stuffed animal in the attic of Klein Furniture. I thought the police tried to keep information like that a secret."

"They do. Bill thinks there's a leak in the department."

Myra raised an eyebrow. " 'Bill'? The chief of police? You two close?"

"His sister is Suzanne Ryan. She married Frank Hardison after her first husband Patrick's death and I was a friend of Frank's son Doug. I got to know the family years ago."

"And Molly is Patrick Ryan's niece. How is she holding up?"

"Not too well. I had to sedate her after Bill gave her the news about the stuffed toy."

"What horrible news to bring."

"It could have been worse."

"Yes, but with the blood and all—" Myra broke off. "Someday you'll have children and you'll know how something like this is a parent's worst fear. I worried constantly about my two girls. I thought when they grew up I could relax, but you never really do. But when I think of what this poor woman is going through, I realize how good I had it. Nothing bad ever happened to my kids." A crease formed between Myra's eyebrows. "And this has happened twice in the same family. Of course they have money."

"Molly doesn't."

"She has access to it. Her parents."

"Bill says they're trekking merrily around the wilds of Africa taking photographs. They don't even know. They're not close to her anyway."

"Her own parents? Is it because she's never married?"

"Yes and no. When she got pregnant, they weren't morally outraged—they just didn't want to be bothered. Suzanne stepped in to help Molly and they gladly let her."

"Certainly she'd help Molly with ransom money."

"I'm sure she would, but money didn't save Jonnie Ryan."

"No, it didn't." She shook her head. "What a world. I hope Molly isn't alone."

"She isn't. Doug and his father see her all the time. And Bill Garrett." He finally broached the subject that had made him impulsively sit down with Myra. "Her next-door neighbor is Jean Wright. I think she's on vacation. She's been spending nearly all her time with Molly."

"Really? Hmmm. Well, I guess it's good Molly has a full-time medical professional to watch over her."

"You sound a little uncertain."

"I do?"

"Come on, Myra. What bothers you about Jean Wright?"

Myra hesitated, apparently deciding whether or not to

commit herself. "All right. I don't know the woman very well. I've worked with her and she's extremely competent. And caring. Her parents died when she was about nineteen and she suddenly had a much younger brother and sister to look after. They were twins—"

"And they died?" Clay asked anxiously.

Myra grinned. "My, aren't you melodramatic today? No, they didn't die. They left for college last year. They're both spoiled rotten. The boy insisted on going to Princeton even though he could get only a *partial* scholarship there but a full one to West Virginia University. Wendy isn't the studious type and her grades didn't qualify her for a scholarship anywhere. She's going to WVU and spending at least twice what she gets in financial aid. Money was so tight Jean was working overtime here and freelancing night-sitting with elderly homebound patients. She nearly collapsed from exhaustion. She's not on vacation—she's on leave."

"Oh."

"Now you sound disappointed. What's the matter?"

"I just thought there would be more than that to her. Something about her seems a little off. She doesn't like me at all—"

"Then clearly she's unbalanced."

"My feeling exactly," Clay returned with a straight face. "But it's not her appalling lack of taste in men that disturbs me. She's odd. Are you sure she didn't have a breakdown?"

"Well, I wasn't going to say it, but she was a little rocky emotionally before she left. She made some mistakes—nothing serious—and she cried a lot. Maybe she's pulled herself together but it was such a short time ago . . ."

"You don't think she's in any condition to be looking after Molly."

"Honestly, no, especially in such an emotional situation. And I'm surprised she'd try. She knew how important it was for her to rest. At least if she wants her job, which she needs desperately. Oh well." Myra looked troubled, glanced at her watch, then stood up. "This has been nice, but I've spent too long gabbing. Good to see you and . . . well, just forget what I said about Jean."

But of course he wouldn't.

2

"You pull this again and you're out of here, Cochran," old man Maloney growled. He'd always reminded Larry of a bloodhound, and now with his jowls flapping and his voice lowered in menace, the resemblance was even stronger. "Did you hear me?"

"How could I help it?" Larry muttered.

"You are a smart-ass. I should never have let Frank Hardison talk me into hiring you. Get on out in the garage and get to work."

Larry limped out. On good days his limp was barely noticeable. Today was not a good day. The leg ached badly although the orthopedic surgeon who'd operated on it said when he healed, he would have no pain. At the time Larry had been too hopeless to care. After all these years, though, the constant pain often had him on the edge of control.

"Take the Buick Regal next," one of the guys yelled to him. "Needs a front brake job."

Larry went out and turned on the car. Country music blasted in his ears. He savagely flipped off the radio. He hated country music almost as much as he hated gospel. He pulled the car carefully onto the lift, emerged trying to hide his limp, and raised the lift to head level.

The other guys were openly snickering at him. When he got the job, Doug had told him to "be cool," to "roll with the punches." Well, that had never been his and Lynn's way and he was proud of it. He didn't intend to sell out like Doug, whom he'd come to hate with all his clean living and good advice. The jolly little ball of dough, that's how Larry thought of him. Also, Larry had made no effort to befriend anyone at the garage. He'd actually gone out of his way to be aloof and superior, letting them know he neither needed nor cared for their friendship. The result was that no one liked him. Old man Maloney couldn't stand him.

Larry reached for the impact wrench and went to work on the lug nuts, reveling in the wrench's loud hammering noise as it twisted the nut, the high-pitched whine as the nut loosened.

So he'd missed a day of work, Larry seethed inwardly as he pulled off the tires and inspected the brake rotors, seeing the grooves that meant the car needed new brake pads. One lousy day in six months. Maloney said he was pissed off because he hadn't called in. Larry had claimed illness. "I don't believe it," Maloney had thundered. "Even your sister came here looking for you."

"We don't live together. She didn't know I was sick."

Maloney hadn't bought it. Rightly. Larry had not been sick—as Lynn had seen when around noon he'd walked up to his tiny apartment to find her planted outside the door.

"Where have you been?" she'd demanded.

A wave of white-hot anger had flowed over Larry. "What business is it of yours?"

"You didn't show up for work. You weren't home when I called last night." She'd looked like she was going to cry and nearly shouted, "What about Skeeter Dobbs?"

The harridan in the apartment next to his had swung open her door and stuck out her head, glaring. He'd glared back, then hustled Lynn inside. Lynn kept going on and on, loudly, and he'd turned on the television to cover her voice. On the noon news Kelly Keene had rattled on about murder victim Carson "Skeeter" Dobbs while Larry coldly denied having even seen the old creep for weeks.

"Then where *were* you?" Lynn had persisted.

"You mean if I wasn't murdering Skeeter, which is the most likely answer? Not everyone in this town hates me. I have a girlfriend, Lynn. I stayed with her."

"All *night*? Till *noon*? Have you forgotten that you're on *parole* and you have *curfew*?"

Her platinum hair and light eyes seemed to vanish in the

glare of the sun coming through the front window. She was only a pair of cruel crimson lips. "Will you stop screeching?" Larry snarled. "God, you sound like Mom. Always shouting, demanding, accusing, always afraid we'd embarrass her."

"Gee, I wonder why she worried about that?" Lynn said sarcastically.

Larry shot her a murderous look. "Maybe if she hadn't always expected the worst of us, punished us for stuff we hadn't done, we would have turned out different."

"And maybe she just saw us for what we were: a couple of self-centered, lazy snots who only cared about getting high!"

"What this? Another chapter from the Douglas Hardison Clean Living Manual? 'Lesson One—Take Responsibility for Your Own Mistakes'?"

"What's wrong with taking responsibility? It's not Mom's fault we messed up. At least I had the sense to turn myself around. I thought you had, too, but look at you! Bloodshot eyes! Two days' growth of beard! I guess this girl doesn't like you for your looks. Who is she?"

"That doesn't concern you."

"Everything about you concerns me."

He'd looked at her levelly. "I'm over twenty-one, little sister. Way over."

"You also have a job. Frank worked hard to get you that job!"

"He did not. Most people in this town owe him a favor. He just called one in."

"That is beside the point."

Larry had felt as if his head might split. He told her to sit down and be quiet while he took a couple of aspirins. Then he said as calmly as possible, "Look, I drank too much. And her alarm didn't go off. I screwed up. It's not her fault so you don't need to go nosing around trying to find out who she is. And I won't let this happen again."

Finally he'd gotten rid of Lynn and put his pounding head in his hands. He might as well be back in prison for all the freedom he had. With Lynn, Doug, his parole officer, and old man Maloney breathing down his neck, he had about as much freedom as he'd had a year ago in the penitentiary. For the first time in his life he hated his sister almost as much as he did Doug. Her love and concern had become just as imprisoning as bars.

Larry had gotten through the rest of the day, then braced himself for a return to the garage. Now he'd gotten the expected verbal assault from Maloney, much to the delight of his co-workers, and he had another whole day in this place ahead of him. But he could get through it. He had to get through it.

Because better days were ahead.

3

Deputy G. C. Curry stepped into Bill's office. Bill noted how haggard the man looked. He clearly hadn't been getting much sleep. "What's up, Chief?" he asked.

"Got the ME's report on Skeeter. Come on in and get a cup of coffee. You look like you could use it."

Curry poured coffee and picked up a Danish. Bill couldn't help thinking of Skeeter Dobbs and his ecstasy over the "foreign food" offered to him on the last night of his life. Curry sat down with the groan of an old man even though he was only thirty-four. "So what does the ME have to say about Skeeter?"

"Want me to wait until you've finished eating?"

"I don't have a weak stomach. But you can skip all the mumbo-jumbo and just give me the basics."

"Okay, basically Skeeter died of a puncture wound to the brain, causing severe hemorrhage."

"We needed an autopsy to know that?"

"Lungs were pale and light. Petechial hemorrhaging poorly limited in right eye."

"So we know Skeeter died almost instantly and we assume the killer was facing him to jab him in the left eye, so he or she must be right-handed," Curry said. "That's helpful."

"We also know the incised wound must have been swift and unexpected because there are no defensive wounds on Skeeter's hands and arms. He'd probably been dead less than twelve hours because there was only redness and swelling around the wound. Scabbing starts after about twenty-four hours. Pus after thirty-six."

"You could have left out the part about pus," Curry said, laying down his last bit of cream-filled Danish.

"I thought you didn't have a weak stomach."

"Even I have limits. Murder weapon?"

"Common ice pick. Metal handle so no convenient traces of skin left in wood. Also no fingerprints. A couple of traces of latex where the handle joins the spike. Killer must have worn latex gloves."

"So how easy is it to get latex gloves?"

"They're everywhere: around a hospital. Dentist's office. Vet's office. Of course you don't have to work in one of those places to get them. Just *be* in one. And there are medical supply stores everywhere."

"This gets easier and easier. Killer might as well have signed his name at the scene for all the trouble we'll have finding him," Curry said dryly. He sipped his coffee. "Is that all the ME came up with?"

"No. There's one bit of information I found fairly interesting. It seems our Skeeter was loaded with Valium."

"The tranquilizer? I didn't know he was a user."

"He wasn't. No track marks, no presence of any other drugs in the body. Just a bloodstream full of Valium. There were also tiny bits of undissolved Valium in his wine bottle. That must be how it was administered. He didn't even know he was getting it."

At last Curry looked interested. "I know in mystery novels they're always slipping undetected drugs in people's drinks, which is such crap. People *do* have taste buds. Okay, we know that if the Valium was in Skeeter's wine, then someone gave it to him without his knowledge. But why didn't he taste it?"

"Would you taste a little medicine dissolved in something like lighter fluid? Skeeter couldn't afford the finest spirits and he didn't have a refined palate like the characters in mystery novels."

"But when would someone have had a chance to drug his wine?"

"Skeeter kept a couple of bottles hidden behind Klein Furniture. Bought them on Saturday to see him through Sunday, when the liquor store's closed. Thought he was being real sneaky about it, but a lot of people knew. Skeeter didn't know how to be sneaky."

Curry leaned forward. "I assume Skeeter didn't drink wine with corks. So someone just unscrewed a lid and put in the Valium when he wasn't around." Bill nodded. "Well, why the hell would someone want to drug his wine? If they didn't want him to put up a fight, why didn't they just wait until he got drunk?"

"You've forgotten about the tolerance to alcohol he'd built up over the years. It would take a lot more than one bottle of wine to get Skeeter drunk—and someone wanted him relaxed and even more fuzzy-headed than usual." Bill looked at Curry and smiled bitterly. "That would have made the murder even easier, maybe even a laid-back kind of sport."

CHAPTER NINE

1

When Rebecca entered the Ryan house at eight in the morning wearing the clothes she'd had on the night before, Betty looked at her disapprovingly. "I suppose you're too old for a lecture—"

"Yes, I am."

"And it's not my place—"

"No, it isn't."

"It's just that I love you like a daughter."

Rebecca had kissed Betty's cheek. "And I love you. And don't worry—my virtue wasn't compromised last night. I had a rough evening. Clay was just looking after me."

"In my day a doctor made a house call and gave you a bill. He didn't take you to dinner and then spend the night with you." Betty grinned. "But if someone's goin' to take such a personal interest in you, I'm glad it's Clay. I was always especially fond of that boy. And so were you, if I remember right."

"No comment." Rebecca laughed and went upstairs to greet an ecstatic Sean, who'd obviously missed her.

Afterward she took a shower and went to see Molly. Bill had told her about Rebecca's vision at the restaurant and Molly asked for a report. Rebecca obliged, going lightly on the physical and mental pain Todd was experiencing. Throughout the recap, Jean had stared at Rebecca with both dislike and disbelief. Rebecca had tried to make conversation with her but received monosyllabic answers. "I guess you're no longer looking after your elderly patient in the evenings," she finally commented just for something to say.

Jean had flushed and said firmly, "No. Friday was my last night. I arrived there at seven P.M. and didn't return until morning. It was an exhausting night. The woman needs to be in a convalescent home. I simply couldn't handle her alone anymore."

Rebecca had tried to look casual, but she couldn't help noting how precise Jean had been about leaving her home at seven P.M. and not returning until morning. She was emphasizing that she hadn't been home when Todd was abducted. Why?

After a couple of hours Molly had looked tired and Rebecca couldn't take much more of Jean's hostility. With promises to return soon, she went home, more puzzled about Jean than ever. She hoped Clay wouldn't forget his promise to ask around the hospital about her.

Back home, Rebecca had poured a cup of fresh vanilla-flavored coffee and wandered through the house looking for her mother. When she neared the open patio doors, she heard Suzanne talking. "Do you like it here? Are you having a good time? Becky says you're temperamental, but you seem like a pretty good guy to me."

She peeked out on the patio to see her mother lying on a chaise longue holding a cigarette in one hand and stroking Sean's head with the other. This is the mother I remember, Rebecca thought with a pang. She used to love talking to and petting their Irish setter, Rusty. Sean had been rather cool this morning, his feelings clearly injured by her absence last night; but as soon as he saw her, he rushed forward, jumping up to put his legs around her waist. Obviously, he'd forgiven her. "Hi, Sean. Hello, Mother."

"Hello. Sean and I are getting to know each other."

"So I see."

"I think he's very bright."

"You can tell that by petting him?"

"I can tell by the alert look in his eyes. He also shakes hands like a gentleman. Besides, I did a bit of reading about his breed. I believe he ranks number two or three on the canine intelligence scale."

"That's just your usual Australian. Sean is number one."

Suzanne half rose from the chaise and looked at Rebecca, smiling. "Why don't you join us, proud mother?"

Rebecca sat down on a lawn chair with thick cushions in a bright floral pattern that matched the chaise. Between them was a round table bearing an ashtray, a glass of iced tea with mint, and a Harlequin romance. Two improbably gorgeous people gazed into each other's eyes on the cover. "Good book?"

Suzanne eased back on the chaise. She wore tan slacks and a loose top. She looked frail and exhausted.

"Yes, it is a good book. It's bright and happy." A hint of amusement appeared in her blue eyes. "I'm not sure whether or not the heroine will get her guy. Things aren't looking good right now."

"Would you like to place a wager?" Rebecca returned lightly. "I bet fifty cents that she does."

"You've read one of these before!"

"Try a hundred."

"I know they're predictable, but I like that. Real life is so uncertain." Suzanne tapped her cigarette against the edge of her ashtray. Her slender hands trembled and Rebecca knew there was no alcohol in the tea. "Have you heard anything about Todd?"

Rebecca had decided not to tell Suzanne about her vision. She wouldn't want to hear about it anyway. "If I'd heard anything about Todd I would have told you."

"Would you?"

"Yes, Mother. You've imagined this conspiracy of silence."

"I haven't imagined it," Suzanne said easily, "but I guess I deserve it. I've never been a tower of strength but I've been particularly useless the last few years. I'm tired of being that way."

Rebecca was surprised. Suzanne had never been quick to admit faults. She'd always preferred playing the injured party. "If you want to be of use, you could give me some information."

Suzanne looked at her sharply. "I don't know what information you think I might have that could possibly help."

"Who is Todd's father?"

"Oh, not this again," Suzanne said tiredly. She closed her eyes. Sean walked over and put his paw on her arm. She smiled and began stroking him again. "I can't tell you how many times I've been asked that question since Todd's birth."

"I'm not asking out of curiosity," Rebecca said. "It might bear on his abduction."

"You think the father might have taken him?"

"Most child abductions are committed by people who aren't strangers."

She'd remembered this from when Jonnie was taken. The police had told them over and over as they grilled everyone in the family. Frank had finally exploded with a wrath she still found hard to believe. "His father is dead," Suzanne said. "Besides, he didn't even know Molly was pregnant."

"But who was he?"

"You and Molly are like sisters. She'd be much more likely to tell you than me."

"She has never even hinted to me; besides, she warned me not to ask. And you've seen more of her the last few years than I have. You've been like her mother. She adores you."

"I adore her, too."

Rebecca was ashamed of the jealousy she felt. She loved Molly. She knew how much Molly needed Suzanne and she was glad Suzanne had always been there for her. But Rebecca had needed her, too. She'd longed for Suzanne's love.

She forced the thoughts from her mind and returned to the subject. "You have *no* idea who Todd's father is?"

"I just said I didn't."

"I have a feeling you're not saying all you know." Suzanne stared out over the lawn to the gazebo, white and elegant in the bright sun. Her face had taken on a closed, stubborn look. "Mother, this is so important."

"Don't you think I know that?" Suzanne snapped.

"Molly told me Todd's father is dead. I can only rely on what people tell me. I'm not psychic like you!"

The words vibrated in the hot summer air. Rebecca felt detached, as if she were watching two other women squabble on a lovely patio. She was embarrassed for both of them.

"Frank would tell me that remark was inexcusable," Suzanne said meekly.

"It was."

"I'm sorry. I promised myself . . . oh hell."

"Forget it. We're all tense."

Sean flopped over, offering his belly to Suzanne for a rub. She lowered a hand and obliged. "I really *don't* know who Todd's father is," she said after a full minute, "but I've picked up a clue here and there. One time Molly said something about the 'fling.' So I assume the affair was brief. She also said, 'I guess I got what I deserved. He belonged to someone else.' She was in labor. You remember that she had to have a cesarean and she'd already been sedated. I don't think she remembers saying it and I've never reminded her."

"Do you think he was married?"

"Probably. And I believe he was at West Virginia University with her. She couldn't get away from there fast enough, as if she didn't want him to see her pregnancy. That's why we sent her to New Orleans to be with you. You'd always been so close no one thought it was odd that she'd changed her mind and wanted to transfer to Tulane. And we thought she'd give up the baby. No one was more shocked than I when she not only decided to keep him, but to return to Sinclair."

"I've wondered if he was a married professor and she refuses to give out his name because she's afraid the police will question his family and then the secret would be out. She could be impulsive enough to have a 'fling,' as she called it, but she'd never want to cause pain."

"That makes sense. She was impulsive. And she was romantic. You both were."

"So are most teenage girls." Rebecca smiled. "But Molly did give me my first Harlequin to read."

"That doesn't surprise me. I pass all of mine on to her." Suzanne stopped rubbing Sean's belly. By now he was asleep with his mouth open. "Once she said Todd didn't look like his father."

"No, he looks like Molly only with blond hair. A lot of kids have blond hair when they're young, then it darkens."

"Jonnie's didn't."

"It was the color of yours." Rebecca touched the heart-shaped locket she always wore, where Jonnie's picture nestled. She almost handed it to her mother, then stopped. Suzanne's lower lip twitched. Her throat muscles worked.

"Can you remember anything else Molly said about Todd's father?" Rebecca asked awkwardly, trying to recapture her mother's attention. But she knew that faraway look in Suzanne's eyes too well. She was seeing her beautiful, laughing boy again. He filled her mind and her heart, leaving no room for anyone else.

"I can't think now," Suzanne finally managed. "I'm tired. I'm just going to close my eyes before lunch."

She never ate lunch. Suzanne simply didn't want to talk to her anymore. She wanted to be alone to dream.

Rebecca stood up and turned abruptly, just in time to see Walt Sykes backing away from the patio doors. Their eyes met and Walt flushed. "Just wanted to ask Mrs. Hardison about putting more mulch on them flower beds out front."

If he hadn't looked so guilty, Rebecca would have thought nothing of his presence. But the deep red of his cheeks and the shifting of his gaze let her know that he'd been eavesdropping.

2

TUESDAY, 11:15 A.M.
Molly sat rocking, staring at Todd's photo. He'd been concerned about his school picture, telling her he wasn't going

to smile because one front tooth was out and the other space was occupied by a permanent tooth halfway in. "I look weird," he'd explained earnestly. "So no smiling." But the photographer had made him laugh and there he was, a boy with blond hair, cinnamon colored eyes, and a strong little chin beneath the temporarily unfortunate teeth. Molly could feel the joy radiating from him.

And now he was out there somewhere. With someone. Someone kind? No. No kind person would take her child. It was either someone unbalanced or someone who'd taken him for money and didn't give a damn about him. Just like someone had not given a damn about Jonnie.

Molly's stomach muscles clutched at the thought of Jonnie's lifeless body being thrown on the vacant lot a block away from Klein Furniture. It had been the only vacant lot downtown, the building destroyed by fire the year before. Since then a video store had been built there. But was it only coincidence that Tramp had been found so close? Rebecca claimed to think so, but Molly wasn't fooled. Becky thought there was a connection between the kidnappings. But what could it be?

Molly rose abruptly, too nervous to sit still. Jean had gone home for a couple of hours. She'd fretted about leaving, saying Molly shouldn't be alone. She'd nearly insisted on asking one of Molly's friends to stay with her. Molly had said, "They're all working. Maybe Rebecca could come." That had stopped Jean. She disliked Rebecca although she denied it.

She'd wanted Jean to leave because she hadn't been alone since Todd's abduction. How long ago that night seemed. She'd returned home tired but happy and relieved to have her work finished. And then she'd found Sonia, unconscious, bleeding. She'd rushed to Todd's room to find it empty. And the world spun out of control when she knew her worst terror had at last come true.

The next few hours had been a haze of questions and activity. Molly only remembered feeling a savage panic and an overwhelming need to see Rebecca. Rebecca had ESP, she'd thought with the simplicity of a child. Rebecca had "seen" all those things years ago and found Molly's lost cat Taffy and saved the man wrongly accused of killing Earl Tanner. She'd even found a couple of children who'd tumbled into an old well at a deserted house. Rebecca could find Todd.

But it was Tuesday now and Todd had been gone since Friday night. Rebecca had *not* found him. The only real lead had come from Skeeter Dobbs, miserable old wretch. Bill had reminded her they would have paid no attention to Skeeter if Rebecca hadn't said Todd was in a hot, deserted place. She was having visions, but they weren't good enough because Rebecca couldn't tell them *where* Todd was.

Molly's arms started to itch and burn from nerves. She ran her hands up and down them as she paced, going first to the refrigerator, then Todd's room, then to the living room to peer around the closed draperies at the five people trying to look casual as they watched the house, and back to Todd's room. She watched the fish swimming calmly. Todd had named them Rocky and Bullwinkle. She sprinkled fish food in the bowl.

"You guys need to stay healthy because Todd will want to see you as soon as he gets home." The fish nibbled their food, smooth, golden, oblivious.

Todd had been conceived in an ill-advised moment of passion. When Molly found out she was pregnant, though, she hadn't been entirely sorry. She'd loved Todd's father. He didn't love her—there was someone else and she would never force herself on him or make claims—but she would have part of him now. Someone to love, someone who wouldn't abandon her like her parents, and Uncle Patrick, and Rebecca who'd run away to New Orleans. At ten she'd understood that Patrick hadn't deliberately left her. And at nineteen she'd understood Rebecca's reasons for permanently leaving Sinclair, but she'd never let Rebecca know she'd been deeply hurt. Throughout the years Rebecca had thought Molly was strong because that was what Molly wanted her to think. No one liked a weakling and Molly was desperate to be liked, to be accepted. But inside she had always felt like a small, deserted child left to cry in the darkness.

And then there had been Todd. In some places no one would bat an eye at an unwed mother. Sinclair wasn't one of those places. A lot of people in the area thought of her as "disgraced." She hadn't cared, but she didn't think she could have managed without Suzanne. She'd been frightened, not because she'd been penniless as everyone thought—her parents weren't that unfeeling. But they hadn't gone out of their way to help in any way except monetarily. They'd been annoyed, not morally outraged, and they did not like to be annoyed. They saw their grandson a couple of times each year, but that was enough. They didn't care to be reminded they were old enough to be grandparents.

Molly had doted on her child, happily finished college, and then taken a good job at Grace Healthcare provided by Frank. Her life had been work and Todd. He'd brought her love, peace, joy, and fulfillment.

And now he was gone.

"Damn it, Becky, *do* something!" Molly burst out. She knew she wasn't being fair. She knew Rebecca was trying. But she also knew that if Todd did not return to her, she would never be able to look at her cousin the same way. For years she'd thought Suzanne completely unreasonable, even cruel, for holding Rebecca partly responsible for Jonnie's death. Now she was holding Rebecca responsible for Todd's life. She hated herself but she couldn't change her feelings.

3

Rebecca continued to wander the grounds of the house restlessly, even taking Sean out to see the beautiful gazebo. She didn't want to admit it, but she was waiting for another vision to strike, which was useless. In the meantime she searched her mind for something constructive to do. Only one thing presented itself: a few hours at the volunteer center.

She arrived around one, parking her mother's Thunderbird down the street and walking back to the building that had once housed Fanny's Fine Fabrics. There was no Fanny. There had been a Stanford from Baltimore who'd bought the little store on impulse when he'd spent a week in Sinclair, then mistakenly decided that all women in West Virginia liked only gingham, calico, denim, and other inelegant but serviceable materials. He'd also been huge on country prints. The store had staggered along for two years, a succession of three managers arguing futilely with the less-than-savvy Stanford, until he'd finally tired of the whole thing and sold the building to Frank Hardison at a rock-bottom price.

Rebecca knew that when Frank bought the place, he'd never dreamed what dreadful use he would find for it. Nevertheless, he'd acted quickly and efficiently, having the volunteer center up and running less than twelve hours after Todd's disappearance. It would have been a good place for the city and county police to coordinate their efforts also, but their tartar of a county sheriff had decided to make things difficult. Rebecca had never liked Sheriff Martin Lutz, and the feeling was mutual.

Now she walked into the volunteer center and gazed around at the five women and two men who were copying, faxing, answering phones, and chatting. A young woman with a child's face and a body heavy with pregnancy walked toward her, smiling. "You look like you haven't been here before!"

"I haven't. I want to help, though. Will you show me what I can do?"

"Oh, I sure will! We appreciate this so much, and I'm sure Molly Ryan does, too. Isn't this just the most awful thing?"

"It certainly is."

"Do you have kids?"

"Not yet."

"Me either." She giggled. "But soon. Just three months! I can't wait." She held out a small hand. "I'm Amy Tanner."

"Hello. Rebecca Ryan."

Amy shook hands, then frowned. "Ryan? Are you related?"

"I'm Molly's cousin."

"Oh! Rebecca Ryan. Goodness gracious!" Rebecca could see awareness flickering in Amy's great blue eyes. She'd heard of Rebecca Ryan and all the stories of ESP. Rebecca would have liked to have presented a blank slate to this sweet-faced girl. "Well, how nice of you to come down! We'll just start you off answering the phones. Now Chief Garrett wants us to take the caller's name . . ."

Amy had rattled on, repeating the instructions as if Rebecca were slightly slow or her head too full of visions from the netherworld to concentrate on the present. After Rebecca took her first call, she looked up to see Amy watching her with a mixture of curiosity, trepidation, awe, and suspicion. She smiled quickly, though, hurried over to make sure Rebecca had taken the message properly, then scurried back to her own post. Rebecca knew she should probably be offended by the girl's hovering, but she could tell Amy only meant to be helpful. She was terribly earnest about her duties and about the search for Todd.

One woman brought her a cup of coffee and pointed out the refreshment table. A man instructed her on how to load copier paper. She thanked him, although she'd been loading copiers for 15 years. On the whole, though, the other volunteers tended to steer clear of her. During her years in New Orleans she'd almost forgotten what it felt like to be an oddity—a source of wonder for some, a source of fear for others. No wonder she'd been so miserable during her teenage years, she thought. No wonder she'd never considered returning to Sinclair to live.

Fifteen minutes later her phone rang again. An elderly

man reported the presence of a new child next door. "It's a boy, about the age of that Todd kid," he said. "The guy next door, I think he's one of *those*, if you know what I mean."

"I'm sorry, sir, but I don't. One of what?"

"You know, homeosexuals. He's good looking in a girly kind of way, dresses to beat the band, and never has a girl in that I've noticed. Then out of the blue comes this kid. He told me it's his nephew."

"But you don't believe him?"

"I never heard about no nephew before."

"And you talk to this man often?"

"No oftener than I have to. Say, what're you givin' me the third degree for? I'm tryin' to help you."

Rebecca reminded herself that she wasn't a cop and her job wasn't to weed out cranks from sources of solid information. Amy had told her this three times. And just because she had a feeling this man simply disliked his neighbor due to real or imagined sexual orientation, she couldn't dismiss his information. He might be absolutely correct. This new nephew might be Todd.

But her hope faded as the boy was described as blue-eyed and unable to speak plainly. Still, he might be someone else's lost child. Rebecca dutifully wrote down the man's name, address, and telephone number and twice promised to pass on the information to the police.

Amy had stopped by again to see how things were going. Then she looked at the door and her big blue eyes grew even bigger. "Alvin!" she exclaimed.

Amy Tanner. Alvin *Tanner*. The name hadn't registered with Rebecca when Amy had introduced herself. Now she felt herself freeze. She'd been responsible for sending Alvin's mother away for life. Slim Tanner had claimed to be protecting herself and her child when she killed Earl Tanner. After she went to prison, a ten-year-old Alvin had been sent to live with an aged grandmother who'd raised him in poverty. Because of Rebecca, Alvin had lost a mother and a comfortable home.

Rebecca looked down at her notepad and began writing additions to the account she'd just taken from the elderly man. Anything to keep from facing Alvin, who was saying, "Amy, you told me you'd only stay a couple of hours. It's been four."

"Oh, has it?" Amy exclaimed almost convincingly. "Gosh, the time just slipped away, honey. We've been really busy."

"And you need to rest."

"Yes, well . . ."

"Well . . . I want you to come home."

"Oh!" Amy sounded startled and Rebecca had the feeling Alvin Tanner did not often issue orders, even if they were mild. "Okay, honey. If you'll just wait another few minutes."

"No. I think . . . no, I want you to come *now*."

"Miss Ryan, could you help me here with these copies?" a woman asked in a louder-than-necessary voice. Rebecca rose, furiously aware that the woman had wanted to announce her presence to Alvin. She had to walk past him to reach the copier and she tossed a casual smile, trying to act as if nothing was wrong. Alvin did not look surprised to see her. He just stared at her, his dark eyes enlarged slightly by his glasses.

"I'll get my purse, honey, and we'll go right home. You don't look like you slept one wink," Amy chattered, scampering around the room in search of her handbag. "I'll make you some hot cocoa—it's nice even if it is summer—and we'll watch a TV show and then we'll both take a good, long nap. Won't that be fun? Okay, I'm ready. 'Bye, everybody. See you tomorrow."

Overly cheerful good-byes chased Amy and Alvin out the door. Rebecca gave the woman at the copier a long, level look. "Now what was it you wanted me to do? Shut the lid for you? Or push the Start button?"

"I guess I can manage," the woman murmured, her face turning red.

Rebecca forced herself to stay another hour. She would

not give anyone the pleasure of seeing her flee. She took five more calls, none of which seemed too important, grabbed up a handful of flyers, and at two-thirty left the volunteer center, imagining the flurry of gossip she left in her wake.

She sauntered down the street looking in store windows, then headed for the car. She'd locked the doors but left the windows down a couple of inches on both sides so the leather seats wouldn't be so hot they'd burn her thighs through the thin material of her slacks. Sun bounced off the windshield as she climbed in and her foot touched something lying on the floor. Leaving the door open, she bent down to see a narrow, braided length of leather. She picked it up, turning it over to inspect it more carefully.

The letters *JPR* had been burned inside. Rebecca felt as if she were falling through space as she recognized the bracelet Jonnie had made in Boy Scouts, a bracelet no one had seen since he disappeared.

Chapter Ten

1

TUESDAY, 2:45 P.M.

Matilda Vinson had been terrified since she found Skeeter. They were exactly the same age. She'd known him since he'd attempted to go to first grade and Mrs. Esther Hardison had been their teacher. Way back then Matilda had been his champion when other kids made fun of him. She'd missed him when he was forced to drop out to attend the special classes from which his father constantly found excuses to withdraw him. Nevertheless, for the rest of his life Skeeter had considered Matilda his best friend and waved to her through the windows of the drugstore, although he rarely came inside unless he had a bit of money to buy some antacids for his ulcers.

Sunday morning Matilda had been in the store. She came every day because the big drugstores at the mall had hurt business and Matilda still answered to her father, who was in his late eighties and in the local Gracehaven Nursing Home. Every month he insisted on looking at the accounting books and if profits were markedly down, he became agitated and sometimes cried. Once he had even run away and tried to climb up to the ramshackle treehouse Matilda had shared with her sister fifty years ago. He'd broken his hip and spent three months recovering. Matilda could never fudge a second set of books for his eyes only to prevent such disasters. Her father was deeply religious and the thought of lying to him filled her with as much fear as lying to her God. Instead she opened on Sunday mornings without telling him. The drugstores in the mall did not open until one o'clock on Sundays, and she caught the extra business.

The last time she'd seen Skeeter before his death, he had

careened into the store at ten. "Tildy!" he'd called. "Tildy, wait till you hear!"

"I have a prescription to fill." She counted pills with the speed of a machine. "Mr. Scarpatti will be here in five minutes to pick this up, so tell me your big news before he arrives."

"It's Grandfather! He's been on top!"

"Oh, for crying out loud, Skeeter. You're taking up my time with this nonsense? Your grandfather is dead."

Skeeter drew himself up and said in a dignified voice, "I know he's dead. He's a ghost."

Matilda had huffed in exasperation, then softened. "I'm sorry, Skeeter. Certainly he's a ghost. You say he's been on top. On top of what?"

"The Presidential Suite."

Matilda's lightning movements had stopped. "You mean he's been in the attic? Of Klein—of the hotel?"

"Sure as can be." And then he'd launched into his tale of the ghost who paced and looked out the windows of the attic, a first for Carson Dobbs. "And I just don't know what to make of it, Tildy."

Matilda had looked at him carefully. He was not drunk. And with the exception of thinking he saw his grandfather jump from the top floor of Klein Furniture each night, she'd never known him to spin tales. He didn't have the right kind of imagination for it. "Skeeter, are you sure you saw someone in the building last night?"

"Grandfather. I told you. And sure I seen him. Gave me a turn. What do *you* make of it, Tildy?"

"I don't know," she'd murmured stiffly, her mind drifting back to Saturday night; she'd stayed late at the store to do paperwork. Even though she'd extended evening hours from nine until ten, profits were still down. She'd thought about raising the prices of medications. Then the faces of so many of the elderly had flashed into her mind, people who had been friends of her father's and who'd remained loyal to Vinson's. Not all of them had good insurance that paid for their drugs. No, she would hold drug prices down as low as possible. Maybe she could charge a bit more for her scanty selection of cosmetics . . .

At 10:45 Matilda had stared at her accounting books and let out a little groan. She had been up since five and in the store since seven. Her eyes burned and her head hurt. She was worried, not because she was having trouble making ends meet, but because she didn't want her father to be upset when he saw this month's figures. She adored him. His approval meant everything to her and the doctor had told her he would not live out the year.

Matilda had walked to the front door and looked out. Skeeter was not at his usual post on her stoop. The storm had let up and he'd gone wandering. The theaters and two bars, the only places where people remained at this time of night, were two blocks away. Across from her sat Klein Furniture. The display windows had been lit, showing a huge cherry sleigh bed with matching dresser, and a living room suite in beautiful shades of cream, blue, and rose. The second and third floors had been dark. Some windows on the fourth and fifth floors had glowed with light from apartments. The sixth floor had remained dark. And above—

Matilda had frowned. Never in all the years she'd worked at the store could she remember seeing lights in the attic of Klein Furniture. But there was a faint one in the south end. She'd had the impression that it was not a light glowing from the ceiling. No, the steady light had seemed to come from something like a strong flashlight left resting on a table.

Matilda had unlocked the front door and stepped out on the sidewalk to get a better look. She couldn't imagine Herbert Klein rummaging around in the attic at this time of night. Still, she would feel silly if she called his home to report an intruder and found out that the building owner was working in his attic and thought she should mind her own business.

And then she'd caught a glimpse of a face. It was so brief, the light so bad, she wasn't sure if it was a man or a woman. But no more than five seconds later the light had gone out. She'd started back inside when she'd felt a gaze traveling from her feet to her head. A penetrating, malevolent gaze.

Matilda had rushed into her store, slammed the door, and locked it. Then she'd fled to the back room and stood shivering for nearly ten minutes, during which time she'd called Herbert Klein to find no one home. So maybe he *was* in the attic, and wouldn't she feel stupid if she called the police?

At last she'd crept out and turned off the store lights. Then she'd waited another five minutes and almost crawled to the front of the store to peer out the front window. The attic was dark. She'd taken a deep breath, telling herself she was ridiculous.

Then someone had pulled gently on the front door, which mercifully she'd locked.

Matilda had collapsed onto the floor, her breath coming fast and loud. The pulling had started again. Slow but firm. Once, twice. Matilda had thanked God the old-fashioned door she'd always hated was not made of glass, like the slick doors on the new drugstores in the mall. It had only a small square of glass at eye level. Even if someone broke it, they could not reach the lock. But she had felt that awful gaze again sweeping through the store, looking for her like a cat looking for a mouse. She'd shrunk against a set of shelves, perspiration running down her neck.

And then she'd gone rigid as she wondered if she'd locked the back door.

Matilda had not been able to make herself move, to traverse the length of the store, race through the back room and check that door. It was too late, anyway, she'd told herself. Whoever had tried the front door had already had ample time to go around back. She would be best off to stay up front. That way if she heard someone coming in the back, she could unlock the front door and run into the street screaming.

She'd mentally rehearsed this plan three times although she was too terrified to move an inch much less take such decisive action. She couldn't even crawl the 30 feet to the counter where the phone and its link to police headquarters awaited. She'd hated herself but that hadn't changed anything. She'd been paralyzed, remaining in a frightened little knot for nearly half an hour until abruptly she'd realized the stalker was gone. That was how she'd thought of him—because she was now almost certain she'd seen a man—as the stalker. She'd unwound her painfully tight body, finally called police headquarters, and fifteen minutes later been escorted to her car by a ludicrously young deputy who'd smirked at her skittishness and told her it was probably just some teenager trying to scare her.

On Sunday morning Matilda had tried to put the whole incident out of her mind. Her father had always said she made too much of things. Someone had been in the attic of Klein's, probably Herbert Klein himself, and someone had tried the door of the drugstore, probably a teenager or even Skeeter, although he'd always respected locked doors. Those were the only concrete things that had happened. Her imagination had invented the malevolent gazes. She spent too much time alone. She was getting strange. She'd probably end up a batty old woman who saw danger around every corner.

Then Skeeter had come in babbling about someone in the attic Saturday night and she knew in her heart it hadn't been Herbert Klein. "You must go to the police," Matilda had told Skeeter, deeply alarmed but trying not to show it. Skeeter was already wound up, his eyes blazing with excitement.

" 'Course I'm goin' to the police," Skeeter had assured her. "I'm gonna talk to Chief Garrett. He'll take care of Grandfather. I'll come back when I'm done, Tildy, and tell you what he's gonna do."

While Skeeter was gone Matilda had told herself again she was being a coward. No one would listen to Skeeter. She should go to the police herself, although she didn't like the idea since the deputy had so easily dismissed her. He'd looked at her as if she were a fool and his smug attitude had stung. Besides, stirring up trouble with the police might get back to her father and he'd be upset. She couldn't stand for him to be upset. Still . . .

And then she had arrived at the store Monday morning filled with ideas for improving business and the energy to carry them out and nearly fallen over Skeeter's body. Nausea rose in her as she thought about the ice pick protruding from his eye. Poor exasperating, hopeless, pitiful Skeeter. She would miss him, although she would never admit it to anyone. But her real grief for Skeeter would come later. Now she was lost in terror over what his murder might mean. She knew Chief Garrett had actually followed up on Skeeter's story and found Todd Ryan's bloodstained toy in the attic. He'd been held captive up there. What Skeeter had thought was his grandfather's ghost "acting up" was actually the kidnapper. And if Skeeter had seen the abductor of Todd Ryan, then she'd seen him, too. Not clearly, of course. Not well enough for an identification, but the abductor might think she had. He might come after *her* with an ice pick.

Matilda shuddered slightly, then told herself to get control as she counted out Mr. Moreland's cholesterol medicine in groups of five with her metal spatula. Matilda considered the price of the medication exorbitant, but at least the Morelands had great insurance from all of Edgar Moreland's years as an employee of Grace Healthcare. He'd been in earlier in the day, telling her how he'd once discovered that Herbert Klein had left the attic door open and Skeeter Dobbs had been creeping up the stairs. "Wouldn't steal or damage a thing, poor soul. So one night Helen and I put cookies and juice up there for him. Not a drop or a crumb left the next morning. I think he had himself quite a time."

Mr. Moreland said his wife was scared to death, knowing that Todd had been held in the attic right above their apartment. Said she blamed herself, too, for not calling the police sooner when she sensed something was wrong. Matilda knew exactly how she felt. Mr. Moreland said he didn't want it known, but he was paying for Skeeter's funeral. He couldn't bear to have Skeeter shuttled away to some potter's field. The funeral wouldn't be anything elaborate, he'd told her. Just a nice coffin, a simple graveside service presided over by Father Brennan at Shady Mount Cemetery, and a simple granite headstone. Matilda had promised she would attend. Poor Skeeter. The ice pick, the blood, the *horror*—

"Miss Vinson?"

Matilda jumped, jerked the spatula, and scattered pills all over the counter. She glared at Lynn. "What is it?"

"I didn't mean to startle you. Tess says we're running out of chocolate syrup at the fountain."

"I suppose Tess has also turned mute," Matilda snapped.

Lynn lowered her voice. "She's a little bit afraid of you."

Matilda glanced at Tess, who blew a pink bubble with her gum and stared back dully, not looking at all afraid of Matilda. She was simply lazy. She was also the granddaughter of an old customer and Matilda's father had insisted she hire the little twit. It was a waste of money. The fountain did hardly any business. "Tell Tess to order one gallon of chocolate syrup," Matilda ordered, suddenly furious at having to pay a salary to the bovine Tess. "And Lynn, would you mind mopping the stoop again?"

Lynn's cold eyes suddenly smoldered. She had mopped up the area where Skeeter had been found exactly four times. You could eat off the recessed entrance, she thought acidly. "Why don't I wait until this evening?" She sounded pleasant and helpful. "That way it will be fresh for morning." And fewer people would see her doing menial labor. She wasn't a janitor, for God's sake.

"All right." Matilda gathered the pills to start another count. "But use ammonia in the water. The stoop still feels sticky to me."

Her imagination, of course. She knew Skeeter's blood was long gone. Maybe she was becoming like him. He always saw his grandfather plummeting from the Presidential Suite and the blood splattering over him. Matilda would always see the ice pick protruding grotesquely from Skeeter's eye, his gooey blood all over her new white pumps, the flies swarming around his limp body ripe with death in the hot morning sun.

Matilda shuddered and lost count of the pills again.

2

"I'm telling you this is Jonnie's bracelet," Rebecca said shrilly. "He made it in Boy Scouts."

Bill looked at her wearily. "I know Jonnie had a bracelet like it—"

"Not *like* it. This is *it*. He was wearing it when he was kidnapped."

Bill turned the braided leather strap over in his hands. It certainly didn't look like the work of a professional. And it did bear Jonnie's initials. But it had the smell of new leather. Jonnie's bracelet would have been at least eight years old. "Honey, I know you're upset—"

"Don't patronize me!" Rebecca and Bill rarely argued and he didn't believe he'd ever seen such resentment in her eyes. She was furious that he wasn't fervidly jumping on the discovery of the bracelet in her car. "Do you think I put it in the car myself to draw attention?"

"For heaven's sake, Becky, I'd never suspect you of a thing like that. But to think that after all these years Jonnie's bracelet just happened to show up in your car. Your *locked* car—"

"A locked car with the windows rolled down a couple of inches. That's plenty of room to drop in the bracelet."

Bill looked at her intently. "Just what is it you want me to do, Becky?"

"I would like for you to act interested. I might as well be in here arguing about a parking ticket for all the emotion you're showing."

"I *am* interested. I care. But I'm puzzled. Hell, I'm baffled by this whole damned mess! But everyone keeps looking to me to do something miraculous and I don't have any miracles up my sleeve."

"Then maybe you know how I feel most of the time," Rebecca said in a subdued voice. "I know Molly is disappointed in me. Actually, I think she's furious with me for not finding Todd. And as for Mother—"

"Has she been giving you a hard time like with Jonnie?"

"No, not like with Jonnie. She's not at me all the time, begging for answers, recriminating when I don't have them. But she's as disillusioned with me now as she was eight years ago."

"You know a lot of this has to do with our mother. Suzanne can't accept that you have the same talents. She was frightened of our mother. She's frightened of you."

"Well, that's just too bad," Rebecca snapped. "Besides, Mother isn't the point here. Neither is Molly. I want to know what's going on with this bracelet, Bill."

"I don't know what's going on."

"Yes, you do. Someone is trying to scare me. Do you know who I saw today at the volunteer center? Alvin Tanner, whose mother is in the penitentiary because of me."

Bill looked at her with interest. "You think Alvin put the bracelet in your car? Rebecca, how could he have known you'd be at the volunteer center? Or do you think he carried around the bracelet just in case he saw you?"

She glared at him. "And where would Alvin have gotten Jonnie's bracelet? When Jonnie was kidnapped, Alvin was fifteen."

"I'm not saying he kidnapped Jonnie, but he hates me!"

"You don't know that."

"How could he not? His mother killed his father to protect him. Because of me she's been locked away for years."

"Rebecca, she wouldn't have gotten such a harsh sentence if there wasn't some doubt about why she killed Earl. Let's think about that big life insurance policy she had him take out four months before she killed him. She waited to ambush him outside that bar and she was willing to let another person get the death penalty for her crime." Rebecca didn't answer. "And this bracelet . . . I'm telling you, it smells new to me. I don't see any sweat stains. We don't know that it's Jonnie's."

Rebecca drew a deep breath. "All right, let's say it's a copy. Who put it in my car?"

"Someone who wants to scare you away," Bill said flatly. "I don't want to sound cruel, but I'm not telling you anything you don't know. A lot of people in this town are afraid of you, people who don't understand ESP. A lot of people don't like you because they think you're a charlatan. Do you know Sheriff Lutz was in here not an hour ago raving about how you'd come to town and purposely had a wreck and caused a scene at Dormaine's simply because you're trying to cash in on Todd's disappearance to promote your book?"

Rebecca felt as if she'd been slapped. "I've always known Martin Lutz didn't like me, but I didn't believe he thought me so low as to take advantage of a little boy's abduction!"

"I gave him a piece of my mind. I nearly had him thrown out. He made a lot of threats, but there's nothing he can do except spout his theories to that obnoxious journalist Kelly Keene. Together the two of them could cause real trouble for you, Rebecca, not to mention for this investigation. So I want you to keep quiet about this bracelet."

"I understand the need for discretion, Bill, but keeping quiet is another matter." Her voice rose. "This bracelet is important, don't you see that? Aren't you going to do *anything*?"

Deputy G. C. Curry passed by and glanced in the chief's office. Bill said quietly, "Rebecca, would you tone it down a little?"

"Why? Am I causing a scene? That's all I seem to be good for these days."

Bill looked at the ceiling. "I can see I'm rubbing you the wrong way. Leave the bracelet with me and I'll get a couple of people working on it. You go home and take a nap."

"Take a *nap*?" Rebecca was suddenly so angry she couldn't think. Bill was treating her like a willful child. She stood. "Thank you for the coffee. And for the extreme interest and support. I'll get out of your way now before I embarrass you further."

"Rebecca—"

But she flung out of his office, steaming past deputies and a wide-eyed secretary who looked as if she were stifling laughter. Well, let them look and let them laugh. At 26, Rebecca was accustomed to it.

Once on the sidewalk, though, she felt as if the steam had drained from her. Her whole body ached from strain and fear and her hands trembled. Even her legs felt weak. She had to sit down before she fell down.

Slightly panicked that she might faint in the street, she ducked into the nearest store. Cool air washed over her and she glanced around, quickly locating a dainty chair upholstered in blue brocade. She sat down, closed her eyes, and drew deep breaths.

"Ma'am, are you all right?"

Rebecca opened her eyes. A beautiful girl with long black hair and violet eyes stood over, frowning. "I hate to trouble you," Rebecca said, her face growing even hotter with her embarrassment, "but could I have a cup of water? I don't feel so well. Just the heat, I guess—"

"Be right back." The girl immediately turned away. Rebecca took another breath, then looked around the store to see how many people were staring at her.

But the place was empty. Thank goodness, she thought, as her heartbeat began to slow a bit. She wasn't making *too* big a fool of herself this time.

The store had been decorated with an eye toward understated elegance. The carpet was dark blue and thick, the wallpaper cream with delicate swirls of gold. Strains of Vivaldi filled the cool interior and Rebecca detected the delicate scent of jasmine. She realized she'd entered The Jewelry Box.

The girl returned quickly with a glass of ice water.

"Drink it slowly or you'll get a wicked pain above your eyes," she advised.

Rebecca drank slowly, then smiled. "Thanks. I feel better."

"Are you sure? I can call for an ambulance—"

"No!" Rebecca cringed at the thought of an ambulance screaming down the street for her. "Really, I'm fine." She smiled. "I used to come here a long time ago. The place has been redecorated. It's beautiful."

"I think so, too. I love working here. It's such a pretty place and all this gorgeous jewelry. I'll almost be sorry when my job ends in the fall and I go to college full-time."

Rebecca rose just to prove to herself that she could and walked over to a display case. Rings sparkled up at her, their beauty enhanced by artful lighting, but one caught Rebecca's eye. "I like that emerald ring. The princess-cut stone."

"Oh, isn't it exquisite? It's my very favorite!" Rebecca could tell the girl was sincere. "Would you like to try it on?"

Rebecca hadn't the slightest need for a ring, but the store was cool and comfortable, the girl friendly, and the ring lovely. "Sure. Why not?"

The girl withdrew the ring in its small green velvet box lined with white satin from the display case. "Now this is a size five. That's rather small, but it can be enlarged—" She broke off as the ring slipped with ease onto Rebecca's right ring finger. "Well, how about that! Perfect fit. And it's gorgeous with your coloring."

Rebecca wiggled her finger beneath the lights carefully set to display gems at their best. "I don't suppose you know the carat weight."

"The center emerald is one and a half carats. The emeralds on each side are eight points and ten points. And the gold is eighteen karat." The girl smiled. "I told you I've admired that one. I'd buy it for myself, but one summer of work here and two years of baby-sitting just haven't put enough money in the bank for college *and* the ring. And

I'm not baby-sitting anymore. I don't think I ever will again."

Rebecca looked up. The girl's violet eyes were somber, her smile gone. Good heavens, Rebecca thought. Hadn't Molly said Todd's baby-sitter worked at The Jewelry Box? "Excuse me for asking, but is your name Sonia Ellis?"

The girl immediately looked wary. "Why? Are you a reporter?"

"No."

"But you came here looking for me."

"I didn't. Honestly, I came in because I wasn't feeling well. I just guessed you were Sonia Ellis. It was something about the way you looked so sad when you mentioned baby-sitting."

"I don't want to talk about Todd Ryan," Sonia said firmly. "I don't mean to be rude, especially if you're not a reporter like that awful Keene woman who keeps following me around, but Chief Garrett doesn't want me talking about the kidnapping."

"Chief Garrett is my uncle, Sonia. I'm Rebecca Ryan— Todd's second cousin."

Sonia's eyes widened. "Rebecca Ryan? The one who's supposed to have ESP?"

The stigma of ESP seemed to follow her around like a dark cloud. "Yes," she replied with forced ease, "but right now I'm trying to help find Todd through traditional methods. Would you mind talking to me? I *am* a relative and I know Bill Garrett wouldn't mind."

Sonia lowered her gaze. "The store owner wouldn't like me standing around blabbing."

"I could meet you after work."

"I have to go to the library. I'm taking a college class this summer and I have a paper due. No talking there, either. Besides, I'll be very busy."

"Sonia, I only need a few minutes. Perhaps I could speak to the owner."

Sonia sighed. "You're not going to give up, are you?

Okay. He's not even here right now so I'll give you ten minutes. That's all."

"Thank you. It means a lot to me."

"I'll put the ring back first."

"No, don't," Rebecca said quickly. "I really am interested in it. Let me wear it while we're talking. Maybe I can make up my mind about whether or not to buy it."

Sonia looked at her doubtfully, clearly thinking she was only using the ring as a ploy. Nevertheless, she didn't object and Rebecca left the ring on her finger. "I know the police have asked you this over and over, but please answer one more time. The neighbors on either side of Molly's house were gone, right?"

"Wrong." Rebecca looked blank. "I keep saying this but no one believes me. That nurse, Ms. Wright, was home."

Rebecca's eyebrows rose in surprise. "She says she was doing private duty nursing from seven P.M. until morning."

Sonia's face took on a stubborn look. "I don't care what she says. And I don't care that her patient says she was with her all that time. My mother knows her patient. She's senile and on a lot of medication. Ms. Wright could have gotten there at seven or midnight and she probably wouldn't have known the difference. And I *saw* her, Ms. Ryan. A little before nine I heard a cat meowing. It was loud, like a Siamese. I know Ms. Wright has a Siamese and I went out into Molly's backyard to see if something was wrong with it. Just as I stepped out, I saw Ms. Wright's back door open and the cat ran in."

"Couldn't someone else have opened the door?"

"Someone who called the cat 'Sabu' in *her* voice? It was starting to get dark and I couldn't see very well, but I could tell that the person had short dark hair and those awful white nurse's shoes she wears with *everything*. Doesn't that woman have a clue about fashion?"

Rebecca almost smiled at Sonia's distress over Jean Wright's clothes. Dowdiness was almost a sin in the eyes of many pretty teenage girls. "You didn't see her face?"

"No, but the voice, the hair, the *shoes*. I think the police call that stuff circumstantial, but I'm sure it was her."

"You're sure you didn't get the time wrong."

"It was right before *Basic Instinct* started on cable. I was looking forward to it because my mother never lets me see it. It came on at nine. I'd just made it to the couch from the back door when it began."

"Weren't there any lights on at Jean's?"

"No, which is something else kinda weird. Who hangs around in a dark house?"

"What about her car?"

"The garage door was down. It could have been in there way after seven o'clock." Sonia looked at her closely. "You don't believe me either. I'm just a teenager and she's Florence Nightingale."

Rebecca looked into Sonia's beautiful, earnest violet eyes. She felt something about this girl—a certainty about the goodness of her character, an inability to lie about anything serious. And for some odd reason, she felt a link with her. She knew what it was like to tell a truth and be doubted by everyone who counted. "I *do* believe you, Sonia," she said intensely. "And I intend to tell my Uncle Bill I believe you."

"You do?" Sonia brightened. "Because a lot of people think my boyfriend Randy Messer had something to do with the kidnapping. They act like we were in on it together. That's nuts. What would Randy do with a seven-year-old kid all this time? Besides, he likes kids. And I love Todd. I'd *never* let anything happen to him if I could help it. But the grief I'm getting from my mom!" Sonia rolled her eyes. "I sure would appreciate any help you could give me, Ms. Ryan."

"It's Rebecca," she said absently. "And I can't guarantee Bill will believe me, but I can certainly put in my two cents' worth."

The door opened and Sonia stiffened, then relaxed. "I thought it was the owner," she hissed. Rebecca turned to see Clay. She felt an abrupt surge of embarrassment over the fact that she'd spent the night in his bed and hid it behind banter.

"Why Dr. Bellamy as I live and breathe! Are you following me?"

"Yes. Doing a sly job of it, too, aren't I?" He smiled at Rebecca in a way that made her embarrassment vanish.

Rebecca was aware of Sonia watching them avidly, sensing a hint of romantic tension. Clay smiled at the girl. She smiled back with a slightly starry expression, clearly dazzled by golden hair and gray-blue eyes and the title of "Doctor." "I'm really here looking for a gift for Gypsy. She's partial to rubies."

Sonia appeared slightly disappointed that he hadn't come in to see Rebecca, but she said helpfully, "We have some pretty ruby earrings. And four ruby tennis bracelets, two with diamonds."

Clay frowned thoughtfully. "Well, Gypsy doesn't have pierced ears and clip-ons are so easy to lose. I don't know how she feels about tennis bracelets, either . . ."

"Then perhaps a nice ring."

"Gypsy is his dog," Rebecca said dryly so Sonia could stop trying to please.

The girl blinked at her, then laughed. "Okay, sir. I guess you're not really here for a gift for Gypsy."

"Well, I do admire that ring Ms. Ryan is flashing around."

"So do I," Sonia said. "I think it was made for her."

"Me, too. Wrap it up and send the bill to Peter Dormaine of Dormaine's Restaurant. I've heard he'd like to buy her something exquisite, the more expensive the better."

Sonia appeared confused and Rebecca blushed and glared at Clay. The last person in the world who would want to buy her a gift was Peter Dormaine. He'd probably like to have her run out of town before she completely destroyed his restaurant. "He's joking," she said. "And I suggest he keep his rapier wit to himself and buy what he came in here for. Unless, of course, he really was following me."

Clay was unabashed. "I'm sorry to disappoint you, Rebecca, but I did come in for a gift. Sunday is my father's birthday. I'm buying him a watch. He won't like anything I get, but his is a disgrace." He paused. "Could you wait five minutes while I pick out something and then go next door for coffee with me? I have something I need to talk over with you." He sobered. "Something important."

Sonia had seemed to enjoy the exchange between the two, her teenage mind creating sparks of romance. Rebecca crossed the room and sat back down on the dainty blue-upholstered chair. Clearly Clay had been asking some questions and might now have some pertinent information.

Clay looked at three watches before hastily picking one and pulling out a credit card. While Sonia took care of the purchase, Rebecca said, "That didn't take long."

"I told you Dad won't like anything I give him. Gifts are a gesture. And the Sunday birthday party should be the usual gala occasion." He raised an eyebrow. "Want to come?"

"What? Me? I don't even know your father."

"Doesn't matter. Mom's a good cook and doesn't mind surprise guests. You could take Sean and I'll take Gypsy. At least they'll have a good time. They can chase cows or something."

"That would please your father. May I think about it?"

"Sure, but don't take too long. Shindigs like this draw people by the hundreds. Have to reserve your place."

Clay was smiling, his tone bantering, but Rebecca saw the unhappiness in his eyes. She knew little about his home life except that he'd grown up on the most prosperous farm in the area. The Bellamy clan was known to be quite comfortable in the money department, but they rarely socialized and lived as simply as if they had to watch every dollar.

When Sonia handed him the gift-wrapped watch, Rebecca returned to the counter. "I want to thank you for talking with me earlier."

"It's okay. It's just nice to be believed for a change."

Clay looked puzzled. Obviously he had no idea the pretty clerk was Todd's baby-sitter.

"I hope to see you again, Sonia," Rebecca said. "Goodbye."

"Nice to meet you." Sonia's smile faltered. "But, uh, Ms. Ryan? I mean, Rebecca?"

"Yes?"

"You're still wearing the emerald ring."

"Are you trying to pull this trick again?" Clay demanded. He looked at Sonia earnestly. "Everywhere we go she walks out the door with something valuable. An out-and-out kleptomaniac. I tell you, miss, it's downright embarrassing."

Sonia dissolved into giggles as Rebecca pulled the ring off her finger and handed it to Sonia. The girl's brows drew together. "You don't want it?"

"No. Well . . . that is . . . I'm not sure. It *is* beautiful—"

"Beautiful!" Clay agreed fervently.

"Oh, *will* you be quiet!" Rebecca snapped as Clay blinked innocently and Sonia tried to swallow more giggles. Clay was being extremely annoying and just about to make her laugh, too. "Sonia, could you put the ring away for me until tomorrow? Just twenty-four hours until I make up my mind?"

"Well, I can't refuse to sell it if another customer wants it," Sonia said, then winked. "But I could sort of forget to put it back in the window until tomorrow afternoon. I have some of the store's business cards here. They have our telephone number. I'll also write my home number on one," Sonia said, reaching for a pen. "That way if you make a decision before the store opens tomorrow, you can let me know and I'll be sure the ring is put away until you can get in. Okay?"

"That's very considerate. I appreciate it," Rebecca said, taking the card. She then looked at Clay. "You said you wanted to have coffee so you could talk to me."

"Right you are, my dear. Let's go next door. I have extraordinary news to impart."

"You do seem full of it today. I absolutely can't wait to hear. 'Bye, Sonia."

"Yes, good-bye," Clay said. "Thanks for the assistance."

They walked in silence to the Parkview Café next door. Just as they had for Dormaine's, people had predicted failure for what they considered a precious little gourmet coffee and pastry shop in downtown Sinclair. "This isn't New York or San Francisco," some hard-line proponents of the "simple life" had announced. "People want a good old-fashioned cup of joe and a doughnut. Period. None of those brioches and croissants and flavored coffees with whipped cream." But two years later the Parkview Café thrived with its lovely periwinkle blue and raspberry interior and its huge picture window overlooking Leland Park.

Rebecca ordered a vanilla decaf and a croissant. Clay ordered a double espresso. "Espresso?" she asked. "You seem so wound up today, that should blow you right through the roof."

"I'm not as wound up as I seem. It's been a hard day. I got someone to relieve me for an hour so I could pick up this gift, then I have to work until ten. I need the energy boost. But may I say you seem fairly wired yourself today?"

"I haven't had a great day either, and I have a blazing headache that's making me snappish. I let Bill have it right before I went in the jewelry shop."

Clay was instantly all concern. "You've been too active after the wreck. You haven't even had your sutures removed yet. Are they bothering you?"

"They itch."

"That's normal. And good. It means you're healing. I want you to come into the hospital and let me check them tomorrow."

"You checked them last night and changed my bandages. And I'm taking my antibiotics. Could you take out the stitches tomorrow?"

"No. It's too early. But I'm concerned about the headache."

"It's partly the result of the vision last night. It's a pattern. The pain starts in my right temple around the area of the crescent scar by my eye."

Clay removed a small pill container from his jacket pocket and handed it to her. "Take these two tablets."

"What are they?"

"Cyanide. After you take them you won't even think about your headache anymore."

"You just want me to convulse, die on the floor, and make another scene in a restaurant."

"That *would* make you the talk of the town, but I'm afraid they're only Excedrin. They work better on headaches than plain aspirin. Now take them." As she dutifully swallowed them with water, Clay added, "But as for restaurants, I don't think we'll return to Dormaine's for a while."

"You actually think I'd go back to where I humiliated myself so royally?"

He smiled at her, his eyes turning gentle. "Don't worry about it, Rebecca. It was an incident in a small town restaurant. I don't think it even made *Entertainment Tonight*. And according to the hostess, Frank is taking care of the bill for the damage, which looked a lot worse than it was. Forget it. In the great scheme of things, it was nothing."

Rebecca sighed. "I guess I'll take the doctor's advice, both about forgetting Dormaine's and about coming into the emergency room tomorrow. Believe me, I can't wait for these cuts to heal and to get rid of these stitches."

Clay smiled. "Now, do you want to hear what I dragged you in here for? Rhetorical question. Of course you do. Well, first let me tell you that I'm thinking of giving up medicine to become a private eye. In less than twenty-four hours, I've come up with interesting information about Jean Wright."

Rebecca's attention quickened. "Well, don't make me wait. What's her story?"

Quickly Clay told her about the younger brother and sister away at colleges they couldn't afford and Jean's near breakdown less than two months ago caused by frantic overwork to pay their expenses. "My source, who shall remain nameless, is surprised that Jean is spending so much time with Molly in such stressful circumstances. She says Jean knows she has to take it easy if she's going to pull herself together enough to get her job back."

"You mean she was fired?"

"The words were *on leave*. I think she was suspended."

Rebecca thought for a moment. "Well, she could just be a very kind-hearted person—without charm but kind-hearted—who's more concerned about Molly than about getting her health back."

"Getting her health back so she can get her *job* back. A job that supports the two spoiled brats that seem to be the center of her life. That strikes me as being a little odd, especially since you said Molly had only mentioned her a couple of times in the past. Now she's a fixture at the house, and it's not like there's no one else to watch over Molly. I know Doug would spend time with her. You'd spend more time with her if Jean the dragon weren't there breathing fire at you. Even your mother and Betty would if they were needed, but Jean seems to be driving everyone away. *Why?*"

"Because she's not just being helpful? She has some self-interest?"

"My conclusion exactly."

"What self-interest?"

"She needs money, Rebecca. Desperately. After all, she may not get back her job."

Rebecca set down her coffee cup. "My God, Clay, you don't think that she might have something to do with taking Todd?" He lifted his shoulders. "Well, you weren't the only one doing some detecting. I went into The Jewelry Box because I wasn't feeling well, why I'll explain later. The salesgirl was Sonia Ellis, Todd's baby-sitter. I'm beginning to wonder if . . . well, I know this sounds kooky, but—"

"That was Sonia Ellis?" Rebecca nodded. "So you wondered if you'd been drawn in there."

"Yes." She looked closely at Clay. There was not a hint of doubt or ridicule in his expression. "Anyway, I got her talking about Jean. Jean insists she left her house at seven the night of the abduction. Sonia claims a little before nine someone opened the back door to Jean's house to let in the cat. The light was dim, but she saw short dark hair and white nurse's shoes. And the person called the cat's name in Jean's voice."

"But what about the patient who says Jean was there at seven?"

"Sonia says she's senile and takes lots of medication. It could have been seven or much later when Jean arrived for all the woman knew."

Clay leaned back in his chair. "Well, that puts a different spin on things."

"I'd say so. I'd like to talk to Sonia some more, but she says she's going to the library tonight and I don't want to interrupt her there. Maybe I'll stop in the store again tomorrow."

"For conversation and another look at that ring?"

"For conversation. She might reveal something else she was too frightened to tell Bill, although I know he likes her."

"He's still the chief of police and she's a teenager who was left in charge of a child who was abducted. I'd be intimidated, too."

"Looks like this is the place to be on a Tuesday afternoon."

Rebecca glanced up to see Doug standing over them. "Well, hi. Did you just come in?"

"I've been here about fifteen minutes sitting right behind you. You two were too engrossed in your conversation to notice me. Actually I've been downtown all afternoon." He was heavy-lidded as if he hadn't slept a wink and he hadn't shaved that morning. Some men could get by with stubble. Doug looked unkempt. "Why aren't you at the hospital, Clay?"

"They give me a break after every thirty lives I save.

Nice to see you again, Doug. What's it been? Three or four months?"

"More like six. At the Christmas parade you stood with Lynn and me."

"And Larry. We went to The Gold Key afterward for some Christmas cheer," Clay said.

Rebecca smiled. "That seems like an odd place to go for a festive holiday drink. I remember it as pretty grungy."

"That's just because of all the Hell's Angels clientele and the floor sticky from beer and the country music blaring from the jukebox, and the occasional fistfight," Clay said. "Since you've moved to New Orleans, you've gotten too sophisticated for the more rustic ambience of our local tavern."

Rebecca smiled. "Nice try, but I'm afraid The Gold Key can't compare with some of the dives on Bourbon Street. I'm certainly not a little hothouse flower."

Doug's eyes turned stern, his voice repressive. "Better watch what you say, Becky. This is a small town. Things can be misunderstood."

Rebecca looked at him in amazement. Doug used to have a sense of humor. His tight expression told her it had temporarily disappeared. She glanced at Clay, who only stared back in faint amusement. "I'm going to the volunteer center," Doug said. "I haven't seen the two of you there."

"I've been working," Clay said shortly.

Rebecca's tone was equally clipped. "And I already put in a couple of hours today but didn't feel it was the best use of my time."

"Helping to find Todd is the best use of *anyone's* time I can think of," Doug snapped.

"I didn't mean—" Rebecca began, but Doug was already heading out the door. "Well, for God's sake," she sputtered. "What's gotten into him?"

"Ice water. Sanctimony."

"Reformed whore syndrome?"

Clay's eyes widened in pretend shock. "Rebecca, please! Watch what you say. This is a small town. Things can be misunderstood!"

"People often choose to misunderstand if it makes life more interesting. Gee, I liked Doug even when he was a bad boy, but I'm not fond of this holier-than-thou guy."

"Now you know why we're not good friends anymore. And do I even have to describe that evening at The Gold Key with Lynn and Larry at Christmas? Doug was insistent or I wouldn't have gone. What he really wanted to do was keep an eye on Larry; I think he wanted a little extra muscle with him in case he had trouble keeping Larry under control. Lynn was shooting lasers from her eyes at me and Larry looked like he would gladly have slit my throat. I felt lucky to make it out of the place alive after one warm beer with the merry crowd."

Rebecca frowned. "Doug said he'd been sitting behind us for fifteen minutes but he didn't make himself known. Why?"

"Absorbed in his coffee before he was off to do more good works?"

"Or listening to us. Listening to what I said about Sonia."

"Is there any harm in that?"

"I guess not, although I don't like the idea of him eavesdropping, if that's what he was doing. But there's another thing. He said he's been downtown all afternoon."

"And the crime in that is?"

"Something I didn't tell you earlier. One of the things that gave me my terrible headache." Clay looked at her alertly as she told him about her encounter with Alvin Tanner and about finding the leather bracelet.

"What?" Clay exploded, then lowered his voice when people looked at him. "Good God, Rebecca, what did you do with the bracelet?"

"Took it to Bill. His reaction was strange. He says it smells new and he doesn't think it's Jonnie's at all. It didn't smell new to me, but even if it *is* new, someone put an exact copy of my dead brother's bracelet in my car. I naturally thought of Alvin."

"But now you think it might have been Doug?"

"He could have seen my car—or rather, my mother's car—parked here. He could have said something to Lynn or even Larry. Vinson's Apothecary is only a couple of blocks away from the volunteer center, Maloney's Garage just a little more."

"But Rebecca, Larry or Lynn would have had to have the bracelet ready for just such an occasion."

"And is it so hard to believe they might not have? They both knew about the bracelet, and it would be so easy to make one like it. An opportunity to slip it in the car or my purse would have to come up soon. And neither one of them wants me here, especially Larry." She paused, scowling. "*Especially* Larry, if he had anything to do with Todd's kidnapping."

Chapter Eleven

1

"Where have you been?" Suzanne demanded. "We're not running a hotel here. You could at least show up for meals!"

Rebecca looked closely at her mother. Her eyes were bleary and she stood unnaturally straight, her thin shoulders thrown back in a poor attempt to indicate perfect equilibrium. Apparently her latest try for sobriety had failed, Rebecca thought sadly. "Mother, dinner isn't for an hour."

"I'm tired. I decided we'd dine early tonight."

"Well, I'm not a mind reader."

"Was that supposed to be a joke? This is still *my* house. You are a guest."

Rebecca felt like flaring back, but the last thing she needed to do was fuel her mother's hostility. "If I've missed dinner, I'll just have a sandwich. It's not a big deal."

"You haven't missed dinner. It's in fifteen minutes."

Rebecca hadn't realized Frank stood behind her. He spoke calmly but when she turned to look at him, she saw the anger in his eyes. She knew he loved Suzanne, but nearly 16 years of her nerves and drinking had to be taking a toll on the marriage. She was surprised life in this house moved along as semi-smoothly as it seemed.

Twenty minutes later they sat around the table pretending to enjoy Cornish game hens and wild rice. Suzanne, with a wine bottle placed possessively near her plate, was having trouble removing meat from the tiny hen. Rebecca and Frank pretended not to see her clumsy efforts with knife and fork until one hacking movement sent the carcass onto the floor. Frank calmly laid down his cutlery and looked at his wife.

"I think you should excuse yourself from the table."

"You think I should do *what*?" Suzanne sizzled.

"You heard me. When you're too drunk to keep your food on your plate, you're not fit company at dinner. Go to your room. I'll have Betty send up something."

"Go to my room!" Suzanne spluttered. "Who do you think you are? My father? The damned bird is greasy as hell. It slipped."

"Along with half of your rice, which is now scattered around your plate like the rings of Saturn. And perhaps you haven't noticed that your dinner roll is in your lap."

Suzanne's gaze flashed to her lap. She picked up the roll and flung it against the wall. Then she scooted back her chair, nearly sending it toppling, and stalked from the room, carrying the bottle of wine with her.

Neither Frank nor Rebecca spoke. Betty immediately dashed in, picked up Suzanne's plate, the remains of the hen and the roll, and returned to the kitchen without a word. At last Frank said, "I'm sorry. I should have ignored her."

"I think you've ignored her behavior too long," Rebecca said gently. "She can't go on like this."

"Am I supposed to have my own wife put away? To humiliate her in this town where she's lived all her life?"

"You wouldn't be putting her into a mental institution, Frank. You'd be sending her to rehab. And I think most people in town already know about her condition. She's already humiliated herself, whether she realizes it or not. Besides, what does it matter if it saves her life?"

Frank smiled at her. "When did you get to be so wise?"

Rebecca was aware of the absolute silence in the kitchen, where she usually heard the murmur of Betty's and Walt's voices. She decided they needed to get off the subject of Suzanne. "I'm not feeling very wise these days. I haven't been able to help at all with Todd."

"Because of you we know he's still alive."

"But I have no idea where he is."

"Someplace dark. But he's being fed and kept warm."

"Oh, that's immensely helpful, isn't it? We might as well call off the police." She sighed impatiently. "I should be doing more. Joining the air and ground searches, for instance."

"You're not up to that after your wreck and you're not trained."

"Not trained? Half the town has been on these searches and they aren't trained."

"They got some introductory lessons. And frankly, for all their good will, I'm not expecting much to come from the volunteers. It didn't . . . before."

"With Jonnie. No, I seemed to be his best hope, and I failed."

"Don't be so hard on yourself, Rebecca. This gift of yours doesn't make you omniscient."

"You never really believed in my 'gift,'" she said without rancor. "And maybe you were right not to. I haven't been too successful the last couple of times. Perhaps traditional methods are the best." She continued casually, "I met Sonia Ellis today. I can see why Bill likes her."

"She's very pretty and very bright. Maybe a bit too bright for her mother to handle."

"Is Mrs. Ellis lacking in some way?"

"No. She's a fine woman, just very traditional and rather naïve. I think Sonia is much more sophisticated than her mother. Sonia is an enigma—which would make any mother nervous."

"Tell me about it," Rebecca said dryly. "I am the quintessential enigma."

Frank grinned. "Perhaps you could start a club."

"I'll get to work on it as soon as I return to New Orleans. I'll have to think up a club motto and a password. Something classy but not *too* obscure." Rebecca paused. "Anyway, Sonia had some things to say about Jean Wright."

Frank looked mildly interested. "Such as what?"

"That she was home near the time that Todd was taken even though she insists she wasn't. Sonia saw her call in her cat a little before nine."

"Or so she says now. I was there when she told it the

first time to Bill after Todd was taken. She didn't say anything then about a cat."

"Maybe she just remembered."

"How convenient, especially since I know the police have been questioning that lowlife boyfriend of hers." He sighed. "Oh well, I'm no doubt being far too hard on her because Todd was in her care when he was taken. She probably didn't have a thing to do with what happened, but if Todd dies, she'll have an unbearable burden of guilt to carry around with her, which won't be fair. I just hope she's not still seeing that Messer kid."

"She isn't—at least not tonight. She said something about going to the library."

Frank laughed. "Oh, the *library*. What do you want to bet her mother has forbidden her to see Messer and she's really sneaking off to meet him somewhere?"

"She sounded sincere about having to work on a paper. Once Sonia goes away to college, though, Mrs. Ellis can't watch her day and night. If she doesn't see Randy now, she will then." Rebecca looked over at the mess around her mother's plate. "The women of this family seem incapable of having a dignified meal. What a scene I caused at Dormaine's last night!"

"Livened up the place, that's all."

"I'm sure that's how Mr. Dormaine put it. He was horrified."

"He's easily horrified."

"Frank, I'll pay for the damage to the lawn, the tree, and the dining room. That's not your responsibility."

Frank smiled. "Dear, I'm an investor in Dormaine's. Peter doesn't want people to know that—he wants to play the big cheese—so it's just a secret among you, me, and Peter. But you don't owe him a penny. Forget about the money and forget about being embarrassed. People are more interested in what's happened to Todd and to Skeeter Dobbs."

"I suppose it was fairly egocentric of me to believe everyone is thinking about me instead of those disasters. Frank, who do you think murdered Skeeter?"

"Not everyone in this town thought Skeeter was harmless. He had a bad habit of wandering around town poking into things he shouldn't, rummaging through trash, looking in windows, begging, pestering, trying to talk to children. He might have just pushed one of our less patient citizens too far. I'm surprised he lasted as long as he did."

"But what about him seeing someone in the Klein attic on Saturday night?"

"He thought he saw his grandfather every night. He might have just seen a light."

"But if he saw more than that?"

"We'll never know now." Frank suddenly rubbed his eyes. "I've lost my appetite. I've also been letting my work slide because of Todd. I should go back to the office for a few hours and catch up. You don't mind, do you?"

"Of course not." Rebecca remembered her mother saying Frank often returned to the office when he was annoyed with her. She thought he'd long passed the point of annoyance with Suzanne tonight. Maybe he merely wanted to escape the house. "I think I'll take Sean for a walk," she said. "I've been neglecting him lately."

After Frank left the table, Betty came in. "I made a fresh apple and raisin pie. Want a piece?"

"I'd love some, but I'll have it in the kitchen with you and Walt."

Betty looked pleased. "Now that would be a treat for us."

As usual Walt nearly bolted to his feet as soon as Rebecca walked in. "Walt, relax. It's just me, not Queen Elizabeth." Rebecca laughed. "I see your pal is keeping you company."

"He's a fine dog." Walt sat down and reached under the table to touch Sean, who lay close to Walt's feet. "We understand each other."

Betty cut large slices of pie and everyone dug in. "Betty, you've outdone yourself," Rebecca said. "Frank and Mother don't know what they're missing."

"It didn't sound like either one of them was too interested in food tonight," Betty said. "We can't help over-hearing right in here."

Rebecca nodded. "I know. I wish I could do something about the situation with them."

"Married folks have to work these things out for themselves," Betty said sagely, as if she'd been married for fifty years instead of two.

After finishing the pie, Rebecca headed up to her room with Sean. When she reached the top of the stairs, she heard strains of "A Whiter Shade of Pale" coming from her mother's room. The song sent chills through her and without thinking, she opened the bedroom door and burst in.

Suzanne lay on the four-poster bed in her blue silk robe, propped up on pillows, smoking. A full glass of red wine sat on a nightstand and a boom box rested on the floor beside her bed.

"Why are you listening to that?" Rebecca asked loudly.

Suzanne raised up angrily. "I'm listening to it because it was your father's and Jonnie's favorite song," she said with a slight slur to her words. "And how dare you barge in here? Can't I have any privacy?"

Rebecca marched to the boom box and flipped it off. "*Rebecca!*" her mother snapped, but she paid no attention. She opened the cassette case. Her father's old cassette had been playing, not a new compact disc. "What are you doing?"

"I just wanted to see something," Rebecca said distractedly.

"You wanted to know if I have a CD like the one you found in the car." Rebecca looked at her sharply. "I wasn't supposed to know, but Bill told me. He wanted to make sure I didn't have any CDs around here. Good God, do both of you think I'm trying to terrorize my own daughter?"

"We just thought the CD might have come from this house. No one thought you put it in the car."

"I'm sure it crossed *your* mind." Suzanne stared at Rebecca sullenly. "Did Frank send you up?"

"Frank left for the office."

"Typical."

"You can hardly blame him. You aren't your most congenial self this evening."

"I'm having a bad day."

"It seems to me most of your days are bad."

Suzanne glared. "The expert who has been here since Saturday evening after an eight-year absence. Thank you for your opinion."

"Oh, Mother, can't we stop fighting and just talk?" Rebecca sat down on the bed. Her mother drew away slightly. "What is wrong?"

Suzanne puffed on her cigarette and gazed into the distance for a moment. "I miss Jonnie."

"I know that. I miss Jonnie, too, but I don't wallow in my bed drinking myself silly because of it."

"Oh, you are *so* strong, aren't you? You're not like me. You're like my mother. You two put me to shame with your stalwart spirits!" Suzanne looked at her fiercely. "But don't think you're fooling me, little girl. You're as obsessed with Jonnie as I am. My God, do you think I don't realize that 'Sean' is the Irish form of John? You named your dog after your brother."

It was true. Sean, on whom she could bestow so much love and tenderness. Sean, who'd been abused, whom now she could protect as she'd never been able to protect Jonnie. The knife of her mother's accusation plunged deep, but she knew the tactic. Her mother was trying to divert the subject from herself and her own failings.

"Mother, missing Jonnie isn't the point—"

"And I miss your father," Suzanne plunged on. "If Patrick had been here, Jonnie would never have been taken."

"We don't know that."

"*I* know it. When we got married, he promised he'd never leave me. But he did. He broke his promise. And look what happened."

Rebecca looked at her mother. Suzanne was a child, she thought bleakly. She was a once-beautiful child who'd been coddled and loved and couldn't understand when her magical life had fallen apart. What she'd never realized, though, was that the world did not revolve around her. To Suzanne everything was personal. She could acknowledge Rebecca's pain about Patrick and Jonnie but she could not empathize because she could only feel her own devastation. And she felt she had the right to make everyone suffer with her.

"Mother, you may not feel the same about Frank as you did Daddy, but you do love him," Rebecca said quietly. "He's been so good to you—so good to all of us for so long. Please try to pull yourself together. Otherwise you're going to lose him."

She expected a sharp retort, but Suzanne only stared stonily at her, then refilled her glass of wine. In a mixture of disgust and hopelessness, Rebecca left the room. As soon as she reached her own, "A Whiter Shade of Pale" began to play once more, louder than ever. She sat down on the bed, slipped her locket off her neck, and looked at the smiling picture of Jonnie inside. "Nothing has ever been the same since you've been gone," she said. "I wonder if things will ever be right again."

Sean jumped up on the bed beside her. She slipped on the locket again and stroked his head. "Let's go for a walk and get out of this madhouse, boy."

The sky had been an unusually pale blue-gray when Rebecca arrived home and now she saw dark gray thunderheads forming in the distance. Summer humidity was always high in the Ohio Valley, but temperatures had been running about five degrees above normal for late June. The frequent storms didn't surprise Rebecca and she knew farmers welcomed them after last summer's drought. Sean had a different opinion.

He lagged behind her and a couple of times looked at the sky and whined. Rebecca kneeled and rubbed his ears. "Is this any way to act over a few clouds, Brave One?"

They plowed on, veering off Lamplight Lane onto a narrow asphalt road with a simple wooden sign reading Mockingbird Court. Once the lavish home of Carson Dobbs had presided as the lone occupant of the Court, but the house had burned down shortly after the his suicide. Insurance investigators proved arson, and the family collected nothing. After World War II, a developer planned to start a colony of cheap houses, but Rebecca's grandfather had bought the land to prevent the plethora of what he'd called "tinderboxes" from blooming. He'd willed the land to Patrick, whom he knew would not sell it for a quick profit, and it now belonged to Suzanne.

The land was overgrown although Frank sent out a crew with mowers and heavy equipment to clear the worst of it once a year. Rebecca knew her father had reserved it for fine homes for her, Jonnie, and Molly, imagining the three of them living forever in happy proximity to him and Suzanne.

During her teenage years she could remember Frank trying to talk Suzanne into doing something with the land, but she nixed all ideas, still hanging on to Patrick's dream. Now that Jonnie was gone, that could no longer be her reason for letting the land lie fallow. Perhaps she'd simply lost interest.

Rebecca tilted her head, closed her eyes, and drew a deep breath of air filled with the smell of coming rain. Somehow it made her feel calmer. Then she opened her eyes. A hawk flew over, low, with a mouse wriggling in its claws. The calmness shattered, replaced by repulsion. She knew all creatures had to eat. Still . . .

From somewhere close by came the sound of a cat crying. She looked to the right and saw a bird sitting on a shrub. It was slate-gray with a black cap. A catbird, named for its mewling call. Many people said Carson Dobbs, who had named Mockingbird Court, had mistaken the catbird for the mockingbird, which is known for a prettier song. Rebecca was no bird expert, but this bird's particular catlike sound made her think of Sonia hearing a cat and Jean Wright letting it into her house shortly before Todd was taken. Sonia seeing Jean, Jean probably seeing Sonia watching her, *knowing* she was home when Jean claimed to be gone.

Rebecca stopped in the middle of the road. A familiar, dreaded pain started beside her right eye. The surrounding shrubs and trees slowly blurred, then disappeared. Instead she saw stacks of books, felt the chill of air conditioning, watched a slender girl with long black hair sit at a table reading a book, then writing in a spiral notebook. Rebecca's vision had become one of a watcher who scanned the room, which was empty except for the girl and one young man who was clearly not with the girl, someone who gave the impression of leaving soon. Rebecca experienced the watcher's feeling of satisfaction. It was all right to wait. Just fine to wait until the girl was alone.

Until Sonia was alone.

The overgrown world of Mockingbird Court came back into focus. Rebecca stood rigid, her hands cold, perspiration popping out on her forehead. Sean looked up at her, whined, then pawed at her leg. "Oh God," she muttered. "Someone is going to kill Sonia."

2

TUESDAY, 8:20 P.M.

Rebecca turned and began running back toward Lamplight Lane. She had dropped Sean's leash, but he raced along next to her, pulling ahead with the natural speed of the Australian shepherd. The image of Sonia in the library had vanished, but Rebecca's panic remained. She'd felt an odd sort of connection with the girl earlier today. Now she sensed that Sonia was in danger, and she didn't for a moment doubt her feeling.

She was panting by the time she burst out of Mockingbird Court onto Lamplight Lane. She had no doubt some neighbor was watching her run like a wild thing through the evening, but she didn't care. Public opinion had already seemed to cast her into the role of oddball. She might as well keep on giving people something to talk about.

Once again the scenery around her seemed to fade. Projected over it was a pallid reproduction of a long table behind which loomed towering shelves of books. And a gaze through a space in the books at the back of Sonia's head. Rebecca saw through this gaze, watched it move over the sheen of Sonia's black hair, the back of a blue T-shirt, the tight waist of blue jeans, smooth curve of hips, sandals lying beside small bare feet crossed at the ankles as she sat on a plastic chair pulled close to the Formica-topped table. She even saw the band of the girl's watch on her left arm and the pink frosted polish on her fingernails. The gaze noted all this with fondling, obscene detail. Rebecca felt faintly nauseated.

She rushed up the front walk and almost slammed into the locked front doors. Frantically she rang the bell and Betty answered. "Good Lord, honey, what's wrong?"

"I don't have time to explain," Rebecca called as she raced up the stairs, Sean at her heels. In her room she grabbed the phone and called police headquarters. Bill wasn't in, but a young deputy listened while she poured out her story of a girl in danger at the library. "And how do you know this, ma'am?"

"I just know," Rebecca said, hearing the futility in her voice. "Please go there. The girl's name is Sonia Ellis. She has long black hair—"

"And what did you say your name is?"

"Rebecca Ryan. As I said, she has black hair—"

"Oh, Rebecca *Ryan*. With the ESP?"

Rebecca fell silent for a moment. "Go to the library. If you don't, you'll regret it."

"Is that a threat, ma'am?"

"Oh for God's sake," Rebecca snarled and hung up. She called Bill's home. Just the machine. In three minutes she had the car keys in hand and was heading for the Thunderbird. "Honey, what in the world's wrong with you?" Betty demanded, trundling along behind her to the car. "Where are you goin'?"

"Just take care of Sean for me. I'll be fine."

Rebecca roared out of the driveway with Betty desper-

ately holding on to an agitated Sean's leash. It would take
her at least ten minutes to get to the library even if she hit
every green light and didn't get stopped for speeding. That
was too long. Her mind raced, trying to come up with a
solution. If only that damned deputy had listened to her. If
only Bill had been home. Maybe he was at Molly's. She
grabbed her cell phone and dialed Molly's number. Someone answered but so much static cut in, Rebecca couldn't
make out a word. She shouted her name and an order for
Bill or a deputy to go to the library, not knowing whether
or not she'd been heard.

"Damn, damn, *damn*!" she muttered, throwing a murderous glance at a stop sign. At this rate she'd never get to
the library in time to help Sonia.

If Sonia *was* at the library. What had Frank said? That
Mrs. Ellis didn't want her seeing Randy Messer and that
she probably wasn't going to the library at all but to a secret
meeting place. In that case, Rebecca's vision would be
completely wrong. That had never happened. Sometimes
her visions were vague, but never imaginary, like dreams.

She fished in her purse for the card Sonia had given her
at The Jewelry Box bearing her home phone number. She
called and a slightly nasal male adolescent voice greeted
her charmingly with, "Yeah?"

"Is this Sonia Ellis's residence?"

"Yeah."

"May I speak with her?" More static. Rebecca groaned,
then repeated the question.

"I told you she's not home."

"Could you tell me where she is?"

"You a reporter? That Kelly Keene chick?"

"No, I'm Rebecca Ryan. I met Sonia today at the jewelry
store. It's extremely important that I speak with her. May
I ask who you are?"

"Cory."

"Hello, Cory." Static. Rebecca wanted to scream at the
noise and the inarticulate kid, but she forced herself to
sound polite when the static died. "I know this is an odd

call, but Sonia gave me her number." She started to say something about her being in danger, but Rebecca had a feeling the boy might hang up on her. "I was thinking of buying a ring. I couldn't make up my mind, so Sonia asked me to call if I decided I wanted it so she could put it away for me until I can get to the store tomorrow afternoon."

"Oh. So you want the ring?"

"*Yes*. That's why I must speak with Sonia tonight. She said she might go to the library. Would she be there now?"

"She could be." Rebecca was on the verge of losing patience when Cory suddenly turned into a geyser of information. "I'm her brother. She said somethin' at dinner about a woman bein' in the store and tryin' on a ring. Guess that was you. Said you were flirtin' it up with some hot doctor." Oh wonderful, Rebecca thought. *Flirting*. "Anyway, she told Mom she was goin' to the library. She's prob'ly there, but she goes to meet Randy Messer sometimes. She's not s'posed to be seein' him, but she is. I keep quiet 'bout that, she keeps quiet . . . well, 'bout some things I do. Anyway, she said you were cool, so I guess I can tell you she's at the library, only if you go there to tell her you want the ring and she's with Randy, don't tell my mom." He added darkly, "That would be *major* uncool."

Cory's tone implied being uncool was tantamount to complete personal downfall. "Don't worry—I won't. Do you have any idea where in the library she might be?"

"Hey, *I* never go there." Cory sounded appalled at the thought. "Shouldn't be too hard to find her, though," he added helpfully. "It's not like it's the New York Public Library. Hey, you ever see *Beneath the Planet of the Apes* where that guy finds the ruins of the New York library underground and it like freaks him out?"

"Well, yes, I've seen the movie several times—"

"And I really like the one where the apes come to Earth and they go on talk shows and then the woman has a baby ape and the scientists wanna take it—"

"Cory, I'm losing you," Rebecca yelled, finally glad for the static. "Thanks for your help."

Good Lord, she thought. Would the country someday be run by the Corys of the world? If so, it wouldn't be long until the apes *did* take over.

So Sonia probably was at the library. At least she knew where the girl was. The bad thing was that she also knew her vision was accurate. Someone was watching Sonia, biding his time.

A light turned red and she nearly rear-ended a gigantic Explorer in front of her. Rebecca saw the driver glare at her in his rearview mirror before the sport utility vehicle went fuzzy. Her heart speeded up. She felt her body heat increasing.

The young man sitting near Sonia closed a book, put it with two others on the table, and stuck his pen in his shirt pocket. He smiled tentatively at Sonia, but she wasn't paying attention. *Loser*, the watcher thought. The guy hesitated, picked up the books, and walked around the table, casting one more hopeful look at Sonia, who was now writing furiously. He walked past the watcher without so much as a glance.

A horn blasted behind Rebecca. She snapped back to her immediate surroundings to see the Explorer four car lengths ahead of her. That's great, she thought. With time so crucial, she was sitting through a green light.

Fourth Avenue. The library was five minutes away. Sonia could be killed in five minutes. Once more Rebecca punched in Molly's phone number. Once more she got a busy signal. Calling the police again was useless. The library. Send someone on the staff in search of Sonia, Rebecca thought. The watcher certainly wouldn't attack two people, even if both were unarmed. She called directory assistance, then the library. The phone rang three times before an officious male voice said, "Sinclair Library. May I help you?"

"Yes. Thank God." No, she must not sound frantic. Rebecca took a breath. "A girl is at the library. It's very important that she be brought to the main desk. She's about eighteen and slender with long black hair. Very pretty."

"I see. Has there been an accident? Are you calling to give her bad news?"

"No. I mean yes. I must speak with her. It's urgent."

"Oh, I'm sure it is."

"What?"

"You are referring to Sonia Ellis. I know who you are— Kelly Keene. You've tracked her to this library before, trying to badger her with your insulting questions, and she as well as her mother instructed me to keep you away from her. Now, Ms. Keene, I consider Sonia a very fine young woman. Polite. *Quiet.* I will not have her bothered, and I resent your using this clumsy trick to get to her. Do you think I'm stupid?"

Yes, I think you're a self-important idiot, Rebecca thought angrily. "This is not a trick—"

"Not working, ma'am. Try your cheap reporter's tactics on someone more gullible."

The phone clicked in her ear. What a wonderful protector Sonia had chosen. But Rebecca had already gotten a taste of Kelly Keene's persistence. No wonder Sonia was trying everything to escape her and still live a normal life. But of all the horrible luck. Or maybe it wasn't luck. Maybe Rebecca was just fated to see disastrous circumstances and be unable to do anything about them.

The thunderclouds that had frightened Sean earlier now rolled directly overhead, billowing ominously across a grayish yellow sky. Normally it would not be this dark for another hour. Wind swept along the streets, sending birds soaring for cover.

Rebecca made a right turn onto a less busy side street that led to the Ohio River. The Ohio was wide here at Sinclair, nearly a quarter of a mile, and the wind was now so strong it had whipped up whitecaps that beat at the sides of laden coal barges being pushed by a towboat.

Rebecca slowed the car when her sight began to blur again. Once more she saw a translucent image imposed over the real world around her. She saw the river. She saw a wooden raft with merry passengers drifting on the sun-dappled water as the raft neared a log cabin placed improbably close to the shore. Beautiful blue-green hills loomed above the cabin and an eagle floated against an azure sky.

What on earth was this? Rebecca wondered as she struggled to see through the image and keep the car under control. What did this fairy-tale scene have to do with Sonia? It couldn't be real. It had the quality of a painting.

Or a mural. Abruptly the image faded as Rebecca remembered the idyllic, amateurish mural on the wall of the library's third-floor "Pioneer Room." She was still seeing through the watcher's eyes, eyes trained momentarily on the mural, eyes that were giving her Sonia's location.

Rebecca turned right onto First Avenue, which ran parallel to the river. Now the water churned, looking dark and depthless as the evening deepened to slate and lightning glowed wickedly in the depths of the huge clouds.

She raced down one block, then the library abruptly popped into view. Built shortly after the turn of the century, the place had been designed by an architect with a love of the gothic. It brooded, a dull gray stone monster with too much ornate detailing and too few windows. Rebecca used to think the only thing it lacked were gargoyles glowering from the roof.

The parking lot was nearly empty. She spun into a handicap spot nearest the front doors, sprinted from the car and up the steps, and burst into the main room of the library. Behind the main desk stood an impeccably groomed middle-aged man whose jaw dropped when she yelled, "Call the police! Send someone to the Pioneer Room!"

"What the—what are you—ma'am, stop! Stop!"

"Call the police!" Rebecca shouted frantically. "Someone is going to be murdered. *Do* it!"

"Are you crazy?" the man blustered. "Stop! I said—"

Rebecca ignored the elevator, remembering that it moved with the speed of a glacier. She rushed for the stairs, taking them two at a time. When she reached the second floor she nearly fell as the landing disappeared into the

perspective of Sonia's watcher. Sonia stretched, looked
around, glanced at her watch, then swept her long hair over
her shoulder, exposing a tender white neck before she again
bent over her book. *Easy prey*, her watcher thought before
drawing closer to the girl. Closer, closer . . .

"Sonia!" Rebecca screamed as the girl's image faded.
"Sonia, get *out*!"

If the girl responded in any way, Rebecca couldn't see
her. The landing and the next set of stairs came into focus
again. She felt chilled and feverish at the same time. She
also felt dizzy, as if she might pass out, but she pushed
ahead, bolting up the steps without looking down at her
feet.

Do it now. The watcher's thoughts beat in Rebecca's
mind. *Hurry. She's lifting her head.*

Rebecca mentally saw the room. She watched a hand
extend something toward Sonia, saw the girl begin to turn
her head just as a metal object touched her neck, then crackled softly, emitting blue light. Sonia gasped, then tumbled
out of her chair. A stun gun, Rebecca thought. Sonia's as-
sailant didn't want any screams. He wanted an unconscious
victim before the hideous work of murder.

Rebecca burst into the room and gasped as a figure in
jeans and a hooded black nylon windbreaker rose from
Sonia. Keeping his head down, the watcher surged past
Rebecca toward the light switches in a swift, animal-like
movement. The fluorescent tubes went dark. The only light
in the room flowed through two high, narrow windows.

Rebecca heard the faint sound of many voices shouting,
but it seemed to be coming from far below. No doubt the
librarian was still standing behind his counter uselessly
squawking and fluttering. Maybe someone with a cooler
head had called the police, although she heard no sound of
feet pounding up the stairs or the elevator creaking, slow
but relentless.

Rebecca's lungs didn't want to pull in deep breaths.
Quick, shallow ones were all she could manage, making
her heart beat faster. She was afraid she would hyperven-

tilate and pass out. She dropped to her knees, out of the glow of the weak pre-storm light coming through the narrow window. She knew the watcher could not be in the process of killing Sonia. He'd wasted precious moments diving for the light switch. Besides, she could feel him lingering behind her. She had to reach Sonia before he returned to the girl's unconscious form. Rebecca had no doubt he would attack both of them, but killing her would not be as easy a task as murdering Sonia. She was alert and strong, unless he took her by surprise and managed to zap her with the stun gun just as he had Sonia.

Rebecca went still for a moment, trying to get her bearings. She crouched between Sonia and the door leading from the Pioneer Room. As best as she could remember, the room was about 500 square feet. The size was daunting until you realized how many bookcases and display cases filled with local artifacts occupied the area.

She heard a slight shuffling movement that seemed to be coming from where Sonia lay. Rebecca dropped prone from the crouch and slithered closer to Sonia. By now rain was lashing against the narrow windows. Where in the name of God were the battalions of police that should be rescuing them? Had that twit behind the counter even called anyone? If *he* hadn't, certainly someone else would have, thinking a lunatic was loose in the form of Rebecca.

All this time she'd been creeping toward Sonia, feeling the watcher keeping track of her movements. At last she touched a spill of silky hair spread on the carpet. She drew nearer to Sonia, wondering what she would do if she were attacked. She had no weapon. Except her own body. And she had her wits. She wasn't stupid or a coward.

She wished she had a gun.

Rebecca reclined on her side, gently sheltering Sonia's body. She didn't want to put her full weight on the girl because she didn't know how much damage had been done to Sonia's neck by the stun gun. Each breath she drew seemed long and noisy.

And then the watcher was there. Rebecca felt body heat,

heard heavy breathing, smelled some kind of fabric softener from jeans. Her heart was a frozen thing in her chest, but her mind was working at top speed. "Is someone there?" she asked pitifully. She sounded weak and terrified. She felt strong and determined. "Please don't hurt us. I didn't see anything."

"Seeing. That's the key, isn't it, Rebecca?" somebody whispered. "You don't have to see with your eyes to *see*. That's what makes you so dangerous."

"Oh, no, *please*." She added a pathetic tremble to her voice. "I'm only twenty-six . . ."

In the weak light she was still able to see the outline of a dull metal object nearing her neck. The stun gun.

Rebecca's strong right leg shot out as she grunted to give herself more force. The heel of her shoe connected with something. Not something as soft as a crotch, but perhaps the inside of a thigh. The watcher yelped, emitting a guttural curse. Finally people began pounding on the door to the Pioneer Room. Of course the watcher had locked it after turning off the lights. "Help!" Rebecca screamed. "Break down the door!"

A hand closed around her neck, pinning her to the floor. The threat of the stun gun terrified her. She could be shocked into unconsciousness and killed in seconds. Rebecca kicked again, making no connection. She kept her hands rigidly by her sides, knowing flailing them would make them easy targets for the stun gun.

Then a weight lowered itself over her. Good God, was she going to be raped before being killed? Raped with a crowd right outside, a crowd who shouted and pounded ineffectually while the overgroomed nitwit librarian searched for a key? That would give this sick twit a thrill, wouldn't it? Silencing her and Sonia would be the main objective. A brutal rape would be an added attraction.

But no one tore at her clothes. No one ground a crotch against her in simulated sex. Rebecca felt only fingers caressing her neck, breath in her ear, contained lust mixed with panic. Rebecca moved beyond fear to revulsion.

Sonia groaned at the same moment glass shattered explosively and voices grew louder. "Are you all right in there? The police are here. Dozens of them!"

A familiar, slightly nasal male adolescent voice. Rebecca knew that voice. Cory Ellis, Sonia's younger brother. "We broke out all the glass in the door. We're comin' in! I'm unlocking it! Listen, you son of a bitch, you leave my sister alone!"

"Get out of the way, son," a deep male voice commanded, then repeated Cory's words. "We're coming in!"

Oppressive weight rolled off Rebecca. Then a hand slapped the side of her face so hard she felt her teeth loosen. "Bitch! Always ruining everything!" The watcher grabbed her wrist and she felt a slight tug on the tender underside. Then the other. All within seconds. The watcher moved away from her. The Pioneer Room door flew back and hit the wall. More glass shattered and she closed her eyes against a burst of fluorescent light. Trying to untangle the jumble of voices, she heard someone yell, "Goddammit, he's gone!"

Finally Rebecca fainted.

CHAPTER TWELVE

1

Rebecca and Sonia shared an ambulance although Rebecca felt perfectly capable of driving herself to the hospital. "Is she going to be all right?" Rebecca asked a paramedic as she stared over at Sonia's parchment-white face and closed eyes.

"Blood pressure and heartbeat are normal. She's got a couple of nasty places where that damned stun gun burned her neck. Delicate skin there." The blond female ambulance attendant looked at her. "You didn't get a look at the creep who did this?"

"No, I didn't."

"I see. Last time I hauled you in, you claimed to be blind. Guess you can't use that as an excuse this time."

Finally Rebecca recognized the voice. The woman who'd been so sharp with her after her wreck at Dormaine's. She'd clearly thought Rebecca had plowed her car into the tree because she was drunk. She rose and started toward Sonia.

"Sit down, ma'am. You're dripping blood all over my rig."

Rebecca looked down at her arms. The tugs on her wrists before the watcher had run. He'd cut them. "If I'm dripping blood, why don't you put better dressings on me?" Rebecca snapped.

"They'll do that at the hospital. You just chill out and quit making such a fuss."

"I am not making a fuss," Rebecca started, then shut up. The woman didn't like her. Nothing she said would make a difference.

By the time they reached the hospital, Rebecca felt dizzy. She stumbled out of the ambulance and someone came to help her. Before she could see his face, however, she passed out. When she awakened, she was in an examining room. A nurse's face was about three inches away, and blurry. Rebecca almost screamed before the woman said, "It's all right, sweetheart. You're safe at the hospital."

"Where's Sonia?" Rebecca demanded.

"Being treated by Dr. Bellamy. My name is Myra. Myra Kessel. I don't usually work the emergency room, but we're doing a landslide business tonight." She took Rebecca's hand. "You really are all right, Miss Ryan. Just cuts on the wrists. Not as deep as they could be, but you've lost some blood."

"People will think I tried to commit suicide."

Myra smiled, a dozen laugh lines shooting out from her warm brown eyes. "People think you're a hero."

"But I'm not. Sonia's hurt . . ."

"Sonia is alive thanks to you. Now I want you to lie back and rest. We're keeping your arms elevated and a physician's assistant is going to suture those wrists for you."

"Okay." Rebecca was suddenly dizzy again and lay back, closing her eyes against the bright light. The last hour seemed unreal. She still couldn't quite comprehend what had happened. But the nurse had said Sonia was alive. That's what mattered.

"Sonia's brother," she said as the nurse prepared a suture tray. "He was at the library, Mrs. Kessel. Is he here now?"

"My name is Myra to heroes, and yes he is."

"What about Mrs. Ellis?"

"We haven't been able to locate her. The brother said she was at choir practice but when they called the church, no one had seen her." She smiled. "But your father is here. Would you like to see him?"

"He's my stepfather," Rebecca said, "and I'd love to see him."

"All right. On the condition that you lay down that pretty head and quit worrying. I told you everything is fine now. I'll be right back."

Everything is fine now. The words echoed in Rebecca's

head. Everything was fine except that someone tried to murder a seventeen-year-old girl. Someone would have murdered her, too, if Cory Ellis hadn't led the charge to break down the library door. Yes, everything is just dandy, Rebecca thought, except that there was a murderer on the loose.

Frank rushed into the examining room looking as if every drop of blood had drained from his face. His hazel eyes were too wide and for once his black-and-silver hair was askew. He stood beside her, touched her forehead, and muttered, "Good God, Rebecca. Are you all right?"

"I think physically I'm okay. Psychologically I'm not so sure. I just can't believe what's happened, Frank. This is more bizarre than anything I could think up for a book. I guess Mother isn't here."

Frank still looked nonplussed but he answered calmly. "You know she wasn't well at dinner. I didn't even tell her what happened because she wasn't up to coming . . ."

"You mean she's still drunk. Well, that's okay. I've heard Mrs. Ellis isn't here, either. Not at choir practice where she's supposed to be."

At last Frank smiled. "Because you're hurt, I'll tell you a piece of juicy gossip to cheer you up. I think Mrs. Ellis has been fibbing about going to choir practice. I'm fairly sure she's having an affair."

Rebecca feigned deep shock. "The *minister's* widow?"

Frank nodded solemnly. "They're the worst kind. I'm drawing conclusions, but in the last three months she's lost about ten pounds, started wearing makeup, and been perkier than I've seen her for years. She's really quite an attractive woman now."

"You should have been a detective, Frank. Does Cory know?"

"Certainly not. And I'm in a quandary. He's not only upset about his sister, he's worried about his missing mother although he's trying to hide it. I'm sure she hasn't told the children about a man in her life because she's so uptight. So if I tell Cory to put his mind at ease, I expose her horrible secret."

Rebecca grinned. "You're clever enough to come up with some excuse for her that will calm Cory. But tell him something fast. It's awful to let him think something bad might have happened to his mother after what did happen to Sonia."

"You're right. I said you were wise." He sobered. "Dear, how on earth did you know to go to the library to save Sonia?"

"She told me she was going to the library. Then I got a vision of someone lurking around, planning to kill her. I know you don't believe in my visions, but—"

"I'm fast becoming a believer. I'm sorry I doubted you all these years."

"It never bothered me. Really. But I do have them and I have to live with them."

"And thanks to you, Sonia will live as well." He sighed. "Since her mother isn't here, I think I should play surrogate father. Do you mind if I leave you for a few minutes to check on her?"

"I'm frantic to know how she is. Please look after her, Frank. She needs someone strong."

As he left the room, Rebecca felt sad for him. After Patrick died, Frank had been strong for Suzanne. Rebecca didn't know what would have happened to her mother without him. Then he'd been strong for her again after the death of Jonnie. And he'd always been strong for Rebecca, too, supporting her decision to go to New Orleans, even making the first trip with her and staying a couple of days until she got settled. She remembered their visit to the French Quarter and the lovely dinners he'd treated her to. And she remembered the money he'd pressed on her, insisting that she eat well and try to have some fun. After all, she wouldn't come into her trust fund until she was 21. She shouldn't have to wait until then for pretty clothes and a trip over spring break.

Then he'd been strong for Molly when she gave birth

to Todd. And now he was stepping in with Sonia. Being the rock seemed to be his lot in life, and Rebecca was certain the strain was showing. Frank looked older, his movements were slower, and some of the sparkle had gone from his fine eyes. He didn't even smile as easily. She suddenly felt angry with her mother for not being kinder to him.

And then she was out again. Just like a light that had been flipped off. When she awakened, she was covered with an extra blanket and a young man was suturing her wrist. "What happened?" she asked in a blurry voice.

"You passed out again. You've been through a lot, Miss Ryan. Do your arms hurt?"

"I'm not aware I even have arms."

He smiled. "You have two good ones. And I'm going to suture them so well you'll barely have scars. I'm a master of sutures."

"Clay Bellamy says he's the master of sutures."

"So *he* thinks." The young man grinned. "I'm kidding. You can do that with him. Joke around, I mean. Some doctors think they're God on high. Not Doc Bellamy. Anyway, he's been in twice to check on you. He'll be back. And that Ellis kid wants to see you."

"Sonia?"

"No, the brother. You don't have to see him."

"I'd like to, really. When you finish, would you send him in?"

Shortly afterward a reed-thin boy of around fourteen with shaggy black hair and acne crept into the examining room. He wore baggy jeans that looked ready to slide off his nonexistent hips and a Megadeth T-shirt. Sonia was a beauty. Cory reminded Rebecca of Ichabod Crane with his long neck, prominent Adam's apple, and huge darting eyes. "So how're you doin'?" he asked.

"Fine, thanks to you," Rebecca said. "You broke down that door to the Pioneer Room."

"The glass was double-paned with wire mesh in the middle of the panes."

"Heavy security. I guess the library board is afraid some-one will break in and steal those flint arrowheads in the display cases, as if you can't find one buried in the ground every six inches in this area." Cory's laugh emerged as a two-octave squawk. He blushed furiously and shuffled his feet. "Why did you come to the library, Cory? You didn't seem worried about Sonia when I called."

"I wasn't then, but after I got off the phone I got this weird vibe about her. I mean, she keeps talkin' about no-body believin' her about how the kidnappin' went down. I mean, about that nurse bein' home when she said she wasn't. And you sounded funny—funny creepy, not funny ha-ha. Then I started thinkin' about the *Planet of the Apes* movies."

Rebecca stared at him, baffled. "What did *Planet of the Apes* have to do with anything?"

"Well, in the movies things weren't what they seemed to be and you understood and didn't think they were stupid so maybe you see what's underneath the surface." This maze of logic escaped Rebecca but she nodded. "Then I talked to someone who knows you and they said you have ESP. That is *so* cool, so *X-Files*. I think maybe I have it, too. What do you think?"

"I don't know," Rebecca said faintly.

"But if I have it, looks like I'd know where my mom is," Cory said, clearly disturbed by the absence of his mother although he was hiding his anxiety under chatter about ESP. "I mean, she never misses choir practice. But she hasn't made Sonia and me go to church every Sunday lately. Maybe that means somethin'."

Maybe it means she hasn't been at choir practice so she can't be in the choir on Sunday and you'll want to know why if you attend services, Rebecca thought. "I believe Frank—Mr. Hardison, your mother's boss—might have an idea about where your mother could be. Why don't you talk to him?"

"Why would he know where she is?" Cory asked, his voice jumping again. "You think she might lose her job?"

"No, I'm sure she won't. He thinks very highly of her." And I am exhausted, Rebecca thought.

"Oh, it's your ESP," Cory said excitedly. "You know that *he* knows. This is just *too* cool. I gotta work on mine, sharpen it up." Rebecca smiled wanly. "I'll go find Mr. Hardison right now. Hope you feel better. And thanks for savin' Sonia. I mean, sometimes she's a real pain, but I wouldn't want her to die or anything."

With this eloquent expression of sentiment for his sister, Cory dashed from the examining room. Rebecca sighed in relief, then smiled at Cory's excitement over his possible ESP. He didn't know what he was hoping for.

Clay arrived after what seemed an interminable time. He, too, looked pale and worried, but he tried to joke. "Is it possible to keep you out of trouble?"

"I don't think so."

"I've gotten a dozen jumbled stories about what happened. Promise to give me the true version later?"

"I promise, but it was bizarre even for a weirdo like me. How's Sonia?"

"A couple of burns from that stun gun. A concussion. Some pulled ligaments in her neck. Mostly shock. Her mother finally arrived and that seemed to soothe her. Naturally she'll be here for the night so we can run more tests."

"I'm so relieved about her. When do I get to go home?"

"Tomorrow."

"What? Why not tonight?"

"Because whether or not you want to admit it, you're not Superwoman. You've put in one hell of a week and it's drained you. You fainted twice. Once you were on the verge of going into shock."

"I hate hospitals, Clay."

"I'm sorry, but you'll have to be a big girl and bear it. I'll give you something to help you sleep and first thing you know, it'll be morning and you'll be going home."

"Can you smuggle in Sean?"

"Not without causing yet another scandal." He lifted her

wrist. "Pretty soon you're going to be completely held together by sutures."

Rebecca frowned. "The watcher wasn't trying to kill me."

"The watcher?"

"I could see through his eyes so that's how I thought of him. Or her. Anyway, the purpose of these cuts wasn't to murder me. I don't understand why he did it."

"He was trying to brand you."

"Brand me?" Clay nodded. "Here I thought you were going to be a private investigator and now you're a criminal profiler."

"I admit that my talents are legion." Clay said solemnly. He was trying to sound light, but his eyes were dark with worry. "I don't know how I came up with the branding theory, but it feels right. You're correct—he certainly couldn't have been trying to kill you by severing surface vessels. The cuts aren't even deep enough to injure tendons and ligaments and cause permanent harm, thank God. But there will be scars."

"I told that nice nurse Myra Kessel that people would think I tried to kill myself."

"Exactly. They're scars that will make you self-conscious, something you'll try to hide, try to explain if they're spotted. They'll make you *look* suicidal, unstable. So maybe it's a punishment for screwing up a murder attempt."

"Wow, you're deep. I had no idea."

"I try to hide my astounding perceptiveness beneath boyish charm."

"You do an excellent job."

"Well, I see you're back to normal. I was afraid you'd come out of this all serious and sweet." He cast her a sideways look. "Maybe even in love with me?"

"I think I'm going to faint again," Rebecca said and closed her eyes, smiling.

2

Bill and G. C. Curry stood on the front porch of Jean Wright's house, ringing the bell for the third time. For the first time in days the news van was not sitting across the street. Tonight it was parked at the hospital, with the omnipresent Kelly Keene prowling the halls trying to get information about the attack on Sonia Ellis.

A Siamese cat with incredible blue eyes leaped up on the windowsill and looked out at them. "The cat Sonia said she saw Jean Wright take in the night Todd was kidnapped," Bill said.

"Sonia didn't say she saw *Wright* take the cat inside," Curry corrected politely. "She said she saw *someone* take in the cat."

"Someone with short dark hair, nurse's shoes, and Wright's voice. I wish I'd paid more attention to the girl when she first told me."

"No sign of Jean?" a female voice asked.

Bill almost jumped and hoped Curry hadn't noticed. Molly had slipped silently through the darkened yards and stood at the foot of the porch steps. "No lights. Door's locked. And you said you haven't seen her since when?"

"Around six. Maybe a little after. She got a call. She said it was her sister, who needed her to come to the university. Jean didn't say what the trouble was, but she seemed awfully upset. She apologized for leaving me alone, rushed over here and packed, and was gone in half an hour." She glanced at the window. "I hope she remembered to put out plenty of food and water for Sabu."

Bill and Curry didn't have a search warrant and didn't have enough evidence to get one from the notoriously cautious Judge Burberry, who was the only judge available tonight. But if Molly needed to get inside to check on the poor cat . . .

"Molly, do you have a key to Jean's place?" Bill asked casually.

"Sure. We look after each other's houses when we're on vacations. Why?"

"You seem concerned about the cat. Hate to see it starve to death or suffer from dehydration. You might want to go in and check on it."

"Oh, that's a good idea!" Molly exclaimed.

"Curry and I will go in with you. Don't want you caught outside here with all these damned reporters and sight-seers." Molly looked at the empty street. "They could show up any minute," Bill said. "You know how that Keene woman is."

"You're right. I'll be back in a minute with the key. You're an angel, Bill."

"Saint Bill," Curry muttered as Molly hurried across the lawn to her house.

"I feel like sinking straight down in the ground where I belong. I shouldn't be tricking her this way."

"She won't mind if we find out something that might help us get Todd back."

"The only problem is that without a warrant, nothing we find will stand up in court."

"You'll think of a way around that," Curry said and grinned in the darkness. "You're a lot cagier than I realized."

"I'm going to take that as a compliment. Here she comes."

Molly unlocked the door and reached for the light switch. Two lamps snapped to life, the cat fled yowling from the living room, and Molly moaned. "I hope Jean closed the cat door. Otherwise Sabu will carry on all night in the backyard."

The cat making a racket in the backyard. Just like Sonia had said. Bill and Curry exchanged glances. "I'll help you look for him," Curry said. "Then we'll check out the food and water situation."

Molly smiled her thanks. Bill knew Curry was trying to

keep Molly diverted while he did a little illegal poking around.

The house's aged furnishings were almost pathetic. The carpet was worn through in places; and although Bill was no expert about interior design, the couch and chairs looked like they dated from the early seventies. Metal television trays substituted for end tables. Above an unused fireplace hung an oil painting of a boy and girl around twelve years old. The famous spoiled twins Clay had told him about, Bill thought. They were both dark-haired and dark-eyed like Jean and already had superior expressions Bill didn't like. We're special and the world owes us, they seemed to be thinking.

"Why, all Jean left out for Sabu was half a handful of dry food and about an eighth of an inch of water!" Molly declared from the kitchen. "She said she wouldn't be back for a couple of days. This cat weights twelve pounds. He can't exist comfortably on this for two days. I can't believe it! She loves Sabu!"

"Maybe she was flustered over some emergency," Curry was saying.

"Or counting on me to look after him. Not that I mind, but for all Jean knew I might have been too distracted by my own problems to think about Sabu!"

"Well, thank goodness you weren't!"

Bill smiled. Curry sounded sincere and outraged when Bill knew he didn't care that much about the cat. "Want me to look for canned cat food? And how about milk? Is Sabu a milk-drinker?"

With tenderhearted Molly fussing over the cat who was playing his neglected state to the hilt, Bill was free to wander down the hall. Two small bedrooms, too orderly to be recently occupied. One had a green-and-tan quilt on the bed and a poster Creed on the wall. The other room's bed had a frilly white spread; a large framed photo of a dark-haired girl jumping in a cheerleader outfit, her skirt flying up to show her underpants as she smirked at the camera, no doubt thinking she looked sexier than she did, hung on the wall.

The third bedroom clearly belonged to Jean. A pale blue spread covered the bed and a white heart-shaped decorative pillow rested against the bed pillows. A small glass lamp with a cheap shade sat on a slightly scarred oak nightstand. An array of drugstore colognes and lipsticks sat on a dresser along with five jasmine-scented candles that had recently been lit.

Bill quietly opened the closet door. Pristine nurse's uniforms. Three pairs of wool slacks, two cotton, a navy blue suit, several synthetic sweaters, the requisite simple black dress. Two pairs of nurse's shoes, loafers, a pair of black heels and a pair of white heels, both in Payless boxes. Everything in the closet was presentable but cheap. Bill knew about women's clothes because his ex-wife had lived for them. During their short marriage, she'd maxed out his credit cards on beautiful outfits she had nowhere to wear. What he also noticed in Miss Wright's closet was the absence of jeans, T-shirts, and sneakers. He knew she owned some—he'd seen her wear them. She must have taken them with her.

He paused and listened. "Maybe I should take Sabu home with me," Molly was saying. "He might be lonely."

"You might just disturb his routine. Cats are particular about litter boxes and all," Curry said seriously. "Hey, do you think Jean changed the litter? Smells a little strong to me. Let's get to work on that."

Bill almost laughed. This was above the call of duty. Curry deserved a raise. He'd bought Bill a little more time.

He opened one of Jean's dresser drawers. Three pairs of underpants and one bra. Certainly she owned more undergarments than this. In another he was surprised to see a couple of sexy negligees, a blue low-cut nightgown and a white teddy. He had difficulty picturing stern-faced Jean in a teddy. But her lack of attractiveness was the result of demeanor, not poor features or body. Perhaps in these clothes . . .

"Oh look, he's using the new litter already!" Molly

trilled from the kitchen. "Thank you for taking that horrible stinky stuff out to the trash, Deputy Curry."

This time Curry didn't answer and the screen door slammed with unnecessary force. Bill snickered and turned to the small desk by the window. First he found a scrawled note from a girl named Wendy asking for the money to buy a "to die for" bikini. That had to be the ex-cheerleader. Next he discovered an index card bearing a phone number with no identifying name. That should be easy to track down. At the bottom of a drawer lay a letter from the bank threatening to repossess Jean's small car for her missing two payments. Next he discovered three credit card bills. She'd overstepped her credit limits, missed her last two payments on all three, and as punishment was facing substantially increased interest rates.

Bill jotted down the phone number and replaced the bills. Jean Wright was in financial trouble. Jean Wright had been acting strange all year and been forced to take a leave of absence from her job. Jean Wright claimed to have been gone when Todd Ryan was kidnapped. The girl who'd insisted Jean was lying had been attacked with intent to kill. And now Jean Wright had fled. Maybe there truly had been a family emergency. He needed to check out that, too.

Bill was about to leave the bedroom when his gaze fell on a cheap stereo system tucked behind the door. If the door had been completely open, he would never have seen it. Clearly it was meant to be played in private. Maybe with the candles burning and Jean in her teddy, Bill thought. Out of curiosity he glanced over the various buttons and dials. He turned it on and opened the cassette player. Empty. Then he punched the button that controlled the compact disc player. The CD drawer slid out and Bill's lips parted in shock.

Jean had been listening to Procol Harum's "A Whiter Shade of Pale."

CHAPTER THIRTEEN

1

Rebecca's night was miserable. Anyone who expected to get rest in a hospital was crazy. The elderly lady in the room next door had screamed constantly that she was being raped. She'd been sedated, but she continued to mutter, fighting off an imaginary man who first wanted to hurt her, then wanted to lustfully possess her shriveled body.

The nurses kept up a steady chatter at their station. One was elated because she was dating a doctor. Another was depressed because she was pregnant. Two other nurses repeated with relish stories of horrible deliveries that elicited shrill squeals of dread from the pregnant one. Every time Rebecca started to drift into sleep despite the noise, a nurse entered the room to ask if she were comfortable.

By morning Rebecca was exhausted and irritable. When Clay showed up she snapped, "What do you want to do with me now? Operate on my brain to find out why I have ESP?"

"Had a pleasant night, did you?" Clay asked amiably. "If you don't sweeten your tone, young lady, you'll be leaving here without a lollipop."

"Am I ever going to leave?"

"You're too mean to stay and I can't think of any more tests to run. Of course if I really put my mind to it, I can probably come up with a few new tortures."

"Please don't tax your brain on my account. How's Sonia?"

"Physically fine. Emotionally a little rocky. She'd like to see you before you go."

"I want to see her, too. I should have gotten to the library sooner."

Clay shook his head. "After that spectacular feat you

pulled off to save her life, you're still not satisfied."

"I'll feel better when I get home."

"Which will be soon. I'm taking you."

"Don't you have to work?"

"I pulled a twenty-four-hour shift. I get the day off to recover."

Had Clay stayed all night because of her? Rebecca wondered. Of course not. How egotistical. He'd stayed because of Sonia. Still, she was glad he would be taking her home even though she could easily have gotten a cab.

Thirty minutes later she was showered and dressed. With no makeup, no hot rollers to smooth her hair into some kind of shape, and only the rumpled clothes she'd worn last night, she knew she looked like she'd had a particularly raucous night at Mardi Gras, but there was nothing to be done for it.

Before she left the hospital, Rebecca briefly dropped in on Sonia. The girl looked wan and shocked but said the doctors had assured her she'd be fine.

"Your brother pulled off some real heroics to save you," Rebecca said.

Sonia managed a smile. "Isn't that the weirdest thing? Cory, a hero. He rode his bike to the hospital, of all things. I don't picture heroes riding bikes."

"I guess they come in all forms, even skinny fourteen-year-olds."

"Yeah." Sonia bit her lip, then motioned Rebecca closer to the bed. "I have no right to ask a favor of you after what you did last night, but—"

"Sonia, I can't call up visions at will." Sonia looked puzzled. "I don't know who attacked you and I can't go home and just conjure up his face."

"Oh, I don't expect you to find the killer. I don't even want you to try. He might kill *you*." She frowned. "It's Randy I'm worried about. Randy Messer, my boyfriend. Everybody's down on him and I'm afraid they're going to blame this on him."

Rebecca looked at her steadily. "Sonia, are you certain

Randy didn't have anything to do with Todd's kidnapping or the attack on you?"

"Absolutely certain!" Sonia replied fiercely. "But the police have already questioned him. And now, after this—" Her eyes filled with tears. "I haven't heard from him and I know it's because he's afraid. Could you maybe locate him? Maybe find some way to tell him that I'm okay and I love him and everything is going to be all right?"

Rebecca hesitated. Sonia was only seventeen. Randy Messer didn't have the greatest reputation in town. And Sonia's mother didn't want her to see him, or even talk to him on the phone. But Sonia looked so sure of his innocence, so desperate to protect and comfort him . . .

"I can't make any promises," Rebecca said gently. "But I'll do what I can."

2

"Beautiful day, isn't it?"

"I wouldn't care if we were having the worst snowstorm of the century," Rebecca said, looking out the car window. "I'm just glad to be going home."

Clay smiled. "No one ever claimed the hospital offered four-star accommodations."

"I would have been thrilled with a third of a star. It seems to me people would recover best in a restful environment."

"I'll speak to the concierge," Clay said. "We'll try to do better, your ladyship."

Rebecca burst into laughter. "I'm being bitchy, aren't I?"

"Choleric, grumpy, peevish, irascible. Not bitchy."

"Thank you. And I'm going to start consulting you instead of a thesaurus."

"Does that mean I get to help write the next book?"

"If there is one. I'm not making much progress. I've haven't written one sentence of the synopsis of my second book. I haven't even *thought* about it. I'll never get another contract. I'll probably be a one-book writer."

"Please stop," Clay said shakily. "I'm going to cry."

Rebecca almost laughed again. "I deserved that one. You don't let me get away with much."

"I suppose I should spoil you after what you've been through."

"Okay, then do me a favor." Clay looked at her. "We're about a quarter of a mile from Shady Mount Cemetery. Please stop there before you take me home."

"What for?"

"I want to check the family mausoleum."

Clay frowned. "Rebecca, I'm not teasing now. This seems a little morbid."

"When I was able to drift off to sleep a few times last night, I kept dreaming of Jonnie. He was at the mausoleum—"

"He *is* at the mausoleum."

"In the dream he was alive. He wanted to tell me something."

Clay sighed. "Oh, Becky, I don't know—"

"Clay, *please*. I promise I'm not cracking up. I know his ghost isn't going to be lurking around to pass on secret messages."

"Then what are you expecting?"

"Nothing. It's just that I haven't visited the mausoleum since I've been back. I feel a need to go there today and leave these flowers I bought in the gift shop before we left the hospital."

Clay seemed to relax. "Well, that doesn't sound bad. I guess it would be all right. But it's going to be a short visit."

Last night's storm seemed to have blown away all murkiness to leave a cool, saffron sun glowing in a sky the color of thistle. The air at Shady Mount smelled of flowers and new-mown grass, and a flock of robins strutted around inspecting the moist ground for hapless earthworms brought up by the rain.

"I'd forgotten how pretty it is out here," Clay said. "For a cemetery, that is."

"You don't find cemeteries pretty?"

"Depressing."

"Maybe. But they're a fact of life. The cemeteries in New Orleans look so different. There's one only a block from my house. There everyone is buried above ground because the city is below sea level."

"So mausoleums like the Ryans' aren't such an oddity."

"Well, I've never seen one quite like ours. It's sort of grand."

"And black."

Rebecca smiled. "Grandfather Ryan was rather dour. Only he would have chosen polished black granite. He was also a show-off."

"I'm not a connoisseur of mausoleums. Or graves. I don't like thinking what's going to happen after I die. Maybe it was cutting up all those cadavers in medical school." Rebecca made a face. "I'm going for cremation myself. Quicker. Space-saving. None of that nasty rotting stuff going on."

"Oh, Clay, that's so gross."

"Death is gross. You spend all your life trying to learn, trying to better yourself, then you drop dead and become food for the worms." He paused. "I'm not making you feel a whole lot better about visiting the family mausoleum, am I?"

"I'm trying not to listen to you."

"When I turn philosophical, that's usually wise."

"I didn't find your pronouncements deeply philosophical. Just creepy."

"I never claimed to be Plato or one of those guys who sat around and thought all day. I'm just a poor working slob." He slowed. "Well, here we are at the Ryan shrine to the dead. I feel like we're standing in front of the Taj Mahal."

"I think we're supposed to." Rebecca walked up the

steps and pulled the handle on the wrought-iron door. "Damn, I forgot the place is kept locked."

Rebecca looked down at the slender bouquet of six red roses she'd found in the gift shop. When she bought them, she hadn't noticed the "Get Well Soon" written in gold on the white ribbon. She could be guilty of bad taste and leave on the ribbon, or take it off and have the roses scatter in the bronze vase mounted on the wall of the mausoleum. She opted for bad taste.

"No prayers?" Clay asked as she turned away.

"I don't think the dead really need prayers. It's the living who need help." She frowned into the sun. "Here comes Mr. Hale."

Avram Hale walked briskly toward them, dressed in a suit and tie. He was in his late sixties, six-three with perfect posture, an African-American with startling white hair who had owned the cemetery for thirty years. He smiled and shook hands with Rebecca, who introduced him to Clay.

"Oh, one of that exclusive Bellamy clan." Mr. Hale grinned. "None of them buried here; have their own private cemetery out on the farm. But I'm sure you're a good fellow anyway."

Clay smiled. "Actually, I find the family cemetery downright scary-looking. I think I'd rather break with tradition and be buried here, sir, if that's all right."

Avram laughed softly. "That's fine with me, young man. Got a real pretty spot overlooking a little brook."

"He wants to be cremated," Rebecca said.

"That's all right, too. We'll just bury his urn. He'll take up less space that way." Mr. Hale looked at Rebecca. "You wanting to get in the mausoleum, Miss Ryan?"

"Rebecca, and yes, but I don't have my key."

"I could get mine, but it's back at the office and we're just about to begin a funeral for Skeeter Dobbs."

"Here?" Clay asked in surprise.

"Right over there." Mr. Hale gestured toward a small gathering of people standing near an oak tree. "Mr. Edgar Moreland is paying for his funeral. Now isn't that a nice thing? 'Course it's a real simple little service. Just Father Brennan saying a few words and my wife Chloe singing a hymn. Would you like to join us?"

Rebecca glanced down at the bandages on her wrists, suddenly self-conscious. "Oh, I don't think—"

"Yes, we would," Clay interrupted. "Come on, Rebecca. Let's say good-bye to Skeeter and hear Mrs. Hale sing."

Clay wasn't going to let her be embarrassed, to shy away from people as she had during her teenage years. He took her arm and walked to the graveside. The coffin was metal, which Rebecca knew was cheaper than wood, and topped with a blanket of daisies. Only three small baskets of flowers rested near the coffin. Five people stood in a group as if huddling for moral support. Rebecca didn't see Bill, but she had a feeling he was around. She recognized Edgar and Helen Moreland. Mr. Moreland had been in the accounting department of Grace Healthcare since her grandfather's reign.

Matilda Vinson looked small and frightened in a pale blue dress that hung on her. Her blue eyes kept darting at Rebecca, making her uncomfortable. The woman had found Skeeter's body, which would have been a shock. And she'd probably heard about the attack on Sonia at the library. Those incidents could account for her nervousness, but certainly not for the wildly haunted look in her eyes. Rebecca had known the older woman casually most of her life and she was certain Matilda was no timorous soul. Something had her spooked.

At the end of the service, Chloe Hale sang "Amazing Grace" in her rich voice. Tears filled Rebecca's eyes when she thought about long ago, before Skeeter was afraid of her, when she'd told him stories in the park about the constellations.

Chloe's voice soared through the clear air and Avram looked at her proudly. They had been married for forty years. Many people claimed Avram's great-great-grandfather had been a slave of Sinclair's founding family, the Lelands. Leland descendants hotly denied their ancestors would have ever sanctioned slavery. Avram wisely said nothing on the subject.

After the service Rebecca spoke briefly to the Morelands, complimented Mrs. Hale on her singing, and began to walk away from the grave. In a moment she felt cold fingers pluck at her upper arm. "Rebecca? May I speak with you?"

Rebecca turned around and looked down into the panicked eyes of Matilda Vinson. "Yes, Miss Vinson. What is it?"

"Well, I probably shouldn't trouble you with this. I know you've been through a lot. And maybe I'm exaggerating. Or even imagining. I just don't know anymore. These last few days have been so awful and—"

"Miss Vinson, please calm down and just tell me what's bothering you," Rebecca said kindly. "Would you be more comfortable talking to me alone?"

Miss Vinson glanced at Clay. "Well, I don't mean to be rude, but maybe that *would* be best."

"It's not rude at all," Clay said. "I'll just wait over here." He took a few steps away, fumbled in his pocket, and withdrew a peppermint drop, becoming deeply absorbed in unwrapping it.

Rebecca looked at Miss Vinson and said gently, "Please tell me what's bothering you."

Miss Vinson twisted her hands. She had short nails, no rings, and dry skin from constant washing. "I'm not a busybody. I believe in people minding their own business. I know other women my age who are bored and like stirring up trouble. Well, actually I haven't known many. But I'm not one." She took a deep breath and lightly patted her chest as if it felt tight. "I shouldn't tell you this unless I'm absolutely certain. But I'm mostly certain and I just can't live with it all anymore. I keep thinking if I'd said something earlier, Skeeter would be alive and if I keep quiet, maybe someone else will get killed . . ."

Sun and exhaustion and the trauma of last night's events were making Rebecca feel slightly dizzy. She had an urge to shake Matilda and yell, "Just say it!" Instead she smiled encouragingly. "I understand that you're trying to be precise, but please just tell me what's wrong."

"Yes. All right. I realize I'm babbling." She blinked rapidly. "It all started Saturday night. I saw someone in the window of Klein's attic—"

"Where Todd was?" Rebecca blurted.

"Yes. I didn't realize there was anything wrong at the time. I saw someone at the window, but the light was dim and the figure was in silhouette and I didn't really see clearly at *all*. I thought maybe it was Mr. Klein. But Skeeter saw something odd, too, and he went to the police and well, we don't know he was murdered because of what he saw, especially because he thought he saw his grandfather, the sweet, frustrating fool—Skeeter, not his grandfather. Anyway, maybe Skeeter *was* murdered by someone who thought he saw more than he did. Maybe the person in the attic killed Skeeter because he thought Skeeter could identify him, and in that case, he could think the same about me because I saw someone in the attic, too, only I *didn't* see a face!"

"But the person saw you?"

"Well . . . yes, I'm fairly certain. Someone came to the door of the drugstore and tried to get in. Stealthily, not like a regular customer. I reported it to the police, but that young deputy acted like I was an old fool and . . ." Matilda's voice came rapidly with no breaths between words. Rebecca was afraid she would hyperventilate. She also knew a clumsy response might stop Matilda from divulging things she felt were important but had been too frightened to tell Bill. Rebecca knew she had to get as many details as possible. She glanced at Clay and was relieved: She could tell he was listening intently, although he gave the impression of being completely absorbed in his candy and perusing the sky.

"Just slow down and take a deep breath," Rebecca said calmly. "You're probably getting all worked up over nothing. That's right. A slow, deep breath. Good." She placed a comforting arm around Matilda's thin shoulders. "Now go on."

"Last night," Matilda continued, "I suddenly remembered I hadn't returned two videos. *The English Patient* and *Titanic*. If I didn't turn them in before nine, I would have had to pay nearly five dollars in late fees! I left Lynn in charge and decided to take the shortcut through the alley that runs between the video store and the library—"

"The library?" Rebecca echoed.

"Yes. You know where I'm going with this, don't you? Well, I was just walking along, hurriedly, and then someone came charging down the alley, bumped right into me, nearly knocked me down—"

Matilda's gaze snapped to the right. The little bit of color left in her face fled and her pale lips parted.

"Miss Vinson?" Rebecca asked. "What's wrong?"

The woman's gaze remained fixed, her face frozen into a mask of pure fear. Rebecca turned to face the tiny chapel located at the top of a knoll about forty yards away. She saw a blur disappear behind the chapel, then nothing. "Miss Vinson?"

Matilda's throat muscles worked. Her breath grew even more rapid. She swayed. "Clay!" Rebecca called. He rushed toward her. "I think Miss Vinson is going to faint."

"Let me help you to this bench over here and take your pulse," Clay said calmly. "Then I want you to concentrate on breathing slowly and deeply. You're going to be fine."

"I have to go." Miss Vinson shook his hand off her arm. "I have to go!"

"But you're not well," Rebecca protested. "Please rest for a few minutes."

Matilda Vinson's eyes grew huge and terrified. "I have to go!" she shrilled.

"Miss Vinson, who did you see on the hill that scared you?" Rebecca pleaded. "Please tell us. There are two of us here—Clay and me. We'll protect you."

"I thought I'd be safe saying something out here in the open, but I'm not. Don't you dare try to keep me here!"

Her voice rose to a shout. "I don't even *know* you! I didn't see *anything*! What are you talking about?"

Rebecca drew back in surprise. Matilda tore away from her and Clay and nearly ran across the cemetery to the parking area.

Clay looked at Rebecca in astonishment. "What on earth was that about?"

"She claimed to have seen someone in Klein's Saturday night although she didn't recognize him. Then she said she'd been in the alley beside the library yesterday evening and someone came racing past her, nearly knocking her down—"

"She saw who attacked Sonia and you and escaped out the back way!"

"And I'm fairly certain she recognized him. Clay, I think she saw the person from the alley at the chapel."

"That's why she was yelling that she didn't know you or what you were talking about and that she didn't see anything. All for the benefit of the person hiding around the chapel." He frowned. "Or she saw Bill or a deputy sent to scope out the funeral."

"Should we go up and check out the area?"

"No, I'll do that," a voice said from behind them. Rebecca jumped, then turned to face Bill. "You might disturb evidence," he continued.

"Then neither you nor any of your people were at the chapel," Clay said.

Bill's jaw was tensed, his expression grim as he walked away from them toward the small, charming chapel. Rebecca shivered and Clay put his arm around her. Without thinking, she laid her head on his shoulder. "Clay, do you realize the person who attacked Sonia probably killed Skeeter and then had the nerve to come to his *funeral*? That's sick."

"Whoever killed Skeeter is sick." He sighed. "Let's just hope the next funeral out here isn't Matilda Vinson's."

Chapter Fourteen

1

Rebecca felt tired and shaken when she arrived home after the funeral. Sean greeted her joyously, jumping up to wrap his front legs around her waist and bathing her face in kisses when she lowered her head. "Oh, my beautiful boy!" Rebecca crooned, rubbing his ears. "Did you miss me?"

"Sean, she didn't give me a greeting like that this morning in the hospital," Clay said, smiling.

"You didn't deserve one, keeping me prisoner in that noise box all night. Besides, I didn't know you liked ear rubs."

"Love them. Hey Sean, how do you feel about beagle/German shepherd mixes? I know a real doll named Gypsy."

Sean dropped down, looked carefully at Clay, then walked in a slow circle around him. Clay held perfectly still but asked, "He's not going to wet on my leg, is he?"

"Not unless he's proposing to you."

Betty appeared bearing a plate of cookies. "A bird told me you'd be bringing Rebecca home, Dr. Bellamy, and I remembered how much you liked my Toll House cookies." She was beaming all over herself, clearly thrilled that Becky had brought home a "fella." Rebecca felt her cheeks growing hot and was glad Clay didn't look at her.

"I see Sean is doing fine," Rebecca said quickly.

"He wasn't last night. Prowling all over the place looking for you, so I took him out to the apartment over the garage with Walt and me. Walt wasn't feelin' so good so I let him have the bed and I took the couch. When I went in to check on him about two in the morning, he and Sean were all cuddled up together sound asleep. Wish I'd had a camera."

"Well, I'm glad Sean had a pleasant night," Rebecca said dryly. "Where are Mother and Frank?"

"Your mother isn't feeling too well today," Betty said evasively. Code, of course, that meant Suzanne had been drinking. "And your stepfather is resting. He was up all night takin' care of you and that Ellis family. Didn't get home until about nine this morning. I put him in the guest room so he could get some sleep away from your mother."

Betty immediately looked stricken, realizing her gaffe. Frank couldn't get any sleep in the room he shared with Suzanne because she was probably smoking and slurring along to music the way she always did when she'd been drinking.

Clay obviously sensed Betty's distress over her loose tongue and smiled like a little boy. "I sure do love these." He took a cookie. "You always used plenty of butter."

Betty looked relieved. "Butter! Yes, that's the secret!" she announced as if divulging the mysteries of the pyramids. "Some use margarine. Margarine!" She snorted in disgust. "Imagine!"

"While you two are discussing recipes and Sean is giving Clay the once-over, would you mind if I call Bill?" Rebecca asked. "I want to talk to him about Matilda Vinson."

"What about Matilda Vinson?" Betty demanded.

"I'll tell you in the kitchen," Clay said. "Now 'fess up, Betty. Butter isn't the only secret to these heavenly creations."

"Well, I *have* made a couple of alterations to the recipe," Betty confided as the three of them trouped down the hall toward the kitchen. "Every *real* woman has to put her own personality onto a recipe, that's what I always say."

Rebecca skittered into Frank's study and sat down at his massive desk, reaching for the phone. She said a silent thank you when she was put straight through to Bill at police headquarters. "How do you feel?" he asked.

"Like running a marathon." Bill was silent. "Oh no. What's happened?"

"We found an earring in the Pioneer Room right beside

where Sonia was attacked. Randy Messer wears an earring."

"Well, he can't be the only person in Sinclair who wears an earring, Bill. I don't consider that very damning evidence."

"It matches the description of an earring he wears."

"A no doubt expensive and distinctive earring," she said sarcastically.

"Well, now, Rebecca, I didn't know you'd become Randy's lawyer."

"I'm just a mystery writer asking questions my readers would ask. And you haven't answered."

"No, it wasn't expensive or distinctive. Something they call a stud. We went to his house this morning to question him. His father hasn't seen him since late yesterday afternoon. He's an old son of a bitch, but at least he was cooperative. Half-drunk at nine in the morning, but cooperative. No sign of Randy's earring."

"Maybe he's wearing it."

"His father said no. Lately Randy's been wearing, and I quote, 'Some silly circle thing like women wear.' "

"A hoop." Rebecca felt a strange sinking sensation as she pictured Sonia's beautiful, slightly battered, and very sad face. "Well, there are other explanations."

"Sure. But it looks bad for Randy."

"Bill, Sonia doesn't know any of this, does she?"

"Not yet."

"Don't tell her today. Give her some time to recover from last night."

"*I* won't tell her, but I can't guarantee Sheriff Lutz won't. He knows and he loves being the bearer of bad news. I've posted a guard on her door and he can keep out casual visitors, even Kelley Keene, but not Lutz."

"The jerk." Rebecca picked up a pen and tapped it absently against the blotter. "I have a contact at the hospital. Let me see if I can get him to limit Sonia's visitors to family and claim she's not yet up to being questioned by the police."

"Oh, I imagine you can get Clay to do just about anything for *you*."

"What's that supposed to mean?"

Bill laughed. "You know very well what it means. Half the town is talking about you two."

"About us? What about us?" Rebecca's voice was too loud. She tried to sound more nonchalant. "Of all the silly topics. Are people around here so bored that they make something out of one dinner together? Since when did that mean anything?"

"Oh settle down, Becky." Bill was still laughing. "You're protesting too much."

Oh great. She was. "Well, I thought people were only talking about *me*, that's all. I wouldn't want Clay to be embarrassed by a lot of stupid gossip."

"I think it would take a lot more than being romantically linked to you to embarrass Clay Bellamy. He hasn't exactly been dodging your company, niece." Rebecca felt foolishly flustered at the thought of her and Clay being considered an item. Flustered, excited, and scared. She didn't want to betray her feelings to Bill, though, so she rushed on. "Have you learned any more about the bracelet I found in the car? Jonnie's bracelet?"

"I took it to the local shoe repair shop. The owner naturally has a lot of experience with leather. He says the leather is new, Becky. It can't be Jonnie's bracelet."

"I see," she said slowly. "But what was the point of making a replica and putting it in my car?"

"I've told you. A lot of people are frightened of you, especially after some of the things that have happened lately. The scene at Dormaine's, for instance, has the whole town buzzing. Someone just wanted to scare you off."

"Someone who knew what Jonnie's bracelet looked like and went to all the trouble of reproducing it? And someone who happened to be downtown when I had the car windows partially rolled down?"

"Now I've been thinking about that. Do you keep the

car locked and in the garage all the time when you're home?"

"No. Since I've been using it so often, I often leave it in the driveway. And I don't lock it at home."

"So the bracelet could have been slipped into the car at your house and you just didn't notice it until you got downtown."

Rebecca was quiet for a beat. "Bill, I hadn't considered that. It was on the floor. Maybe my foot just missed it when I drove downtown. But who at this house would do such a thing?"

"I can't think of anyone in that house who would do it. But Lamplight Lane isn't guarded. Everyone has access. It would be easy to make a quick stop at night, open your car door, and drop the bracelet in. None of your neighbors have dogs to raise a ruckus. And I think your dog stays inside."

"Sleeping like a log." Rebecca sighed. "Well, this puts a new spin on things. And makes tracking down the culprit harder. But someone certainly went to a lot of trouble to scare me. Why not just send me creepy mail or make spooky phone calls?"

"Mail and phone calls can be traced. Besides, crank mail and phone calls wouldn't have quite the effect that bracelet did."

"I guess you're right. And I have made quite a spectacle of myself since I came home. No wonder people are talking, some of them frightened. They know there's a lunatic on the loose, but they think it's me." Rebecca paused. "Speaking of people in town talking about me, maybe even watching me, Clay and I were in the Parkview Café yesterday afternoon. You know how close the tables are, and the place was crowded. I was telling Clay that Sonia would be in the library that evening. Anybody could have heard me. Even Doug—he was sitting right behind us."

"You think Doug attacked Sonia?"

"Of course not. I'm just saying that a lot of people knew where Sonia was going to be that evening thanks to my big mouth. Randy Messer shouldn't be your only suspect."

"You don't even know this kid. Why do you keep defending him?"

"I'm not defending him. I just want you to keep an open mind."

"Because Sonia means something to you, and he means something to her."

"Because you're a good policeman," Rebecca said firmly, although Bill had been half-correct. "Now brace yourself, because I have more exciting news for you."

"My God, I don't think my heart can stand it."

"Then take a pill or have a shot of bourbon or whatever it is you do to maintain that uncanny calm of yours. You're going to need it. Matilda Vinson saw the face of the person who tried to kill Sonia last night. She saw that person again at the cemetery today. She is scared out of her mind and I'm scared for her."

2

WEDNESDAY, 4:30 P.M.

"Miss Vinson, normally I'd assign someone to watch you, but I'm stretched thin because of Todd Ryan and Sonia Ellis," Bill Garrett said as he sat lost in the giant flabby recliner that had belonged to Matilda's father. He knew she considered it the seat of honor in her living room. He felt as if he were being swallowed whole. To make things worse, Matilda had served unbearably sweet hot tea, which he was sure would turn him into a diabetic. "So I would suggest that you leave town for a few days."

Matilda smiled shakily. "Chief Garrett, I know your niece meant well when she sent you here, but there is really nothing wrong."

Bill realized the necessity of being careful with the woman, who was obviously suffering from fright and denial. "You told her you saw someone in the attic of Klein Furniture Saturday night."

"Yes and I reported it. Your deputy acted as if I were a dotty old lady."

"I'm very sorry about that. He's new and young and cocky. He's been severely reprimanded for treating you so cavalierly—especially for dismissing the fact that someone tried the drugstore door."

"I'm glad you spoke to him. I was quite frightened and I thought that as a taxpayer, I deserved a bit more attention and respect." Matilda seemed to remember she wanted to downplay the incident. Her expression quickly changed from incensed to indulgent. "But he was probably right. It was just some teenager at the door."

"Teenagers can be a menace, too," Bill said seriously. "And even if the person at the door wasn't the person you saw in the attic, I don't like the idea of someone trying to get into a drugstore. People in search of drugs can be dangerous."

"I've been in this business a long time, Chief." Matilda took a sip of tea from a delicate cup. "I'm very careful about locking up and keeping controlled substances highly protected."

"I know that. There's never been the slightest bit of trouble at Vinson's Apothecary. That's a credit to you and your father." Matilda looked pleased with the compliment and relaxed a bit, just as Bill had intended. "Rebecca also said you saw someone in the alley leading from the library right after the attempt on Sonia Ellis's life."

Matilda's cup rattled in her saucer. "I did not see a face. Just a person in a hurry. Someone in a windbreaker with the hood up. The wind was getting bad. I didn't see a face."

"Man or woman?"

"I couldn't tell."

She was lying. Bill knew and she knew Bill knew, but she stared at him stubbornly. "Didn't you get the slightest impression about the person's sex?" he asked kindly.

"Absolutely not. Shapeless clothes everyone wears these days. And I didn't see a face. I *didn't*."

"The person didn't even grunt when they bumped into you?"

Color rose and fell in Matilda's face. "No."

"Because you can get an idea of sex just from a grunt. You know—high-pitched or low."

"No grunting. No."

Another lie. "All right. But why were you so frightened about it at the cemetery?"

Matilda sloshed tea and finally set down the cup and saucer. "I think dear Rebecca misunderstood what I was saying. I just wanted to express sympathy for what happened to her at the library. And I was upset over Skeeter. It meant nothing except that I was upset over all that's happening. I chatter when I get upset. I'm calmer now and I feel silly for making such a fuss, especially because I don't know if the person in the alley was a man or a woman or even if that person had a thing in the world to do with what happened to Rebecca and the Ellis girl."

"And you didn't see anyone around the chapel at the cemetery? Someone who frightened you?"

Matilda gave him a ghastly smile. "Did Rebecca tell you that, too? Really, she's a dear child but her imagination is running wild. I didn't see *anyone* at the chapel. I simply got a bit overheated in the sun."

"Well, now, Rebecca thinks she saw a blur of movement, like someone darting behind the chapel."

"Really?" Matilda squeaked. "Her wonderful writer's imagination, as I said. I read her book. Scared me silly late at night. But of course it was fiction. I know the difference. And I wasn't frightened at the cemetery. I was just overheated and upset and wanted to get home."

"Not back to the store?"

Matilda batted her eyes at him. Getting back to the store would be characteristic behavior. "Not returning to the store was showing respect for Skeeter. I've known him since he was a child. He was quite salvageable, in my opinion. It was that awful father of his who ruined him. Most people don't understand. They don't know Skeeter's history. These days people just don't get to know each other like they used to. Hurry, hurry. Everyone's in a hurry. Such a fast-paced world. Give drugs instead of working with people and learning their strengths and weaknesses. Of course drugs are my business—I shouldn't complain."

She'd managed to skillfully and completely sidestep the subject of her fear at the cemetery. Bill realized getting information from Matilda Vinson was hopeless. All he could do was try to keep an eye on her, although under the circumstances he could do only a poor job of it. There would be no help from Sheriff Martin Lutz, either. He had dismissed her as easily as Bill's young, chastised deputy had done. Lutz was another one who thought no one over 60 had any sense. It was one of the things that made him an idiot in Bill's book.

Bill stood. "Sure I can't talk you into leaving town just for a few days?"

"I couldn't leave my father."

"He's in a fine nursing home."

"But he expects to see me every Sunday. He gets very upset when he doesn't. And then there's the store. It won't run itself."

"You have Lynn Hardison."

"Lynn is not a pharmacist, and I couldn't get a replacement so soon. No, Chief, I appreciate your concern, but I can't leave. And there's no reason to leave. I'm perfectly fine. I didn't see anything. You be sure people know. That I didn't see *anything*." She clearly caught the anxiety in her voice and added lamely. "So they won't worry."

No, so the killer will hear it and not see you as a threat, Bill thought, but he merely nodded agreeably. "I'll spread the word, Miss Vinson, you be sure of that. And you take care now."

"Oh, I certainly will."

"Thank you for the tea."

"It's Earl Grey, my favorite. I'm glad you liked it."

As he stepped out the door, Bill added impulsively, "And that's one fine recliner of your dad's. Beautifully constructed and worn in just right. Wish I had one."

Matilda beamed. Later Bill was glad he'd given her that compliment, even if it was insincere. It was the last time he ever saw her smile.

3

Frank spent the rest of the afternoon in bed. Rebecca could not remember a time when he'd retired with even a headache. At three o'clock she tapped on the door to the guest room where he was staying. After a moment he'd called, "Come in," in a tired voice.

"I hope I didn't wake you," Rebecca said, noting the closed draperies and the soft light coming from a lamp halfway across the room. Frank seemed lost in shadows and she paused in surprise.

"Come nearer the bed, dear. I don't think I'm contagious." Frank's voice held a hint of humor, but it was forced. "How are you feeling?"

"*I'm* fine. You know bullets bounce off me. I'm concerned about you."

He smiled. "You're twenty-six. I'm in my fifties. Unfortunately bullets no longer bounce off me, but it's not the end of the world. I'm just tired. My heart's running a little fast and I have a damnable headache."

"Your *heart*?"

"It's called tachycardia. I've had it all my life. Hits me when I've been under tension, and there's been a bit too much of that this week."

These last few years, Rebecca thought with guilt. Everyone had depended too much on Frank. No one had been concerned enough about *his* welfare.

"No, I'm not the selfless, suffering martyr you're turning me into in your mind right now," Frank said, grinning. "See, you're not the only one with ESP. But it *has* been a tough week and I'm not as young as I used to be. That's all that's wrong with me, honey. Things just look worse because I'm in a separate bedroom like an invalid, but you understand the situation."

"All too well. In between sips of wine, Mother's been crooning her heart out to old tapes all afternoon."

Frank nodded solemnly. "You know, your father was my dearest friend, but there is one thing I absolutely can never forgive him for." He paused and Rebecca looked at him, shocked. He never criticized Patrick. "He told your mother she had a lovely voice and encouraged her singing."

She burst into giggles. "Oh God, he did! And he hated her voice as much as everyone else, but he didn't want to hurt her feelings because she so loved to sing. But you know who *didn't* mind hurting her feelings? The Irish Setter Rusty. He threw back his head and howled down the roof whenever she sang 'Blue Bayou.' She never got the hint."

"She probably thought he was howling because he was so moved by her heartfelt rendition."

They were both laughing now—snickering, really, like guilty children, and Rebecca felt better. Seeing Frank ill had frightened her more than she would have believed. She hadn't quite realized what a rock he'd been in her world for so many years.

As soon as they'd recovered, Frank put his hand on Rebecca's. "Dear, I've made a decision. As soon as this mess is cleared up, I'm putting your mother in rehab. She'll hate me for it."

"Oh Frank, she won't hate you when she's well. And you have to do it."

"Then you won't be upset if there's a minor scandal here in Sinclair?"

"After all this family has been through, Mother going into rehab would hardly cause a ripple. And I don't even live here anymore. Certainly I won't mind. I'd just like for her to be well again. And as happy as she's capable of being."

"Good. That's settled then." Frank smiled. "Now on to

our more immediate problems. I talked to Bill, they haven't tracked down Jean Wright. She's not with her brother or sister."

"No. She just vanished. Maybe she did take Todd. She certainly needed the money, but something tells me this crime isn't really about ransom."

Frank raised his eyebrows. "Not about ransom? How do you know?"

"One of my spooky feelings. It's about something else. Perhaps revenge. The problem is, I think it's revenge against me for something I did with my ESP. But as much as I love Todd, it's Molly who'll suffer the most if that's the motive. Then again, it could be someone who desperately wants a child." She shook her head. "No, no one who wanted a child to cherish would treat him as Todd's being treated." She frowned. "It's about something else, Frank. Something I can't quite get a bead on. But I will. I swear on my brother's memory I will."

Frank looked taken aback by her ferocity. Then he clutched her hand. "God, honey, I hope so. For your sake as well as Todd's and everyone else's." He kissed the back of her hand, then released it. "We were speaking of the less-than-charming Jean Wright. I'm not sorry she's gone. However, her absence leaves Molly alone. I have a favor to ask of you."

"You want me to move in with Molly."

"No. I don't think that would be best for either of you. You need time to concentrate on yourself, to heal and to . . . well, to clear your mind for visions. Yes, I believe in them now. And having Molly making constant demands on you for information wouldn't help. I'd like you to ask Aunt Esther to stay with Molly. She adores Molly and Todd."

"But she's sick."

"She's functioning like a well woman. And she needs to feel like a well woman, which to her means being needed. However, I'm afraid she'll keep overdoing it at the nursery. Having her stay with Molly is the perfect solution for both of them."

"Frank, you're brilliant, but why do you want me to ask her instead of you?"

"Because she always puts up a fuss with me out of sheer stubbornness and I'm tired. She'll fuss with you, too, but not as much. She's never been able to say no to you."

"How Machiavellian of you!"

"Oh, I have depths and depths! You couldn't even guess."

"Now you sound like Clay Bellamy."

Frank smiled. "Kind of like that young man, don't you?"

"He's nice."

"*Nice?* Such a bland word from a writer! How about good looking, smart, man with a future?"

"Frank Hardison, are you trying to marry me off?"

"I'd like to see you be happy, Rebecca," he said seriously, then added with a grin, "and think of all the free medical care we'd get."

"You need to get some sleep. You're delirious."

But she was smiling as she left the room.

4

Frank was right. When Rebecca called Esther from Frank's study and approached her with the idea of staying with Molly, she had been resistant. "Honey, I'd do anything to help that poor girl, but this nursery needs my full-time attention until I leave for the hospital. People are still planting—"

"And you have two full-time helpers. Don't tell me you hired people who know nothing about plants or who are incapable of going out and digging holes."

"Rebecca, there's more to nursery work than digging holes," Esther said, sounding a bit offended. "If that were so, I'd just hire a couple of dogs."

"Dogs dig where they want. They won't take directions. It would never work." She could feel Esther smile on the other end of the line. "Look, this would mean so much to

Molly. She's always loved you. And believe me, I'd do it myself, but I'm afraid devoting my energies to trying to keep Molly from being depressed might interfere with any visions I might have. Oh, gosh, that sounded pretentious. What I mean is—"

"I know what you mean," Esther said gently. "You've already had visions of Todd. Because of you we knew he was in that attic. And we now know he's been moved to a different kind of place and he's still alive. You might not be quite pleased with your contribution, but it's been a great one. And I'm being silly. I'll gather up some clothes and come to Molly's tonight."

"Good. I'm going to visit her, so I should still be there when you arrive. I'll see you then. And thank you, Aunt Esther," Rebecca said as she hung up.

"What good works is Esther doing now?"

Rebecca looked up to see her mother standing in the doorway. Her hair hung messily around her shoulders. She wore a white robe and held a cigarette in a shaking hand. Her face was drawn and pale, the eyes huge. "Mother. I was talking to Aunt Esther."

"Yes, I gathered that much when you called her 'Esther.' I wanted to know what you were thanking her for."

"She's going to stay with Molly tonight and tomorrow. Jean Wright has taken an unannounced vacation and Molly is all alone."

"Oh." Suzanne took a deep drag off her cigarette. "I suppose everyone is angry because *I'm* not staying with her."

Suzanne was swaying slightly. Rebecca imagined she could smell the wine seeping from her mother's pores. "I don't think anyone expects *you* to stay with Molly."

"Why?" Suzanne asked aggressively. "Because I'm a drunk?"

"As a matter of fact, *yes*."

Suzanne glared at her with hostile blue eyes. Then, abruptly, she began to cry, not the pitiful weeping of someone trying to elicit sympathy, but deep, heartfelt sobs. "Oh God. I know. And I hate myself."

She sat down on a chair and held her head in her hands. Rebecca hesitated, then kneeled beside her and draped her arm around her mother's surprisingly thin, shaking shoulders. "Mother, crying isn't going to help anything."

"It's a release. Oh I know what you're thinking. She's been releasing all day—drinking, smoking, singing. But those releases don't help. They do for some people, but not for me."

"Then why do you keep indulging in them?" Suzanne was crying harder, clearly headed for a jag, and Rebecca couldn't resist trying to joke her out of it like Jonnie used to do. "My God, isn't the singing enough to inflict on yourself and everyone else, Mother? Sean's requesting earmuffs."

Suzanne went quiet for a moment. Then she started to giggle—long, wet, messy giggles but giggles nevertheless. "You never appreciated good music."

"Yes I do. That's the trouble."

Suzanne hid her eyes, still giggling, still crying, then lapsing into hiccups. "God, what a fool I am."

"No. Just a little self-indulgent these days, but I see flashes of the mother I used to know. My beautiful, sparkling mother who loved life and enjoyed it like a child."

"Yes, I did, didn't I? I didn't think anything bad could ever happen to me. Or my children." She wiped at her eyes on the sleeve of her robe and looked up at Rebecca. "When I heard what happened at the library, I went to pieces. Of course I was already a mess—wine all day, that scene at dinner when Frank sent me to my room like a naughty kid—but I can pull myself together in an emergency. Usually. But when I heard you'd not only saved that girl from being murdered but were attacked while doing it, I simply couldn't take it in. Betty told me you were all right, but Betty soft-pedals everything with me."

"Neither Sonia nor I was nearly killed. She was hurt worse than I was—hit with a stun gun—but she's all right."

"But still, Rebecca, what you did! You got a vision that this girl was going to be *murdered* and you rushed right in without a thought for yourself! I could never have done that. My mother would have, but not me. It makes me feel worthless. And it makes me feel a little afraid of you and also a little resentful that my daughter has so much strength that I don't."

Rebecca tightened her grip on her mother's shoulders. "Mother, you don't have ESP like Grandmother Ava and me. And I know you don't even want it because it scares you. Believe me, she didn't understand it and neither do I. And we didn't ask for it. But my vision of Sonia made me run to the library to protect her, just as you would have done to protect Jonnie if you'd known where he was. We're all capable of things we don't know we are—you included. I'm not saying this to cheer you up. I really believe it. You just fall back on alcohol because you think you don't have any inner strength. But you do. Ava was the strongest woman I've ever known. You think *I'm* strong—do you believe all those strong genes just skipped you? Does that make any sense?"

Suzanne sniffled. "It's possible."

"I don't accept that. I think Grandmother was just a dominating personality who unwittingly taught you that your function in life was to be decorative. And Daddy, adore him though I did, did the same thing. I think your problems are the result of training, not insufficiencies of character."

Suzanne looked at her, batted her tear-laden lashes, and said with a hint of a smile, "You're making my head spin. I should never have let you go off to college. I can't understand anything you say anymore."

"Yes, you can." Rebecca squeezed her mother. "So please go in, give Frank a hug, and make a new resolution to quit drinking." She grinned. "And please, for the love of heaven, stop singing."

"I'm swearing it off for the whole evening." Suzanne laughed. "I shall retire to my room and *read*. How's that?"

"Much easier on everyone. I'm heading for Molly's."

Somewhat hesitantly, Rebecca kissed her mother on the forehead. "Have a nice evening, Mother."

Suzanne hugged her fiercely. "You, too, my dear girl. And be careful. I don't want to lose you, too."

Rebecca dashed up to her room, feeling incredibly light. She'd felt real affection in her mother's teasing, in her hug. She realized how much she hungered for that affection. Receiving it could make up for a multitude of traumas, including last night's.

Sean looked at her appealingly as she smoothed a bit of cheerful wine lipgloss on her pale mouth and grabbed up her purse. She looked back at him. "You and I have spent too much time apart lately. I think you'd like Molly's, and I could use a protector. How about being my escort to-night?"

As soon as she reached for his leash, Sean turned in a circle, his stump of a tail wriggling in excitement. At home she lavished attention on him with daily walks around the Garden District and weekends at Audubon Park. Here he'd been passed off too often to Betty and Walt.

Rebecca was relieved to see no news vans or loiterers around Molly's house. She'd already called ahead to say she was coming, and Molly greeted her at the door with a distinct lack of warmth. In fact, her emotions seemed flat, as if she felt nothing. This seeming detachment worried Rebecca more than agitation. It was as if Molly had given up.

Molly, who loved dogs, paid no attention to Sean. He in turn kept his distance from her. "Would you like something to drink?" she asked Rebecca. "Coffee? Wine?"

"I smell fresh coffee. I'll fix myself a cup. You want one, too?"

"No thanks. I've had about a gallon today."

"I'm going to let Sean off his leash. He's housebroken and he won't destroy anything."

"I don't care about anything in this house except Todd's room. I'll never move one thing in Todd's room. *Never!*"

Rebecca ignored the outburst although it disturbed her,

since it only underscored Molly's hopelessness. When Rebecca came back from the kitchen, Molly sat on the couch staring at Todd's photo. "I don't suppose you've had any more visions of him."

"Not for a couple of days," Rebecca said gently.

"Too busy out saving Sonia."

Sarcasm had never been a trait of Molly's. Rebecca bristled at the criticism. "What do you think I should have done, Molly? Left her to die? Besides, the person who tried to kill her is probably the person who abducted Todd. There was a chance of catching him."

"But you didn't, did you? You just stirred up a lot of publicity for yourself."

Rebecca set down her cup. "I feel absolutely miserable about what has happened to Todd and what you're going through, but I will not tolerate this attack. I'm doing the best I can for you, Molly, but I'm not a miracle worker."

Molly closed her eyes. She was quiet for so long that Rebecca had begun to think she was no longer going to acknowledge her, that she was just going to sit there like a rock until Rebecca left, but at last she said meekly, "I'm sorry. That was horrible of me."

"It wasn't horrible. Just undeserved."

"I'm really, *really* sorry."

"Don't worry about it, Molly. Honestly. It's forgotten."

"I'm just so scared." She looked at Rebecca with tragic eyes. "Do you still feel that Todd is alive?"

"Yes," Rebecca said truthfully. "Although I haven't had a vision, today, I feel . . ."

"*What?*"

"It sounds stupid. His life force."

"Did you feel it with Jonnie?"

Not an innocent question. A test. Again, Rebecca answered honestly. "Yes, I did. For a few days." She paused. "About twenty-four hours before he was found, the feeling went away. I didn't want to believe it, but I knew Jonnie was dead. I've never told anyone that before, but I wasn't surprised when his body was found. Devastated, but not surprised."

"But you don't feel that way about Todd. That he's gone."

"No." Dear God, don't let me be wrong about this, Rebecca prayed. She was being totally sincere, but desperately hoped her gut feelings were accurate. "Todd is alive."

Molly closed her eyes again. This time she seemed to be marshaling strength. She didn't need idle chatter to distract her. "I'm going to look for Sean," Rebecca muttered. "I haven't seen him for a few minutes."

She found him lying on Todd's bed. She turned on the Lava lamp, closed the door to the room, and joined him on the bed. "Whatcha doing in here?" she asked, rubbing the thick hair on his neck. "Getting the scent of the little guy who's missing? Maybe that's not such a bad idea." She flipped back Todd's quilt and held a bed pillow to Sean's nose. "He has strawberry blond hair. I know they say dogs can't see color, but it can't hurt. Now give this pillow a good sniffing." Sean obeyed, sniffing for all he was worth.

"Great." She looked around the room, then got off the bed and opened Todd's closet. She took out a pair of jeans and a sweatshirt lying on the floor. "Now try these." She reached down for two pairs of shoes. "And these." Sean sniffed assiduously. "Got a head full of Todd now?"

The bedroom door opened and Rebecca jumped, fearing it would be Molly angry that the sanctity of Todd's room was being violated. But it was only Esther with her long, fluffy white hair and bright blue eyes. "Thought I might find you in here. Letting Sean get Todd's scent?"

"How did you know?"

"When Jonnie was missing, you did the same with Rusty, although the dog already knew his master's scent. Molly doesn't know you're here and frankly, dear, I don't think she'd like it."

"She's in a foul mood tonight."

"So I gathered. I suppose she's entitled. She's been pretty brave through it all."

Rebecca stood and hugged Esther. "Thank you so much for agreeing to stay with her. I know how you hate to leave home."

Esther made a face. "I'll be forced to leave next week when I go to the hospital. And maybe I can help Molly. She used to enjoy my company."

"She loves you. You could always make her laugh and feel secure. Her last caretaker—Jean Wright—was hardly a thrill ride."

"But she *was* a nurse. If something should happen to Molly like a panic attack or hysterics or a fainting spell—"

"You'll call 911. Or Clay Bellamy. I think he's on duty at the emergency room." She hugged Esther again. "You'll do fine."

Rebecca decided that although her visit had been brief, Molly had seen enough of her for one night. Her hostilities flowed because Rebecca had not been able to work wonders. Rebecca was familiar with the syndrome. Still, she did not like to be around it. Neither did Sean. He sensed the tension and acted jittery, which Rebecca feared would result in a defensive nip on someone's ankle or a nervous splatter of urine against a wall. It was definitely time to leave.

Molly bade her a wan farewell. Esther winked at her and told her they would be fine. She also told Sean to take good care of his mistress.

Unlike last night, the evening was windless. A wispy fog crept slyly down the street, making the houses and trees look as if they were shrouded in a thin sweep of gauze. Lights in houses were muted, indistinct, and the few passing cars made a dull, distant sound.

As Rebecca neared the Thunderbird, she pulled her keys from her purse. Then Sean stopped dead and let out a low, menacing growl. The image of a hooded man with a stun gun flashed in Rebecca's mind and her blood seemed to stop flowing. Her grip tightened on Sean's leash and she pointed the notched end of the car key outward, ready to jab it into an eye if necessary.

"Who's there?" she asked in a surprisingly strong voice.

"It's Randy Messer. Sonia's boyfriend. Please keep the dog away from me. I need to talk to you."

Randy Messer. Some people thought he'd taken Todd Ryan. The police thought he'd lost an earring in the library when he attacked and tried to kill Sonia. Sonia believed completely in his innocence and Rebecca believed in Sonia's instincts.

Still, she hesitated. It was dark. The street was deserted. This was no boy—he was 18. He could stab her, or shoot her, and be gone before anyone knew a thing was wrong.

"Please, Miss Ryan. Sonia says to trust you. I gotta talk to someone."

Pain and fear reverberated in his voice. I'm being a fool, Rebecca thought, still clutching the key, but she made a decision. "I'm holding tight to the dog's leash. Don't get too close to me and don't make any sudden moves or I'll turn him loose on you. He'll go straight for your throat." Sean would have to jump six feet to go for Randy's throat, but it sounded good. "He's maimed people before. Do you understand me?"

"Yeah, yeah, I get it. And I'm not gonna hurt you or the dog. Please, Miss Ryan, I don't have all night."

"Step into the light."

"I'm not standing under any damned streetlight. The police are looking for me. I'll take two steps forward. You can see me then. Okay?"

"Fine," Rebecca said, then remembered she had never seen Randy Messer before. She hadn't the faintest idea what he looked like.

But when he came forward, she knew him instantly. Blond hair, blue eyes, chiseled features. Except for the soulful yet keen look in the eyes and the lines added by thirteen years, he could have been Clay's brother. No wonder Sonia had seemed so smitten with Clay. He looked like her own true teenaged love.

"How's Sonia?" Randy asked.

"Last I heard she's doing fine, but her doctor is letting

in only immediate family. And Chief Garrett is keeping a guard on her room."

"Thank God." Randy closed his eyes for a moment. "I kept thinking of her lying there all alone, unprotected, and some creep coming in and smothering her."

"Can't happen," Rebecca reassured him.

He reached up to his pocket. "Just a cigarette," he said when she tensed. He pulled it out and lit it with a lighter held in a shaking hand. "I've been hiding all day."

"They found an earring in the Pioneer Room right beside where Sonia was attacked. They thinks it's yours."

"They found an earring? Jeez, do I have the only earring in town? Or have they done their DNA tests on it and proved it's mine?"

Rebecca smiled slightly. "I don't think the Sinclair police department works that fast. No DNA tests yet."

"Good, because I meet Sonia in that room all the time. It *could* be mine." Randy looked at her closely. "But you don't think I tried to kill Sonia, do you?"

Rebecca drew a deep breath. She should watch what she said to this young man. But he was too perceptive to fall for subterfuge. She could see it in his eyes. "No, I don't think you hurt her. But I have no way of convincing the police of that. I didn't see the face of the person who attacked her. And in spite of our tussle, I didn't get much of a sense of body size. All I know is that the person was strong."

"And agile. The back door of the Pioneer Room is at least two feet above the fire escape. Someone had to nearly fly out of that room, make that jump, then take the fire escape fast. And the bottom three stairs are broken. Another jump."

"You certainly know a lot about the layout," Rebecca said slowly, fear beginning to ebb through her again.

"Every time I've met Sonia I've come and gone by the fire escape so that prissy ass behind the desk doesn't call her mother. Yeah, I know the layout."

"Okay. That makes sense. But what are you going to do

now? You can't go home. The police will be looking for you there."

"I couldn't go home anyway. My old man and I finally had the knock-down-drag-out that's been brewing for years. But I'll be okay. Really. I just don't have any other way to get word to Sonia except Cory. He's sort of a friend. He's also sort of a nerd who talks too much." Rebecca smiled, thinking of Cory with his octave-jumping voice and chatter about *Planet of the Apes*. "Will you tell Sonia I'm all right and that I love her?"

Rebecca nodded, thinking of what she would have felt like at Sonia's age if someone as gorgeous and as seemingly dangerous had loved her. She might be meddling in things that didn't concern her because she was reliving her own teenage fantasies. Or she could be meddling because her instincts were accurate. "I'll tell her, Randy. I promise."

"Good. Thanks, Ms. Ryan. You're all right."

Randy tossed down his cigarette and ground it out with his shoe. As he turned to go, a muted glow from the streetlight fell on his right ear. The lobe was freshly slit and slightly swollen, as if an earring had recently been torn from it.

CHAPTER FIFTEEN

1

On her way home, Rebecca suddenly began to shake. She realized she'd taken a foolish chance talking to Randy Messer. She had no tangible proof that he hadn't tried to attack Sonia. True, Sean had been with her for protection, but Sean had never really been put to the test before. She'd never wanted an attack dog—just one who could make a good show. Aside from the possible lawsuits that could result from a dog attacking someone—no matter how justified the attack—she never wanted to put a dog's life in jeopardy. She did know from Sean's behavior with Doug at Esther's pond that the dog would make an attempt to protect her, but a serious attacker could have made quick work of him. No, she had been silly, even though she felt in her heart that Randy was innocent.

But the police had found an earring near where Sonia had been assaulted, and Randy's ear bore the unmistakable slit caused by an earring having been torn from the lobe. Wasn't that too much of a coincidence?

When she pulled onto Lamplight Lane, she became aware of a car following her. Her heart pumped harder. Could this be Randy? No. He'd had the perfect opportunity to harm her outside of Molly's. Why follow her home to attack her in front of her own house? She pulled into the driveway and sat still with the doors locked. In a moment a uniformed policeman tapped on the window. Rebecca looked at him closely, then recognized a young deputy she'd seen briefly at police headquarters. She powered down the window.

"Did I run a stop sign?"

"You talked to a fugitive and let him get away."

Rebecca stiffened. "I don't know what you're talking about."

"Randy Messer. You talked to him outside of Molly Ryan's house."

"How do you know that?"

"Your uncle assigned me to keep an eye on you since you were involved in the library fracas. Did you think Sonia Ellis is the only one he's been keeping under guard?" His tone was insolent and Rebecca instantly disliked him. "You know the police are searching for Messer. Yet you did nothing when he approached you."

"What should I have done, Officer? Wrestle him to the ground and handcuff him? I thought *you* were protecting *me*. If you saw me talking to him, why didn't you come forward and arrest him?"

Even in the shadows Rebecca could see his face darken. "I didn't see him until about five seconds before he disappeared into the trees."

"Oh. You were dozing."

"The light was bad."

"Chief Garrett will love that excuse." She turned off the ignition, unlocked the door, took Sean's leash in her hand, and began to exit the car. "Randy Messer didn't threaten me, but if he had, you wouldn't have been one bit of help so don't take that arrogant attitude with me and don't treat me like a criminal. I haven't done anything." She paused. "And neither did you, in spite of your orders. And why the hell didn't you pursue the archcriminal Messer instead of me? Oh yes, Bill will be quite impressed. Now step back. I can't guarantee this dog won't attack you."

The deputy stepped back, resentment burning in his eyes. Then his gaze shot up as a vehicle careened onto Lamplight Lane, red lights flashing, siren wailing, and pulled up to the house. Emergency technicians exploded from the ambulance.

"What is it?" Rebecca cried.

"You'll have to move, ma'am," a technician said crisply, maneuvering a gurney past her. "Keep the area clear."

The double front doors of the house opened and Betty stood with the light behind her, waving madly as if she stood on the deck of a flight carrier. "In here!" she screamed. "He's in here! Please hurry!"

"Betty!" Rebecca called. "What is it?"

"It's your stepfather," Betty wailed. "He's having a heart attack!"

2

They weren't allowed to see Frank. At least, *Rebecca* wasn't allowed to see Frank; her mother had remained in her bedroom. While Rebecca sat in the emergency waiting room by herself, she worked up a ferocious anger toward Suzanne. By the time Clay came out to talk to her, she was thinking of spending the night in a motel rather than go home to face a woman too emotionally weak to face anything herself.

Clay looked tired. He took Rebecca into a small, private waiting room. "Frank has had a cardiac incident."

"What's that?" Rebecca demanded. "I don't know what that means. Why don't doctors say what they mean?"

"Rebecca, calm down. He had pain in his left arm. He also had elevated heartbeat and blood pressure—those could have resulted from panic over what he thought was a heart attack, but he also had sweating and nausea. His electrocardiogram was slightly erratic as well."

"Did he arrest?" Rebecca asked in fear, remembering her own four-minute cardiac arrest, the one during which the pretty young nurse had declared she'd "died."

"No, he didn't. And he remained outwardly calm, considering the circumstances. He hasn't had a second incident. I'm encouraged. We don't have all the lab tests back, but of course he'll have to stay here tonight."

"I'd throw a fit if you *didn't* keep him." Rebecca sighed. "Frank is so stoic you have a tendency to think he can handle anything and not consider the strain he's under."

"The strain of Todd's abduction couldn't be avoided, Rebecca."

"But I've added to everything with my wreck and my scene at Dormaine's and the library stunt last night."

"The library stunt, as you call it, saved a girl's life. And you didn't wreck on purpose, you weren't seriously hurt, and the scene at Dormaine's was simply an embarrassment for you. I hardly think it threw Frank into a financial tailspin. Let up on yourself."

But I'm not all of the trouble, she thought. There's Mother with her constant drinking. There was no reason to mention this problem to Clay, though. He already knew about it. All of Sinclair did.

"Are you sure I can't see him tonight?"

"He's much calmer than when he came in. He's also drowsy. As soon as he's settled in his room, I think he'll go to sleep."

"And I would only disturb him."

Clay took her hand and held it tightly. "Listen, sweetheart, Frank is in excellent health other than this episode, which doesn't seem to have been a heart attack. I don't think there's any real reason to worry. If he doesn't have any more trouble, he'll be home day after tomorrow."

"Thank God," Rebecca breathed.

It was only ten minutes later on her way to the car that she realized Clay had called her "sweetheart." The endearment warmed her to the core.

3

After Bill Garrett left, Matilda washed the teacups and saucers, straightened the kitchen, then walked straight back to the bathroom and threw up. She was annoyed by her cowardice and by its disgusting manifestation. She was frustrated that after the funeral she'd babbled her head off to Rebecca Ryan. She was distressed that she'd been too nervous to return to the store. No prescriptions could be filled, so she called Lynn and told her to close at five although this was one of Lynn's nights to stay until ten. Matilda would go in two hours early tomorrow to catch up. Maybe three hours. A good night's sleep would put her on her feet again, she reassured herself. She'd be calm and businesslike and put all this melodrama out of her sensible head.

Matilda had always been contemptuous of what she considered "silly" women. Her mother had been a dear, sweet ninny afraid to stay alone at night, afraid of scary television shows, afraid of crowds, afraid of animals, afraid of business, basically afraid of life outside her home. The idea of turning out like her mother had frightened Matilda above all things, and she'd therefore determined at age twelve to be independent and strong although her mother had desperately tried to turn her into a carbon copy. Matilda had followed her father's lead, though, and made him proud of her. She hadn't necessarily meant to end up alone, but throughout the years she'd considered it the price she had to pay for her hard-won self-sufficiency and meeting her father's expectations.

Now it all seemed to be slipping away from her. She was as jittery and excitable as her mother and it depressed her, no matter how sound her reason for feeling fear. So after her bout of nausea, she decided to act as if nothing were wrong in her world. She would go on just as she had for the last sixty-two years—self-possessed, competent, a bit autocratic to hide the lingering insecurities.

She decided to put the rest of the day to good use. She did two loads of laundry. She ran the vacuum cleaner all over the house, even though she'd just vacuumed three days ago. She organized her already organized dresser drawers. She carefully copied four recipes that had been given to her by her church group.

At ten o'clock she watched a law drama although she had trouble concentrating. Afterward she washed and creamed her pale face, slipped on a cotton nightgown, read a chapter of *My Antonia*, took a melatonin pill, and finally began to doze. She was dreaming of a store full of people furious because she'd filled every prescription incorrectly when the phone beside her bed rang. At first, still lost in her dream, she thought it was a police siren. They'd come to haul her off to prison for incompetence. Not until the third jingle did she realize she was hearing the phone. Her hand shot out for the receiver. "Matilda Vinson here."

"Miss Vinson?" A weak female voice with a terrific twang jittered over the wires. "Is this Miss Matilda Vinson?"

"I just said so. What is it?"

"Oh. It's your father. He's . . . well, he's not doin' so well."

"What! My father? What's wrong with him?"

"He's not doin' so well."

"You said that. Could you be more specific? Is it his Alzheimer's? His heart?"

"Yes."

"Which?"

"Well, both." The woman paused. "See, his heart's actin' up and it's got him scared." She paused again. "He thinks it's World War II and he's going out to kill Japanese in his plane."

"He didn't fight in the Pacific theater."

"You don't understand. He's not talkin' about a movie, he's talkin' about a war."

Oh God, the ignorance of the young, Matilda thought. Did they ignore World War II at Sinclair High?

"He's just plain out of control and he's yellin' for you. The head nurse thinks you should come."

"Where's his doctor?"

"We can't reach him right now. But we're all doin' our best with your daddy. Maybe you can do more." She paused again. "*Please*, Miss Vinton, it's awful important."

"*Vinson*," Matilda said automatically. "I'll be there immediately. And don't put him in restraints. That sets him crazy."

But then he's already crazy, she thought, filled with guilt and despair. What a handsome, intelligent, kind man he'd been, full of more quiet common sense than anyone she'd ever known. And now, in his eighties, he was ready to wage

World War II again, only this time as a pilot when he'd never flown a plane in his life. Matilda hoped in twenty years she would simply have a huge, catastrophic brain aneurysm. It would be painful and terrifying for a moment, but far more dignified and compassionate than this slow disintegration of the mind.

Matilda pulled on slacks, a bulky sweater, and combed her thick salt-and-pepper hair. She never wore jewelry or cologne, not that she would have bothered with them in an emergency. She turned on a lamp in the front window so whoever might be watching her would think she was home. Then she grabbed her purse, which was always set on a metal cart beside the door leading from the house to the garage. In a moment the automatic opener sent the garage door humming up, and Matilda pulled out onto the alley that ran behind her house. Her father had always hated garage doors that faced the street. The cop stationed in a car parallel with the front of her house never saw her leave.

Grace Haven Nursing Home was only two miles away from Matilda's house. When she had first tearfully signed the papers to place her father in the home, she'd felt as if it were two hundred miles away. They had lived together all her life; and although he had a phone in his room and they talked at least once during each day and she visited on Sunday evenings, the closeness seemed mechanical and forced. After two years of it, though, Matilda had grown used to his absence. He was still alive. He was still lucid at least half the time. But if what the nurse had said tonight was true, this could be the beginning of the end of those lucid times. Matilda could be losing her father in all but body.

Before Matilda turned off her car ignition, she glanced at the clock on the dashboard. Twelve forty-five. Usually her father was asleep by ten. What on earth had set him off after midnight? It couldn't have been something he'd seen on television. Perhaps a dream.

The Grace Haven parking lot was behind the facility and

nearly deserted at this time, with only staff members' cars parked close to the building. No one came visiting at nearly one in the morning. Matilda knew no one would care if she parked in one of the staff spots, but she had never been one to break rules. So she parked where she always did, off to the right at the edge of the lot near a stand of evergreens the staff lavishly decorated every Christmas.

Matilda stepped out of the car, pushed down the lock button, and closed the door. She slung her large purse over her shoulder, straightened her sweater, and ran a hand through her hair.

"Miss Vinson?"

"Yes?" she said absently, jerking her hands down from her hair. "I'm just on my way inside."

"I'm afraid not."

An arm shot around the right side of her neck so fast she didn't even get out a gasp. The arm jerked tight, the elbow just left of her Adam's apple, the bicep pushing into the area of her vocal cords.

"Wha—" she managed before someone pulled back her head. She saw the tops of the towering evergreens and the dark shape of a bird lighting on a top branch. The bird seemed to be watching with interest.

"You always did talk too much, didn't you? Skeeter watching, you talking. What a pair. You should have married him, Miss Vinson. He was just about the best you could do."

So this was the person who had killed Skeeter, Matilda thought with an odd numbness. The person whose arm was around her throat had stuck an ice pick in Skeeter's eye because of something Skeeter hadn't really seen. But she *had* seen something. She knew. And there was no use pretending she didn't know. Even if she'd had the breath, her tone would have betrayed her. Matilda had never been a good liar.

"Well, let's get this over with." Here there was a little

snicker. "I know how you hate to waste time. Busy, busy, busy, that's our Matilda."

An arm crossed over the top of her head, the hand splayed and firmly planted above her right ear. She didn't even try to struggle. She felt like a rabbit brought down by a wolf, helpless, in shock. But unlike the rabbit, she wouldn't squeal. No, Matilda Vinson would go out with dignity.

But as one arm jerked right and the other jerked left, breaking her slender neck with a decisive, sickening snap of bone, she rasped out one last word:

"Daddy."

Chapter Sixteen

1

Suzanne crept into Rebecca's room as soon as Rebecca returned. "How's Frank?" she asked meekly.

"You'd know if you'd gone to the hospital with him." Rebecca didn't look at her mother. She removed her earrings, then her contacts. "It doesn't appear that he had a heart attack. His EKG is erratic. Not all the tests are back so he has to stay, but he's resting comfortably, as they say. I didn't get to see him. They wanted him to stay quiet and sleep."

"Then you think he's going to be all right?"

"I'm not a doctor, Mother," Rebecca said tightly. "Why don't you get dressed, go to the hospital tomorrow, and consult with one? Frank *is* your husband."

Suzanne sat down on the bed. "You know why I didn't go this evening. It's obvious I've been drinking. What would people say?"

"I have news, Mother. People already know you spend half your time drunk." Suzanne winced. "I'm sorry. That was cruel. But it's true."

"I know it." Suzanne's voice was weak. "I try to pretend no one knows the shape I'm in, but it's hard to hide. That's why I rarely go out." She paused. "I was so frightened this evening, Rebecca. I thought Frank just had a touch of flu. Or maybe he just didn't want to sleep in the same bed with me. He's having an affair, you know."

"Oh, Mother!" Rebecca whirled away from the vanity mirror. "For God's sake, do you have to start this paranoid nonsense *now*?"

"It isn't paranoia," Suzanne said calmly. "It's true. And it's all right. Well, it isn't all right, but I certainly understand it. I haven't been a real wife to him for a long time.

He's a charming, attractive man. Naturally he'd look for female company."

Suzanne was too calm to be spinning a fantasy. She was clearly telling something she knew to be true and had accepted. "Who is the woman?" Rebecca asked.

"I don't know. He's very discreet, bless him. Maybe it's someone from work."

Sonia's mother. Suddenly Rebecca was sure Frank's "lover" was Mrs. Ellis. She seemed to have confided a lot in him about Sonia and Randy. He said she'd been looking better and acting happier lately. He spoke glowingly of her. He hadn't been the least concerned when she hadn't really been at choir practice during Sonia's attack and Cory couldn't find her afterward. He wasn't surprised by her lie or worried about her true whereabouts because he'd known where she was. After all, he'd been gone earlier in the evening, too. They'd probably been together and she'd stayed wherever they met until choir practice was supposed to be over. He'd returned home earlier and received the call from the hospital.

Rebecca wanted to be outraged for her mother, but she couldn't. She couldn't even be disappointed in Frank. She had never felt that he was truly in love with Suzanne. He had married her because of fondness for her and obligation to his best friend. And she'd made him a poor wife. Still, he had conducted himself with patience and dignity, but he couldn't help being a man, needing someone for attention and affection.

"Affair or no affair, I think you should go to the hospital tomorrow," Rebecca said gently. "You are Frank's wife. He's been good to you and to this family—"

"Oh, I know!" Suzanne said fervently. She might have been intoxicated earlier in the evening, but she was almost completely sober now. "I'm going to do better, Rebecca. I know you've heard that before. I've even tried before, but I've never felt this much resolve. I owe it to everyone, especially to Frank." She smiled almost shyly. "And to you. No matter what you think, no matter how I've acted, I've always loved you, Rebecca. And I'll prove it to you. Those aren't hollow promises. I *swear* to do better."

Rebecca knew most alcoholics thought they could handle their problem by themselves. She knew they all swore to do better and usually failed. Still, Rebecca didn't remember ever seeing such flinty earnestness in Suzanne's eyes. In spite of Frank's heart problems, in spite of Todd's abduction, Rebecca went to bed feeling more settled about her mother than she had since before her father died. he'd always known she longed for her mother's love. She just hadn't known how much.

She fell promptly to sleep around midnight. She didn't remember dreaming, although she knew she had, but at four in the morning she sat straight up in bed, her eyes open, perspiration drenching her dainty cotton nightgown; the familiarity of her bedroom vanished as she realized her mind had taken her to another place, a cold and frightening place, a place that did not exist except in her dreams.

His hands and feet were manacled, arms behind his body. He lay on his abdomen on a series of dusty cushions—he could feel the breaks between them. Three. A couch. An old couch that had gotten wet and mildewed. The smell was faintly nauseating. Still, his stomach roared with hunger and his dry mouth longed for water, no matter how foul. His throat hurt. His lungs felt constricted. He knew he was in a cabin and it was late October. There was no heat in the cabin, and the nights dropped into the forties and thirties. He had only a thin wool blanket for warmth.

At first he'd tried to get free whenever he was left alone. He'd scuffled and slithered on the floor, and ran his head into walls, until finally he was one mass of sore and bleeding injuries. Even then his will hadn't died, but his body wouldn't cooperate anymore. He shivered uncontrollably through the nights and in the mornings, he was just too tired, too spent, to try much of anything. Then his captor had decided to feed him a decent meal and he'd eaten as much as his shrunken stomach could hold. Later that night when he was alone he'd thrown up. Gagged, he had thrown up.

"You don't look too good. You feel all right?"

He shook his head. "Water," he croaked.

A long pause. He thought his request was going to be denied. Then arms lifted the top half of his body, twisting him at the waist, letting his back fall against the couch. The blindfold was tight and he had the feeling he'd never see right again, as if the eyeballs had been pushed back too far for too long. Someone took the gag off and water poured into his mouth.

"Drink."

The water was warm, musty. Probably rusty if he could see it. Rusty. His mind filled with images of the dog and he felt tears run into the material of the blindfold. If only Rusty could find him.

He choked. Water poured down his chin onto his chest. "Damn it, now you're wasting it and there's not that much."

But he couldn't stop choking. And with each cough, he felt mucous rise in his throat. Thick gobs of it spewed from his mouth, landing on his chest.

"Jeez!" his captor exclaimed. "That's gross!" Then after a moment, the person asked, "You got a cold or something?"

This morning the tightness in his chest had started, causing him to grow breathless after the least exertion. And then the awful cough that seemed to be bringing up his lungs. Was it possible to cough up your lungs? Maybe pieces? If you did, would the pieces grow back? Oh God, he was so miserable.

The strong hands retied his gag, only looser this time "so you can cough easier," and pushed him back on the couch. "I'm gonna get you some cough syrup. You'll be okay. It's all gonna be okay. It has to be."

But as the door closed behind his captor, Jonnie knew it wasn't going to be okay. Sometime in the deepest, coldest part of last night, the last bit of hope had died in him and he'd known he'd never see home again. Maybe he would be buried in the woods and no one would ever find him. Maybe he would be stored in the awful black Ryan mausoleum that had always scared the wits out of him.

Rebecca came back to herself and her breath labored in her chest. She coughed, loudly and raggedly, just as Jonnie had in her vision, but nothing had come from her lungs. Of course not. The autopsy had shown that during his capture he'd vomited, but no one had removed his gag so some of the vomit had rolled back into his lungs, causing aspiration pneumonia. Even if he'd been found the day before someone had bashed in his skull, he probably could not have been saved.

And now, because of her vision, she knew he had realized death was inevitable. All of these years she'd prayed he'd kept hope until the last, brutal minute. But he hadn't. He was a smart boy. He'd guessed the inescapable.

After a vision, Rebecca always felt shaken, her equilibrium unreliable, her mental focus nonexistent. But today was different. Her senses thrummed. Her body longed for action. It was only five, still dark outside, but she could not force herself to lie in bed, waiting even for light. She flung back the covers, splashed water on her face in the bathroom, threw on a robe, and went downstairs.

The kitchen was empty and seemed completely unfamiliar without Betty's presence or the smell of cooking. At least of coffee. That's what she needed. A good strong cup of coffee. In her wired mental state, decaf probably would've been best, but she craved caffeine, no matter what the results. She filled the coffeemaker, flipped it on, then walked through the house to the front in search of the morning newspaper. She turned on the porch light, unlocked the double doors, swung them open, and gasped.

On the walkway lay the wilted remains of the roses she'd left at the mausoleum yesterday, the golden script of "Get Well Soon" glittering under the light.

2

Within fifteen minutes Rebecca, dressed in jeans and a T-shirt, had pulled the red Thunderbird out of the driveway. She carried a thermal cup of coffee and Sean sat in the bucket seat across from her.

"Twice I've envisioned Jonnie at the mausoleum," she chattered in her nervousness to the dog. "Yesterday I was there. I left *those* flowers, Sean. Not some *like* them. *Those*, with that ridiculous message." Her eyes filled with tears. "What in the name of God is he trying to tell me?"

After finding the flowers, Rebecca had run back to the kitchen and headed for the Peg-Board. Even here Betty's sense of order reigned. The Peg-Board measured nearly three feet by two feet and hung at eye level. Rebecca scanned the dozens of sets of keys hanging from it, all carefully labeled. Keys and spares to every car. Keys and spares to every door on the property. Keys to Esther's house. Keys to crucial offices at Grace Healthcare. Finally, when she was ready to scream, she spotted them: Mausoleum Keys.

After throwing on clothes, Rebecca looked at Sean. She wasn't afraid to go alone to the cemetery in the day, but in the semidarkness she wasn't going without her protector. He displayed his usual excitement as soon as she attached his leash.

Blue streaks ran like spilled paint across a slate gray sky as Rebecca pulled into Shady Mount Cemetery. The car headlights sparkled on the dewy, perfectly trimmed grass. Many of the granite headstones still gleamed with night moisture, and recently placed fresh flower arrangements burst with damp color.

She slowed as she neared the Ryan mausoleum. Its black granite lines didn't look imposing in the early light—it looked menacing, a perfect site for unhappy ghosts. Rebecca shivered and suddenly decided that when she died, she wanted to be buried on that rise overlooking the brook Mr. Hale had described to Clay. Maybe she'd even be buried *with* Clay if he wouldn't mind since neither would be with their families—

"Oh for crying out loud!" Rebecca exclaimed in exasperation. She was procrastinating because she was scared. She'd come flying out here like a superhero to the rescue and now she sat in the car dithering about where she wanted to be buried. She had no time for this.

She looked around and didn't see anyone. She checked her watch. Six-fifteen. Far too early for gardening work to begin in the cemetery. She could always go to Mr. Hale's cottage a quarter of a mile from here and have him accompany her to the mausoleum—but if there was nothing wrong, she'd look like a nut, not to mention the fact she'd have disturbed his morning.

Rebecca took a deep breath and emerged from the car, Sean scrambling behind her. He immediately lifted his leg, and suddenly Rebecca was glad she hadn't gone for Mr. Hale. He was a good-natured man, but a tyrant when it came to the appearance of his cemetery. He would not appreciate a circle of dead grass.

"Sean, must you do that *everywhere*?" she hissed.

Sean gave her a look that said clearly, Yes I *must*. I *will*. She sighed, grateful that humans didn't feel the need to mark territory in this manner.

Slowly they climbed the three steps to the columned portico of the mausoleum. Of course her offering of roses was missing. They were lying in front of her house. Wrought-iron gates, always kept locked, protected the carved wooden doors of the mausoleum. Rebecca twisted an iron handle, and the gates swung open. Next she pulled on the brass handles of the wooden doors. They opened without a squeak.

The first thing that hit her was the music. Low, haunting: "A Whiter Shade of Pale." The hair on her arms raised and her neck felt icy. She forced herself not to run out the door.

Inside, soft lights burned in lavender glass sconces. In

spite of them shadows lay everywhere because there were no windows. Rebecca felt the coldness of the floor beneath her thin-soled shoes. She suddenly felt as if someone were going to walk out of the shadows, offer her a skeletal hand, and say, "We've been waiting for you." She shivered and shook off the image. Lights and music did not equal welcoming skeletons. And she would not be a shaking, hallucinatory coward.

Bracing herself, Rebecca walked to the end of the first row of plaques. First she saw Rusty's. The dog had died searching for his beloved master, and Suzanne had insisted he be buried in the crypt, no matter how outraged some family members had been. "If that dog didn't have a soul, then no one does," she'd said staunchly, and Rebecca had been so proud of her. Next to Rusty's crypt was Jonnie's, on which Suzanne had allowed no date of birth or death to be added, as if the missing dates alone could change reality:

Jonathan Patrick Ryan
And death shall have no dominion

Rebecca's eyes filled with tears. Then she looked below the copper plaque to the polished granite beneath it. There, in chalk, someone had inscribed a symbol:

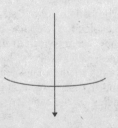

"Oh God, an inverted cross," she gasped, backing away. "Is it meant to be the sign of Satan?"

But Sean was paying no attention to his horrified mistress. At the back of the mausoleum sat a small altar covered with white lace. A crucifix hung above it, and candles burned in front of a statue of the Virgin Mary. Sean was not interested in the altar itself, though. He nudged something lying on the floor in the shadows a few feet in front of the altar. He pawed at it, whining loudly.

Rebecca's heart skittered in her chest and she turned away from the inverted cross to face Sean, who whined again, louder. She stood still for a moment. Then she walked toward the dog and kneeled beside him.

The object was a bit over five feet long, slender, and wrapped in a thin, white blanket. Rebecca extended a shaking hand, feeling as if the world might fall away if she unrolled the cloth. Still, she could not stop herself.

She pulled the edge of the blanket and the cloth spun open, rolling toward the altar. Sean drew nearer to her, his body tense yet shivering. Rebecca remained motionless, still balanced on the balls of her feet, until she saw a limp hand fall free and land against the altar.

She drew a deep breath. Finally she stood and walked around the edge of the blanket, picking up a lit candle. Then she kneeled, holding the candle low and squinting in the semidarkness.

Rebecca's mouth opened but no scream emerged when she saw the white, twisted face of Matilda Vinson.

CHAPTER SEVENTEEN

1

Rebecca felt oddly calm as she stared into the still face of Miss Vinson. She even gently touched her cheek. It was cold. The woman had been dead for hours.

When she stood, her legs felt stiff and old. She almost groaned with the effort. Then she walked to the front of the mausoleum, down the steps, and all the way back to the Hale cottage, ignoring the car. She never took Sean's leash, but he remained within a foot of her, whether from fear or an instinct to protect she didn't know.

On the road to the cottage, she didn't think. It seemed perfectly normal to be walking briskly in this beautiful blue and pink dawn, breathing deeply, swinging her arms at her sides to burn off extra calories.

As soon as Chloe Hale opened the door swathed in a yellow wraparound robe, though, Rebecca felt tears flood her eyes. Chloe's dark face showed surprise, then concern before she said, "Why, child, what are you doing out here so early? What's *wrong?*"

"The mauso-mausoleum," Rebecca managed.

Tears ran down her face. Chloe took her arm and drew her inside. Sean marched in without being invited and stood staunchly by her side. "Now what's wrong with the mausoleum? No, don't answer now. You come right in the kitchen and have a fresh cup of coffee. Lord, you look like you're gonna faint."

Rebecca followed dutifully into the kitchen. Mrs. Hale nearly pushed her into a chair, poured a mug of coffee, and set it in front of her along with a pitcher of milk and a sugar dish. Then she sat down across the table from her, her amber eyes full of curiosity and a bit of alarm. "*Now* tell me about the mausoleum."

Rebecca took a sip of hot coffee. "I had a . . . dream about something being wrong at the mausoleum." No sense shaking everyone up with talk of visions. "It wasn't the first one, and I just had to come check out the place."

Mrs. Hale stared at her. "Honey, if you thought something was wrong out here, you should have called Avram. That's what he and the staff are here for. My goodness, young thing like you wandering around in the dark, and you weakened by all the awful things that have happened to you this week."

"I didn't think. And I didn't want to seem silly."

"Child, my grandmother taught me to have respect for second sight. I've believed in your visions since you were a little girl. If you'd called at three in the morning and said you thought something was wrong out here, Avram and I would have been out to that mausoleum in a shot. But you didn't. You found out something for yourself." Chloe Hale covered Rebecca's cold hand with her own. "Honey, what is it?"

"The doors of the mausoleum were unlocked. I went in. There was an inverted cross marked beneath Jonnie's plaque."

By this time Mr. Hale had appeared at the door wrapped in a terry-cloth robe, his hair wet. "What!" he exploded. "Some hooligan broke into that mausoleum—"

"Not broke in, Mr. Hale. The doors were unlocked."

Avram Hale disappeared for a moment, then reappeared with a gigantic ring of keys. "My keys stay with me at all times during the day. At night they're locked in a drawer, just like they were this morning. My spares are in a safe-deposit box. There's got to be an extra key to that mausoleum out there, because no one in the Ryan family would commit such a sacrilege. It just makes me burn—"

"Mr. Hale," Rebecca said, trying to make herself sound calm. "That's not the worst of it." His white eyebrows rose. "Matilda Vinson's dead body is lying in front of the altar."

2

THURSDAY, 5:00 P.M.

The early morning had been a haze of police cars, photographers, an ambulance, the crew of Shady Mount standing around watching what for the police was the routine of homicide. After intense questioning by Bill, Rebecca had been allowed to return home just as the ambulance left the cemetery taking the small body of Matilda Vinson to the funeral home. At least she won't be worrying about her father tonight, Rebecca thought.

The rest of the day she'd felt oddly numb. Since last night her mother had been planning a coming home celebration for Frank. Betty fretted about the appropriateness of a celebration in light of Matilda's murder, but Rebecca was determined they would not spoil the first positive step her mother had taken in months. They would not talk about Matilda. She had said the mausoleum was broken into and she hadn't told the family about the inverted cross in the mausoleum. That was one horror Suzanne would not be able to ignore for the evening.

Now, however, Rebecca talked quietly with Bill on the phone in Frank's study. Clay was off at six and had volunteered to bring Frank home and then stay for dinner. Rebecca was relieved there would be a doctor in the house to make sure Frank was doing all right on his first night home. Molly and Esther were coming. Molly had barely left her house for five days. Esther felt a couple of hours away in a social setting filled with loving people might help her. Rebecca and Bill had agreed.

"About Matilda," Rebecca said. "Was there any evidence about who killed her?"

"The broken neck was the only injury. There may be hair and fibers, DNA evidence, but I won't know anything about that for a couple of days."

"Was she killed at the mausoleum?"

"I don't think so. Her car is at Grace Haven Nursing Home. No one saw her there. Maybe she got a call to go there about her father, and someone was waiting for her in the parking lot."

"The person she saw in the cemetery."

"Seems to make sense. I believe the killer used his or her own car to transport the body because there was too much chance of leaving some incriminating evidence behind in Matilda's—his hair, fibers, that kind of thing."

"What about fingerprints on the boom box or the CD?"

"None but yours. I didn't expect to find any. Our killer is too organized."

Rebecca sighed. "I wish Matilda had said more at the funeral."

"She didn't get a chance. Someone was watching her. But the killer doesn't know how much she told you. Obviously she didn't reveal his identity or he'd be under arrest, but maybe he's afraid she said enough to give you a clue. So now he's trying to scare you away before you make any damaging connections in your mind. That's why he put her in the mausoleum and left your bouquet on your porch. It was all staged for *you* so maybe you'd be so frightened you'd leave town. After all, you're quite a threat with your ESP."

Rebecca raised her gaze to the ceiling. "I haven't been much of a threat yet."

"You *have* had visions and given us help. And maybe the next time your vision will tell us exactly where Todd is and who took him."

"Oh God, if only that were true." Rebecca shook her head. "Bill, look at this nightmare. Skeeter and Matilda dead. Sonia attacked with intent to kill. All of this because of Todd. There wasn't so much mayhem when Jonnie was kidnapped."

"Maybe it was a different kidnapper. Or . . ."

"Or what?"

"I hate to bring up a painful subject, but you weren't as much of a threat when Jonnie was taken as you are now.

You weren't seeing anything. Now you are and that puts you in real danger, Rebecca."

3

Suzanne wore a pale blue dress, pearls, and high heels. Her makeup, applied by Rebecca, was perfect. She'd had one glass of wine "to steady my nerves," but she definitely had her wits about her. With her blond hair gleaming in a loose pageboy and small diamonds sparkling at her ears, she looked beautiful when Frank walked in the door.

"Darling!" she cried. "I'm *so* glad to see you!"

She kissed his cheek, giggled, then wiped away a trace of cherry-colored lipstick. Frank looked taken aback by his wife's beauty and open affection, but extremely pleased. "How do you feel?" she asked.

"Perfectly fine."

"You look a bit tired to me. Clay, do you think he looks tired?"

"Rebecca can tell you the hospital is the last place to get a good night's sleep," Clay said easily. "And he had a roommate who mumbled and moaned all night."

"A roommate!" Suzanne exclaimed. "Why didn't you let him have a private room?"

Clay grinned. "I remembered when I was seventeen and he gave me the devil for taking his Porsche for a joyride. It was payback."

"It was nothing of the sort." Frank laughed. "Suzanne, dear, I'm capable of answering for myself. First of all, if I was going to buy a car like a Porsche, I should have expected hijinks from teenagers like Doug and Clay. But as for the room, *I* requested a double. I wanted to know another living being was in there with me throughout the night. I know it was silly, but fear does strange things to the mind."

"Were you scared?" Suzanne asked innocently. It was a

child's question and Rebecca felt a twinge of embarrassment.

"Well, I did think I was having a heart attack," Frank said smoothly. "But I don't want to hear another word about that tonight. I'm just glad to be home. And look who's agreed to come with me. Suzanne, you haven't said one word to Dr. Bellamy."

She flushed. "I'm sorry. We're so pleased you could come to dinner."

"I'm pleased to be invited."

"And you look so grown up!" Rebecca closed her eyes briefly, fearing what would come next. And it did. "Last time I saw you, you had your hair cut in those awful spikes like on the music videos."

"To annoy my father."

Suzanne looked perplexed. "Why do children always want to annoy their parents?"

"Because their parents annoy them," Frank supplied, smiling.

"Well, you certainly look clean-cut and handsome now."

"Thank you. And you look beautiful tonight, Mrs. Hardison."

"Oh, you are just as charming as ever!" Suzanne beamed all around. She was so happy tonight with her looks and her new resolve to make Frank a good wife that all old resentments seemed to have vanished. So Rebecca knew absolutely she was not being malicious when the awful words bubbled from her perfect, cherry-colored lips: "Rebecca, didn't I always say Clayton Bellamy was a doll?" Suzanne looked archly at Clay. "Not as if I had to convince *her*. Our poor little Rebecca just suffered with her crush on you, didn't you, dear? Worst case of lovesickness I've ever seen."

Clay raised an eyebrow at Rebecca, his lips twitching. Rebecca thought if any more blood rushed to her face she'd turn blue and pass out. For once even Frank looked flummoxed. It was Sean who saved the day, bounding in and jumping up on Clay the way he always did Rebecca, wrapping his front legs around Clay's waist.

"Well, what's this?" Frank nearly exploded, trying to cover the dreadful moment. "Our Sean is enraptured by a *man*?"

"I think it might be the scent of my dog, sir," Clay said. "Her name is Gypsy and I think she's quite the femme fatale."

Frank laughed. "I'm Frank, not sir, and I'm sure your Gypsy is lovely." He turned to Suzanne. "Something smells very good."

"Betty is fixing a special dinner for you. Italian food—your favorite. But nothing too high in cholesterol."

"Actually Mr. Hardison's—Frank's—cholesterol is perfect," Clay said. "No worries there."

"Oh, that's wonderful. Even more reason for having a little party. I hope you don't mind, Frank, but we're having guests. I talked Esther into bringing Molly."

"It'll be good for Molly to get out," Frank said.

Suzanne's smile inched down a notch. "There's one off note, though. I invited Douglas, which is fine, but I'm sure he'll bring Lynn."

Rebecca's gaze met Clay's. He seemed to be thinking the same thing she was: Oh no. Doug would be polite but no one could predict what Lynn might do. She hated Rebecca.

Frank continued smiling. "We'll make the best of Lynn. Maybe since she thinks I'm dying, she'll be nice."

"Oh Frank, don't even joke about such a thing! Honestly!" Suzanne rebuked with a smile. She's giving it her all, Rebecca thought in admiration. Frank couldn't help but be impressed.

Still, she had to say a word to her mother before Molly arrived. "Mother," she whispered as the men moved into the living room.

"Yes, dear," Suzanne trilled. "Isn't this fun? Clay is *so* cute. And a doctor. This is so exciting."

"Mother, he's just here for dinner. He brought Frank. There's nothing serious—" She broke off, trying to get back to her point. "Mother, I know you're glad to see Frank and relieved he's all right. And you look lovely—ebullient—but we have to remember that Todd is still gone. We must be sensitive to Molly's feelings. Maybe when she comes, you should act a little less, well—."

"Merry," Suzanne said flatly. "What on earth was I thinking? I wasn't thinking, as usual. You're right. We'll try to keep things upbeat, but not jolly. That's entirely the wrong note to strike for Molly. Or any of us. Thank you for the advice, dear."

Rebecca's lips parted in surprise as her mother walked into the living room to join her guests. She'd expected Suzanne to be defensive, but once again she'd astounded Rebecca. "Thank God," Rebecca breathed. "Please let this evening go well."

She had her doubts about her prayer being answered when Doug and Lynn arrived ten minutes later. Rebecca ushered them in. Doug's greeting to her was overly hearty. Lynn snapped, "Hello," and tried to freeze Rebecca with her eyes. Rebecca managed a bland smile and complimented Lynn on her earrings. She saw with satisfaction the compliment enraged Lynn. Smirking to herself, Rebecca trailed after them into the living room.

Doug hugged his father stiffly. In the old days there had been so much trouble between them. Rebecca could still remember the shouting coming from Frank's study, the nights he'd stormed from the house to bail Doug out of jail for some infraction, the tumultuous return home and Suzanne's persistent wail, "Douglas, *why* can't you be more like Jonnie?" Those had been awful days, but in spite of Doug's rebelliousness and the trouble he caused, Rebecca had felt sorry for him. He'd been miserable in this house. He hadn't belonged. What he hadn't seemed to realize in that unhappy past was that she hadn't belonged either.

Everyone now swore the past was buried. Rebecca was not a great believer in pasts ever being buried. She thought people were largely the product of their environments, their presents and futures molded by the lives they'd already led. Worst of all, she felt that unfortunate pasts had a way of bubbling, hidden, for years before they burst forth like geysers, refusing to stay quiet. Not a pleasant scenario.

Rebecca had felt the evening should be alcohol-free, but Suzanne insisted this would make everyone more conscious of her effort at sobriety and embarrass her. Frank was offering drinks in the living room when Molly and Esther arrived five minutes later. Esther was smiling brightly, but Molly's smile was forced, a strained slit in a tight and pale face. Her eyes were bloodshot and heavy-lidded. She hadn't been sleeping. She wore slacks and a blouse that was buttoned unevenly.

"I'm so glad to see both of you," Rebecca said warmly. "Frank has been home for about half an hour. Clay Bellamy is here with him. And so are Doug and Lynn."

Esther maintained her smile although at the mention of Lynn Molly's disappeared. "Oh dear, she'll cause trouble. She doesn't like us, Becky."

"We will ignore her," Rebecca said blithely. "Two against one."

"But I don't feel like having a fight with her tonight."

"There won't be a fight," Rebecca reassured her. "Aunt Esther won't allow it, will you? She's a former teacher. She knows how to break up childish arguments."

"I certainly do," Esther said, stepping in and removing a scarf from her fluffy hair. She wore a simple blue dress and her ever-present cross necklace. Rebecca thought of the inverted cross on Jonnie's plaque and shivered. "I can put Little Miss Lynn in her place if I have to, so don't you worry, Molly."

"I don't intend to be put in my place."

Everyone turned to see Lynn lounging in the door holding a glass of wine. "Ganging up on me already before I've said one word?"

"Building our defenses on the basis of *past* words," Rebecca said easily. "I think we could all use a glass of wine."

"Doug doesn't want me to have any. I usually don't drink anymore, but I figure family gatherings certainly warrant at least one glass of wine."

"On that I agree with you," Rebecca said, herding Esther and Molly past the cool-eyed Lynn. "Molly, have a drink and try to relax for a few hours."

Molly turned a pinched, anxious face toward her. "Rebecca, you haven't—"

"No, I haven't had any visions," she said gently. "Maybe relaxing, clearing my head will help. Tonight could help me to concentrate . . ." She trailed off, feeling duplicitous. Concentration didn't help call forth visions that had a mind of their own. But Molly was deeply uncomfortable in this situation. She had to get her through it. Thinking she was helping Todd would help Molly.

Sean had curled into a corner, either trying to be a gentleman or trying to make himself invisible so he wouldn't have to leave the festivities. Frank was expansive, amiable, and Suzanne was fluttering around being the perfect hostess, casting Frank flirtatious smiles and loving looks. He seemed slightly at sea with her attitude. Clay and Doug talked quietly. Or rather Doug talked. Clay nodded, clearly deciding it was best to let Doug pick which topics were acceptable. Lynn floated around the room looking both resentful and preoccupied. Rebecca wondered how she felt about Matilda Vinson's death. She knew Lynn hadn't liked the woman, but certainly she felt *something*. Did she plan to attend the funeral?

Esther stayed close to Molly. No one talked about Todd. Suzanne told Molly she liked her hair longer and Molly smiled slightly. Esther drank mineral water while Molly took Rebecca's suggestion and had wine. But Rebecca noticed she was sipping too often, probably from nerves, and a subtle way would have to be found to slow her down. Well, stopping too diligent a drinker was a familiar task in this house, Rebecca thought. Frank and Betty must be masters.

Molly was in the midst of asking for a third glass of wine when Betty announced dinner, to Rebecca's relief. They all trooped into the dining room, where the best china, crystal, and silver glowed in the candlelight. Rebecca no-

ticed Sean slipping unobtrusively into the kitchen, where
he would take up his accustomed place under the table at
Walt's feet.

Fifteen minutes later they dined on light veal ragù with
tomato. Frank seemed to be enjoying his meal but was
rather quiet. Lynn ate sullenly and mechanically. Molly put
food in her mouth with a distracted air. Clay, Doug, Suzanne, and Esther led the conversation, for which Rebecca
was grateful because she felt a dull headache forming beside her right eye. She also felt a vague sense of uneasiness
nothing caused by events happening at the table, which
made her feel more uneasy. The feeling usually preceded
vision. Perhaps that was good if it meant she'd learn more
about Todd.

"Rebecca, your bangle bracelets almost completely hid
your bandages," Lynn piped up, then slipped a bite of oven-
roasted potato into her mouth. "Did the guy really slit your
wrists?" Doug glared at her but she didn't look at him.

"He cut them a little," Rebecca returned casually. "Nothing serious."

"I wonder why he did it?"

"I don't think any of us wants to understand the mind
of someone like that person and *I* don't want to talk about
him. I'm sure no one else does, either," Esther said repres-
sively. "Lynn, what plans do you have for your new store?
Do you have plenty of inventory to fill your shelves?"

Lynn had been pouting because no one was paying attention to her. Esther's ploy was perfect. Lynn came to life
talking animatedly about her latest ceramic pieces and how
she planned to set up the interior of the store. Doug's face
relaxed. Molly took another slug of wine in what seemed
relief. Clay winked at Rebecca. Suzanne reached over and
lightly touched Frank's hand.

By the time Betty delivered dessert—almond me-
ringues—Rebecca's headache had intensified. Frank had
left the table twice to go to the bathroom, assuring everyone
in a self-deprecating way that he was fine except for
build-up of fluids due to all those "cursed IVs" he'd re-

ceived at the hospital. So when Rebecca excused herself, no one seemed to notice.

She bypassed the downstairs hall bathroom and rushed up to her room. In her own bathroom she held a washcloth under cold water, wrung it out, and lay down on her bed, placing the cold cloth on her forehead. A moment later she rose, turned on the radio component of her clock, and lay down again. No music now. Just a weather report. Fair and warm tomorrow with a high of—

The vision hit her like a blow. She grimaced with the pain, pulling herself into a tight ball. Her lovely room disappeared, along with the voice of the weatherman on the radio. Even with her eyes open, it was dark. Rebecca was lost in the vision.

Something cried pitifully not far away, a sound that had become painfully familiar. His mind felt foggy. His head hurt. His throat hurt. He was hot, but he couldn't stop shivering. And within the last couple of hours, he'd developed a pain in his right side, slightly below his waist. It wasn't too bad, but it was constant, like it was saying, "I'm here. I'm here." He was too tired to try to stand up anymore or work on the bonds that held his hands and feet and covered his eyes and his mouth. He felt almost too yucky to be scared. Almost.

He was hungry and desperately thirsty. The Dark Warrior hadn't come around for ages. Was he just going to be left here? Was he just going to die here in the dark? Someday would somebody find his bones and say, "Gee, I wonder who this was? Oh well, it's just bones. It doesn't matter"? And no one would know the bones had belonged to Todd Jonathan Ryan, who was a great swimmer and had goldfish and meant everything to his mother.

He wondered if Mommy was still thinking about him. He wasn't sure how long he'd been gone. Sometimes it seemed like a couple of days, sometimes it seemed like forever. But he was pretty sure Mommy wouldn't forget him. He knew she loved him an awful lot. He loved her an awful lot, too, although he didn't tell his friends. They'd think he was weird.

For a while he'd had the hope that his cousin Rebecca would find him. Mommy said she had special powers. Also, one time he'd felt like Rebecca was in his mind. That sounded really creepy, but it also sounded kind of like something a Jedi Knight could do—entering someone's mind, poking around, sending messages to be strong. He wondered if Rebecca was a Jedi. But if she was, wouldn't she have found him by now? Or had she given up?

He started to cry. He felt worse than worst. He was lonely. He was getting sick. And what in the world was that poor thing that kept wailing into the night, something that sounded like a baby getting killed? It frightened him. It made him want to help. But he couldn't do *anything*, not for himself, not for whatever was hurting.

He cried harder, holding his right side. For the first time, he was sure he was going to die.

"I feel yucky, I'm afraid. I feel yucky, I'm afraid. I feel yucky, I'm—"

"Rebecca. *Rebecca!* Come out of it. You're shaking. Come back. Come back *now!*"

Slowly Rebecca returned to her surroundings. She lay partially reclined on the bed, Clay's arms around her. "I don't . . . where . . ."

"You're in your bedroom. You're safe." He pulled her closer to him. "Calm down, Rebecca. Concentrate on your breathing. You're hyperventilating. You're also soaking wet."

"But I have to help—"

"Not now. Now just be quiet." He pulled the bedspread over her. "Lie back in my arms, relax, and slow your breathing."

Rebecca did as he said, leaning against him, enjoying the feel of his strong arms around her. Why did they make her feel so secure? Just because she was terrified of being alone? Or was it something about Clay, his feeling of steadiness and assurance in spite of all the lighthearted teasing?

He stroked her right arm, and she thought she felt him lightly kissing the top of her head, murmuring to her. Music now played on the radio. Sarah McLachlan's "I Love You." Rebecca murmured, "My favorite song." She drifted with the music and the warmth of Clay. It was all so seductive. She could drift like this forever, forget the problems, forget little lost Todd—

She pulled herself back with a jerk.

"I'm all right now," she said, sitting up so fast Clay looked startled. "I had another vision, needless to say. About Todd. He's alive, but he's not doing well, Clay. His head and throat hurt. He feels hot yet he's cold. And he has a constant pain. Here." She pointed to her side.

Clay frowned. "Has Todd ever had his appendix removed?"

"No. Molly would have told me." Clay looked even more troubled. "Oh God, you don't think he's developing appendicitis?"

"Well, I can't do a physical examination and I don't have any blood tests to go on, but I don't like the sound of it. Hot skin, yet chills—fever. Pain in the right place."

"If he *is* getting appendicitis, how long does he have before the appendix ruptures?"

"It varies."

"Twenty-four hours? Forty-eight?"

"Forty-eight would be pushing it."

"And if it ruptures?"

"If he got immediate help, there would be a chance. If not, there's peritonitis and—"

"And it's all over."

"Probably."

Rebecca stood up. "Oh God. I have to do something. Fast."

"Did you see where he was?"

"No, damn it! Just that same dark, cold place. And there was something crying outside. An awful sound like a child or an animal being killed—slowly, horribly. Does that help?"

"No. Not immediately, anyway. Maybe if I think about it a little. No other clues?"

"The Dark Warrior—that's how Todd thinks of his captor—hasn't been around to feed him. He's starving and thirsty. And he feels so bad. He probably *does* have appendicitis. How do I go down and tell Molly this?"

"You don't," Clay said firmly. "Bill's manning her phone tonight while she's here. First we tell him. Make the call now before anyone comes up to check on us, like I'm supposed to be doing on you."

Rebecca called and Bill answered almost immediately. Without preamble she launched into her vision. "But you still have no idea where he is," Bill said, sounding disappointed.

"He's blindfolded—he sees nothing. He feels cold."

"And he hears what?"

"A high-pitched crying. Shrill. Like a baby being tortured."

"Do you only know what he thinks he hears, or can you hear it?"

"I can hear it."

"Then imitate it."

Rebecca was too agitated to feel silly. She tried a couple of times and failed. She adjusted her voice a third time until she got a rough rendition. "Does that ring any bells?"

Bill was silent for a moment. "Are you sure you're not making it sound more human?"

"I don't think so. It *does* sound human."

"Then I might have an idea. A long time ago when I was out in the woods, I heard something similar. Raised goose bumps on my arms. I ran through the woods, Garrett to the rescue, and what do you think it was? A fawn."

"You mean like a deer?"

"Yeah. A very young fawn in the nest. The mother had left it, probably to look for food, and it was afraid. She came charging back, ready for a fight with me. I backed away and she went straight to her baby and it stopped that godawful noise. But believe me, it was horrible. And I heard it again another year. This time the fawn was in danger from a fox. I scared the fox away. Mama returned shortly."

"Are you sure the noise is *that* bad? That frightening?"

"Both times I heard it, it spooked the hell out of me."

"Bill thinks Todd could be hearing a frightened fawn?" Clay asked.

"Yes."

Clay snapped his fingers and nodded vigorously. "So Todd could be in or near the woods!"

"I'd bet on it," Bill said, overhearing Clay's exclamation.

"Well, that's something!" Rebecca felt elated for a moment. Then her spirits fell. "The trouble is, Sinclair is surrounded by woods."

4

Rebecca and Clay decided to mention nothing about her vision or Bill's suggestion that Todd was in the woods to the family. They would simply say Rebecca had suffered a headache from her injuries but had taken aspirin and was feeling better now. Certain they looked and acted calm, they descended the stairs and entered the living room, where the family had gathered.

"Why Rebecca, you and Clay have been gone so *long*," Lynn purred. "And you look so dewy, so *flushed*."

"Shut up, Lynn," Rebecca said absently.

Lynn flushed and turned to her husband. "Doug! Did you hear what she said?"

"Glad you're feeling better, Becky," Doug said smoothly. "Clay, what do you think of West Virginia University's football schedule for this year?"

Lynn poured another glass of wine and went into a dramatic smolder by the piano. Suzanne looked up at Rebecca and murmured, "Hope you feel better, dear."

In a moment Walt appeared at the doorway and motioned to Rebecca. She went to him quickly. "Is something wrong with Sean?"

"No, ma'am. Took him for a little walk after his dinner. He's right as rain. But Mr. Hardison has a phone call. Betty's in a cleaning frenzy so she sent me to tell him, but I don't look presentable to come in the living room."

Rebecca turned. "Frank, you have a phone call."

Frank smiled. "Take a message and tell them I'll call back later."

Rebecca smiled at Walt. "Will you do that?"

"I can't," Walt hissed.

"Frank, Walt says he can't—"

"Walt, quit hovering in the doorway. Come in here and tell me what's wrong."

Walt took a reluctant step onto the forest green carpet. "Sorry, Mr. Hardison. This person won't take no for an answer. Insists on talkin' to you. I sure am sorry to interrupt, sir, but it sounds real important. And the person sounds mad. I'm sorry, sir . . ."

"Damn it all," Frank said, rising. "Don't apologize, Walt. Every day I get a hundred of these life and death calls that really mean nothing. I'll take it and get rid of the person."

As Rebecca turned back to the room, she looked at Molly, who'd fallen into a deep study of her own shoes. Molly had cranked her spirits as high as she could to come to this dinner, but she'd had about all she could take. And if she only knew what Rebecca knew, that Todd was cold and frightened and sick . . .

Molly looked up at Rebecca as if she sensed something. Rebecca smiled encouragingly. Clay was right. She couldn't possibly tell Molly what she knew. Molly might break completely, particularly if she knew what they feared—that Todd had appendicitis. Rebecca's smile felt stiff and false, even treacherous, but she didn't know what else to do.

Frank returned with heightened color and annoyance, even agitation, written on his face. "Damn people expect immediate service no matter what!" he blustered. "That was nothing—absolutely nothing. Could have waited until tomorrow. Could have waited until next week!"

Frank was usually more sanguine about business affairs and Rebecca noticed Doug looking at his father in consternation. She couldn't tell if he was worried about Frank's health or if some of his old teenage fear of his father's sudden angers, usually elicited by him, had crept into the body of the man now in his thirties. Frank recovered quickly. He glanced around and smiled. "Never mind me. A short stay in the hospital and I come home a curmudgeon. Now what were we talking about?"

"Really, Frank, I think Molly and I should wend our way home," Esther said. Molly instantly came out of her reverie, looking relieved. "I know Molly doesn't like to be away from the phone for long and I'm not used to this wild nightlife."

"Yeah, it's been a real blast, hasn't it?" Lynn sniped.

Esther and Molly stood, followed by Suzanne. "We hate for you to run off, but we understand. I'm just so glad you could come." Suzanne hugged Molly. "Dear girl. Keep up your spirits. You know we all love you."

Everyone followed Molly and Esther to the front door. Molly was the first to see the envelope lying an inch beyond the foot of the door on the dark carpet. "Secret messages slipped under the door?" she asked with an attempt at levity.

She bent to pick it up, but Clay said, "Stop!" Then he withdrew a handkerchief from his pocket and lifted the envelope by the corner. It had not been sealed. The flap hung open and, still using the handkerchief, he withdrew a folded note and read aloud while Rebecca looked over his shoulder:

Ransem for Tod Ryan: $500,000.00
Leave un-marked bills in trash can in brown paper bag in mens rest room between 9:00 and 10:00 Friday nite during the concert in Leland Park. You will be watched. All park will be watched. Any sign of cops or FBI Tod will *die*. No second chances. Remember other Ryan boy.

Chapter Eighteen

1

Everyone stood frozen. Here it was at last. Concrete proof that Todd had been taken for ransom. But it was Thursday evening. He had been taken the previous Saturday. Why the long wait?

"I don't care why they waited so long!" Molly blurted almost hysterically when Rebecca voiced her doubts. "Money! That's all they want. Money, and I can have Todd back. But I don't have five hundred thousand dollars."

"I do," Frank said crisply. "What's mine is yours, Molly."

Molly's eyes filled with tears. "Oh Frank, I can't ask—"

"Molly, dear, don't be silly. What's money compared to a child's life?" He paused. "But we must be careful this time. Not like with Jonathan. The note says no FBI. We made the mistake of showing Jonathan's ransom note to Sheriff Lutz and he brought them in anyway. They bungled everything. Or maybe Lutz did, trying to horn in on the glory. In any case, Sheriff Lutz can't know."

"I agree," Molly said fervently. "Please don't tell Lutz."

"Maybe Bill shouldn't know either," Frank added. "He might feel some official obligation to tell the FBI."

"I don't think he would," Suzanne said. "He has no love for the FBI. He thinks they let local police do the work, then step in and take the credit. But there's this other thing about *no* cops. Bill is my brother. I know him. He won't stay away from this drop."

"If he knows how important it is for him to stay away, he might," Molly offered.

"No, Molly. If Bill knows a kidnapper is going to be in that park, he'll have police there," Suzanne insisted. "Maybe *he* won't show up, but he'll send someone he trusts."

"Like that Deputy Curry," Rebecca said. "Bill has tremendous respect for his abilities. Mother is right. Bill would send him. Disguised, of course, but still . . ."

"Then we can't take the chance," Molly said frantically. "We *can't.*"

Doug looked at his father as he spoke. "I agree. We'll do exactly as the note says. *Exactly.* And none of us"—he looked around, especially at Lynn, Clay, and Esther—"none of us will say a word about this. To anyone. Agreed?"

"That's brilliant, darling," Lynn drawled, "but don't you think someone's going to get suspicious when Frank draws five hundred thousand out of the bank tomorrow? The most confidential information travels like wildfire in Sinclair."

"All of Frank's money is in Sinclair, but *I* have an account in Charleston," Suzanne said. "I have certificates of deposit worth well over five hundred thousand. Rebecca can take me since my driving isn't what it used to be. I will have that money for you by tomorrow afternoon, Molly."

"Oh, Suzanne, I don't know how to thank you," Molly choked out.

Suzanne waved her quiet. "Don't you worry. We're going to get Todd back. And Douglas is right. This is all to be kept secret." Suzanne turned and gave Lynn a surprisingly steely look from her beautiful blue eyes. "Do you understand that, Lynn? This is absolutely a *secret.*"

"Jeez, I understand," Lynn said in a bored voice. She made the motion of a key turning at her lips, sealing them like a vault. Doug seemed dismayed by her insouciance. Rebecca clearly wanted to slap her for being a smart aleck. Molly looked wounded. They all thought she was an unfeeling jerk, Lynn thought. If they only knew. Underneath her dress, her heart felt as if it might pound out of her chest. Perspiration popped out on her upper lip. She was more frightened than she had ever been in her life.

Matilda Vinson, the gorgon, was dead. Her neck had been snapped like a chicken bone, snapped the way Larry

had showed her how to do years ago. Shown her an
laughed. "Can you believe it's so easy?" he'd crowed. An
Matilda had been placed in the Ryan mausoleum. Lyn
could just see Larry, drunk out of his mind, loading Vin
son's skinny body into his trunk, hauling it to the mauso
leum. And how had he gotten in? Years ago when he ha
been friends with Doug he'd visited this house. No one
not even Doug, knew that he'd stolen the key to the mau
soleum, had a copy made, and replaced the original. He'
wanted access to the place because he thought it was s
freaky. He'd actually had a party in there one night, man
aging to escape detection by picking a time when Avran
Hale was on vacation; Hale's minions didn't keep a hawk'
eye on the cemetery like he did.

Larry probably still had that key somewhere. He woul
have thought it was the funniest thing in the world to pu
Matilda's body in that horror of a place. He would hav
thought Lynn would get a secret kick out of it, too, whe
she heard. And Frank had told her about the inverted cros
drawn on Jonnie's plaque. It had shaken her to the core
When she'd confronted Larry, his denial of drawing th
symbol hadn't been convincing. He'd just sounded furiou
with her for asking him about it.

Now she wanted to scream at all these well-dresse
well-mannered people in frustration for warning her, *spe
cifically*, not to talk about the ransom note. If anyone her
believed she might run blabbing to the police, they wer
crazy. After all, the person who turned up at that ranso
drop might be her own brother.

2

"Becky, I have a favor to ask," Molly said as they walke
out to her car.

"Anything."

"I want you to go to Leland Park and make the drop."

Rebecca looked at her. "Why me? I would have thought Doug."

"Oh, I want him to go, too, if Lynn will let him."

"Lynn can't stop him when it comes to this," Rebecca said. "But I still don't understand."

"I don't quite understand it either. I just know that I want you there. That you are supposed to *be* there." Molly raised her shoulders. "It doesn't make any sense. Maybe I'm going crazy. It's just so important to me . . ." Her eyes filled with tears. "But it could be a dangerous situation. It's not fair to ask you—"

"Danger is my middle name," Rebecca said with a rakish tilt to her head. "I don't care about any possible danger. What's going to happen to me in a park full of people?" She hugged Molly. "I'll go. Count on it."

Chapter Nineteen

1

Tension thrummed through the Ryan house. Even Sear
seemed aware of it, following Rebecca relentlessly, frequently touching her leg with his paw, waiting for her to
bend down and rub his head for reassurance.

Rebecca had not slept all night. She felt tired as she and
Suzanne started off for Charleston, Rebecca driving her
mother's Thunderbird. They listened to music. When the
Eagles' "Peaceful Easy Feeling" came on, Suzanne sighed
and closed her eyes. "Your father and I loved this song. He
used to sing along. And *he* had a great voice."

Rebecca smiled. "I remember."

"Jonnie inherited it."

"And I inherited yours."

"Poor child." Suzanne grinned. "Must you drive so
slow?"

"I'm doing the speed limit. You and Daddy always
flew."

"And had the speeding tickets to prove it. But it was
fun. When he was young, he had a Harley. We soared
around the countryside. I never felt so free."

"You seem in a good mood today in spite of everything
that's happening."

"I feel hopeful, Rebecca. So much time went by without
a ransom note that I was sure Todd had been taken by a
crazy and there was no chance of getting him back." She
was silent a moment. "I know what you're thinking—we
got a ransom note for Jonnie, too, but ransom didn't save
him. But that time we didn't do what the kidnapper wanted.
Sheriff Lutz and the FBI were sure they knew best. They
didn't. Now neither Lutz nor the FBI knows. Not even Bill
knows. He's my brother and he wants to do what's best,

but he's still a policeman to his bones, even though he loves Todd."

"He told me he's been dating Molly."

"It's more than that. He's in love with her. He has been for months. Maybe over a year. He's never said anything, but he *is* my brother. I could tell at family gatherings." She sighed. "Wouldn't it be wonderful if we could get Todd back and Molly and Bill got married?"

"Married?" Rebecca thought. "Do you think Molly loves Bill?"

"Oh yes."

Rebecca looked at her mother sharply. "You said when Molly gave birth to Todd and she was under the anesthesia she said Todd's father belonged to someone else. Bill was married to that clotheshorse masquerading as a woman then."

"Until Bill proved she'd been seeing another man for months."

"Don't change the subject. What about Bill? Was he in love with Molly then? Could *he* be Todd's father?"

Suzanne looked at her openly. "I've thought about it, Rebecca, but I honestly don't know."

The rest of the day went smoothly. Suzanne withdrew the money and afterward insisted they stop at a nice restaurant for lunch.

"Mother, are you sure you want to go in a restaurant? Do you know how much cash you have in your tote bag?" Rebecca asked.

"Certainly enough to cover lunch," Suzanne replied airily. "And I have a craving for lobster salad and a nice white wine. One glass. I promise." She looked at Rebecca and smiled. "Please, dear, one mother–daughter lunch when things are going so well. It would mean so much to me."

So they lunched. Then Rebecca acquiesced to Suzanne's request and went five miles over the speed limit all the way to Sinclair. They sang along to Carly Simon CDs and arrived home at three sharp. Frank was watching a soap opera, which he hastily turned off as soon as they arrived.

Sean sat in the kitchen, waiting for Rebecca. And for Walt.

At five-thirty the phone rang. Rebecca answered. It was Doug. "I fell down the basement stairs and sprained my ankle. I can't go with you tonight."

Rebecca sat silent for a moment. "You did *what*?"

"Sprained my ankle. It was so dumb. There was something wrong with the water heater and I went tearing down and missed the last five steps. I'm really sorry."

He did not sound sorry. He sounded ashamed. "Have you been to the hospital for X-rays?" she asked.

"No."

"Then how do you know your ankle isn't broken?"

"Oh, I'm sure it isn't. Just hurts like the devil. I've taken plenty of aspirin."

"If you can't go, you can't go," Rebecca said stonily. "I hope you feel better."

"Rebecca, I'm really sorry—"

She hung up.

Rebecca leaned back in her chair and covered her eyes. Now what was this all about? Certainly Doug wasn't so spineless that he'd back out simply because Lynn didn't want him to go. He cared for Todd. She knew he did. But she didn't believe Doug's story. He just didn't want to go.

So she would go by herself. What was the alternative? Frank was in no shape. Bill couldn't go, couldn't even *know* what was happening. But the money was to be left in the trash can of the men's rest room. Maybe she could wear a cap and slip in unnoticed. Yes, that could be managed easily. But surveillance? The family didn't want cops patrolling the park, but they had hoped to get a glimpse of whoever went into the rest room. The kidnapper would obviously be watching. He couldn't see her go in, leave the money, then hang around, keeping an eye on the rest room. He'd know he was being watched. No, the rest room had to be watched by a second person.

After ten minutes, Rebecca called the hospital and asked to speak to Clay. He had to call back, but when he did, he sounded as if he already knew something was wrong. "What is it?" he asked urgently.

"Doug called. He said he sprained his ankle. He's not coming tonight."

"Not coming? What the hell? Rebecca, we've had a light day. He hasn't been in for an X-ray, bandaging, painkillers . . ."

"I know. He said he was sure he didn't need to come to the hospital. He's just not able to come with me tonight."

"With *you*. You didn't tell me you were going."

"Molly asked me to. Begged me to, really. I can go alone—"

"No, you can't. I'm supposed to be on duty, but I can get off. I'm going. But you're not."

"I am."

"You're not."

Rebecca huffed. "Clay, we need two people there as lookouts. That park is eight acres."

"Two people can't cover eight acres."

"Two people can cover a half-acre around the men's rest room. I'm not arguing about this. I'm going. Are you?"

"God, you're stubborn! What time should I pick you up?"

Rebecca couldn't help smiling. "This isn't a date. It's a top-secret mission, remember? How about I meet you at . . ."

After a pause Clay asked, "Am I supposed to guess?"

"I'm thinking. We shouldn't enter the park together. We'll look suspicious if either of us is recognized. I'll meet you two blocks away from the park, in Dormaine's parking lot at eight-fifty. I'll give you the money there. You walk on to the park and put the money in the trash can in the men's rest room. I'll follow about fifteen minutes later. We'll stay close, but not team up. How does that sound?"

"Like you're with the CIA. But good except for you walking two blocks in the dark to the park. I can't let you do that."

Rebecca closed her eyes in exasperation. "Am I supposed to station myself right outside the park in my mother's flaming red Thunderbird with the vanity plates, or would it be better to take Frank's silver Mercedes S600?"

"How about Betty's car? It's nondescript." Rebecca was silent. "I insist."

"Doctors are *so* bossy. All right. I'll make up some excuse to borrow her car."

"Good. See you tonight at eight-fifty."

"Right. And Clay?"

"Yeah?"

"Thank you."

"Anything for you, Stargazer. Ten-four over and out." He hung up and in spite of the whole mess, Rebecca grinned.

2

FRIDAY, 8:50 P.M.

"Is that you?" Clay asked.

Rebecca took off her baseball cap. "Hides the hair, hides the bandages on my forehead. Apparently a pretty good disguise."

"Complete with your glasses. Love the tattered jeans. And isn't it kind of warm for a long-sleeved shirt?"

"The jeans weren't tattered until an hour ago when I took Betty's shears to them. The shirt sleeves cover the bandages on my wrists."

"I hope you have bug spray on your face. The mosquitoes are wicked."

"Sean fell in love with the scent. I'm thinking of substituting it for Chanel No. 5."

They stood in Dormaine's parking lot, Clay beside his small white compact, Rebecca beside Betty's behemoth of a Dodge. She hadn't been able to think of an excuse for borrowing the car from Betty. She'd just taken the extra set of keys off the Peg-Board in the kitchen and driven away.

She removed a paper bag from her white tote bag. "Here's the money."

Clay took it gingerly. "My God. I don't even want to think about how much is in here. And I'm going to stick it in a trash can. I'll throw a few wadded paper towels on it. And I'll act casual. No darting in and out. No furtive looks. Cool is the word. How's my outfit?"

"Stylin', dude. We look like twins with our caps."

Clay smiled. "Even with caps, we don't look like twins. You're still all girl."

"You never quit teasing, do you? Even at a time like this."

"Hey, I'm trying not to let nerves get the best of me. Believe it or not, this is my first ransom drop. But I meant what I said about you being all girl."

"In spite of all my stitches?"

Abruptly Clay pulled her into his arms. His kiss was quick, insistent, hot, and temporarily made her forget murder and ransom drops and everything except the sunny smell of his skin and the tender stroke of his tongue on her lower lip. "See you later, gorgeous," he said before just as abruptly letting go of her and turning away. She nearly fell down.

"Wow," she muttered to herself like a fourteen-year-old as she watched him loping across the parking lot of Dormaine's, heading for the street. "Clay Bellamy, what have I been missing all these years?" She glanced at her watch. "And what will I miss if I don't stop acting like a lovelorn adolescent and get back to work?"

In ten minutes Rebecca found a parking place near the park. It was a lovely night and a crowd had turned out for the concert. She didn't know if this was good or bad in the kidnapper's eyes. Her parallel parking was always bad, but Betty's huge car made it nearly impossible. She seesawed back and forth, cursing, until she finally gave up in frustration. When she emerged from the car, she saw that it was a foot from the curb. She'd probably have a ticket when she returned, but the street was wide. She wouldn't be blocking traffic and she couldn't spend all night trying to park. It was nine-fifteen.

The park lights were on, drawing moths. Lights glowed in the bandstand. High above the crowd stood the players in uniform, sending a merry rendition of "The Band Played On" into the night. Each summer they added one new song. One. Rebecca wondered what this summer's selection would be. But the Sinclair devotees never seemed to mind. The concerts were a meeting place where they could bring children, listen to fairly good renditions of old classics, and have soft drinks and lemonade on pretty summer nights. They had always been enjoyable for Rebecca.

Until tonight. Now there seemed to be too many people. The music was too loud. The lights were too bright, shining on her face, which she wanted to keep hidden. Her heart was going like a trip-hammer. Her bug spray wasn't working. She slapped at a mosquito biting her shoulder, then realized her shirt covered it. Nerves were making her itch. Great. A nervous rash on top of everything else.

Rebecca sauntered toward the refreshment stand and bought a lemonade. Then she walked nearer the bandstand. Children ran past her. She spotted Helen and Edgar Moreland and quickly ducked her head. All she needed was Edgar Moreland booming out her name. She sucked down the lemonade in less than a minute, her throat dry from tension. She wanted more, but returning to the refreshment stand so quickly might call attention. This undercover stuff was tough, she thought. It made you self-conscious of every movement.

The band finished to happy applause then launched into "A Bicycle Built for Two." Rebecca thought of Cory Ellis's Megadeth T-shirt and smiled. He'd be as likely to attend one of these concerts as he would be to spend an evening at the library.

Slowly she walked away from the bandstand toward the white-painted, concrete-block building housing the rest rooms. She was on the men's side and suddenly saw Clay emerging. Rebecca jerked her head the other way, then rebuked herself. Hardly a nonchalant movement. But what had taken him so long to place the money? He'd had to wait until the rest room was empty, of course. He was careful. He was calm. She must be, too.

Rebecca strolled the brick paths through one of the rose gardens, but all the beautiful blooms were lost on her. She returned to the refreshment stand for another lemonade and tried to pace herself, but she felt as if she were going to die of thirst. This waiting and hiding in plain sight was driving her mad. The band plowed on with "Ciribiribin." People were now a mass of blurry faces to Rebecca. She neared the rest rooms again. This time she saw Clay leaning against a tree talking to a pretty young woman. She blazed inwardly. Of all times to be flirting! Then she noticed his eyes continually straying toward the door of the men's room. Certainly he couldn't just stand and stare at it. The woman was a convenience. Rebecca felt impatient with herself that she'd even cared if he was flirting. She also felt better that he wasn't.

By ten-thirty the band had rocked through "Home on the Range," "Au Claire de la Lune," "Oh, Susannah," and "Funiculi, Funicula." Exhausted by mental strain, Rebecca sat down on a bench about thirty feet from the men's room and angled slightly away from it. She was on her fourth lemonade. She wished it was a margarita with a double shot of tequila.

She didn't know what she had expected of tonight, but it wasn't this *nothingness*. She was too influenced by books and television. She'd expected a burst of action, but all she could do was wait and sip her lemonade.

3

"This town is turning into Murder Central," Burt, the bartender at The Gold Key, said to Larry Cochran after watching the latest reports on the murder of Matilda Vinson on the fifteen-inch television suspended above the bar. "First

Skeeter, then Miss Vinson. And there was that attack on Sonia Ellis. Poor kid. Just a teenager."

"Two more minutes and that girl would have been a bloody pulp. That's what I heard," a beefy man sitting beside Larry stated to the room at large. He had gigantic arms covered with garish tattoos, a shaven scalp, one gold front tooth, and the tiny mean eyes of a boar. "Pretty little teenager. Choice meat." He sneered. " 'Course that redhead that saved her isn't bad either."

"Know both of 'em well, do you, Densh?" the bartender asked with a careful smile.

"Know every good-lookin' woman in this town, Burt," Densh boomed. "Had most of 'em, too, if you get my drift."

"Subtle as it was," mumbled a thin, dark-haired man in a booth directly behind Densh.

Densh whirled on him. "What's that, wimp? You callin' me a liar?" He pronounced the word "lar." " 'Cause I don't put up with nobody callin' me a liar."

"I was merely talking to myself," the young man said.

"So you're just a nut, that it? Talkin' to yourself like a damned lunatic? You tryin' to take over for Skeeter Dobbs?"

"I didn't mean anything."

"The hell you didn't. But you're just jealous. You don't look like you ever had a woman in your life, much less scored like I have. Had my first when I was nine." The bartender rolled his eyes and a few patrons smiled mockingly, but Densh was focused on his dark-haired victim. "What's your name, wimp?" The young man continued to stare into his beer. "I said, what's your *name*?"

"Alvin."

"Alvin!" Densh guffawed. "Now there's a helluva name. Damned *manly* name, that is. Alvin *what*?"

"Tanner."

Larry Cochran's head shot up. "Alvin Tanner," Densh repeated. "Sounds kinda familiar to me. I know you?"

"I don't believe so. No, certainly not."

"Whattaya mean, certainly not? You mean you wouldn't have nothin' to do with the likes of me?"

"Hey, Densh, leave him alone," Larry Cochran intervened.

Densh glared down the bar at Larry. "And what's he to you?"

"Nothing. I'm just trying to think and you're making it hard."

"Oh, you're *thinkin'*." Densh looked around. "Hey everybody, the ex-con is tryin' to *think*. Whatcha got on your mind, Cochran? Computers? Brain surgery? The meanin' of life?"

Larry suddenly looked angry. "Just give it a rest, Densh. Leave me alone. And leave Tanner alone."

"Who's Tanner?"

"The guy whose name you asked two minutes ago, genius. He's minding his own business. Why don't you give it a try?"

Densh surged off the bar stool. "Why, you son of a bitch! I'll break you in half. I'll tear off that bad leg. I'll make you scream like the stupid pig you are, you . . . you . . . you stupid pig!"

Burt nodded at a man taller and even more muscular than Densh, about ten years younger, and incredibly handsome except for a pair of soulless green eyes. He approached Densh slowly, his chiseled lips stretched in a smile. "Think you've had your limit, Densh," he said pleasantly. "Why don't you go home to the little woman?"

"And why don't you shut your mouth?" Densh roared.

Larry knew the bouncer's name was Strand: He'd had his own run-ins with the guy, who was one mean specimen, pumped up on steroids physically and mentally. Strand took Densh's right arm, twisted it until Densh yelled, then dragged him toward the door.

"I said to go home," Strand said above Densh's bawling. "Give your little woman the thrill of her life in bed."

"In his dreams," Larry muttered.

Densh tried to whirl on Larry, but Strand pinned his

arms. Suddenly Strand had the front door open and Densh was standing on the sidewalk, reeling. Strand slammed the door.

"Nice going, Cochran," Strand snarled as he passed Larry. "Never know when to shut up, do you?"

"Go to hell," Larry snapped, then turned hurriedly back to his scotch when Strand looked like he was going to punch him. After Strand moved on, Larry climbed off his bar stool. The pain in his leg had been worse for days. His limp was more pronounced and lines of pain dug into his forehead. He scooted into Alvin's booth. "Bad news, that Densh," he said.

Alvin glowered at him from behind his glasses. "You didn't have to come to my defense. I could have taken care of myself."

"Oh really?" Larry had expected gratitude. "And how would you have taken care of yourself?"

"Reasoned with him."

Larry threw back his head and laughed. "Oh sure. Reason is *very* big with guys like Densh."

"You made me look like a fool," Alvin accused.

By now Larry was growing furious with the skinny twerp who didn't appreciate being saved. "I didn't have to make you *look* like a fool. You *are* a fool if you think you could have handled Densh." Then he squinted. "You're Slim Tanner's boy."

Alarm flashed in Alvin's eyes. "What if I am? Did you know her?"

"I know she knifed your old man to death right outside this bar. Saved your life. But she suffered just like I did thanks to that bitch Rebecca Ryan."

"I don't know Rebecca Ryan," Alvin said stiffly.

"You know who she is. She sent your mom *and* me to the penitentiary. She tried to wreck my life, but she's got a surprise coming." Larry was starting to slur. "She's got herself one *big* surprise coming."

"Please get out of my booth."

" 'Please get out of my booth,' " Larry imitated in a

prissy voice. "What the hell's the matter with you?"

"Thank you for helping me with Mr. Densh, but I'd like to be alone now. Please move."

"My pleasure, asshole," Larry sneered. "I should have let Densh kill you, but you don't look like you've got the balls your mother had." His eyes narrowed as he lurched from the booth. "What are you doing here, anyway? Dredging up fond memories?"

Alvin's face flamed. Dear God, what *was* he doing in this hellhole? Remembering, that's what he was doing. Remembering the times his mother had sent him, a little boy, here to look for his father. Remembering his father full of sloppy, drunken gaiety, holding him up so he could play the pinball machines and saying he was smart as a whip. Remembering the young waitress who clung to his father and sweetly called Alvin "Little Man." Remembering a big man like Densh who'd called Slim a whore, been punched by Alvin's father, and later been accused of killing Earl Tanner. Remembering creeping back here two days after his father's murder to see the bloodstain on the concrete in the alley.

Today had been one of the worst days of Alvin's life. But he had to hang on. Soon it would all be over.

4

It was eleven-twenty. The band had stopped promptly at eleven. The park was emptying. By now Rebecca and Clay had given up avoiding each other. Clay had joined her on a bench ten minutes ago. He sat over a foot away from her and acted as if they weren't together. They had a view of the men's room door, but neither looked directly at it. Rebecca looked at her hands. Clay looked at the sky.

"When you were about fifteen, you told me a story about a constellation, Stargazer," Clay said suddenly. "Something about bears. I can't remember it. Tell me again."

He was losing hope, trying to take up time, but Rebecca

obliged his effort. "Lycaon, a king of Arcadia, served Zeus human flesh so Zeus changed him into a wolf in retaliation. But Zeus didn't stop there. Lycaon had a daughter named Callisto. Zeus fell in love with her—"

"Zeus fell in love with every woman."

"True. He was a cad. Anyway, Hera got mad and turned her into a bear. It was her intent to have Callisto's son Arcas kill her, thinking she was an ordinary bear. But Zeus got wind of Hera's plan and put Callisto in the sky where she'd be safe. She's known as the constellation the Great Bear. Later Callisto's son Arcas was also put in the sky as a constellation. He's known as the Lesser Bear. But Hera wouldn't let matters rest. Infuriated, she talked the God of the Sea into not letting the Bears sink into the ocean like the other stars. So the Bears are the only constellations that never get to descend below the horizon." She paused. "What made you think of that story?"

"Molly and Todd. Mama and Baby Bear. Wouldn't it be wonderful if they were both safe up there in the sky?"

Rebecca was touched, both by his remembrance of the story and the sentiment it had aroused in him. "They had a powerful protector in Zeus."

"Todd and Molly have you."

"Not quite the same," Rebecca said dryly.

"I'd put my money on you rather than Zeus anytime." Clay continued to stare at the sky. "You, of course, can pick out Mama and Baby Bear."

"Yes. Right up there."

Clay looked intently, then said, "I've never been able to pick out constellations."

"Maybe you're just too impatient." Rebecca fell silent. Finally she asked, "Do you think this guy is going to pick up the money?"

"He may have already."

"Should you go back in the men's room and check?"

"No. If he's watching, I might scare him off." Still not looking at her, Clay said, "As a matter of fact, I think we

should leave now. For all we know, he's been watching us
all along."

"But if he goes in—"

"And comes out waving the money triumphantly we'll
jump him? Rebecca, he'll tuck away the money. We won't
know if he has it or not."

"Then why were we out here?"

"To see if someone familiar came out of that rest room
at the right time, someone that could have taken Jonnie,
too. After all, no kidnapper would leave five hundred thousand dollars in a public restroom all night."

She sighed. "The park is almost empty. We're beginning
to look conspicuous."

"Then we have to go home," Clay said. She finally
looked at him. "Face it, Rebecca. We won't know if we
have a chance of getting Todd back until tomorrow."

5

"One more scotch," Larry told the bartender.

"Sorry. I told you last call."

"Yeah, so I want my last call. One more."

"The one *before* was last call. Besides, you've had
enough."

"I already got one mother. Or let's say a Medusa that
passes for a mother."

"What's a Medusa?"

"A woman in Greek mythology whose look could turn
a man to stone. An ex-friend of my sister's told me about
her a long time ago."

The bartender smiled. "Cochran, you're always coming
up with weird shit like that. You're a damned scholar.
Maybe you should go on one of those quiz shows. Make a
fortune."

"Other ways to make a fortune. And don't call me a
scholar. I read a lot in prison. Nothin' else to do but read
in there. Read and fend off a few inmates that got romantic

'tentions." Larry's lips were numb by now. The pain in his leg had also subsided by half. "Come on. One more."

"Can't do it. I make one exception and I'll get my license pulled. That's my luck. Don't give me a hard time, Cochran. We've always been friends."

"Got no friends."

"Suit yourself. But leave. Vamoose. Hit the road." He leaned forward. "Leave under your own steam or you'll land on the sidewalk like Densh."

"Oh hell, all right," Larry mumbled, suddenly seeming to lose interest in scotch and The Gold Key. "Mind if I hit the facilities first?"

"Just make sure you *do* hit the facilities. You miss the commode, and I'll make you clean it up."

Larry nearly fell off the bar stool laughing at this. The bartender had no idea he was so funny, but at least the guy wasn't going to give him trouble. He set about loading the last of the glasses into the dishwasher while Larry lumbered down the hall toward the rest room, occasionally bumping off a wall.

The odor of Pine-Sol made Larry draw back as soon as he opened the door. As a frequenter of the bar, Larry was used to the smell, but it seemed particularly strong tonight. Of course, his head felt like a pumpkin propped on his shoulders. He'd heard people talk about migraines but he'd never had one. Now he wondered if he were experiencing his first. The light hurt his eyes and sound reverberated painfully around his brain. He also felt like he had an ice pick jabbing into the base of his skull.

An ice pick. Skeeter Dobbs. No loss to the world, Skeeter. The guy had always given him the creeps. Gave Wendy Wright the creeps, too. God how he missed her. But she was back at school, making up in summer the classes she'd failed in the spring. Not that it really mattered that much. If she were home, she'd have to stay with her sister Nurse Jean, who kept an eagle eye on her and pronounced Larry strictly off-limits. In fact, she hated Larry for sullying her pretty little sister with his ex-con body. But Wendy sure didn't hate it and sneaked back to town whenever she got the chance. At this time in his life, Wendy was the only bright spot, the only person who gave him joy, not grief. He intended to marry her, no matter how much of a howl Jean put up, no matter how much she threatened him. Said she'd get his parole revoked. Said all kinds of weird shit. Damned uptight nutcase. Wendy detested her, couldn't wait to get free of her.

Larry relieved himself and left by the back door. That was what Burt would expect. A few feet of concrete separated The Gold Key from the back of what used to be Fanny's Fine Fabrics but would soon be Lynn's store. He hoped it would be a success. Then she'd be so busy she'd get off his back.

An overloaded Dumpster sat under a sodium-vapor lamp. On this warm night, the smell emanating from the Dumpster was revolting. Burt really should have the thing emptied more often, he thought virtuously. Should keep the place clean.

He'd take the alley out to Second Avenue, then cross the park on his way home. It was midnight now. The park would be empty. Great timing. Then just three blocks to his apartment.

A lot of people had stupid ideas about this alley and avoided it because it was where Slim Tanner stabbed her husband to death. People seemed to think it was haunted or something. Larry snickered. Of all the damned nonsense. Haunted. Poor old Earl Tanner didn't have the guts to haunt anything. He'd scare himself. Larry remembered him from when as a teenager he'd sneak in The Gold Key under the protection of older, tougher friends. Earl had been a good-natured drunk, always buying rounds for the house. Sometimes his dorky kid Alvin had come in after him. He'd been skinny with big glasses and a cowlick, but Earl acted proud of him, of all things. That had never made sense to Larry. They said Earl beat the kid near to death, but he'd been affectionate to him in the bar, holding him up to play pinball, letting his girlfriend make over the kid like he was

something special. People were hard to figure. Maybe Earl
was one of those split personality types.

As Larry staggered down the alley, he wondered if Slim
Tanner regretted what she'd done. Sure, she probably regretted getting caught. Everyone in the joint did. But when
Alvin came to visit her, did she look at his woebegone face
and wonder what she'd gotten herself in so damned much
trouble for? Larry had thought there might be a bond between him and Alvin. They'd both suffered because of Rebecca the bitch Ryan. But Alvin didn't seem to feel any
bond. He just seemed prim and sanctimonious. Sir Douglas
Do-Right's type. Larry was sorry he'd defended Alvin to
Densh. Sorry he'd pissed off Strand in the process. Both
were hot-headed, dangerous enemies.

Larry thought he heard something behind him. A foot-
step. He turned. There were no lights in the alley and it
was long. A little artificial light filtered in from the street,
but he saw nothing. Probably just an echo of his own footsteps, he thought, and slogged on.

A moment later he heard something else. He turned
again. Nothing. But the skin on his neck prickled. "Okay,
Cochran, this week's been a little too much, even for you.
What you expect to see? Ghost of Earl Tanner?" He tried
to snicker again, but the sound came out a sickly gag. He
faced the street and picked up his pace.

Sixty or seventy feet to Second Avenue. That's all. Just
keep walkin', Cochran, he told himself. Keep walkin' and
stop thinkin'.

Was that breathing he heard? Rough, ragged breathing
not too far behind him? He looked a third time. Was that
a shadow? Something hugging the wall of The Gold Key?
"Hey, Strand, that you?" he called. "Didn't mean to piss
you off earlier. Had a few too many." No answer. It sure
wasn't Densh. Maybe he'd made it home, maybe he hadn't,
but wherever he was, he was passed out. A stray dog or
cat. That's what it was. Scotch played tricks with the vision,
made things look bigger than they were. Think of it—Larry
Cochran, scared by a cat. He'd never repeat that one.

He took a few more steps, wondering what Wendy was doing. He was going up to the university this weekend. They'd spend Saturday and Sunday in bed like usual. He wouldn't drink tomorrow so he'd be up to speed in the love department. "I'm just a love machine," he sang, then broke into laughter. That song was before Wendy's time, but it was true. Nobody ever had any complaints about Larry Cochran in bed.

He stopped. He could feel someone looking at him. Not some*thing*. Not a dog or a cat. *Someone*. "I'm gettin' tired of this shit," he called. "A real man would come out and be seen. That you, wimp Tanner?" Silence. Larry would not turn around. He'd already looked three times. He wouldn't look again. Point of pride, he told himself. No more peeking over his shoulder like he was afraid. But actually, he *was* afraid, afraid to look behind him because someone was behind him, someone breathing hard, breathing excitedly, someone coming fast, someone coming for *him*.

He stumbled through a puddle of water left by the week's earlier rain but the sound of splashing water made him squeal. Squeal like a pig. Densh had called him a pig. He was mildly afraid of Densh, but not *this* afraid. Not afraid enough to have his spine turn to ice, his mind to blur and begin screaming, "Run! Run as fast as you can!"

And he tried. But it was too late. Someone was on him. The weight hit with tremendous force, knocking him to the concrete. He banged his head and his bad leg twisted under him. He cried out, but the sound was weak, mewling, shameful. If only he wasn't drunk. If only he could coordinate legs and arms, fight like he'd learned to fight in prison, kick the shit out of whoever was on him. But his equilibrium was shot. The blow had made his dizzy head even dizzier. His arms were pinned under his own body.

Suddenly he felt something metallic under his ear. Something like the head of a shaver. He heard the sound of electricity crackling. Blue flashed in the darkness. Then he was out.

As Larry lay motionless on the cold concrete of the dark alley, rendered harmless by a stun gun, someone rolled him onto his back and coolly and neatly pushed an ice pick into his closed right eye. Blood trickled. A latex-gloved hand then drove the ice pick deeper, deeper, until it was buried almost to the hilt. The attacker turned Larry's head for a better view, then watched as blood gushed down the side of his face and gathered in the very spot where Earl Tanner's blood had once pooled while his wife coldly looked on with a knife in her hand.

Chapter Twenty

1

Pain. In the right side. Stabbing. Scary. So hot. So thirsty. So scared. Mommy, Mommy. Please don't let me die here.

Rebecca awakened with a scream. Sean scrambled away from her, his ears perked forward, then dived for her, burrowing close. "My God," she murmured, holding him tight. "He's dying. Todd is dying."

Her door flew open and Frank stood there in a robe. "Rebecca, what is it?"

"A dream. A vision. I can't tell which this time. Todd is sick. He's alive but not for long, Frank. He's really suffering. I have to do something—"

She tried to get up but Frank rushed forward and put his hands on her shoulders. "I want you to calm down first." Sean showed his teeth and Frank abruptly removed his hands. "I'm not going to hurt your mistress, so take it easy, boy. I only want her to relax, get her breath."

"Frank, we have to see if someone got that money," Rebecca said urgently. "If they did, then maybe they'll get in touch with us soon about where to pick up Todd. Every minute is crucial."

Frank lowered his gaze. "Clay called about fifteen minutes ago. He's already checked the men's room, Rebecca."

She stared at him. "The money is still there."

"Yes. No one ever picked it up."

She lay back against the pillows. "Then what was this all about? Why all this drama about ransom? I don't understand!"

"There's something else," Frank said gently. "Clay said Larry Cochran's body was found in the alley beside The

Gold Key less than an hour ago. He had an ice pick in his eye, just like Skeeter."

"Larry . . . an ice pick . . . the alley?" Frank nodded. "I don't believe it! I mean, it's so close to the park!" Frank kept staring at her. "Do they have any idea who did it?"

"No. Clay only knew because he's at the hospital. Lynn is probably being informed right now."

"Oh Lord, she's become intolerable, but I feel sorry for her. She adored Larry."

"Yes. I don't feel sorry for Larry, though. He was a lost cause. But you're not thinking of what this might mean. Maybe it was Larry who took Todd, Larry who was supposed to pick up the ransom, only he couldn't because he was murdered before he could get to the money. The owner of The Gold Key says he got in a couple of verbal scraps last night. That's nothing new for Larry, but I suppose the men he insulted were the violent type. They're both being questioned."

"But the ice pick. Certainly they didn't murder Skeeter, too."

"Maybe one of them did. Or maybe someone got inspired by the method and decided to use it on Larry. Anyway, this is what we have. Larry murdered. Ransom money intact. Draw your own conclusions."

Rebecca closed her eyes. "Oh, Frank, if Larry took Todd, if he was only going to give up his location when he got the money, there's no chance of that now."

"I know."

"And Todd's sick. I've had this vision before. Clay thinks he might have appendicitis. If the appendix ruptures—" She broke off, her eyes filling with tears. "Does Molly know about the money yet?"

"No. I'm leaving for her house right now. Clay has gotten someone to fill in for him at the hospital and I asked him to meet me at Molly's. She might need another one of those injections."

Frank rose from the bed and walked slowly to the door,

his shoulders slightly bent. "Frank?" He turned and looked at her. "It's all over, isn't it?"

Rebecca had never seen him look so sad, so beaten. "I'm afraid so, dear." He shook his head. "Poor little Todd."

2

Rebecca tried to lie in bed for a while to piece everything together, to think of a way they could possibly retrieve Todd without a kidnapper safely holding his ransom money, but no answers came. The only hope lay in her. She needed a vision that would tell them exactly where to find Todd. But she felt no headache portending a vision and time was of the essence.

Last night when she'd returned from the park, she'd made a pot of decaf coffee and sat in the kitchen, feeling deflated. Frank had come in awhile later, wanting to know how the drop had gone. He looked awful, gray and tired. She'd told him they'd seen no sign of someone picking up the money.

"That doesn't surprise me," he'd said. "He'll wait until the park is empty."

"But wouldn't that make him more noticeable?" Rebecca had asked. "And don't they lock the rest rooms at night?"

"I'm sure this guy knows how to pick locks. And the rest room was probably crowded last night. Someone would have noticed a man pawing through the trash can. Cheer up, honey. I'll bet the money will be gone tomorrow morning."

But it wasn't. And now the awful news had to be broken to Molly. They couldn't even rely on Bill for this one because they'd kept the whole thing a secret from him, which would enrage him. God, what a mess.

Rebecca decided to talk with her mother. Certainly Frank had already told her. She was probably as upset as

Rebecca. She pulled on a robe and went to her mother'
room.

She entered without knocking and found Suzanne lyin
half out of the bed, her mouth open, a spilled bottle of win
beside her on the floor. Rebecca couldn't believe it. He
mother had been so together yesterday and the previou
evening, so in control. And now here she lay, dead drunk
oblivious. What had happened to all her good intentions
What had happened to her knowledge that everyone neede
her, especially Molly?

Rebecca was suddenly furious, strode to the bed, an
shook her mother hard. "Wake up," she said sharply
"Wake up, damn it. There's bad news."

Suzanne's mouth worked and she mumbled, but she di
not open her eyes. Rebecca picked up the wine bottle, se
it on the bedside table, then hauled her mother back int
the bed. Her face was slack, wine staining the front of he
nightgown. "Mother, open your eyes!" Rebecca com
manded. "How could you do this? Last night was *so* im
portant. Too important for you to face sober? Is that it?
said to open your *eyes*!"

"Beck, where Jonnie?" Suzanne slurred. "Find Jonnie?"

"Jonnie is dead," Rebecca said brutally. "And now Tod
will probably die, too. No one picked up the ranson
money. Do you hear me?"

"Tryin'. Can't think."

"Open your *eyes*."

"Can't. Don't know what's wrong."

"You're drunk, that's what's wrong. Mother, I am s
angry with you I could . . ." Rebecca sat down on the bed
"I've never seen you this drunk. What set you off?"

Suzanne moved her head on the pillows. "Don't know
No dinner. Waiting. Music. Then don't 'member. Sorry. S
sorry. But don't 'member."

"Wonderful. You're a great help, as usual." Rebecc
looked at her mother in disgust and confusion. "Neve
mind. Just lie here and sober up. Leave everything to Fran
as usual. He's the one who has to tell Molly no one picke

up the ransom and we still don't know where Todd is."

"Oh God," Suzanne mumbled. "Oh God. Want to help."

"Well, you've seen to it that you can't. Have a lovely day, Mother," Rebecca snarled, then flung out of the room.

But for all her anger, she was deeply hurt. She'd been so encouraged, so proud of her mother yesterday. The woman had suffered two terrible blows—the death of her husband and her son. Then she'd indulged in a weakness Rebecca knew nothing about. After all, alcoholism was a disease. She knew that. But Suzanne had seemed so sincere about trying to crawl out of the well. And last night, such an important night, she'd crawled in again. How could she?

Rebecca went downstairs for coffee. Betty said, "Mr. Hardison told me he was going to see Miss Molly. He didn't say about what, but I could tell it wasn't good news. Do you know anything about Todd?"

She couldn't tell Betty about the ransom drop. She had to tell Bill first. And without explaining about the failed drop, she couldn't explain how hopeless things looked for Todd. "I know he's alive. I also know he's sick," she said truthfully.

Betty's hands flew to her mouth. "Oh, lordy. Poor little mite."

"Betty, you didn't come over last night, did you?"

"No. Your mother sent me to our apartment early—said I looked tired. Why? Is there somethin' I should've done?"

"No. It's just Mother. She is *so* drunk."

Betty's eyes widened. "What? After her doin' so much better?"

"I know. I'm baffled because she's much drunker than usual. She must have gone on a real bender last night."

"Well, she's mighty upset over Todd. Still . . ."

"I just wondered what could have sent her off the deep end like this."

"I have no idea, honey. Things just seem to get worse and worse around here."

That was an understatement, Rebecca thought as she showered and dressed. A week ago she'd been on her way to Sinclair. Now she felt as if she'd always been here and the trouble had never stopped. Maybe her presence had made things worse. They certainly hadn't made things better.

Which was why she did not want to go to Molly's. Molly already resented her for not being of more help with Todd. Frank had devastating news to deliver. What would Rebecca's presence do, except underscore her failure in Molly's eyes as well as her own? No, for both their sakes she would stay home. Hopefully by now Clay had given Molly a sedative and she was asleep under Esther's loving care. Thank goodness Jean Wright wasn't still around interfering. As far as she knew, the woman had never returned.

Clay called about fifteen minutes later. "I'm back at the hospital recovering."

"Then things were bad with Molly?"

"My God, Rebecca, I've never seen such emotional pain. It would have been better if she'd screamed and railed. But she just stared. She just *left*, went somewhere deep inside and didn't say a word. I gave her a sedative."

"Do you think she'll come out of this or go comatose?"

"People rarely go into comas because of shock. She'll come out. Then what will happen I don't know. She'll certainly need psychiatric help."

"Oh, Clay, listen to us. We're talking like Todd is dead."

"Rebecca," he said hesitantly, "if he *does* have appendicitis and we can't find him today . . ."

"I know. If only things had been different. If only Larry had been able to pick up that ransom money."

"Larry?"

"Yes. Frank thinks he was the kidnapper and never picked up the money because he was killed first."

"Hmmm. Well, I guess it's as good a theory as any. It's just that all this seems out of character for Larry."

"Why? Because he's such a fine fellow?"

"No, because he's such an impatient fellow. This kidnapper waited days to demand ransom. We don't know why, but whatever the reason, I have trouble imagining

Larry looking after a kid for almost a week before asking for money. Larry wants everything and he wants it *now*. At least he used to. And he ran a bigger risk of getting caught, trying to stash the child for so long. It just doesn't make sense." He sighed. "But what do I know?"

"You knew Larry a lot better than Frank and I did." Rebecca paused. "If Larry *did* take Todd, do you think Lynn knew?"

"If she knew where Todd was being held, she would have gotten him back to the family. She's not a likable person, but she's no Larry. And she wouldn't want this scheme to backfire on her brother. She wouldn't give Larry away, but she'd put a stop to this hideous plan if she could. So I'd say if Larry took Todd she either didn't know, or she didn't know where Todd was."

"Wait until she hears Larry was murdered. Maybe you should stop by Doug's and sedate her, too."

"Angel that I am, I thought about that. I called, but no one's answering the phone there. They could be with the police; or if she's hysterical, Doug probably took her to the emergency room."

"I have trouble seeing Lynn as hysterical. I guess Frank is on his way home."

"He should be. He doesn't look too good. Oh, not bad," Clay said quickly. "Just tired. But he won't be home for a while. Esther didn't want to leave Molly, so she asked Frank to go out to the nursery and pick up some things for her since she'll be staying a few more days. She made a list. Frank told me he was glad to be going. He said the nursery needed some work—something about the pond needing dredging and the house needing a new roof—but Esther would never let him contribute a cent to the place. He said he's going to take the opportunity to look things over, get some crews out there on Monday to make financial estimates, and hopefully have the work completed by the time Esther gets home."

"The place does need work," Rebecca said. "I noticed last Sunday that the pond is in awful shape. It used to be beautiful. The whole place was. Frank grew up there, you know. Or rather, his father's brother and Esther took him in when he was a boy after his parents were killed. Jonnie and Doug and I always loved the nursery. I'm sure Frank does, too."

"Well, he sure wants to keep it in good condition. And Esther is a fireball. I'll bet you'll be just like her when you're in your seventies."

"I hope," Rebecca said vaguely, thinking of her mother. Good Lord, what if she turned out like Suzanne?

"What are your plans for the day?"

"To hang around here and see if I'm needed. And you?"

"Back to the hospital. They're going to kick me out if I keep taking time off."

"In spite of all that charm you keep telling me about?"

"You still haven't noticed it. I'll have to try harder."

No, you won't, Rebecca thought. His charm was already almost more than she could resist. But romance had never worked out for her. Eventually her "gift" became too much for men to handle, especially when they decided she could read their minds, which she'd never been able to do. Besides, Clay's life was in Sinclair, and she could never live in Sinclair again, especially if they lost Todd.

"Thought any more about my father's birthday party tomorrow?" Clay asked.

"I really think it's a family affair," Rebecca said, her thoughts making her sound crisper than she meant to. "And I wasn't invited by your mother."

"I'll have her call."

"No. Please. I don't mean to be rude, but I can't go to a party tomorrow."

"I understand." Clay sounded somewhat chastened. "I should have thought of how you'd feel. I'll talk with you later, okay?"

"Yes. Fine. Good-bye, Clay."

She hung up feeling miserable. "The Ice Princess emergeth," she said aloud, baffled at herself. She cared about Clay. She more than cared about Clay. And she'd brushed him off like he was a pesky salesman. After all he'd done for her. In spite of all she felt. She'd have to apologize. But what would she say? "Sorry. I'm crazy about you, but you scare me to death. So go away and leave me to my loneliness."

"Oh hell," she said aloud. She hadn't noticed Sean sitting by her feet. He looked up at her and cocked his head. "You heard me. Hell. Romance is a pain."

Rebecca wandered restlessly around the house for about twenty minutes. Then she thought of Clay saying Frank didn't look well; yet he was walking around Esther's ten acres of land in the heat. She wasn't sure if any staff was working today. If Frank had another cardiac incident, he would be alone.

She attached Sean's leash. "Ready for a trip back to the nursery?" She found Betty in the kitchen. "Frank has gone out to Esther's. I think I'll go out, too, and make sure he's all right. Would you check on Mother from time to time? She's really in bad shape. I want to not give a damn, but I'm worried."

Betty smiled. "Sure you give a *darn*. She's your mother and you love her. But don't fret. I'll look after her," she said. "And you look after Mr. Hardison. We don't want any more upsets in this family."

Rebecca left off the air conditioner and rolled down the car windows. Sean stuck out his head, letting his hair blow and his ears flap as he sported a dopey, happy smile. Rebecca wished she felt like smiling, but all she could think of was Todd. Was he dying, alone and scared? Or was he already dead? She shuddered, remembering his merry cinnamon-colored eyes, the giggle that seemed to come from the depths of his being, his endless curiosity, his delight with life. No matter what happened, Esther's deep faith let her believe that there was a reason for everything. Rebecca wished she could believe that, too. But she couldn't. What possible reason could there be for depriving a pure and happy spirit like Todd from all the years of life ahead of him?

She'd been so lost in thought she almost missed the turn into Whispering Willows Nursery. The Thunderbird kicked up dust in spite of the recent rains, which hadn't had much effect after the long dry spell. Ahead loomed the huge white house and in front sat Frank's Mercedes.

Rebecca parked in front of the house. As she passed Frank's car, she noticed the parking lights were on. He must have accidentally pulled the knob, she thought. She opened the car door and bent in, looking at the dash. She felt as if she were in the cockpit of a jet. How many extras did this car have? While she peered at various knobs, buttons, and controls, Sean leaped by her and settled on the passenger's seat. "We are not going for a ride in this car," she told him absently. "And don't get any nose prints on the window. Frank will kill me."

She continued to peruse the dash. Sean sat impatiently for a moment, then leaped into the backseat. When at last she found the correct control for the lights, he was snuffling in a plaid wool blanket. "Stop that!" Rebecca ordered. But Sean continued to sniff, then tried to drag the blanket into the front seat. "What's the matter with you? Your favorite old acrylic blanket not good enough anymore? Got to have virgin wool? You are one spoiled boy."

She forced him to drop the blanket, earning her a glare from the brown and blue eyes, and dragged him from the car. "We'll stop at McDonald's on the way home and I'll get you a hamburger to make it up to you, okay?" Sean continued to glare. "All right, a Quarter Pounder with cheese. And a sundae. Then you can have indigestion tonight but be triumphant that you proved who's boss. Or are you just in love with the Mercedes? Got news for you, boy—we can't afford one. Now come on."

Sean dragged as they climbed the verandah steps. The front door was unlocked and Rebecca walked into the coolness of the hall. "Frank?" she called. No answer. But she saw a shopping bag sitting by the door. She riffled through it, finding underwear, jeans, a new toothbrush, a copy of *Gone With the Wind*. When the phone on the hall desk rang,

Rebecca jumped like a thief for pawing through Esther's possessions. She picked up the receiver.

"Rebecca, is that you?" Esther asked.

"Yes. Clay told me Frank didn't look too well after he left Molly's and I decided to meet him out here, just to make sure he's all right."

"Is he?"

"I haven't found him yet." She sat down on the chair at the desk. "He has some of your things gathered in a shopping bag by the door, but he must have gone outside to look around."

"Then I'm glad I caught you. I forgot to tell him to get a fresh bottle of Prinivil. It's in my medicine cabinet."

"What's Prinivil?"

"Medicine for high blood pressure. Now don't start worrying."

"All right, I won't, although you never said anything about high blood pressure. I'll put the medicine in the bag for you. How's Molly?"

"Sleeping. Clay said he'd come back this evening and give her another sedative."

"She'll need it. Esther, I don't think there's much hope."

Esther was quiet for a moment. Then she said, "Rebecca, there is always hope. Until we find Todd's body, there is *always* hope."

"I guess," Rebecca said vacantly, not really believing what Esther said. Esther's faith was so great and her belief would not waver. It hadn't eight years ago when Jonnie disappeared, not until she was faced with the undeniable fact of his lifeless body. And even then, she'd not despaired. She had said Jonnie would live on, his soul saved by a benevolent God.

If only I believed that, Rebecca thought as her eyes strayed to the framed piece of needlepoint hanging above the hall desk. It was excellent work. The writing was in deep rose, the symbol above in dark blue on a pale blue background . . .

Rebecca rose from her chair and stared at the piece:

Anchor of Salvation
Anchor of Hope

Rebecca felt as if all systems in her body had stopped functioning for a few moments. She could not move her gaze from the needlepoint. Old memories stirred. New memories flashed. Finally she became aware of Esther asking, "Rebecca, are you there? Is everything all right?"

"Esther, I'm looking at the needlepoint above the hall desk," she said slowly. "How long has it been here?"

"The needlepoint?" Esther sounded puzzled. "My mother made that, dear. The glass covering has kept the colors fresh, but it's been hanging there since I was a girl. Sixty years at least. Why?"

"I liked it when I was little, didn't I?"

"Why yes, you did. Funny you should remember that."

"And someone else liked it, too, didn't they? *Doug* liked it."

"Yes, Rebecca. He was fascinated with ships. Naturally he was attracted to a picture of an anchor. I explained to both of you that in early Christian drawings, the anchor symbolized salvation and hope. I used to find him staring at it." She paused. "I've never told this to anyone, but once I found a tattered photograph of Doug's mother. He'd drawn the symbol of the anchor on the back."

Rebecca's mind flew. The mausoleum. Doug had lived in the Ryan home, knew where all the keys were kept, and was still in and out frequently. And the symbol on Jonnie's plaque, the symbol she'd glanced at in terror and, after years of watching horror movies, immediately decided was an inverted cross. It wasn't. When she thought about it coolly, she remembered that the cross bar had been curved. It was a crude replica of the needlepoint anchor Doug had looked at since he was a child. To him it meant salvation and hope.

"Rebecca, are you all right?" Esther asked insistently. "You sound very strange. I know you're upset about Todd and you want to look after Frank, but maybe you should go home. I can call someone to come get you. Yes, that would be best. You shouldn't drive—"

"I have to go, Esther," Rebecca said abruptly and hung up.

3

Frank. She had to find Frank and tell him about Doug. His own son. Why would Doug draw the emblem on Jonnie's plaque—unless he felt guilt for kidnapping and killing Jonnie, whom he'd never liked. And if he'd done it once—

Rebecca grabbed Sean's leash and they dashed through the house and out the back door. She stood for a moment, letting her eyes adjust to the light. She had a clear view of the greenhouses, but the doors were shut and there appeared to be no activity. It was Saturday, but apparently Esther had given her staff of two the day off.

"Frank!" Rebecca called. "Frank, where are you?"

Nothing but the sound of birds chirping. What had Clay said? Frank was going to inspect the property, especially the pond. He was probably there now.

She started out at a brisk pace past the greenhouses. Sean seemed to think they were on an adventure and he galloped along beside her. She stopped and unhooked his leash, knowing he wouldn't stray far on relatively unfamiliar territory.

Without Esther and her small staff around, Whispering Willows seemed almost lonely in spite of the sunshine. She never remembered it seeming so deserted when she was young. But then she'd usually been with Jonnie and Molly. And sometimes Doug. The very thought of his name made her feel cold. Could he really have taken Todd? He'd seemed so concerned, almost frantic all week. But what about last night and his obviously false excuse for not coming with her to the ransom drop? Could his conscience have gotten to him? Or had he suddenly been overcome by panic, by the fear that Rebecca would discover him? After all, he did seem to believe in her ESP.

As Rebecca neared the pond, she saw no sign of Frank. Damn, she thought. Where could he be? Would she have to cover all ten acres to find him? Or had he doubled back and already returned to the house? If so he would see the Thunderbird and surely wait for her.

Rebecca stopped and was wondering whether or not to keep wandering around the grounds or go back to the house when she heard Sean barking. She looked to the right and saw the dog at the door of the old Leland cabin. He sat solidly, barking rhythmically and looking around as if he expected her to show up momentarily.

"I'm over here, Sean!" she called. "Come on, boy." The dog did not move. "Sean, we're going back now. Come!"

Sean looked back at the door and barked three times. Loudly.

Rebecca took a few steps closer to him. "Sean, no one lives there. There's nothing inside except maybe a couple of mice, and you're not a cat. Now come on."

Sean would not look at her. He jumped up on his hind legs, scratching at the door and whining. He dropped down again, looked at her, then repeated the action.

"What on earth is wrong with you?" Rebecca called at

the same moment she thought, Frank might have gone in the cabin and passed out. His heart—

She ran toward the cabin. Sean danced in a circle, then leaped at the door again.

Rebecca turned the handle on the door that was always kept locked. It swung inward. Just like the doors on the mausoleum. The association sent a tingle of fear through her. So far unlocked doors had not boded well.

Rebecca stepped inside. "Frank?" Her voice had a hollow sound in the old, musty cabin. She looked at the floor. No footprints in the dust. No dust. Did Esther actually clean out this place regularly? It did have historical value and Rebecca knew Esther tried to keep up the structural integrity, but to clean it like she did her home? Perhaps her staff was assigned that task.

Sean was darting madly around the small rooms. In a new place he usually showed cautious curiosity. Not today. Something was wrong, which made her even more certain Frank was in here. Perhaps he hadn't answered because he was unconscious.

The cabin had an area Rebecca had always referred to as the kitchen, although cooking was done in the big fireplace in the main room. The "kitchen" had shelves hidden behind rough cabinet doors, a recessed area for a tub that served for washing clothes and once-a-week baths, and storage bins for vegetables. Off the kitchen were three bedrooms, a luxury number for the time the cabin was built. One bedroom was larger than the other two to accommodate the elder Lelands and a cradle or crib depending on the age of the newest Leland. Now all bedrooms were empty, their antique furniture sold long ago. The cabin sported a back door. Rebecca unlocked it and stepped out onto a narrow porch. The land around had little in the way of bushes or trees. Frank was nowhere in sight.

Rebecca walked back into the cabin. Sean was now in the main room again, pawing at the set of shelves built into the corner. Rebecca opened their doors to see dust and a few dead flies. Sean continued pawing. "There's nothing here, boy. It's time to leave."

She shut the cabinet doors and started toward the main door of the cabin. Sean suddenly darted in front of her blocking the door. Then he growled. "What in the world?" Rebecca exclaimed. "You haven't growled at me since the first week I found you." He came closer, growling. She took a step back and he followed, growling. They continued this routine until she was back at the corner shelves, where Sean again pawed at the doors and barked. And barked. And barked.

And finally Rebecca heard it. A sound so soft she thought she'd imagined it. Just a slight blur of noise. Sean barked again in agitation. "Shhh!" Rebecca hissed. She opened the cabinet doors and tilted her head in between two shelves.

"T-Tramp?"

She jumped. *Tramp?* Could that possibly be what she'd heard? A weak, tiny voice saying *Tramp?* "Todd!" she yelled. "Todd Ryan!"

A sob, rough and weak.

Rebecca went into a frenzy, clawing at the shelves, skinning her hands. Sean leaped and dug at them, too, as if he could paw through the wood. Rebecca pulled at the shelves, wondering if she could loosen them from the wall. Finally she grabbed a corner of the fourth shelf and felt a slight movement. She pulled harder. Another slight movement but with an accompanying creaking sound. She pulled a third time and at last the entire set of shelves swung away from the wall and she looked at rough-hewn planks leading down into darkness. A flashlight lay on the top step. She grabbed it and shone it down the stairs, onto the dirt floor and a small heap under a dirty white blanket.

Chapter Twenty-one

1

Rebecca shone the light on the narrow planks and descended carefully. All she needed now was to fall and break her neck. When she reached the bottom, she folded back the blanket. Strawberry blond hair. A pale, pinched face with cracked lips, dripping with sweat. The eyes were closed.

"Todd," she said softly. "Todd."

Nothing. Not even the eyelids fluttered. She pushed the wet hair off his burning forehead. "Todd, please try to open your eyes. Please speak."

The lips parted slightly. "Tramp," he rasped. "You came like for the baby. Save baby. The rat . . ."

He trailed off without ever opening his eyes. Dear God, he was so sick, Rebecca thought frantically. His gag had been shredded away by his teeth. He shivered violently beneath the thin blanket in this dreadful, dark hole. One look at his face told her he was on the verge of death. What strength of will he'd found to call out when he heard Sean barking!

Rebecca put the flashlight on the floor. She squatted, placed her arms gently beneath him, and lifted. He groaned pitifully. "I'm sorry baby. I don't mean to hurt you, but I have to get you out of here."

She began the upward climb, slowly and cautiously. It would be so easy to fall on these flimsy steps that led from a place where the Lelands must have taken shelter from the occasional marauding Indian parties. She'd never known about the hiding place. Esther had no doubt kept it a secret, afraid the children would hurt themselves trying to explore it. But Doug must have discovered it.

Halfway up the steps Rebecca paused. She'd broken into a sweat and her arms were trembling both from Todd's weight and the strain of trying to place her feet so carefully on the next narrow plank. Sean stood above her, looking down. "Almost there, boy. Please don't come down and get in my way."

After three deep breaths she started up again. Briefly she looked down at Todd. He was breathing, although he still hadn't opened his eyes. Occasionally he murmured, "Mommy." Once, "Tramp." And once, to her surprise, "Becky."

When she reached the top of the stairs, Sean was gone. Good, she thought. The way is clear. The distance from the top step to the floor of the cabin was greater than between the steps. She took another deep breath, raised her right leg, set her foot firmly on the floor, and heaved herself up into the cabin.

"Thank God," Rebecca murmured. Then she turned to see Doug standing just inside the doorway of the cabin. She also saw the revolver in his right hand hanging by his side. He looked at her dully, all expression drained from his face, and said flatly, "So you've found him."

2

Panic rushed through Rebecca with the speed of an electric shock. Then to her amazement, utter calm descended. She knew this was some atavistic response to extreme danger, some genetically buried knowledge about how to survive.

"Yes, Doug, isn't it wonderful!" She smiled radiantly. "I didn't really find him. Sean did." Sean sat looking at Doug. He knew Doug. Doug was making no threatening moves, so the dog was not alarmed. "I can't believe it. And he's still alive!"

"He's alive?" No exuberance. Nothing.

"Yes. But he's very sick. We have to get him to the hospital immediately." Rebecca began moving slowly toward the door. "I don't understand why this place wasn't searched when he disappeared."

"The cabin was searched. Not the hiding place."

"Why?"

"No one knew about it."

"Not even Esther?"

"Guess not. Whispering Willows was her husband's place. He was weird. He had a lot of secrets from her. My dad told me."

"But you knew about it."

"No. I just followed all the noise."

"I see." Clearly a lie, but she had to act as if she believed it. "Well, Doug, we really have to get Todd to the hospital. He's extremely sick. I think he's dying."

Doug stood immovable, turned slightly to the right to face her. The cabin door hung three fourths of the way open behind him, but he made no move toward it or toward her. He simply stared at her, then at the bundle in her arms, his eyes dead, his face haggard, ravaged. "Larry's dead, you know."

"Yes, I know. I think he was the kidnapper. He was killed before he could pick up the ransom money."

"No, he was killed because he was trying to blackmail the kidnapper. There was no other way to shut him up. But Lynn will never get over it. Never."

Rebecca's ploy wasn't working. Doug was not going to pretend he wasn't the kidnapper, wasn't going to help her get Todd to the hospital, wasn't even going to let her out of this cabin. He was going to shoot her right here. Then she and Todd would both die. Her only hope was Frank.

"My arms are cramping," she said truthfully. "I have to put Todd down for a minute." Doug said nothing as she lay Todd's limp body on the floor. This time his eyelids did twitch, although he didn't open his eyes. But at least he was still alive.

Rebecca stood slowly and stretched out her arms, rubbing them. "Do you know how happy Molly is going to be? I think she'd given up after the failure of the ransom." Did Doug hear the tinny cheerfulness in her voice, the complete falsity of her relief? "This is a miracle, Doug."

"But Skeeter's dead. And Miss Vinson. And Larry. Todd will probably die, too. He's so sick."

He looked at the prone child and his eyes filled with tears. How could he cry? Rebecca wondered. How could the son of a bitch stand there and cry after all he'd done? But this was no time to analyze him. Her gaze swept his body, a body only a couple of inches taller than hers, a body grown overweight and flabby. Soft. His gun hand began to tremble. His shoulders sagged.

Rebecca steeled herself, then lunged. Less than ten feet separated them. By the time Doug had lifted his eyes, she was a foot away. She turned slightly, gathered all her strength, and drove her right shoulder into the edge of his right shoulder. He grunted, staggering against the edge of the open door that gave with the force of his body and swung with a crash into the wall. Rebecca swept past him, not looking back to see if he'd fallen although she heard the gun hit the wooden floor. She was out in the open, running as fast as she could, screaming "Frank!" at the top of her voice.

She veered toward Esther's house. Knowing there were animal holes, she kept her eyes on her feet, determined not to fall. In mid-stride a large copperhead slithered beneath her descending foot. She managed to prevent herself from stepping down on it, but the sharp movement sent her stumbling. She caught her balance and began to run again, without thought heading straight for the pond. "Frank!" she screamed hysterically. "Frank!"

The pond loomed directly ahead of her. The pond. What had she been thinking? Now she would have to go around it instead of heading in a straight line. Rebecca lurched into the tall grass, planning to make a quick cut to the left, back toward the house, right before a heavy weight threw her to the ground with a thud.

Doug. He'd knocked the air from her and she lay face-down, almost paralyzed for a moment. "Stop running," he huffed into her ear. "You don't have to run."

Her breath came back with a sharp pang. She reached

forward, digging her hands in the dirt, and pulled herself forward, Doug still on her back. She kicked but she could not dislodge him. His fingers dug into the nerves at the base of her neck, sending pain coursing through her, rendering her motionless.

"Rebecca, *stop it*!"

Where was Sean? He could help divert Doug if not really hurt him. Unless Doug had killed the dog. He probably had. After all, he was letting Todd lie in the cabin and die. Another victim. Another *kidnap* victim. She drew in her breath. "You took Jonnie," she rasped.

A groan wrenched horribly from Doug. "Yes. So easy. The camping trip. He went off in the woods to pee. With the stun gun it was so easy."

Rebecca felt no rage. Only the dull ache of depthless regret. "Why? Oh God, Doug, why?"

"Drugs," he panted. "Lynn and me. So strung out. Larry gone to prison. No money. I thought she was going to die."

"Lynn *helped* you?"

"No. She didn't know. Still doesn't know." Rebecca thrashed, clawed into the dirt again and dragged herself a few inches closer to the pond. "Needed money. So simple. Get ransom." He gasped for air. "Put him in a cave until morning. But I almost didn't get him out of there fast enough. Searchers came too fast. The dog found us first. I had to kill it."

Poor Rusty, Rebecca thought. He'd broken away from the first search party and gone howling through the woods, searching for his beloved master. His body had been found near a cave where police thought Jonnie had been kept for a few hours.

"After I got the ransom, I meant to just drop off Jonnie. He didn't know who took him. Nobody the wiser. But the FBI came. Saw them at the drop. Couldn't get money." He sobbed. "It all went wrong."

The pond. So close. Rebecca hoped people who could not swim under normal circumstances could manage in a panic. In the water she'd have an advantage. She could get

Doug off of her. And by then maybe Frank would find her . . .

"Frank!" she screamed again.

Doug hit her on the side of the head, stunning her. "Shut up! I can't let him find you. Or Todd—"

Rebecca had clawed until she was within arm's length of the pond. Still slightly dazed, she pulled forward until she slipped into the filthy water. She'd pushed off into one of the deeper sections of the pond and sank into mud, with Doug still on top of her. The long, sinuous leaves of pond-weeds and hornworts wrapped around her legs and arms, binding her to the airless bottom.

She kicked uselessly. Doug's hands felt as if they were all over her, pulling, dragging. With the expenditure of energy, her ability to hold her breath was getting weaker. His must be, too. She stopped fighting, trying to make him think she'd lost consciousness. She hung in the water, his hands under her arms, suspending her. Two seconds, four seconds, eight . . .

Abruptly she felt Doug's hands release her. Miraculously she was free. She fought to the surface, gasping desperately for air, and opened her eyes, looking directly into Doug's face. She pushed away from him, off to the left toward the bank of the pond. "No!" he shouted, his gaze fastened on something beyond her. And then she heard what sounded like a roar. Doug's head snapped back. Blood gushed from a gaping hole in his throat. Slowly his eyes glazed over as the life drained out of them. Then he sank back into the murky depths of the pond.

Rebecca started to scream, mindlessly, over and over. She fought to stay afloat amid the dull red slowly spreading around her but she was exhausted, horrified, unable to think. In the water was quiet. In the water was peace. In the water . . . Something grabbed her and she flailed against it.

"Rebecca, stop fighting me! Rebecca, it's Frank. You're drowning! Go limp!"

And she did. Her muscles relaxed, and the lulling water

flowed around her, pulling her down into sleep and dreams. Then arms dragged her out of the water, roughly over the edge of the bank, through the cattails, and out onto the grass. Someone pushed on her chest until she coughed and spit water, rolling partially on her side.

"Rebecca! Dear God, are you all right?"

She didn't want to open her eyes. She never wanted to open them again. But she did. And there was Frank, his gaze anxious, his face white. "Frank," she mumbled. "Frank, it was Doug. He's been shot."

"I shot him," Frank said dully. "He was drowning you. I didn't mean to kill him. I'm not a good shot. I just meant—" His voice broke. "He was murdering you. You're not the first. Oh, dear God, forgive me."

"Frank, I found Todd," Rebecca gasped. "He's in the cabin—"

"Todd? You *found* Todd?"

"Yes." The clouds in Rebecca's mind began to clear. Words, terrible words, echoed. "You said I wasn't the first person Doug tried to murder." Her eyes widened. "You knew he took Todd, didn't you? And you knew Doug killed Jonnie. Frank, how *could* you have sat by and—"

"And let him get away with it all?" Frank turned anguished eyes on her. "I didn't know who'd taken Jonnie until it was too late. I was trying to get Doug off drugs. I cut off his money so he'd go to rehab. I never dreamed he was so desperate and crazy he'd kidnap Jonnie. But after Jonnie went missing, Doug started acting strange. I got suspicious. We had an old hunting cabin in the woods about thirty miles from here. I went there. Jonnie was dead. Doug was hysterical. He said after the ransom pickup failed, he decided to just let Jonnie go and make his own way home. But Jonnie was weak. Doug said he found him about half a mile from the cabin. He'd fallen and rolled down a rocky hill. That's why he was so battered. He was dead. When I arrived, Doug had already dumped the body downtown and returned to the cabin. He didn't know where to go, what to

do. He was in heavy withdrawal, shaking, vomiting.
thought he was going to die, too."

"But he came to the funeral. He was all right."

"I got heroin for him. Enough to get him through th
funeral. Then he supposedly went back to college. Only h
really went into rehab. Lynn, too. When he came out, h
was a different person. Or I *thought* he was a differen
person."

"But you didn't *tell* anyone, Frank. You didn't turn hir
in for killing Jonnie!"

"He didn't kill Jonnie! It was an accident! He'd don
something crazy under the influence of heroin. He didn'
really know what he was doing. It was too late to chang
anything." His eyes were tragic. "He was my son, Rebecca
My only child. Can't you understand?"

No, she didn't understand. Not really. But there was n
time to talk things out, no time for reparations now.

"Frank, Todd is in that cabin," she said coldly. "He's il
Terribly ill. He's dying. We have to get him to the hospi
tal." She clutched his arm, feeling the warmth of his ski
on her cold hand. "We don't have time to call 911. W
have to get him in your car and . . . and . . ."

Pain stabbed at her temple. The familiar pain that pre
ceded a vision. She tried to hold on to the present, bu
Frank's face faded. The sunshine disappeared. Suddenl
she was in another consciousness, one racked by pain
barely able to breathe, unable to see, but still able to hear
Incredibly, in this consciousness Frank's voice yelled fu
riously, "What the hell have you done?"

"I only wanted money. I didn't want to hurt him.
Doug's voice, shaking and weak. "But I didn't get th
money. We've got to get him back home. He's sick!"

"Got to get him back *home*? Are you insane? He's *dying*
you fool."

Jonnie's consciousness, Rebecca realized. She was hear
ing what Jonnie had heard up in that lonely cabin wher
Doug had taken him.

"At the hospital they can save him," Doug said feebly

"And he can tell everyone that his stepbrother Doug kidnapped him."

"He doesn't know. He never saw me."

"He *heard* you. He knows your voice."

"No. I disguised—"

"You're too screwed up to know what you did. Don't tell me he doesn't know. I'd bet my life he does."

Doug began to cry. "I'm sorry. I had to have money. I'm in bad shape."

"You stupid idiot! Do you know how hard I worked to get us to where we are? Do you know I *killed* a man to get us here? Do you know I married that fool of a woman and lived with her all these years to *keep* us here? And now you do *this*?"

"I didn't mean . . . Killed a man? Who did you kill?"

"Patrick Ryan. Did you really think I was in Pittsburgh? I knew he was going up that damned hill to look at some property. I came back secretly, I waited, and I shot his tire. I didn't know Rebecca would be with him. I didn't want to kill her. She's the child I *should* have had, not a sorry specimen like *you*, just like your stupid, screwed-up mother. But it worked out. I made it all work out. And you are *not* going to ruin it!"

"But how do we fix it?" Doug wailed.

"This way." Metal clanked. What was it? The pokers at the fireplace? Then Doug screamed, "No! No!" And something crashed down onto Jonnie's head. Once and the pain was intense. Twice and merciful darkness descended.

Rebecca felt as if she were floating away into a void. There was nothing but darkness and silence. Then the darkness slowly lifted. Sunshine drenched her, warming her skin that felt cold as death. Frank's face hovered above her. Frank, still looking at her with such tragedy, such concern. Frank, whom she now realized was the murderer of Jonnie, of Skeeter, of Matilda, of his own son. She was in mortal danger. And so was Todd. Her head pounded and she was shuddering, but she tried to look back innocently. It didn't work. The shock of the vision had been too much. Frank gazed deeply into her eyes. Then he frowned sadly. "Oh Rebecca, I'm so sorry." He pulled a knife from his pocket, unsheathed the long blade, placed it against the thin skin of her neck covering the carotid artery, and smiled. "I never wanted you to know what really happened."

3

"Why, Frank?" she asked, barely above a whisper.

"Do you know who Todd's father is?"

Rebecca swallowed. "Not you. Please tell me it isn't you."

He shook his head. "No, my dear. I have strayed from your mother—what sane man except Patrick Ryan wouldn't?—but I had better sense than to choose Molly. No, Todd's father is Doug."

Rebecca stared at him. "I don't believe you."

"Would I lie to you at a time like this? Molly was infatuated with Doug for years. And in college, at a party, when Doug fell off the wagon after rehab and Molly had too much to drink, they went to bed. Later she felt awful about it because of Lynn. She also knew he didn't love her." He paused. "Doug didn't remember sleeping with her and she didn't tell him. Even I didn't know when we shipped her off to New Orleans to be with you. But then Suzanne and I came down for the birth and when Molly was anesthetized before her Caesarian, she babbled the truth to me." He shook his head as if amused. "Later she didn't even remember telling me. But I told Doug. He panicked. He's so in love with Lynn, you know. I promised to keep the secret."

"Don't tell me it was out of consideration for him."

"It was self-defense. I was always afraid Doug might decide to tell Lynn the truth about what happened to Jonnie. But after Todd's birth, I had more leverage over him. Lynn would have left him if she'd known."

"So all your secrets were safe. Then why the abduction of Todd? Certainly not for money."

"Because as each year passed, Doug became more eaten up with guilt. I think he was headed for a breakdown. He told me he was going to the police. He was going to tell them he'd abducted Jonnie, turned him loose, and Jonnie had died in a fall. 'I won't involve you, Dad,' he promised. 'I won't say a word about you being at the cabin and killing Jonnie.' Ha! The stupid weakling. They would have broken him in an hour. So I threatened to hurt Todd. He didn't believe me. He didn't think I would do anything to my own grandchild." He sighed. "I'm telling you this so you'll understand everything before I kill you. I'm sorry, but I have to now."

"And how are you going to explain my and Doug's deaths?"

"The story will be that you found Todd, Doug found you, he was trying to slit your throat, and in an unsuccessful attempt to stop him, I had to shoot him. And I'm using *Doug's* knife on you. He brought it along to use on *me*."

Rebecca closed her eyes against the sun. "So you took Todd to show Doug that you'd really do it. But he could have told the police that you'd threatened Todd once and they would have protected the boy from you."

"Even Doug realized that if he went to the police with that ridiculous story, no one would believe him, not with his background compared to mine. No one would believe I'd killed Jonnie, either. I also made him see that if he confessed, he'd be arrested for kidnapping and manslaughter, and I'd eventually find and kill Todd."

Rebecca thought of Doug's frantic air all week. Maybe he'd come to love the child that was his own. He'd known his father had taken the child, but he hadn't known where. No wonder he'd been so stiff with Frank the night of his homecoming from the hospital. He'd had to act normal around the man who'd kidnapped his son—a man who was also capable of murder.

"Your heart attack," Rebecca said abruptly. "If you'd died, no one would ever have known where Todd was."

Frank laughed. "I didn't have a heart attack. Certainly you've heard of poppers."

"Amyl nitrate?"

"Yes. A drug used for heart problems. And I'm told for auto-erotic purposes. It simulates a heart attack. I slept in the guest room that night and used a popper. I needed a night away from home and I needed an alibi."

"So you could kill Matilda Vinson, who saw you in the alley beside the library after you tried to kill Sonia."

"Exactly. I asked for a roommate. A damned zombie is what the man was except for a strong heart. Perfect. I simply hooked my heart monitoring equipment to him. The nurses never noticed a thing out at their station."

"Sonia. You tried to kill her because she knew Jean Wright *was* home near the time of Todd's kidnapping. My mother told me you were having an affair. I thought it was with Mrs. Ellis, but it was with Jean, wasn't it?"

"Yes. Nice body, but no imagination. At least I thought no imagination. When she went off to look after her old lady the night of Todd's abduction, I stayed in her house. It was the perfect opportunity with Molly working late. But I couldn't get clear out here to the cabin in that awful storm so I stashed Todd in the Klein building. Anyway, Jean had become a pest, badgering me to leave Suzanne. Then she started threatening to tell the police that I'd been in her house the night of the kidnapping. She saw immediately that was a mistake."

"Oh God, Frank, you didn't kill her, too?"

"Didn't get the chance. Before I could do anything, she wisely left town—but not before confiding in her idiot sister, Wendy. The girl was seeing Larry Cochran. She told him. He decided to try to blackmail me. That was a mistake."

"And the ransom note was a ruse."

"I didn't use it earlier because I didn't want to take a chance on having the FBI involved. But when you told me you thought this kidnapping had nothing to do with ransom, you threw a little scare in me, dear. I had to make it look as if it *was* about ransom. So I left you and Clay prowling the park like amateur sleuths while I got rid of Larry, my blackmailer. He was the last danger to me because when Todd got sick, I knew I had to let him be found. I never meant for him to die—he was my ace-in-the-hole over Doug. I came out here today to get Todd. I was going to leave him in some conspicuous place where he'd quickly be found. I'd make it look as if Larry took him.

"But you and that cursed dog found the hiding place." He sighed. "You know, I've always cared for you. Your beauty. Your intelligence. I didn't used to believe in your ESP. That's why I didn't fear you when I took Todd. After all, look how you failed with Jonnie."

Rebecca winced. "I tried with Jonnie. I don't know why I drew a blank."

"I think perhaps you were too close to him. I often thought it was as if you two had one mind. Todd is different. You love him, but not like you did your brother. Over the last week, I became a bit wary of you, tried to scare you off: the CD of 'A Whiter Shade of Pale,' my rendition of Jonnie's bracelet, Matilda in the mausoleum. But you're stubborn. Too stubborn, and I'm afraid my soft spot for you has become a sore spot. You're a thorn in my side. You have to go, dear. And such a shame. You're so young and beautiful."

Frank held the knife to her throat but did nothing. She saw the faint trembling of his hand. "If you're going to do it, do it fast," Rebecca said tonelessly. All the fear, all the fight, had drained out of her as she thought of the lives this man had taken—especially when she pictured Jonnie, so sick, being bludgeoned to death by him. "I won't struggle if you just promise one thing."

"And what is that?"

"Don't hurt Todd."

"Very well, my dear. My last promise to you."

Rebecca turned her head. Frank pressed the knife against

her skin and she felt hot blood running over her collar-
bone . . .

A shot rang out. Then another. Another. The top of
Frank's head disappeared in a red spray against the blue
sky. The blood misted down onto her face, hot and hideous.
He dropped the knife and fell backward.

Rebecca fainted.

4

"Todd? Todd?" Rebecca mumbled.

A woman with smiling brown eyes leaned over Rebecca.
"You're in the hospital. You're fine. And it looks like Todd
will be, too." She looked up. "Here's Dr. Bellamy now."

And there he was, his gray-blue eyes serious, his hand
taking hers. "We're going to have to give you yearly rates
in this place. Of course we're higher during tourist season."

"You're a laugh riot," she managed in a rough voice.
"What happened?"

"First of all, Todd's appendix was on the verge of rup-
turing, but we got to him just in time. Another few hours
and it might have been all over."

"He'll be all right?"

"Pretty sure of it."

"Thank God. And Sean?"

Clay looked surprised. "You were worried about Sean?"

"At the pond. He didn't come. Is he . . ."

"He was standing guard over Todd and got shut in the
cabin. You should see the claw marks on the inside of that
door. Anyway, I took him home with me. He's nervous,
but Gypsy is doing her best to soothe him."

"Thank you for not taking him to a kennel."

"He doesn't look like a kennel lover. And just between
you and me, I think there might be sparks flying between
your boy and my girl."

"How romantic." Rebecca smiled. "You were at Whispering Willows? How did you know to come?"

"It was actually Bill and me. Bill had stopped by to see your mother. She was in horrible shape. He called the emergency squad. They brought her in, I was on duty, and one look at those pupils told me she'd been drugged."

"Drugged! Is she all right?"

"Yes. Bill and Betty—Betty climbed in his patrol car and wouldn't get out—swore your mother drank but didn't take pills. Then Suzanne started babbling about Frank giving her wine the night before. It seems Skeeter Dobbs's wine was drugged and Bill made a connection. Betty said you and Frank were out at the nursery. She also said she'd gotten a call from Doug asking where his father was. She'd told him and then he said, 'He's a murderer and I'm going to put an end to him.' Betty was nearly hysterical."

"Frank must have drugged Mother so he could get out for most of the night and kill Larry. Doug must have figured out his father murdered Larry."

"Well, we weren't sure about all that. We just thought Doug was out to kill Frank, and that maybe Frank was dangerous, too, and you were alone at the nursery with both of them. This time I was the one who forced my way into the patrol car with Bill." He closed his eyes. "We got there just in time."

Rebecca ran her hand down the side of his face. "A doctor who's there when you need him. Now I believe in miracles."

And then she slept.

Chapter Twenty-Two

The next week Rebecca drove her mother to the rehabilitation center. Suzanne tried to act lighthearted, but Rebecca saw the sadness in her eyes. "It's only three months, Mother," she said. "I know that seems like a long time—"

"No, it doesn't. I need the time, Rebecca. Not just to get off alcohol. To think about my life. To think about all the mistakes I've made."

"No, not the mistakes. Please not the mistakes. Think about the good things. Think about Daddy, and Jonnie, and Rusty. Think about how much you loved—love—them, and how lucky you were to have them."

Suzanne smiled. "I noticed you left yourself off that list."

"Well, I don't know how lucky you've been to have had me. I've caused my share of trouble."

"You've been a wonderful daughter, Rebecca." She grinned. "Stubborn as a mule, but wonderful. I was just too stupid to realize it. But I'd like to give you something as a symbol of our starting over."

She held out a small green box. Rebecca pulled the car to the side of the road and opened the box. The emerald ring she'd tried on in the jewelry store twinkled in the sun light. "Oh, Mother, it's beautiful! But how did you know?"

"A little bird in the hospital told me. Or rather, a tall gorgeous blond doctor I'd like to have as a son-in-law."

"A son-in-law?"

Suzanne shrugged. "Remember how happy your father and I were and think it over. Clay reminds me a lot of Patrick."

Suzanne refused to let Rebecca walk her into the rehab center. "Too depressing," she said. "Let's just say good bye here."

"Mother, when you get out, I want you to think about moving to New Orleans," Rebecca said sincerely. "You'd love it. There's so much to do, so much to see."

"I've lived in Sinclair all my life, Rebecca. And there's Molly and Todd and Bill."

"Molly and Todd and Bill will probably be a family in a few months. We'll come back for the wedding. But Sinclair . . . Mother, I know Daddy and Jonnie are here physically, but—"

"They're dead. I have to face that. But my daughter isn't." Suddenly Suzanne hugged Rebecca. "I'll give moving serious thought. I've always wanted to live in the French Quarter."

"The French Quarter! Mother, that might be—"

"Too much fun? I'm ready for a little fun in my life. There's been damned little of it the last few years." She started toward the rehab center doors, then turned and waved. "See you soon, dear. And remember that I love you. I always have."

Four days later, Rebecca returned from Columbus, where she had seen Esther successfully through her surgery. She was tired after the ordeal and dreading the return trip to New Orleans. Part of her didn't want to go, but she knew she must. Her life in Sinclair had ended eight years ago. As she'd begun packing, Clay had called. "How about an evening tryst?"

"Not at Dormaine's, I hope." Rebecca laughed.

"No. I was thinking of that beautiful gazebo in your backyard. I've heard all the stars will be out tonight."

"All of them? Sounds nice."

"I'll be there in an hour with wine and music. Oh, and may I bring Gypsy?"

"Sean will be delighted. Will she expect a corsage?"

"Nothing fancy. Tell him not to spend all his allowance. See you soon."

In a fit of depression after dropping her mother off at the rehab center, Rebecca had fallen back on the age-old

cure of shopping. After Clay's call, she impulsively ra
upstairs and after a quick shower and spray of Chane
No. 5, donned a newly acquired filmy mint green slip dress
matching strappy sandals, and her mother's single larg
pearl on a glistening gold chain. Then she carried twelv
fat candles out to the gazebo and lighted them.

"We're both having dates tonight," she told Sean as sh
brushed him gently, smoothing the long hair on the back
of his legs and slicking down his slight cowlick. "I know
this girl is special to you, so I want you to be a gentleman
If you pee on her, I'll die of embarrassment."

Sean licked her nose, which she took in lieu of a con
tract. She hoped Betty and Walt wouldn't come nosing ove
to see what was going on.

In exactly one hour Clay arrived at the door bearin
wine and a boom box. "I thought we could use some mu
sic," he said simply. "I brought some CDs."

"Not 'A Whiter Shade of Pale,' I hope."

"No. 'Baa Baa Black Sheep' and 'Here We Go 'Roun
the Mulberry Bush.' I thought we could dance." Sean an
Gypsy were already touching noses. "A happy reunion."

"Sean's a lothario."

"Gypsy's not exactly playing the shy country lass."

"I think it was love at first sight. Why don't the two c
you come in? I'll grab the wineglasses and corkscrew an
we'll head for the gazebo."

When they climbed the steps to the candlelit gazebo
Clay whistled. "This looks magical."

"My parents used to light candles out here some nights
I thought it was beautiful."

"It is. And so are you. I feel underdressed in my khakis.

"Oh, this dress just looked cool for a warm summe
evening," Rebecca said airily. "Found it at the back of th
closet."

"Well, it will go great with something I picked up fo
you." Clay set down the wine and the boom box an
opened a cluster of tissue paper. He withdrew a cream
white gardenia. "For your hair."

"Clay, it's lovely!" Rebecca breathed.

"Women in old movies wear them. I always liked them."

"Will you pin it in my hair?" He placed it behind her right ear and carefully pinned it in place. "How does it look?"

"Gorgeous. You should always wear gardenias in your hair."

"I will from now on. They'll be my trademark."

"Going to wear one at your next book signing?"

"If I ever write another book. The synopsis of my next one is so late the publisher has probably forgotten me."

"I doubt that. And I'm looking forward to book two."

"You haven't read book one."

"Yes, I have. It was great. And I'm glad you didn't write about real events like Jonnie's abduction and Earl Tanner's murder."

"Speaking of Earl Tanner," Rebecca said as Clay uncorked the wine and poured two glasses, "I got a letter from Alvin today."

"A letter?"

"According to Bill, Alvin would be too shy to call and talk to me personally."

Clay handed her a glass. "I hope he didn't say anything awful."

"His mother died in prison of cancer five days ago. When I read that, a load of guilt descended on me. But he went on with incredible information. He said it had never been his father who beat him. It was his mother. For a long time Earl believed her stories about Alvin having falls, but finally he caught on. He was going to divorce her, charge her with abuse, and take Alvin. So she murdered him and tried to collect the life insurance, which would have worked if it hadn't been for me. Alvin said he knew she would have eventually killed him and he thinks he owes me his life."

"Well, I'll be damned," Clay said. "And all this time you've thought he hated you."

"It seems old terrors die slowly. Every time his mother

came up for parole, she told Alvin when she got out, she'd
come after him. He was terrified, the child part of him
thinking she could do anything. Now that she's gone, he
feels free. And get this—he wants to write a book about
the whole thing. He and his wife are expecting a baby and
strapped financially. A book advance could do wonders. He
asked me as a favor to bring up his proposal to my agent.
I did. She loved the idea. True crime, ESP, the book written
by the former child actually involved in the story—great
stuff. She wants to see a synopsis. I wrote a note back to
him telling him the good news. I didn't want to call him
and scare him to death."

Clay laughed. "If he actually sells the book, he'll have
to get over some of this shyness."

"He'll write it. He sent me some samples of his work.
He's good. Very good."

"That's great. Some of the people at the hospital think
he's strange, but I always liked him."

Rebecca took a sip of wine. "I have three other pieces
of news," she said quickly. She was unaccountably nervous
and couldn't seem to stop talking. "One is about Aunt Esther. Before I left this morning, she told me she's decided
to stay at a convalescent home near the hospital until the
course of radiation therapy is finished. I was so afraid she'd
insist on going back to Whispering Willows."

Clay smiled. "Esther has good sense, Rebecca. She's
also a fighter. I think she'll be around twenty years from
now."

"I hope so. My second piece of news is about Randy
Messer. Remember my telling you they found an earring
in the Pioneer Room after Sonia's attack, then I saw that
his earlobe was torn?" Clay nodded. "Randy's father admitted that he and Randy had a 'ruckus,' as he put it, and
he tore out an earring. It was a hoop. The one in the library
was a stud. I always thought it would be hard to tear out a
stud."

"I guess it would be. I hadn't given it much thought."

"That stud in the library could have been anyone's, even

Randy's, but not from the night of Sonia's attack." Rebecca sipped wine again. "Third piece of news. Todd couldn't stop worrying about the 'baby' he thought was crying when he was hidden in the cabin. So Bill took him into the woods and they found the fawn. It was in perfect health. Todd wanted a policeman posted at the site to make sure the fawn stayed fine, but Bill convinced him Mama Deer might not like the intrusion."

Clay grinned. "What a kid! After all he's been through, he was still worried about something crying in the woods."

"I think he's pretty special."

"And you want one just like him someday."

Rebecca's face flamed. The reaction made her feel absurd. She gulped more wine and asked, "How about some music?"

"Sounds wonderful."

Clay slipped a CD into the player. Sarah McLachlan's "I Love You" came on. "My favorite song?" Rebecca asked. "You remembered."

"Sure." He moved closer to her, took her wineglass and set it down, then held out his arms, his gaze holding hers. "Dance?"

Rebecca stepped into Clay's embrace. The dogs huddled together watching them. Candlelight flickered as Sarah's soulful, haunting voice floated lyrics of love into the warm night air perfumed by nearby roses. "We dance well together."

"We're not doing anything fancy."

"Could you please try to get in the mood here?" Clay asked good-naturedly.

That's the problem, Rebecca thought. This wonderful mood. I could stay in his arms all night. I feel like if he lets go of me, I'll die.

"She's singing about a man she loves but she can't tell him," Clay said close to her ear.

"I know."

"Are you going back to New Orleans without telling me you love me?"

Rebecca's heart pounded. "In the song it's the man who walks away, not the woman."

"I know. You didn't answer my question."

They still danced slowly in the magical, candlelit, perfumed night. "Clay, I can't live here."

"No one said you had to. They have hospitals in New Orleans, don't they?"

"Probably."

"Would you mind if I worked at one?" He leaned back and looked at her. "You're the one with ESP, but I know you love me. And I love you. I think I have since you were a teenager and you told me about the constellations Callisto and Arcas. For once you weren't stammering and blushing. And all I could think of were your beautiful green eyes and your soft lips and the music in your voice as you told story. You were completely caught up in the passion and drama of it, and I saw the woman you were going to become."

Rebecca gazed into his eyes, the sad-keen eyes she adored, and her throat tightened. "Clay, there are problems with me because of my ESP, my visions."

"There are no problems without solutions."

"That's not true."

"Okay, but some problems *can* be worked out if people care enough to try. I certainly care enough to try. I think you do, too. Besides—" He turned her around until she faced Sean and Gypsy, lying side-by-side. "Are you going to be responsible for separating these two?"

Rebecca smiled, her eyes filling with tears. Then she laid her head on Clay's shoulder. "How do you think you'll like living in New Orleans, Dr. Bellamy?"